THE WATER
MEADOWS

Also by Emma Blair

THE WATER MEADOWS

Emma Blair

BANTAM BOOKS
TORONTO • NEW YORK • LONDON • SYDNEY • AUCKLAND

THE WATER MEADOWS

All of the characters in this book are fictitious,
and any resemblance to actual persons, living or dead,
is purely coincidental.

A BANTAM BOOK 0 553 40372 9

Originally published in Great Britain by Bantam Press,
a division of Transworld Publishers Ltd

PRINTING HISTORY
Bantam Press edition published 1992
Bantam edition published 1993
Bantam edition reprinted 1993

Set in 10/11pt Linotype Times by
County Typesetters, Margate, Kent

Bantam Books are published by Transworld Publishers Ltd,
61–63 Uxbridge Road, Ealing, London W5 5SA, in Australia by
Transworld Publishers (Australia) Pty Ltd, 15–25 Helles
Avenue, Moorebank, NSW 2170, and in New Zealand by
Transworld Publishers (N.Z.) Ltd, 3 William Pickering Drive,
Albany, Auckland.

Printed and bound in Great Britain by
Cox & Wyman Ltd, Reading, Berks.

For Jean

Chapter One

Madge Forsyth glanced up from her darning when the outside door banged open. Moments later her husband, John, barged into the kitchen, looking flushed.

'We're out!' he announced, and whooped.

Madge's heart sank. Slowly she laid her darning aside.

'If everyone obeys the TUC's call the whole bloody country should be out by midnight tonight. Britain will be paralysed,' John said, eyes blazing with excitement and fervour. 'Isn't that brilliant?'

'How long do you think it will last for?' she asked quietly.

'Till Baldwin and his Tories are brought to their knees, and the Government falls.' He chuckled with glee. 'Oh, that's going to be marvellous. Bloody marvellous!'

A General Strike, Madge thought, and went cold all over. God alone knew how this was going to end.

'Baldwin and his cronies have asked for it,' John rattled on. 'Imagine expecting the miners to accept longer hours and lower pay. I mean, what did they think was going to happen when they locked the poor sods out? Did they honestly believe that the rest of us would let them treat our comrades in such an humiliating and despicable manner? That we wouldn't retaliate in any way? Well, now they know, and hell mend them.'

John began pacing up and down the floor. 'We took a vote at McCall's and the result was unanimous that we come out straight away. You should have seen us leaving the factory. What a sight! We went out *en masse*, many of us with arms linked together, all of us singing "The

7

Red Flag". That was something I'll remember till my dying day.'

He punched the air. 'George Paterson spoke to us before our vote, giving us the usual nonsense. That their profit margins were wafer thin, and that some weeks they actually lost money. All lies, of course, crude management lies to try and put the fear of God into us. Well, it didn't work. The boys saw through his lies for what they were, and rammed them back down his throat by voting as they did. Unanimous! Not one dissenter. I was proud of them, so proud. I was bursting with it.'

George Paterson was the elder of two brothers who owned McCall's, having bought the firm from its founder a number of years previously. His brother William played a back-up role.

Madge rose from her chair and crossed to the cooker where she lit the gas under the kettle. 'Would you like a cup of tea?' she asked.

He shook his head. 'I have to dash. There's a demonstration I've promised to attend.'

Well, she wanted a cup, she thought. She needed one after the news that had just been broken to her. McCall's out, and a General Strike looming. It was a bad dream, a nightmare, come true.

'There's no strike pay I don't suppose?' she queried.

John laughed. 'Don't be daft, woman! Where would we get the money for that?'

She gazed across at her husband's grinning face, and hated him. How could he be so stupid? Couldn't he see what this meant? She could envisage it only too clearly. All she could pray for was that the strike was short lived and everyone would soon be back at work.

'I'll tell you what I'll have instead of tea,' John said, and strode over to a sideboard from which he took a bottle of whisky that had about six inches of spirit left in it.

'How about you?' he asked, waggling the bottle at her. 'It's a day for celebration, after all.'

Madge shook her head.

He poured a measure into a small thimble glass, and swallowed it off in a single gulp. He then refilled the glass.

'There will be no more of that until the strike is over,' Madge said.

He looked at the bottle in surprise. 'I suppose you're right.'

'Nor of a lot of things,' she added softly.

'What was that?'

'Nothing.'

He put the stopper back in the bottle and replaced it in the sideboard. 'We're expecting a good turn out at the demonstration. We're starting from St Enoch Square and walking round all the main streets in the town centre.'

He sipped his whisky, then went on. 'And there's a big rally at Glasgow Green in the morning at which Ernest Bevin himself is going to speak.' Ernest Bevin was the leader of the transport workers and dockers, and a leading light within the TUC.

'Would you like to come with me to hear him?' John asked.

Madge didn't even consider it. 'No thanks.'

Her tone pricked his ebullience. 'I must say you're not showing too much enthusiasm for all this. Don't you understand the importance of what's happening?'

She regarded him steadily. 'That's your viewpoint. What I do understand is how difficult things are going to be until you get back to work again. I understand that all right.'

'It's sacrifice in the short term to give us a better future. And, of course, it will be difficult, but that's simply something we'll all have to put up with.'

'Well, sacrifice will start with the meal tonight which will be tripe and onions because tripe is cheap.' She enjoyed watching him blanch knowing how much he disliked tripe. He could eat it, but only just.

'Tripe,' he repeated hollowly.

'And onions. Lovely thick tripe that will just slip and slither down your throat.'

She smiled inwardly as he swallowed hard. Was it her imagination or had a faint sheen of sweat appeared on his brow?

'I'd better get on then,' he said, and polished off what remained in his glass.

'And don't come home saying you've had fish and chips or anything like that. From now on nothing in the food line gets wasted.' She paused, then added emphatically, 'By *anyone*.'

He got the message loud and clear. If he didn't eat the tripe that evening it would only be served up again the following day. And the day after that and the day after that until he did eat it.

'Goodbye then,' he said, and left the house, closing the outside door behind him.

When he'd gone Madge poured herself a cup of tea and sat down again. She was both angry and immensely sad at the same time. At least her son Graham, a delivery boy for a grocer's shop, was earning which was some consolation. Not that he earned a lot, but a little was better than nothing at all coming in.

Twelve-year-old Jennie Forsyth came out of the school gates and headed for home. It had been a pleasant day earlier, but had now turned chill. She hunched her shoulders as she hurried on her way.

Gradually she became aware of a strange sound, one she'd never heard before. Puzzled, she glanced about, wondering what was making it.

A male voice bellowed out a command, and seconds later the head of a marching column appeared further down the street.

'Right turrrnnnn!' an NCO screamed, and the column turned right to head in her direction.

Jennie stopped to stare as the soldiers went by. They

were dressed in khaki and carrying rifles on their shoulders. The sound she'd heard was the thump of their boots on the cobbles.

A body of horses clattered past, followed by an armoured car with a mounted machine-gun.

How fierce they all looked, she thought, grim and stern-faced. Why you would have thought they were off to war!

Another armoured car clanked by, this one exuding a strong smell of oil.

A man wearing a scarf tied round his neck and a flat cap, who was standing near to Jennie, jeered at the soldiers.

'You'll not fight the soldiers surely!' a thin woman cried at him.

More soldiers continued to march past four abreast, the thump of their boots, like a rhythm being beaten on a drum, now even louder than before.

Other people crowded round to watch the spectacle, until the amount of spectators on both pavements had grown to quite sizeable proportions.

Further jeering and catcalling took place, while the atmosphere in the street changed to one of hostility and ugliness. It was high time she was out of there, Jennie decided.

She elbowed her way through the press, till at last she was able to escape down an alleyway.

As she strode swiftly away those she'd left behind began to chant.

'Will you listen to this!' John exclaimed, and smashed the newspaper he was reading with the back of his hand. 'I quote . . . "any action taken by the armed forces will receive, both now and afterwards, the full support of His Majesty's Government".'

He looked over at Madge who was in a chair opposite him. 'If that isn't the go-ahead for the soldiers to do as they damn well like then I don't know what is. And what

11

do they mean by "any action"? Does that include rape, murder and massacre?'

'Don't exaggerate,' Madge admonished.

'I'm not exaggerating. Any action means exactly that. Any action. They can do as they damn well please and the Government will simply pat them on the head, give them a medal no doubt, and tell them they've done their duty.'

'I don't think it means quite that,' Madge said. 'I would imagine it's to be interpreted as any action deemed necessary, within the realms of reason.'

John remained unconvinced. He made a harumphing sound and scowled at the newspaper. 'The *British Gazette* edited by Winston bloody Churchill. What a load of sh . . .'

'John!' Madge interjected sharply, and jerked her head in Jennie's direction.

'Sorry,' he muttered. 'It's just that I get so incensed.'

As if I didn't know, Madge thought to herself.

'And how about this,' he went on, another article having caught his eye. '"The Home Secretary is appealing for thirty thousand more special constables to be enrolled at once to swell the total to two hundred thousand."' He glanced up again at Madge. 'That's an army in itself.'

John tossed the newspaper aside. 'I can't read any more of that rubbish. There isn't a line in it that doesn't upset me.'

'It surprises me that you bothered to read it at all.'

'Winston Churchill, Chancellor of the Exchequer,' John said contemptuously. 'Come the revolution that man will be dragged out and shot. And as for yours truly, I would happily be a member of the firing squad.'

'There will never be a revolution in this country. We're not like that,' Madge said.

'Don't be too sure. Don't be too sure at all!'

John's tone caused Madge to lay her mending on her lap and stare at him. 'You don't think . . . it would really go that far?'

12

'I believe it could. And so do a lot of people like me. What's happening now could turn into far more than a General Strike. We could not only bring down the Government but the Monarchy as well. Just as they did in Russia and France before that.'

Madge shivered.

'It's early days yet,' John added ominously.

Madge got on with her mending. And when she spoke again she changed the subject.

John was in the forefront of the crowd as the large metal doors swung slowly open to reveal the inside of the tram depot. From his vantage point he could see dozens of double-decker trams sporting their distinctive Glasgow Corporation livery.

'They shall not pass!' someone shouted. 'They shall not pass!'

John took up the refrain, as did the others pressing all around him. 'They shall not pass! They shall not pass!'

The tram came to within a dozen feet of John and stopped. Its driver, clearly a frightened civilian, peered out at the throng confronting him.

'They shall not pass! They shall not pass!'

A senior police officer appeared inside the depot, walking purposefully forward to take up a position in front of the tram trying to leave.

'If you don't disperse immediately, I shall order my men to make you do so,' he said in a loud, authoritative voice.

'Boo!' a man yelled.

'Bugger your men!' a second voice screamed, which caused others to laugh.

Once more the shout was taken up. 'They shall not pass! They shall not pass!'

The police officer tried to speak again, but was howled down, his voice drowned in the vocal onslaught.

The police officer produced a whistle, put it to his lips

and blew. He then signalled the civilian tram driver to follow him back into the depot which the driver did with great alacrity.

'Christ!' exclaimed the chap beside John when a line of policemen emerged from the depths of the depot. 'How did they get in there?'

The line of policemen was followed by another and then by a third, all of whom advanced steadily with their truncheons drawn.

'Link arms!' a burly man at the front of the crowd instructed. Within seconds John found himself part of a human chain barring the depot door.

The police continued to advance. When they reached the human chain, the front line's truncheons were raised in unison, and fell the same way.

John went reeling, a truncheon having taken him on the side of the head. All around him were screams, shouts and the steady thud of blows.

Fists flew, wood responded. One policeman's mouth opened wide, but no sound emerged, as he was kicked in the crotch.

John saw one striker's nose flattened by a flailing truncheon, blood spurting from both nostrils.

There was a crack which he knew instinctively to be a bone breaking, followed by a shriek of agony.

The police now fanned out to form a single line, as their truncheons relentlessly rose and fell, exacting a deadly toll. The strikers resisted valiantly, but it was only a matter of time before the police won the day.

John saw a girl knocked off her feet and fall to the ground. She desperately tried to get up again, but was unable to do so because of the constant ebb and flow of the people surrounding her. The expression on her face was one of sheer terror.

John struggled over to her and grabbed her by the arm. Using himself as a shield he somehow managed to get her back on her feet.

'Thank you,' she sobbed. 'Thank you.'

'Come on,' he said, pulling her with him as he fought and shoved his way through the mêlée.

People were running in all directions as the crowd began breaking up. 'Fascist swine!' a man screamed in the direction of the police, waving a fist at them. He then turned and bolted.

The girl stumbled and would have pitched headlong if John hadn't been holding on to her. Again he yanked her upright, after which they continued their flight.

John stopped in a doorway to catch his breath, and while there saw the tram, driven by the same civilian driver as before, move out of the depot. And behind that tram came others.

'I thought that was it back there. I really did,' the girl said.

'You all right?'

She nodded. 'Thanks to you.'

He shrugged that off. 'Let's get away from here. That would be best.'

A bell clanged in the distance, its clamour getting louder as it came closer. More bells joined the first.

'Ambulances,' John said.

He grimaced when a man went staggering by, the left side of his face twice its normal size. The man's left eye was completely lost in the swollen flesh.

'I know you,' the girl said suddenly.

'Do you?'

'You work at McCall's.'

'That's right,' he acknowledged, thinking now he looked at her there was something familiar about her.

'You're John something. And I'm Anne Moore. I work in the accounts department.'

He placed her now. 'John Forsyth.'

'We've never spoken, but I've seen you round the factory,' she smiled.

An ambulance arrived on the scene, and moments later another.

'Let's go,' said John, and again took Anne by the arm.

15

The tram depot and fighting taking place in front of it were soon out of sight.

'You saved my life back there,' Anne stated when they halted further on.

'I don't know about that. But you certainly could have been badly hurt.' John swore. 'They were bastards to come at us like that. We in the forefront had no chance at all.'

Her eyes widened. 'Were you right in the front then?'

'By the tram itself.'

'That was very brave of you.'

'Brave?' He laughed. It was, he supposed. There again, he doubted he'd have been where he had if he'd known truncheons were to be used, but he didn't say so.

'There was no need for the police to be so brutal,' she said vehemently. 'No need at all.'

John recognized a kindred political spirit. 'I couldn't agree more.'

'How long were you there for?' she asked.

'I was one of the first to congregate. So I was there for quite some time before the doors were opened.'

'I was on my way elsewhere when I saw what was happening and joined in.'

She was pretty, he thought, and young – eighteen or nineteen.

Anne bit her lower lip, then said, 'Where are you off to now?'

The question caught him by surprise. 'I don't know. I'll probably just wander round to see what else is going on.'

'Would you like a drink?'

He smiled thinly. 'I've no money. I'm skint.'

'I have some, and I'm the one doing the offering.'

'But . . .'

'No buts,' she interrupted. 'It's the least I can do after what you did for me.'

A lassie buying him a drink? Well, why not? 'Where will we go?' he asked.

'There's a pub in the next street. I've never been in it, but I've passed it often enough. We'll go there.'

'All right.'

He smiled at her, and she smiled back.

'How come you've got money to spend like this?' he enquired as they resumed walking, for she was out on strike same as himself.

'I just have,' she replied mysteriously, then, with a laugh, added, 'If you must know it's my holiday money that I'm using. I was going away with two other girls for the Fair to Dunoon, but that's had to go by the board now.' The fair she was referring to was the Glasgow Fair, the middle fortnight in July when all the factories and works in Glasgow traditionally closed down *en masse* for the summer holidays.

That explained it, he thought.

When they went into the pub they discovered it was empty, which was hardly surprising with a General Strike taking place. Anne slipped a ten-shilling note into John's hand and told him to get her a whisky and lemonade, and a pint and dram for himself. As he was ordering she chose a table and sat at it.

While John was at the bar Anne thought back to how close she'd come to being trampled. Thank God John had been there to help her, otherwise she'd have been one of those taken away in the ambulances. Or worse . . . taken away in a hearse.

Her thoughts were interrupted as John arrived with their drinks on a small metal tray. 'This is very kind of you,' he said.

'Not at all.'

He winced when he sat down, and gingerly felt the side of his head.

'What is it?' she asked.

'I got hit by a truncheon. I don't think the skin's broken, but it's painful where the blow landed.'

'Here, let me see.'

He bent over to allow her to examine the sore spot.

Her hands were cool, and extremely gentle.

'No skin broken as you thought, but you do have the beginnings of a bruise. Nothing to worry about though I'd say.'

Anne lifted her glass. 'Here's to you, a real hero.'

He blushed. 'I'm hardly that!'

'You are in my book, John. Most certainly so.'

He clinked his whisky glass against hers. 'Here's how!'

'Cheerio!'

They both had a swallow, then replaced their respective glasses on the table. John then had a pull at his pint, relishing the creamy, tangy beer that brought his taste-buds zinging alive. 'That's good,' he sighed.

'So, where do you live?' she enquired.

He told her. 'And you?'

It transpired they lived within a short distance of one another. 'With your parents?' he further probed.

'With my ma. My father died some years back.'

'I'm sorry to hear that.'

'Ma and I get on all right. We both work which means we normally have two wages coming into the house. Three really if you . . .' She broke off and smiled.

'If you what?' he asked.

'You might think this silly.'

'Try me?'

'My ma is also a spaewife. She reads the Tarot cards, runes, tea leaves and crystal ball.'

'A spaewife!' That was an old Scots word for fortune teller.

'I told you you'd think it silly,' Anne said, wagging a finger at him.

'No, I don't. I mean . . . well . . . it's a woman's thing really, isn't it?'

'The majority of those who come to consult by mother are women, but she does get the occasional man.'

'Is your mother good?'

'Very. She can be quite disconcerting at times.'

'And has she ever told you anything that's come true?'

18

'Lots of things.'

He had another deep swig of his pint. 'Such as?'

'Oh, I can't think offhand. But lots.'

John was fascinated. 'I wouldn't mind having my cards read,' he admitted.

'Really!'

'As a laugh, of course.'

'Of course,' she smiled.

'I'd take whatever was said with a pinch of salt though.'

Anne didn't answer that knowing it to be bluff and bluster, a man trying to be seen as one. She liked this John Forsyth, too bad he was so much older than her.

'Are you married?' she asked.

He nodded.

'Children?'

'Two. A boy and a girl.'

'Called what?'

'Graham and Jennie.'

'And what's your wife's name?'

He frowned, the last thing he wanted to do was talk about Madge. His high spirits deflated a little. 'Madge,' he replied.

Anne saw his change of mood, and correctly guessed the reason: not a particularly happy marriage, or so he viewed it.

'And what does Madge look like?'

He finished his dram, then drank more of his beer. 'All right. Pretty ordinary really.'

'Blonde? Brunette?' She was teasing him now.

'Auburn,' he informed her.

'Auburn! I always think auburn hair is very attractive.'

John wished Anne would change the subject.

'Were you childhood sweethearts?'

'Not exactly.' If she wouldn't change the subject, he would. 'But what about yourself? Is there anyone special?' He'd already noted she wasn't wearing either a wedding or engagement ring.

'Nope,' she replied.

'I'm amazed.'

'Why's that?'

'A beautiful lass like you on the loose? I'd have thought the beaux would have been queuing up.'

She laughed. 'You may be married but you haven't forgotten how to chat up a girl.'

'Chat up! Me!' he exclaimed, feigning innocence.

'You!' she said, and wagged a finger at him.

He looked at his empty whisky glass, wishing he'd money for a refill and that he could buy Anne one.

Reading his mind, Anne indicated the change from the ten-shilling note that was on the tray, and said, 'Finish your pint off and we'll get another round in. And when that money's gone there's more where it came from.'

'You're being generous,' he replied.

'What's a few bob compared to what you did for me. I'm very, very grateful.'

'Anyone would have done the same.'

'But it was you who did.'

A real hero, he thought, recalling her words of a few minutes earlier. Not true, of course, but lovely to be called that just the same.

'This is it, my close,' Anne announced.

John glanced up at the tenement, identical to the one he and Madge lived in.

'How do you feel?' she asked.

'Like I've had a decent drink. And you?'

She giggled. 'The same. Terrific, isn't it?'

'Terrific,' he agreed.

'Listen, why don't you come up and meet my ma? I'll ask her to read the Tarot cards for you.'

'Would you?' he exclaimed in delight.

'Sure.'

'Right then,' he agreed.

They went into the close and climbed four flights of stairs to stop before a brown painted door. Anne produced a key which let them inside.

'She's gone out,' Anne declared, having read the note that had been left for her on the mantelpiece. 'Gone to my Aunt Edna's for the day. She says she won't be back till later tonight.'

John's face fell with disappointment. Having his cards read would have been fun. 'Another time, maybe,' he said.

'Another time, I'll arrange it. That's a promise.'

He hesitated, for he was thoroughly enjoying Anne's company, then said reluctantly, 'I'd better get up the road then.'

But she didn't want him to go either. 'Tell you what, why don't we have another drink? We've nothing in, but there's an off-licence just round the corner. Would you go for me?'

'I feel I'm taking advantage . . .'

'You're doing nothing of the sort,' she interrupted, pressing a pound into his hand. 'When you go out of the close turn right, and right again. You can't miss it.'

'What will I get?'

'A half-bottle. That suit?'

He nodded. 'Aye.'

Her knight in shining armour, she thought, through an alcoholic haze. Her white knight who'd saved her when her life was in peril. Her champion. Her Lancelot. 'On you go then,' she said.

When he'd gone she ran a comb through her hair, gazing at her reflection in the oval mirror hanging above the mantelpiece that had been one of her parents' wedding presents. Her eyes were bright, she noted, her cheeks flushed – no wonder considering the amount of whisky she'd already consumed.

The fire had been made but not lit. Bending, she struck a match and within moments the fire was blazing sending a gorgeous heat throughout the room.

Closing her eyes she thought back to when she'd been knocked to the ground and the fear that had gripped her when she'd been sure she was going to die. Her mouth went dry and she shivered at the memory. Then, when all had seemed lost, John had appeared as though by magic to rescue her.

Her Lancelot, she repeated mentally, visualizing him in armour, mounted on a plunging steed. Just like something out of the pictures. She was a dedicated fan, and usually went two or three times a week.

Anne went through to her bedroom and took off her badly laddered stockings. She wondered about putting on a new pair, but decided to leave it for now. She went bare legged to answer the outside door when John knocked on it.

She and John returned to the kitchen where she poured them each a hefty measure. While she was doing this John stood appreciatively in front of the fire.

What seemed like an electric charge went through John when their fingers touched as she was handing him his glass. He tried to smile, but found he couldn't. He was suddenly acutely aware of her.

'There's no rush for you to get home, is there?' she asked throatily.

He shook his head.

'Good.'

She grasped his shirt, pulled herself up on to her tiptoes, and kissed him.

'I don't scare you, do I?' she asked.

'No.'

'I kissed you, but you didn't kiss me.'

He didn't answer that.

'Don't you find me attractive?'

'Very much so. It's just . . .' He trailed off.

Her hand moved up to his throat. 'Just what?'

'I'm thirty-eight.'

'You don't look it,' she purred. 'I would have taken you for much younger.'

He swelled at this compliment. 'You would?'

'Definitely. Much younger.'

He laughed, and felt himself relax and generally loosen.

'You're my Lancelot. My hero.'

Was she drunk? he wondered. He was a bit that way himself. 'It's nice to be appreciated,' he replied, thinking that was something he certainly wasn't at home. Not with Madge at least. All she could ever do was criticize and put him down.

Anne went back up on her tiptoes and kissed him again. This time he responded eagerly. While they were kissing she took his free hand and placed it on her bottom.

She felt his hand stiffen in uncertainty. 'I'm not a virgin, you know,' she said.

'No?'

'No,' she repeated.

He drank off what was in his glass, closed his eyes, then opened them again. 'Perhaps I'm dreaming,' he said.

'You're not. I assure you. I'm real, and all yours.'

'Why?' he asked.

'Because . . .' she answered enigmatically, and led him through to her bedroom.

John walked down the street feeling ten feet tall. What a day! What a girl! They'd made love, talked, made love again, and then talked some more. She'd been absolutely wonderful!

A real hero, her Lancelot. The words spun round and round in his mind making him want to laugh out loud with sheer, joyous delight.

To hear her you'd have thought he was one of the main architects behind the General Strike; that he himself had personally organized and led the crowd at the tram depot.

Ten feet? No, twenty feet tall!

23

John stuck his hands in his trousers pockets and began to whistle a happy tune.

At one point he did a few jig steps which made a woman coming in his direction gape at him in astonishment.

'I'm hungry!' Jennie complained.

'We all are,' Madge said.

'I've only had bread and dripping today, and that was hours ago.'

'You're lucky to have had that,' a bad-tempered Madge countered.

John caught her glowering at him. 'Well, don't look at me like that, there's nothing I can do about it,' he said.

That was true enough, she thought. There wasn't anything he could do.

'It's not my fault we're all out on strike,' he added.

'Maybe not, but you don't have to be so bloody pleased with yourself,' she riposted.

'I've told you before. Sacrifice in the short term . . .'

'Oh, shut up!' she yelled. It took all her willpower not to pick something up and throw it at him. Stupid man!

'Have a glass of water. That will help the hunger pangs,' she said to Jennie.

'I've already had a glass.'

'Then have another.'

Jennie did as she was bid, wishing it was lemonade she was drinking, or better still, cream soda.

The outside door opened, and banged shut again. Graham, three years older than Jennie, entered the kitchen carrying a cardboard box. 'Ta-ra!' he sang.

'What's that?' Madge frowned.

'A few things Mr Baird said I could have.' Mr Baird owned the grocery shop where he worked.

'You mean food?' Madge asked hopefully.

'Stuff he can't use,' Graham declared, plonking the box on the table.

Jennie squealed and dashed to the box to peer inside.

'Broken biscuits!' she exclaimed as she opened a paper bag.

'Help yourself,' smiled Graham, which she immediately did.

'Hmm! Scrumptious!' she said, cramming biscuits into her mouth.

Madge joined Jennie beside the box, and began to sort through its contents. Besides the broken biscuits there was stale bread, sprouting potatoes, squashed tomatoes, vegetables past their prime and several tins of badly dented corned beef.

'Wonderful,' Madge breathed. Turning to Graham, she kissed him on the cheek. 'Aren't you a clever boy.'

'Better than nothing I thought.'

'Far better. It won't take me long to make something tasty out of this lot.'

'I'll help,' Jennie offered eagerly.

'Isn't he clever?' Madge beamed at John, who merely sniffed.

'I asked Mr Baird if I could have them, pointing out that, with the exception of the biscuits, they would only go in the bin anyway. I could have just taken them, I suppose, but thought it best to ask.'

'You did the right thing,' Madge nodded.

'I also asked if I could take other bits and pieces until the strike ends, which he was agreeable to. So there we are.'

Madge swept him to her and hugged him tight. 'You'll go far in life, son,' she said. 'I just know you will.'

'I always try to do my best as you taught me to, Ma.'

'That's right. Do your best in life and that way you'll succeed.'

John's face darkened, knowing this to be a dig at him.

'Some day you might even own your own shop,' Madge suggested to Graham, eyes glowing.

'That would make him one of the bosses,' John said quietly, his tone one of condemnation.

'Shall I peel these potatoes?' Jennie queried.

'Do that lass. And I'll prepare the other vegetables.'

'Bosses,' John went on. 'They're all tarred with the same brush. I wouldn't give you a penny piece for one of them.'

'They're not all bad. At least Mr Baird isn't,' Graham said.

'And what would you know about it? You're still wet behind the ears.'

Graham went red.

'That's no way to talk to the boy. Not after what he's just done,' Madge rebuked her husband.

'Well, he shouldn't talk nonsense.'

Graham wanted to retort, but felt it best to hold his tongue. When it came to politics there was no winning with his father who was totally blinkered on the subject.

'That's *your* opinion,' Madge replied.

And it's the right one, John thought to himself.

'Thank Mr Baird for us. Tell him we're grateful,' Madge said to Graham.

'It was only stuff for the bin,' John commented ungraciously.

'But it means a great deal to us in the circumstances!' Madge snapped back.

'You can say that again,' Jennie muttered at the sink, where she'd started on the potatoes.

Own his own shop? Graham liked the idea of that. He liked it very much indeed. It was certainly a goal to aim for.

The meal Madge produced was delicious. She made a point of giving Graham the largest portion, which wasn't lost on John. He knew if he'd said anything Madge would have told him that Graham was working while he wasn't.

'I'm going out to a meeting later,' John announced as he pushed his empty plate away.

'If I'm in bed don't wake me when you get back in,' Madge said.

26

He bloody well would, John thought, if for no other reason than simply to annoy her.

Jennie and her friend Moira McKay were on their way to school where a soup kitchen had been set up for the pupils. Soup and bread were doled out twice a day, at noon and six in the evening. They were *en route* for the later session.

'I never used to be very keen on soup,' Moira said. 'Now I think the stuff we get at school's fantastic.'

'I know what my ma would say if she heard you saying that. "Hunger's good sauce", she'd say.'

Moira laughed. 'And she'd be right.'

Moira's laugh died in her throat when they turned a corner to be suddenly confronted by a clash between strikers and mounted soldiers. They both shrank back against a tenement wall as the mini battle raged before them.

A man emerged from the mêlée and staggered in their direction. He was clutching his throat. A few yards from Jennie and Moira, he stopped and sighed, eyes starting from his head, before collapsing unconscious to the pavement.

Jennie looked from the prostrate man to the fight which had moved further down the street, and was continuing to move away from them.

'Is he dead, do you think?' Moira queried in a tremulous voice.

Jennie went and knelt beside the man, and put an ear close to his mouth to hear if he was still breathing. 'He's alive,' she pronounced.

'Look at that blood,' Moira said.

Blood oozed from between the fingers holding his throat. Jennie removed the hand and revealed a deep, jagged cut.

'I've got a hanky. Do you want it?' Moira asked.

Jennie glanced around, but there were no grown-ups handy to assist. 'Run and get help. A policeman, soldier,

27

it doesn't matter. Just get help and get it quickly,' she instructed her friend.

'Aye, right. Sure.' And with that Moira was off, running like the wind.

Jennie recalled a conversation she'd once overheard about holding cuts together to stem the bleeding, and decided that was what she'd try and do. Using two fingers she pinched one section of the cut together, then repeated the action with the remainder.

The striker groaned and opened his eyes. He started to move with the intention of trying to get back on to his feet.

'Lie still,' Jennie commanded.

He stopped, lay back, and stared at her.

'Help's on its way,' she explained, hoping that was true.

He'd lost a lot of blood in a relatively short time, she thought. The front of his shirt was sodden with it.

She saw that she'd got blood on her dress, but that was unimportant. Ma would understand when she explained how it had happened.

The man's eyes closed again and his head fell sideways, but he continued to breathe.

Jennie applied more pressure to the cut, and desperately looked in the direction that Moira had gone. But there was no sign of Moira or anyone else.

The fighting strikers and mounted soldiers had now disappeared leaving the street quiet as the grave. Someone must happen along soon! Jennie thought.

The man's face had gone very white, Jennie noted. A tick had appeared in his left cheek, jumping madly as if some creature was imprisoned under the skin. She wondered who he was and if he was married. He probably was, she decided, he had that 'look' about him.

Jennie sighed with relief, there was Moira now. And the man with Moira was carrying what was clearly a doctor's bag. They hurried towards her.

'He's lost an awful lot of blood,' Jennie said to the doctor as he knelt beside her.

'I bumped into the doctor coming out of a close. Wasn't that lucky!' Moira said to Jennie, her chest heaving up and down from the running she'd been doing.

The doctor quietly asked Jennie to remove her fingers, and when she'd done so he made a quick examination of the wound.

'I hope I did the right thing?' Jennie said.

The doctor flashed her a smile. 'You certainly did, young woman. Precisely the right thing.'

A thrill ran through her to hear that.

'Now, if you'll just hold the wound again as you've been doing I'll suture here and now,' the doctor said. When he saw her puzzled frown he explained. 'I'll stitch him up.'

A woman approached and stood a little way off watching them. She was joined by another woman from across the road.

The striker moaned. 'It's all right. You're going to be all right,' Jennie said in a reassuring, comforting tone. 'Everything's going to be just fine.'

'Nasty wound,' the doctor commented, preparing the site for suturing.

'There was a group of them up against mounted soldiers,' Jennie explained.

'So your friend said.'

'A running battle,' Jennie added.

She watched in fascination as the needle slipped through the man's flesh. Moira, who had no stomach for such things, swallowed and turned away.

'He'll need a blood transfusion as soon as possible,' the doctor said, tying off another stitch. 'Will you girls stay with him while I fetch my car? I'll take him to the hospital in that. It will be quicker than ringing through for an ambulance, all of which seem to be permanently in action since the strike started.'

Jennie nodded. 'Of course.'

The doctor finished his suturing. 'I'll be as swift as I can,' he told the girls and walked away.

It wasn't long before a car drove into the street and pulled up beside them.

'Can the two of you help me get him in the back?' the doctor said, grasping the man's shoulders.

It wasn't easy, but between them they manipulated the striker into the rear of the car where the doctor put him in a sitting position.

'On second thoughts, perhaps it would be best if the pair of you come to the hospital with me. I'll need you to take care of him.'

Jennie and Moira clambered into the car, taking up a position on either side of the unconscious man.

'I hope you don't get blood on your upholstery,' the practical Jennie said as the car moved off.

'It'll wash if I do,' the doctor replied. 'And it wouldn't be the first time either. I can assure you of that.'

White as milk, Jennie thought staring into the striker's face. Dark smudges had appeared under his eyes.

When they reached the hospital the doctor instructed them to stay where they were, and then hurried inside. When he returned he had two porters with him, and a nurse. One of the porters was pushing a trolley.

The porters expertly manhandled the striker from the car and laid him on the trolley where the nurse covered him with a red blanket. The nurse accompanied the porters as the trolley was wheeled away.

'Thank you for what you did,' the doctor said to Jennie and Moira. Then he addressed Jennie. 'And you in particular. As I said earlier, you did precisely the right thing.'

Again a thrill and a warm glow of satisfaction ran through Jennie.

'You'd make a good nurse when you're older,' the doctor smiled at Jennie. 'You want to give it some thought.'

Reaching out he shook Jennie's hand, then Moira's.

'I'll get away in now and see to the patient. Thank you both again.'

'It's a long walk to school from here,' Moira said when he'd left them.

'Let's just hope we get there before they stop giving out the soup,' Jennie replied, breaking into a trot.

As luck would have it they arrived just in time.

'What's all that shouting about?' John asked entering the kitchen, having been to the toilet they shared on the first landing down.

'Search me,' Madge replied.

John went to the window and peered out. 'Some sort of commotion,' he said, and opened the window.

'Hey Chick, what's going on?' he called to one of their neighbours below.

Chick looked up at him. 'The strike's over. The Government has won!'

John was aghast. 'You're joking!'

'It's true I tell you. The TUC has ordered us all back to work. The miners are disobeying though. They say they'll stay out till hell freezes over.'

'Good for them,' John said. At least they had some guts and backbone.

'Surrendered, that was the word used on the wireless,' Chick went on. 'Walter Citrine and Arthur Pugh went to Downing Street and surrendered to Baldwin.' Citrine and Pugh were general secretary and president of the TUC respectively.

John felt sick. Surrendered! 'I'm coming down,' he told Chick, and slammed the window shut again.

'It's over then,' Madge smiled as he reached for his jacket.

'So it seems.'

'When will you return to McCall's?'

'I don't know that yet.' He paused, then said, 'The miners have stayed out.'

God help their wives and families, Madge thought.

31

'They might still break the Government,' John added hopefully.

Madge didn't answer that either.

'Still bring the bastards down,' John added further, striding from the room and house.

Madge took a deep breath when he was gone. It was over and now they could all get back to normal.

It was as if an enormous burden had been lifted from her shoulders.

John arrived at McCall's to find members of the workforce milling around outside the factory. The gates, which should have been open, were closed.

'Someone forgot to tell them the strike's over,' he joked to Jacky Mann, a mate of his, who laughed.

'Seems that way, John.'

'Why are we waiting . . . !' someone began to sing. He was immediately joined by others.

John spotted Anne and made his way over. 'Hello,' he smiled as he approached her.

'Hello.'

'How are you?'

'Never better.'

He lowered his voice. 'When can I see you again?'

'Whenever you like. But we'll discuss it inside, not here.'

He nodded. 'All right then.'

They chatted generally for a few moments, and were then interrupted when a loud cheer rang out. The cheer was because the gates had been partially opened to allow George and William Paterson to emerge. George held up a hand for silence.

When he had it he spoke his piece.

'Closed down!' Madge croaked.

'The firm's gone under according to George Paterson. He said the strike was the straw that finally broke the camel's back.'

Madge went to the nearest chair and sat down. This was dreadful. Appalling! Just when she'd thought everything was back to normal.

'I never imagined . . . none of us did. When they threatened us before the strike we believed it to be all lies on their part,' John went on hollowly. 'Christ! It's a terrible time to be looking for a job with so many unemployed and things the way they are.'

Madge rubbed her hands together, her normally quick-thinking mind more or less frozen from shock.

'I'll find something though, you'll see,' he said.

He'd have to, she thought.

'I'll go out now and start looking right away.'

'Do that,' she said.

He turned on his heel and left the house.

McCall's closed down, John out of a job. Back to existing on what Graham brought in.

Madge covered her face with her hands and quietly wept.

Madge stood in the bedroom staring out of the window. It had been raining but that had now stopped, leaving the street and pavements slick and shining.

John appeared, slouching along. His head was down, as were his shoulders. His hands were rammed dejectedly into his trousers pockets.

He'd failed again to find another job, Madge thought grimly. It was now nearly a fortnight since McCall's had closed, two weeks that seemed an eternity.

Closing her eyes, she prayed. Please God let him find work soon. Please! If for no other reason than the children's sakes.

When she opened her eyes it had started to rain again.

'I wouldn't ask Chrissie, but we're desperate.'

Chrissie McDowell, Madge's younger sister, sighed. 'I wish I could help you, Madge, but we're hardly getting by as it is. We've just nothing to spare. You'd be welcome to it if we had, but we haven't.'

Madge ran a hand through her hair. 'I'm sorry. I should have realized.'

'With four children to feed and clothe it takes every farthing that Bob brings into the house. Wee Billy's boots are through in the sole, but they'll have to wait until we can afford to take them to the cobbler's. It's as bad as that.'

'Times are hard right enough,' Madge said.

'Aye, and so much for their great strike. Fat lot of good that did anyone.'

'That's true,' Madge nodded.

'I feel terrible about this,' Chrissie said in anguish. 'You're my own sister after all. The same flesh and blood.'

'You can't give what you haven't got. That's what it boils down to,' Madge replied.

'You'll have a cup of tea though before you go? That's the least I can do.'

'A cup of tea would be lovely, thank you very much.'

Chrissie swept Madge into her arms and hugged her tight. When she released Madge again there were tears in both their eyes.

'What about John's brother?' Chrissie asked.

'Didn't you know? He'd gone to work at McCall's as well. He and his family are in exactly the same boat as us.'

'I *am* sorry,' Chrissie sympathized.

'At least they've only got the one child.'

'It's wicked so it is,' said Chrissie, taking the kettle to the sink where she filled it.

Later, as Madge was leaving, Chrissie thrust a precious half-crown into her hand. 'Not a lot, but better than nothing,' she said.

'Ta, Chrissie.'

'I only wish it was more.'

They hugged one another again, then Madge made

34

her way downstairs. She could now have taken the tram home, but didn't even consider wasting money on the fare.

She walked the three and a half miles back to her own house.

'I'm sorry, Mrs Forsyth, but I can't extend your credit any further.'

Those words, uttered by Goodhew the factor, were like words of doom in Madge's ears. 'You mean . . .' she trailed off, and bit her lip.

'Yes, Mrs Forsyth, I shall have to ask you to vacate the premises.'

Madge swallowed hard.

'I have no choice in the matter. I'm only the factor after all, operating on the owner's behalf. I merely carry out my instructions.'

Madge could just visualize her, John, Graham and Jennie camped on the pavement surrounded by their sticks of furniture. She'd seen it happen to others. An evicted family was an awful sight.

'How long have we got?' she queried in a trembling voice.

'Till Friday. If you can make at least some payment then on your arrears I'll let you stay on for a short while longer.'

All wasn't lost yet, Madge told herself. 'We'll have something to give you then,' she promised feverishly. 'I don't know how, but we'll have something. You have my word on that.'

He nodded. 'I hope you're right.'

She didn't blame the factor, as he said he was only carrying out the owner's instructions. Goodhew himself was a decent man, well known as such.

'I'll show you to the door,' she said.

'I'll be back Friday,' he repeated on the landing.

As she closed the door behind him she found herself shaking all over. It was ages before she stopped.

*   *   *

'Go on the Parish!' John exclaimed.

'There's no other way.'

'I'll be damned if I'll . . .'

'We're out on the street if you don't!' she yelled at him.

John shut up, then said quietly, 'I'll find a job soon. I'm sure of it. This bad luck can't go on for ever.'

'We haven't got for ever, but until Friday. That's the deadline the factor has given us. We have to pay him something on Friday, or else he'll have the bailiffs round.'

The Parish! John mentally recoiled at the thought. It would be so humiliating. You more or less had to go down on your knees and beg for their charity.

'There's no other way,' Madge repeated.

'Even if we did go there's no guarantee they'd give us anything,' John said.

'I know. But there again, they might.'

'Till Friday you say?'

'Then Goodhew will have the bailiffs round and it's out into the street for us.'

'It's charity, Madge. Is that what we're reduced to?'

'Yes,' she stated bluntly.

He sat and stared into the empty fireplace. He felt physically sick at the prospect of such an ordeal. And they'd have to take the children with them. Graham and Jennie would witness his humiliation.

'Oh God,' he moaned.

'We'll go tomorrow,' Madge stated firmly.

John cudgelled his brains, trying to come up with an alternative, but couldn't. Madge was right, there was no other way.

'Like dirt,' John said, his voice shaking, as they emerged from what had once been a red sandstone building, but which was now a dirty grey from smoke, soot and general grime. 'They treated us like dirt.'

36

'It wasn't that horrendous,' Madge said.

He glanced at her, his eyes flashing. 'Yes, it was. You know damn well it was. Even worse than I anticipated.'

'Can I run to the shop, Ma? I've got a lot of deliveries to make,' Graham requested of Madge.

'On you go, son. And thank Mr Baird for being so understanding.'

'And will I go to school now?' Jennie asked.

'Do that. But don't say where you've been. Tell them you weren't feeling well earlier, but are better now.'

Jennie walked swiftly away in the direction of the school.

'It was good of Mr Baird to let Graham have time off at such short notice,' Madge commented.

John wasn't listening. He was mentally going over the interview they'd had inside. 'It was that Lord Cartvale who was the worst,' he hissed. 'From the way he kept wrinkling his nose at me you'd think I smelled.'

'They did give us money in the end. And the firm promise of more. We should be thankful.'

'Was I sure I really wanted to work, and wasn't a shirker?' John went on. 'And what was it about "moral fibre"? I liked that one.' His tone became bitter. 'I liked that one very much.'

'I suppose they have to be sure they're not taken advantage of.'

'Lord Cartvale,' John muttered, and hawked on the pavement. 'Pig! That's exactly what he is, a pig.'

'John!' Madge admonished quietly. 'We did what had to be done. That's the way to look at it.'

'I saw Jennie staring at you when you were pleading with them. She couldn't believe her eyes and ears.'

That wasn't so, Madge thought. How little John knew his daughter. Jennie had been shocked, yes. But Jennie had also understood the necessity of what she was doing. And hopefully learned the lesson that pride can be a fine thing, but there are times when it has to be discarded as an unaffordable luxury.

'I could murder a pint,' John said. 'That might wash some of the bad taste out of my mouth.'

'There will be no pint,' Madge stated, and stuck out her hand. 'Give me the money for safekeeping.'

'Don't you trust me, woman?'

She didn't answer that. Instead she wiggled her fingers. When she had the money she slipped it into a pocket. The bulk of it would go to Goodhew, but some would be used for food. Her empty stomach rumbled at the thought.

'Like dirt,' John repeated, and shook his head.

They'd survived, that was all that mattered, Madge told herself. What they'd had to go through to do so didn't matter.

She began to plan what they'd have for tea.

'The cards tell of opportunities coming your way. And travel. They indicate that you will be travelling a far distance,' Mrs Moore said.

John had to force himself not to smile. Him travelling a far distance! What utter guff.

Mrs Moore tapped one of the Tarot cards. 'A complete change, that's what lies in store for you. A complete change. A transformation almost.'

Better than a stand-up comedian, John thought. And to think she charged for this!

'You have a son?' Mrs Moore queried.

John nodded.

'He will do extremely well in life. Great things are in store for him.'

Great things in store for Graham! John found that hard to credit. Still you never knew.

Mrs Moore frowned. 'A dark place. I see you in a dark place. You and others.'

'What sort of dark place?' John queried.

'I can't be specific. A cave perhaps.'

A cave! He'd never been in a cave. Never even been near one. This was getting ridiculous.

'I see you spending a long time in this dark place. Time that stretches on and on. Years.'

Mrs Moore spoke further, then declared the reading over. John, out of politeness and because Anne was present, thanked her, saying she'd given him a lot to think about.

'Now, will you stay to supper, John?' Mrs Moore said, replacing her cards in their box. 'We're having Welsh rarebit.'

'Oh, I couldn't!'

'There's plenty to go round if that's what you're worried about. And while I'm making it I'm sure Anne can find you a bottle of beer.'

'Have you told her about us?' John asked Anne when her mother had left the room.

'I explained that we'd become friends after you saved my life. I didn't exactly elaborate on the friendship bit.'

'Did you tell her I'm married?'

'No, but she would have seen that in the cards. She mentioned your son don't forget.'

Opportunities, travel, transformation, a dark place! Total nonsense from first to last.

'I'll get that beer,' Anne said.

'Wait!' he whispered.

He took her into his arms and kissed her lightly on the lips. 'It's a pity your ma's home.'

Anne smiled.

'I'm delighted about your job. I really am.' Anne had landed herself a job in the accounts department of the Scottish General Insurance Company in Hope Street.

'I was fortunate,' she admitted.

'At least that's you sorted out.' He suddenly laughed.

'What is it?'

'I just thought, I know a dark place where I'd most certainly like to be.'

'Cheeky sod!' she admonished, and pretended to hit him on the nose.

39

He kissed her again, then she broke away. 'I'll get that beer.'

Tarot cards. What a waste of time, he thought. Strictly for the gullible, which he most certainly was not.

He felt a twinge of guilt when he sat down to his Welsh rarebit, thinking of the others at home on iron rations.

The guilt vanished with his first mouthful.

He couldn't sleep for thinking about Anne. His body was hot and aroused as memories from the occasion they'd been to bed together flashed through his mind. He could almost feel her, smell her, taste her.

Madge sighed in the dark, and turned on to her back. Breath whistled from her mouth.

He didn't want Madge, he wanted Anne. Young Anne with skin like silk. Madge's skin had been like that once, but that was years ago before the children.

He visualized Madge's stretch marks, those silvery white traces which he so disliked. It was as if some snail had been wandering round her middle and sides leaving trails of slime behind.

Anne, what a gorgeous bottom she had, firm, tight, rounded. Madge's on the other hand drooped, and was all squidgy.

He closed his eyes, but still saw Anne. She was lying beneath him, smiling. Calling him a hero, her Lancelot. And how they'd both laughed when he'd said he liked to lance-a-lot, and could have done so all night long with her.

Reaching out he grasped Madge's nightie and pulled it up.

'Eh? Eh?' she said.

'Ssshhh!' he replied, slipping a hand between her legs.

'Not now . . . tired . . .'

He ignored her. He had to have some relief or he'd never get to sleep. With a grunt he hauled himself into position.

'That hurts,' she complained.

'It'll be all right in a minute.'

'Couldn't you wait?'

No, he damned well couldn't, he thought, thrusting quickly.

It was soon over and he sank back into his own place. He'd sleep now, and hopefully dream of Anne.

'You hurt me,' Madge accused.

'Sorry,' he mumbled in reply.

'You don't sound it.'

'Well, I'm sorry about that too. Now let me get some sleep.'

Lovemaking! She knew another word for it, that had nothing to do with love.

John began to snore.

'I don't want to go to church,' Graham said.

'You're going, and that's an end to it!' John told him.

'But, Da . . .'

'I said that's an end to it!' John interrupted.

'I enjoy church,' Jennie declared, not trying to curry favour, but because she did.

John stared at his reflection in the mirror and slightly adjusted his tie knot. He went to church most Sundays, as he'd been brought up to do, and was a believer. His father had been an elder in the church they were off to now.

At the outside door, as they were about to leave, he put on his stern going-to-church-which-is-a-serious-business look. Going down the road he and Madge walked side by side, but not arm in arm, with Graham and Jennie directly behind them.

During the service John sang lustily and prayed for work. Afterwards they chatted with various neighbours and acquaintances, then walked home again.

That evening, as was their custom, John read extracts from the Bible aloud to the family who listened dutifully.

'Amen,' he said at the conclusion of the reading.

'Amen,' the others echoed.

'Listen to this,' Madge said slowly. 'Workers wanted for Devon copper mine, previous experience in mining an advantage but not necessary. Good wage paid. Tied house. Apply Wheal Tempest, Atherton, Devon, giving full particulars.'

'So?' queried John.

'They're advertising for men.'

'I know, you've just said. But it's of no interest to me, the work's in Devon. What paper is that anyway?'

'Last night's *Evening Times*. I picked it up from a tram shelter when I was out earlier.'

'Funny them advertising up here,' John mused.

Madge shrugged that aside. 'The point is, they are. Which is a chance.'

John frowned. 'Chance for what?'

'For you to apply.'

He barked out a laugh. 'Don't talk daft, woman. I'm a Glaswegian born and bred. This is where I live, always have done and always will do.'

'You're unemployed, with no prospects in sight, and we're on the Parish,' she reminded him.

'I'll find work . . .'

'You keep saying that, but don't,' she interjected sharply.

'I'm trying hard. You know I am. I'm out every single day doing my level best to find something, anything.'

'Without success.'

There was a pause during which she perused the article again. 'It doesn't say how many men they want. It could be a few, or many.'

'You really are serious about this,' John said softly.

'You're darned tooting I am.'

'But . . . leave Glasgow? Live somewhere else?'

Madge ran a hand over her face, and sighed. She didn't relish the thought of leaving Glasgow either, and certainly doing so had never entered her mind until

42

reading this advertisement. But desperate times called for desperate measures.

'I don't want to leave Glasgow,' Graham stated emphatically. 'I like it here. And what about all my pals that I've grown up with? I'd never see them again.'

Jennie, listening, wasn't sure how she felt on the subject. One part of her agreed with Graham, another thought going elsewhere could be exciting.

'We sometimes have to do things we don't want to,' Madge retorted to Graham. 'Anyway, there's no saying your father will land the job, so all this may come to nothing.'

'You're presuming I will apply,' John said stubbornly.

Madge stared at him, a glint of steel in her eyes. 'You will, because you know it makes sense. It's a chance, and any chance that comes our way must be grabbed at with both hands.'

'Let me see that,' John requested.

'There,' Madge stated, pointing out the advertisement.

'Copper mine,' he muttered to himself, thinking that sounded slightly exotic. 'I've never heard of this Atherton.'

'Maybe it's just a small place.'

'Would it be in the country?' Jennie asked.

'Could be,' Madge replied.

'I don't know,' John murmured.

Madge rose and crossed to the sideboard. From a drawer she took out a pad of writing paper, pen and bottle of ink. These she set on the kitchen table.

'If you write tonight I'll see it gets posted first thing in the morning,' she said.

Still John hesitated.

'I'll help you with the letter,' Madge stated firmly.

As she had said, it would probably come to nothing, he reminded himself. So he'd write her damned letter, if for no other reason than to keep the peace.

'Aye, all right then,' he said, and sat at the table.

It took a while, and a number of drafts, but eventually the letter was written to Madge's satisfaction.

As she'd promised she personally posted it first thing next day.

John came into the kitchen, sighed wearily, and threw himself into a chair in front of the fireplace.

'No luck again I take it?' Madge said.

He shook his head. 'No-one's taking on at all. It's the same story wherever I go, nothing doing.'

Madge glanced at Jennie busy with homework, and Graham engrossed in a library book. Now was the moment to spring her big surprise.

'I've got news,' she announced.

'Oh aye?' said John, showing little interest.

Madge dug into her apron pocket and pulled out a letter. 'We've had a reply from that copper mine in Devon. It came in the dinner-time post.'

John sat up in his chair. 'And?'

'You've been accepted,' she said.

He was thunderstruck. 'Accepted?'

'That's right.'

'Bloody hell!' Graham muttered. Normally that would have earned him a rebuke from his mother, but not this time.

Jennie laid down her pencil and listened intently, waiting to hear what was coming next.

'Let me see that!' John exclaimed, and jumped to his feet.

He snatched the letter from the excited Madge and read it through. There was no mistake, he had the job. And the wage wasn't too bad either. But then any reasonable wage would have looked good to him the way things were.

To the children Madge said, 'They'll be notifying us when we've to travel and sending us railway tickets for the journey. There's also to be a small payment of good-will. A few pounds only, but a few pounds none the less.'

One of the words Madge had just uttered exploded in John's brain. Travel! That's what Madge had said, *travel*. And wasn't Devon a far distance!

Travel, a complete change, a dark place that could be a cave. Not cave, but mine. My God, the spaewife witch had got it right after all. She'd been spot on.

Throwing back his head he roared with laughter.

'What's so funny?' Madge demanded, frowning.

The laughter died in his throat with a further thought. Leaving Glasgow would be the finish of him and Anne.

He took a deep breath, then another.

'What was all that about?' Madge queried.

He shook his head. 'Just something that crossed my mind. Nothing important.'

'Isn't it wonderful?' Madge smiled.

'Wonderful,' he echoed.

A little over two weeks later they met up in the Central Station with the other families travelling with them and took the train south.

Chapter Two

'Atherton!'

On hearing that word Jennie Forsyth peered out of the carriage window to see the village they'd come all these many miles to live in. And there it was, a huddle of houses dominated by a tall church spire. They'd arrived.

John sucked in a deep breath, and swallowed. 'We're here,' he said to Madge, sitting by his side.

Madge nodded. 'Aye.'

Graham gave them all a broad grin, the grin suggestive more of relief at ending their interminable train journey than anything else.

'Pink!' exclaimed Jennie in pleased surprise, pointing at a cottage. She'd never seen a pink house before – like something out of a story book she thought.

John stood up and reached for the nearest of their suitcases on the roof rack above their heads. He swung that down on to the seat where they'd been sitting, then reached for another.

'End of the road,' Tam Scott said from the next seat along, he also pulling cases down from an overhead rack.

John smiled in reply to Tam whom he was only acquainted with superficially, as he was with the others in their party. There had been ten families bound for Atherton on the train.

Mrs Scott smoothed down the front of her dress, and thought to herself she could do with a good wash. She was a very pretty woman in her early twenties with flashing blue eyes and jet black hair that she wore shoulder length. During the trip south John had glanced at her more than once thinking her 'a real looker'.

'I wonder if our house will be pink?' Jennie mused to Graham, who shrugged.

The carriage was filled with bustle now as people stood and gathered their things about them.

The train, its speed reduced to a crawl, slid along the platform. ATHERTON, a large sign in the centre of the platform, proclaimed. On either side of it were tubs filled with brightly coloured flowers.

'I feel like I'm going on holiday,' a female voice said, and laughed.

No holiday, Madge thought grimly, coming to her feet. But she knew what the woman meant. After all, Devon was a place renowned for holidays and holidaymakers.

The train came to a halt in a great exhalation of steam, and immediately carriage doors began banging open.

'Excited?' Graham asked Jennie.

'You bet. Aren't you?'

He assumed a pose of indifference, the complete opposite to how he actually felt. 'Not really.'

'Well I am. I can't wait to see where we're going to live, and explore the village, and . . . everything!'

He smiled inwardly. 'Bound to be a lot different to Glasgow, eh?'

'Bound to be,' she agreed.

'Here,' said Madge, thrusting several coats into Jennie's arms. 'Carry those.'

Graham was given a case and small leather bag. John was holding two cases, Madge one.

'Follow me,' John instructed, and led the way to the nearest door.

It was a glorious August day outside, the sky a deep shade of blue and cloudless. How clean everything was, Jennie thought, what a contrast to the dirty streets they'd left behind. The air here was so pure and fresh it almost made her head swim.

John placed his cases on the platform and glanced around. They'd been told they'd be met by someone from the mine.

47

'Isn't it a lovely village,' Emma Law said to Glenda Killock.

Glenda was about to reply when her attention was diverted by the small child beside her tugging at her skirt.

A guard rushed along the platform, and a few seconds later waved a green flag. The engine driver tooted his horn as the train, with another exhalation of steam, moved off again.

'Cows,' Graham said to no-one in particular.

'Where?' Jennie demanded.

'Over there,' he stated, gesturing.

Jennie made out about a dozen of the creatures.

'Friesians,' Graham said knowingly.

'How do you know that?' she queried.

He smiled mysteriously, teasing her.

She regarded him sceptically. How would a Glaswegian boy, who'd never set foot in the country before, know one type of cow from another? But then it would be just like Graham to know.

'Friesians,' he repeated. 'You can tell by them being black and white. I read it in a book once.'

That explained it, Jennie thought. Graham was an avid reader, well known at their local library in Glasgow.

A tall man came striding on to the platform and made his way towards the group. He had a stern face and a large hook-nose which gave him a predatory look.

Steve Campbell, one of their number, removed his hat as the man stopped before them.

'You're the Glaswegians I take it?' the man said.

'That's us sir,' Drew McIntyre piped up in reply.

'This way then.' And with that the man strode back the way he'd come.

'You all right?' Madge anxiously asked Graham who was struggling with the heavy case he'd been given.

'I'll manage.'

'Are you sure?'

'I'm sure,' Graham replied, hoping he wasn't going to have to carry the case too far. It was a ton weight.

As they passed the station master's office Jennie caught sight of him standing a few feet back behind a window staring at them. She frowned at his expression which was one of dislike, if not actually hate. His lips were thinned in disapproval, his eyes hard and glinting.

Now why should he be so hostile? she wondered, and shook her head. She promptly forgot about the station master when they came in sight of two flat carts, each pulled by a brace of shire-horses.

The man halted in front of the carts and turned towards them. 'I'd better introduce myself. I'm Mr Staddon, the mine manager. Sir Reginald himself instructed me to come down and meet you.' Sir Reginald was the owner of the mine, Wheal Tempest.

He continued. 'Now if you'll put your belongings on to these carts, and get up on them yourselves, I'll take you to your new homes.'

Jennie was thrilled at the prospect of riding on one of the carts, and couldn't wait to scramble aboard, which she quickly did.

Madge sat on the largest of their cases, while John sat beside her. He stared at their driver who hadn't made any effort to help, but had stayed on his seat gazing steadfastly ahead. The driver of the other cart behaved exactly the same way.

'What's that?' Jennie queried on hearing a sort of asthmatic wheezing sound, a sound she realized came from above.

She gasped with delight as she glanced up, for the source of the sound was a flight of five swans majestically winging their way overhead.

'They're beautiful,' Jennie stated quietly, admiration and reverence in her voice.

'They are that,' Madge agreed.

'Bonny,' John nodded.

The driver of their cart flicked his reins and the cart trundled into motion. It proved to be a bumpy ride, but one Jennie enjoyed none the less.

They went down the main street, High Street it was called, which gave them all a good chance to view the houses lining either side. Many were thatched with crooked, bent windows. Somewhere a cock crowed, followed by the squawk of chickens.

An elderly woman stood on the pavement gazing impassively at them. When they had gone on by she muttered to herself, then resumed walking along the pavement towards her destination.

'There's that pink house again,' Jennie said to Graham, nodding in its direction.

He thought pink an awful colour to paint a house, but didn't say so.

'Ouch!' exclaimed Jennie as the cart hit a particularly large bump causing her to bounce up and down.

'Hurt yourself lass?' John enquired.

Jennie prodded her bottom. She'd thought for a moment there she might have done, but hadn't. She shook her head in answer to her father's question.

They drew level with a post office-cum-general shop outside which a knot of women were standing. The women ceased talking to stare at them, not one of their expressions friendly, Madge noted.

'They probably don't take kindly to newcomers round here,' John said to Madge. 'It might take us a while to get accepted.'

Not too long, Madge hoped.

'There's the school where you'll be going,' Graham said to Jennie, pointing at a handsome stone building set back off the road.

Nice, Jennie thought, with what appeared to be a sizeable playground at its rear.

Mr Staddon was driving in his motor car in front of the two carts, going slowly so as not to outpace them. It was a lovely car, John mused. He'd always wanted one himself, but there was no hope of that. Workers like him didn't own motor cars, all they could do was envy those who did.

Someday there would be equality in Britain, John told himself. Maybe not in his time, but someday. He thought of the revolution that had taken place in Russia nine years previously. If only the same would happen here, oh what a glorious occurrence that would be!

'Hello,' said a girl about Jennie's age, sitting beside Jennie.

'Hello,' Jennie responded.

'I'm Christine Cook from Springburn.'

'And I'm Jennie Forsyth.'

'I noticed you on the train earlier.'

Jennie didn't reply to that, she hadn't noticed Christine.

'It's the first time we've been outside Scotland,' Christine declared.

'Us too.'

'Down among the English,' Christine went on, and pulled a face.

'My da says they're not that bad. At least so he's heard.'

'My da would never have come down here if things hadn't been so awful at home.'

'Mine neither,' Jennie nodded.

'I miss Glasgow already,' Catherine said.

Jennie thought about that. 'I don't. Maybe I will later, but not yet.'

'And what's your name?' Madge asked, having become aware of the two girls in quiet conversation.

'Christine Cook, missus. That's my ma and da over there.'

Madge looked at the couple, and smiled. They were roughly the same age as her and John she judged. Perhaps they'd become friends.

'Is she bothering you?' Pat Cook called over.

'Not at all,' Madge replied.

'Well, just send her back if she does.'

'I wonder if our houses will be together?' Jennie said to Christine. 'That way we'd be close neighbours.'

51

'I'd like that.'

'Me too.'

They grinned at one another, a bond having been forged between them.

'The mine!' John said, nudging Madge. He then indicated off into the distance where what was unmistakably the mine had come into sight.

Madge gazed at Wheal Tempest, her first-ever glimpse of a copper mine, where her John would make his living from now on, down in the bowels of the earth. At least it was cleaner and less dangerous than working down a coal mine, she'd been assured of that.

The postman on a bicycle went whizzing by. He didn't look at them which John considered strange. You would have thought he'd have shown some interest, but apparently not.

The carts rattled on, continuing along the High Street. Jennie leaned back against a trunk and let the hot sun wash over her. How gorgeous the sun was, she could have lain there with it beating down on her for ever.

'A lot of farms round here,' Christine said.

Jennie blinked her eyes back open and sat up straight again. 'Yes.'

'When it's my time to go to work I wouldn't mind doing so on a farm. I'm sure I'd enjoy that.'

Working on a farm did have a certain appeal, Jennie thought. Heaps better than the factories where lots of Glasgow people worked, or toiled as they called it. At least on a farm you'd be out in the open, surrounded by fresh air.

'Is he your brother?' Christine asked coyly, poking a finger at Graham, now sitting with his feet dangling over the side of the cart.

Jennie nodded.

'What's his name?'

Jennie told her.

'I have an Uncle Graham who's my favourite uncle. He always brings me sweeties whenever he visits.'

Christine's face suddenly clouded over. 'Not that he'll be visiting any more. Not down here he won't.'

'What does he do?' Jennie enquired.

'A fitter in an engineering firm.'

'And what about your da?'

'He was a labourer, but was made idle some while back before the strike.'

The carts left the High Street for a narrow, paved road which had houses on one side, a field on the other.

'I wonder what they're growing in that field?' Jennie said to Christine, who shrugged.

The car stopped and Mr Staddon got out. He was holding a buff-coloured folder on top of which were several sheets of paper.

'Here we are, your new homes,' he announced as the carts came to a halt behind his car.

Jennie gazed curiously at the houses they were in front of. Squat and sturdy they were constructed of red brick and slate roofs. They weren't in the least attractive, but did have an air of solid reliability about them.

'If you could all get down and gather round please,' Staddon requested.

The Glaswegians did as they were bid, for the moment leaving their luggage on the carts.

Mr Staddon eyed the group steadily, waiting for them to quieten. When he had their undivided attention he said, 'Before I allocate houses to specific families I would just like to remind you men that you are to report for work at seven thirty a.m. sharp, Monday morning. As today is Thursday that should give you ample opportunity to get yourselves settled in and sorted out. Any questions so far?'

There weren't, as this had been agreed in Glasgow. They waited for the mine manager to continue.

'If there aren't any questions then I'll get on with allocating the houses. The Campbell family?'

Steve Campbell, his wife Gina and son Douglas stepped forward.

'You're in number one which is this house here,' Mr Staddon said, indicating the house in question.

Steve Campbell immediately moved to retrieve their belongings from the cart.

'The Cook family?'

They were allocated number two. And then, as things were being done in alphabetical order, it was the Forsyths next.

Christine flashed Jennie a broad smile, they were to be close neighbours after all. Their wish had come true.

John directed Graham to get back on the cart and hand their suitcases down to him. Madge meanwhile had gone to Mr Staddon who'd given her a pair of keys held together by string from which also protruded a brown luggage label.

Jennie collected the coats that had been made her responsibility, after which she rushed up the path leading to the front door of number three. She couldn't wait to get inside and look round.

'There's a garden at the back,' Madge said to John as they followed Jennie up the path. There had been no garden where they'd lived in Glasgow, only a communal dirt yard where the rubbish bins had been located. She was thrilled at the prospect of having a garden, and one all their very own!

Madge inserted the correct key in the lock and the front door swung open to reveal a linoleum-covered hall.

'After you,' she said to her husband.

John, a case in either hand, stepped inside and made his way along the hall to a doorway which led into a spacious sitting-room. He entered the sitting-room, placed the cases on the floor, and gazed about him.

'Very nice,' he breathed.

Madge thought so too.

'The kitchen's through here!' Graham called out, staring through the kitchen window at the garden beyond. It was a large garden, about a hundred and fifty feet in length he judged, at least half of which was a vegetable patch, the remainder being given over to grass and flowers.

'Ah, the crate!' John exclaimed coming into the kitchen. The crate he was referring to was one they'd sent ahead containing blankets, bed linen and other household goods.

A quick perusal assured him it had arrived safely and undamaged. 'Shall I open it now?' he asked Madge who'd accompanied him through to the kitchen.

'Leave it till we've been round the house. Then you can open it while I unpack.'

John was pleased she'd said that, as he was as eager as she to look over their new house.

Graham sniffed the air several times. 'Still smells of the previous occupiers,' he declared.

That was true enough, Madge thought. She'd noticed it herself. But the smell would soon go, to be replaced by their own.

'There's a hideyhole under the stairs,' Jennie squealed from the hall.

The hideyhole had an oddly shaped door that opened into a cupboard that sloped at a steep angle.

'I've found a meter,' Jennie informed her parents when they peered in at her.

'Gas, penny in the slot,' John pronounced, having gone in and studied it.

'What about the electric?' Madge queried.

'Not here so it must be somewhere else.'

They all returned to the kitchen which had a door leading out into the garden. The second key Madge had been given opened that door.

'I'm going upstairs,' Jennie said, almost dancing with excitement.

Madge laughed at her. 'Calm down or you'll blow a fuse!' she cautioned.

Jennie's reply to that was to run upstairs, her shoes clattering on the wooden treads.

There had been a carpet laid, John noted as he

followed Jennie up the stairs, a carpet that the previous occupiers had obviously taken with them. Well, it would be a while before he could afford to lay a carpet on the stairs, he thought. There was far too much to buy before that – beds for example. These would probably be the first major items to be purchased.

If it had been possible they would have brought all their furniture and other bits and pieces south with them, but the expense involved had been prohibitive for a family in their situation.

'This is your bedroom as it's the biggest,' Jennie said as Madge and John joined her in the largest of the three bedrooms.

'And it is big,' Madge declared appreciatively.

The house was so different to the tenements they were used to, John thought. Different, and better as far as he was concerned. He loved the idea of having an upstairs – that appealed.

Madge noted that their bedroom overlooked the garden. She approved of that. She'd had many worries about moving south, such a huge step after all, even if they hadn't really had a choice in the matter, but now these worries were beginning to evaporate. The move would appear to have been a good one. It certainly was regarding the house – this house knocked spots off what they'd had in Glasgow.

Jennie left her parents and went into the bedroom she'd chosen for herself, the smallest and, in her opinion, cosiest of the other two. That bedroom was at the side of the house, the other at the front. The latter would be Graham's, with which he declared himself happy.

'Hello!' a voice shouted below.

John frowned questioningly at Madge. 'We're up here!' he replied loudly.

Madge recognized Christine's father from the cart.

'I'm James Cook,' he said, as he arrived at the top of the stairs.

'And I'm John Forsyth. This is my wife Madge.'

James shook hands with John, then Madge. 'Lovely houses, aren't they?' he said with a smile.

'Ours certainly is. No complaints,' John answered.

'I'm sure we're all going to be very contented here,' James went on.

'You're next door, aren't you?' John queried.

'That's correct. Number two.'

'We'll be seeing a lot of one another then,' John said.

All ten families would be seeing a lot of one another, Madge thought, but didn't say so, realizing John was only trying to be polite and make conversation.

'Quite a lot I should imagine,' James agreed. 'But as to why I've come barging in like this. We've had the wrong trunk delivered to our house, but ours hasn't gone to the folk whose we have. I don't suppose it came here by any chance?'

John shook his head. 'Sorry, it didn't.'

'Blast!' James swore softly. He sighed. 'Well, some-one must have it. It's down to a case of knocking on doors until I find out who.'

Madge smiled sympathetically.

'I'd better get on then,' James said.

'You and your wife must come round for a cup of tea soon,' Madge suggested.

'That's kind of you,' James replied. 'We'd like that.'

'Good,' Madge nodded.

'I'll see you again,' James said, raising a hand in salute, and with that he hurried back down the stairs.

'Nice chap,' John commented to Madge.

'I thought so too.'

'Speaking of tea . . . ?' He raised an eyebrow.

She laughed. 'I'll have to go to the shop for some, which I'll do as soon as I've seen everything.'

They toured Jennie's bedroom and Graham's. There was a trapdoor in the ceiling of the upstairs landing which John said must lead to a loft area. He would have had a peek up there if he'd had a ladder, which he unfortunately didn't.

'The garden now,' Madge said when they were again downstairs.

The outside toilet was also built of brick, and at right angles to the house.

'At least we have this to ourselves,' Madge said. In Glasgow they'd had to share a communal toilet with two other families.

'That's certainly an improvement,' John enthused.

Madge couldn't have agreed more, she'd always hated sharing.

They strolled up the garden, admiring the flowers and the late summer vegetables growing in abundance.

'There's enough here to keep us going for a while,' John said, examining some runner beans, of which there were several rows.

'And save a penny or two,' Madge beamed.

She crossed to a tall stand of tomato plants and plucked a handful. 'Just like being in the Garden of Eden,' she muttered to herself with a smile.

'Maybe we could keep chickens?' John proposed, thinking of those he'd heard in the High Street.

'Why not!' Madge answered. There was nothing tastier than fresh eggs, and they couldn't come fresher than straight from the chicken.

When they reached the house again Madge said, 'You make a start on the crate while I nip along to the shop and buy what I need. I shouldn't be long.'

'I'll stick the kettle on when I find it,' John said.

'You'll probably have to put some money in the meter first.'

John went to the kitchen cooker and turned it on. 'You're right,' he informed her when there was no hiss of gas. 'I'll do that straight away.'

'I'll help Da with the crate,' Graham volunteered.

'And can I come to the shop with you, Ma?' Jennie asked.

58

'Of course, darling,' Madge smiled at her. 'Just let me find my bag and we'll be away.'

Jennie waited for Madge at the front door where she gazed out over the field opposite, thinking what a lovely view it was. There had only been other tenements to look at in Glasgow, dirty ugly things covered in soot.

There were a number of men working in the fields, one of whom paused in his labours to stare at her. She waved at him, thinking he would wave back, but he didn't. He bent again to his task, ignoring her.

Mrs Scott came walking up the road carrying a wicker basket. She paused when she saw Madge appear at the door with her handbag.

'I'm off to the shop, are you?' Mrs Scott called out.

'I am,' Madge replied.

'Shall we go together?'

'Come on then,' Madge said to Jennie, and went down the path to join Mrs Scott with whom she'd exchanged a few pleasantries on the train.

Jennie fell in behind the two adults, skipping along as they walked and talked.

'I'm glad that train journey's over. I was getting a right sore bum towards the end,' Mrs Scott said.

Madge laughed at the other woman's candour. 'So was I.'

'Of course being pregnant doesn't help.'

'I noticed you didn't have any children,' Madge said.

'Aye, this will be our first.'

'How far gone are you?' Madge queried.

'Four and a half months. Right in the middle.'

Madge eyed her companion's stomach. 'You're not showing yet.'

'Maybe not, but I feel as though I'm the size of Jumbo the elephant.'

'Well, you don't look it,' Madge assured her.

They walked a little way in silence, then Mrs Scott said, 'It'll be funny not having the baby in Scotland. That

59

weighed heavily on my mind when we discussed coming down here.'

'I can understand that,' Madge sympathized.

'But we had to come. There was no alternative.'

'Nor for us either,' Madge stated softly.

'Life can be a bugger at times, eh?'

'Try to look on the bright side. See things positively. Think of the smashing house you've landed yourself.'

Mrs Scott brightened. 'Aye, there's that. We lived in a right dump before. It was so damp the paper used to regularly fall off the walls.'

'Not a good place to bring up a baby. Unlike here, eh?'

Mrs Scott drew in a deep lungful of air. 'This is the stuff to give the troops and no mistake. My baby will grow up healthy down here, no doubt about that.'

'By the way, I'm Madge.'

'And I'm Jane.'

The two women shook hands.

They turned into the High Street, and headed towards the shop. 'One fact I do know about Devon is that it contains a lot of cows. And that the people who live here make good toffee,' Jane said.

'Devon toffee? I've heard of that.'

'I love it. I've got an awfully sweet tooth,' Jane confided.

Jennie stopped to gaze at two little girls on the opposite pavement. She tentatively smiled, but failed to get a smile in return. With a sudden giggle the girls dodged behind a hedge and were lost to sight.

'How long have you been married?' Madge enquired as they continued on their way.

'Just over a year. We were childhood sweethearts. There's never been anyone else but Tam for me.'

Madge thought of John, and her heart sank. He'd been a disappointment straight from the word go. Though, to be fair, he had given her children she could be proud of – she couldn't have had better.

'Come on, keep up!' she called back to Jennie who'd fallen behind.

Madge and Jane carried on chatting until they reached the shop whose door tinged when they opened it. The man behind the counter looked over and smiled, a smile that died when he saw who it was.

'Good-day,' Madge said cheerfully.

The man behind the counter didn't answer, nor did any of the other customers already waiting. Four of them were women, the fifth an elderly bearded, bespectacled man with an equally elderly, down at the mouth, dog. The dog growled, a low rumble at the back of its throat.

'Anything else, Mrs Coffin?' the man behind the counter asked the woman he was serving.

'Half a pound of nice and tasty please.'

Madge wondered what nice and tasty was? It transpired to be cheddar cheese which the man behind the counter cut with a thin wire.

'Slightly over, is that all right?' he asked Mrs Coffin, who nodded.

The man wrapped the cheese in paper and placed it beside her other purchases.

The dog, which hadn't stopped growling, growled even louder. 'Quiet my beauty,' the elderly man rebuked in a stern voice.

The dog shut up, then sank on to all fours from where it glared at the newcomers.

'Doesn't seem to like us,' Madge ventured.

Again there was no reply.

Madge glanced at Jane. The atmosphere in the shop, which had been warm and friendly when they'd entered, had gone decidedly chill.

Jennie crossed to the sweet display and stared hungrily. There were candy sticks, aniseed balls, gobstoppers, liquorice twists, hundreds and thousands, lollipops – all manner of goodies.

'That's it then,' Mrs Coffin declared, and the man began totting up her bill.

'Two and three pence please, Mrs Coffin,' the man said. He thanked her when she paid him.

Madge had to move aside to let Mrs Coffin out of the shop. Mrs Coffin steamed past her, deliberately not looking at her or Jane.

This is awful, Madge thought. From the way these villagers were acting you would have thought she and Jane had the plague. Life was going to be very difficult indeed if this was how they were to be treated.

'I was saying to my husband John what a lovely village it is,' Madge smiled to Jane, loud enough for the others to overhear. 'Very picturesque.'

'Very,' Jane agreed.

'He said how fortunate our men were to land jobs here.'

One of the customers made a harumphing sound, then turned abruptly round and swept from the shop.

Madge gazed after her in dismay. What had she said? She'd only been trying to be friendly. Break the ice so to speak.

'Baccy Bob,' the elderly man requested of the man behind the counter.

'It's been a lovely day, hasn't it, Les?' Bob said.

'Lovely,' Les nodded.

'Did you take your usual constitutional?'

'Of course. Two mile there and two mile back. Do it every day, rain or shine.'

'You're a wonder,' Bob declared, putting a tin of pipe tobacco on the counter.

'Hasn't come down in price I don't suppose?' Les asked hopefully.

''Fraid not. Same price as usual.'

'Far too expensive,' Les grumbled, digging out some coins from his trousers pocket. He slowly and methodically counted out what he owed, slapped the money on the counter beside the tobacco, then counted it a second time with a finger.

'Can't be too careful,' he said, picking up his tin.

'Of course you can't, Les. Bye for now then.'

Les tugged on the length of string acting as a lead and his dog rose to its feet. It growled and snapped its teeth at Madge and Jane as it went past them.

Bob served the next customer, and the one after that until it was Madge's turn. During this no-one spoke to either her, Jane or Jennie, treating the three of them as if they weren't there.

Bob looked uneasily at Madge. 'Yes?' he asked curtly.

Madge told him what she wanted.

'That all?' he demanded equally curtly when he'd come to the end of her list.

'For now,' she smiled.

He tallied up her bill and informed her of the total.

'Is this the only shop in the village?' she enquired as he rang the till. 'It's certainly the only one we've seen.'

'Only one,' Bob confirmed.

'And what's the population of the village?'

'Just under three hundred.'

'That large, eh?' she smiled.

He handed Madge her change and switched his attention to Jane. 'Yes?'

'Can I have a sweet, Ma?' Jennie asked none too hopefully, knowing how tight money was with them.

Madge was about to say no when, on a sudden whim, she changed her mind. 'How about a gobstopper?'

Jennie's face lit up at this unexpected treat. 'Oh please! Thank you, Ma.'

When Jane was finished at the counter Jennie asked for the gobstopper which Bob gave her in a small paper bag. 'That's a farthing,' he stated.

Madge laid the required coin on the counter. 'I'm Mrs Forsyth by the way, and this is Mrs Scott. We've come to live in the village,' she said.

Bob nodded, but didn't reply.

Madge had the urge to biff him on the nose for his sullenness and rudeness. She smiled sweetly instead. 'And you're Bob?'

'Mr Yendell,' he corrected her gruffly.

'Mr Yendell then,' she said.

He turned his back on them and began rearranging items on the shelves behind the counter.

Jane couldn't help herself, she raised her right hand to her face, placed her thumb against her nose and waggled her fingers at him. When Madge saw that she burst out laughing.

Sensing something, Bob whirled round, but Jane had already snatched her hand away from her face.

'Ready?' Jane said innocently to Madge.

'Ready,' Madge confirmed.

They left the shop with Jennie sucking her gobstopper.

'Not exactly the friendliest of folk, are they?' Madge said.

'Not exactly,' Jane agreed.

'Still, give it time. They'll come to accept us eventually.'

'We hope,' Jane smiled.

It was going to be hard living in Atherton if the locals didn't talk to them, or only did so with the utmost reluctance, Madge thought.

'Funny accents, haven't they?' Jane commented as they retraced their steps.

'They probably thought the same about us.'

'Me, an accent!' Jane exclaimed in broad Scots. 'You must be joking.'

Madge laughed again. Jane certainly made for lively and entertaining company. On parting at Madge's house they arranged that Jane would call the following morning for a cup of tea.

Back indoors Jennie helped with the unpacking, a job that didn't take long as they had neither drawers or wardrobes to put their clothes away in. After that she made up her bed, which consisted of a sheet and two blankets spread out on the floor. John said he'd try and find some sacking the next day and make straw palliasses.

While Madge got on with the evening meal – corned beef she'd bought at the shop, the tomatoes she'd picked earlier plus potatoes from the vegetable patch – Jennie decided to go out into the garden and get the benefit of the evening sun.

It was a beautiful evening, she thought, the sun a huge yellow ball low in the sky, the sky itself tinged with pink that promised the following day would be another fine one.

She swallowed the last tiny piece of her gobstopper, and sighed, wishing she had another.

She strolled further down the garden, and stopped. Tilting her head back she let the sunshine beat against it.

Jennie screamed in pain and surprise when the stone smashed into her cheek, ripping the skin and causing blood to spurt. She clapped her hands to her face and bent over.

'What is it? What's wrong, Jennie?' Graham demanded anxiously, running towards her.

She took her hands away from her face to find them covered in blood. Her damaged cheek was stinging.

'Ma! Da!' Graham cried out as he reached her.

Blood dripped from her cheek on to her dress, staining it at the front and side. She clamped her hands back to her cheek.

'What happened?' Graham asked, gripping her by the shoulders.

She looked up at him and saw two brothers instead of one. Both shimmering at the edges. 'Something . . . hit me on the cheek,' she stuttered.

He stared down and saw the offending stone on the grass, recognizing it because of the blood on it.

Graham glanced quickly about, trying to spot who had thrown the missile but there was no sign of anyone.

Madge was the next to come hurrying down the garden, followed closely by John.

Jennie felt sick, and thought she might faint. She bent over again which seemed to help.

'What is it?' Madge queried on reaching them.

'Someone threw a stone that hit Jennie on the face,' Graham informed her, seething with anger. He clenched and unclenched his fists. If it had been a boy and he got hold of him – well, God help the bugger!

'Let me see, lass,' Madge murmured soothingly.

Graham thought he spotted a movement beyond the vegetable patch, and was off like a flash. But, to his bitter disappointment and chagrin, it transpired to have been a figment of his imagination.

'Rotten lousy bastard,' he muttered to himself.

John had a clean hanky on him which Madge used to wipe away the blood. The cut wasn't as bad as she'd first feared. Although bleeding profusely it was really quite small.

'Will she need stitches?' John asked.

'No, not even one I shouldn't think,' Madge replied.

'It could have taken her eye out,' John said angrily.

'How are you now?' Madge asked Jennie.

'A bit better, Ma.'

'Is it sore?'

Jennie nodded.

Madge wiped more blood away. The site of the cut was already discoloured and swelling. Come morning Jennie was going to have a nasty bruise.

'Why would anyone do such a thing?' John demanded. 'I mean, she's only a wee girl after all. Who'd want to hurt a wee girl?'

'Another wee girl or boy,' Madge said softly. 'It seems the last thing we are in Atherton is welcome. That's being made obvious.'

'But to the extent of chucking stones? I never expected that.'

Me neither, Madge thought.

'Come on in and I'll wash it for you,' Madge said to Jennie, wishing she'd brought some antiseptic south with her.

Then she had an idea. To Graham she said, 'Run next

door to the Cooks and ask if they have any antiseptic. If they haven't, try the Scotts. I don't know what number they're in so ask until you find them.'

'Right Ma,' Graham replied, and rushed off.

'Can you walk all right, Jennie?' Madge then queried.

'I think so.'

'Come on then. I'll help you.' And with that Madge placed a supporting arm round Jennie's shoulders.

'I'll put the kettle on for the hot water,' John said, and strode off briskly back to the house.

By the time Jennie reached the house her vision had returned to normal and her nausea had passed. The cut still pained her however.

In the kitchen Madge removed Jennie's dress and then took her to the sink where she wiped more blood away while waiting for the kettle to boil. The bleeding had slowed considerably she noted, which was good. It shouldn't take long for it to cease altogether.

'It was so unexpected,' Jennie said, feeling sorry for herself.

'I should think so,' John sympathized from where he was standing at the cooker.

Graham came galloping into the kitchen carrying a small bottle. 'We were in luck, the Cooks had some,' he declared, giving the bottle to Madge. 'They were upset to hear what had happened and said if there's anything else they can do just to shout.'

That was kind of them, Madge thought. The Cooks were going to be good neighbours.

When the kettle came to the boil Madge instructed John to pour its contents into the stoppered sink. She then dabbed a corner of the towel into the water to wash the wound and surrounding area.

'Ouch!' Jennie yelped when the antiseptic was applied.

'Right. It's into your pyjamas and straight to bed, my girl,' Madge announced when she was finished.

'Aw Ma!'

67

'Sleep is the best medicine for you in my book,' Madge insisted.

Truth was, she was tired, Jennie thought. It had been an extremely long and tedious journey during which she'd stayed awake the entire time.

'Your mother's correct. Bed's the best thing after a shock,' John said, wishing she was going into a proper bed instead of a make-shift job on the floor. But there was nothing he could do about that.

'I'll come on up with you and stay until you've dropped off,' Madge said.

'Thanks, Ma.'

'I wish I'd found whoever threw that stone,' Graham declared, eyes sparking with anger. He and Jennie were very close, the pair of them adoring one another.

'Probably just as well you didn't,' Madge said softly, for Graham was a very powerfully built, and strong, lad. She also knew how fond he was of his sister.

John went to Jennie and kissed her on her undamaged cheek. 'Good night, lass. Sleep tight.'

'I will, Da.'

Graham also kissed her on the same spot. 'See you in the morning Jen.'

'See you then,' she said.

Madge tucked Jennie into the make-shift bed as well as she could then, although Jennie was twelve and past such things, she sang a lullaby that she'd used to sing when Jennie was younger, a lullaby she'd learned at her own mother's knee.

The journey and stone business had taken even more out of Jennie than she'd realized, and within minutes she was sound asleep. Madge crept from the room, quietly closing the door behind her.

'A bad start,' John said to Madge when she rejoined him in the kitchen. 'I just hope we haven't made a mistake in coming down here.'

'We haven't,' Madge stated emphatically. 'You need the work.'

'Still . . .' He trailed off, and shrugged.

'I never knew there was such a thing as red soil,' Graham commented from where he was sitting on the floor. 'There was quite a lot of it just before we arrived in Atherton.'

'I noticed it as well. Pretty I thought,' Madge said, refilling the kettle at the sink. 'Would you like a cup of tea?' she asked John, who nodded.

He wouldn't have minded something stronger, he thought. A glass of whisky and a pint would have gone a treat. His imagination caused his mouth to water, and he wondered if English beer was very different to what he was used to. Bitter was what he'd been told they called it down here as opposed to 'heavy' in Scotland.

'She'll be all right, won't she Ma?' Graham queried.

Madge glanced at him over her shoulder. 'You mean Jennie? Yes, she'll be all right. A nasty experience though.'

They drank their tea, and continued talking. Time ticked by, and they were beginning to think of an early bed when there was a knock on the front door.

'Now who can that be?' John said, frowning. Rising to his feet he went off to answer the knock.

When he returned to the kitchen he was accompanied by one of the men who'd travelled down with them.

'It's Mr Law,' John announced, reminding Madge of the man's name. They had been introduced briefly before their departure from Glasgow.

'Hamish please,' Law said, shaking hands with Madge.

'And I'm Madge.'

'Hamish says there's to be a meeting tonight,' John stated, frowning again.

'Tonight?' Madge queried in surprise.

'That's right,' Hamish nodded. 'In our house at number six. It's to discuss something my wife and I have learned which is very disturbing indeed.'

'Disturbing?' Madge echoed.

'Regarding the village and us being brought down

here. But I won't say anything further until we're all foregathered.'

'Can't it wait until tomorrow?' John asked.

Hamish shook his head. 'I don't believe so. The sooner we discuss this the better. For all concerned.'

How mysterious, Madge thought. 'I suppose we'd better attend then,' she said to John.

'So I'll see you there, at number six, in a few minutes,' Hamish declared, giving them a strained smile.

John saw Hamish out, then came back to a pensive Madge. 'Well, what do you make of that?' he asked.

She shrugged. 'Search me.'

'Something they've learned which is very disturbing indeed,' John said, repeating Hamish's words. 'I don't like the sound of that at all.'

Madge went and tidied herself up a little. That done she said, 'We'd better get along then. You'll be fine by yourself for a while, won't you Graham?'

'Don't worry about me.'

'I only meant it is a new house and . . .'

'Ma!' he interrupted, a pained expression on his face.

Outside it was balmy; a gentle breeze blowing in from what Madge judged to be the west. All around crickets were chirping, while off in the distance an owl hooted several times.

'The winters will be mild here compared to what we're used to,' Madge commented as they made their way along the road.

'I certainly won't complain about that.'

'Nor me,' Madge said, taking John's arm.

They stopped when there was a whistle, and waited for the Cooks to catch up.

'How about this then?' James Cook said when he reached John and Madge.

'Hamish wouldn't give us any information. Only that he thought it important that we attend this meeting,' Pat Cook chipped in.

'Well, we'll soon find out what it's all about,' John said, looking worried.

The door to number six was wide open so they went inside to find most of the other couples already present. 'I would have made tea but I don't have enough cups to go round,' Emma Law, Hamish's wife, apologized to them.

Jane Scott came over. 'A gathering of the clans, eh?' she said to Madge.

'Have you any idea why we're here?'

Jane shook her head. 'We're just as much in the dark as everyone else. All we know is that the Laws felt it necessary to call this meeting without delay.'

Shortly after that Hamish started counting heads. 'One couple left to come,' he declared at the end of his tally.

The last couple were the Killocks, Wally and Glenda. They arrived with their son Ian, who was too young to be left on his own. Other small children and babies were there for the same reason.

'Oh hello,' Madge said to Beattie McDonald whom she'd had a conversation with on the train. Beattie was a small redhead with an inturned eye. 'Do you know Jane Scott?'

Jane and Beattie shook hands. 'We've been generally introduced but haven't spoken,' Beattie replied.

Beattie's husband Bobby was a giant of a man who sported long hair and a bushy beard. They made an incongruous couple, known in the Glasgow street where they'd lived as 'the long and short of it', a nickname they'd both thought rather funny.

'This is all very exciting, isn't it?' Beattie said to Madge and Jane, John and the Cooks standing slightly apart talked among themselves.

Madge wasn't sure that exciting was the right word.

'Here we go,' Jane said, pointing to Hamish holding up his hands for silence, which he soon got.

'Thank you all for coming here at such short notice.

And just let me repeat that we wouldn't have bothered you if we hadn't thought it so important.'

He cleared his throat, then went on in a grave tone. 'Earlier on Emma and I decided to go for a walk round the village, and during that walk came upon a field on the outskirts of the village where a number of tents were pitched. We naturally assumed the occupants of these tents to be holidaymakers which, when accosted by several of them, we soon found out wasn't the case. The fact is the occupants of those tents were living in these very houses (and here he indicated the floorboards) up until recently, from where they've been evicted, I repeat *evicted*, by the mill owner, Sir Reginald Tempest.'

He took a deep breath, then said, 'I have to inform you that we have been misled about our jobs at Wheal Tempest. The truth of the matter is we have been brought down as strike breakers.'

Pandemonium broke out, everyone suddenly talking at once.

Strike breakers! Madge couldn't believe she'd heard what she had. Surely there was some mistake?

'What exactly was said, man?' Wally Killock demanded of Hamish.

John was shaking his head in disbelief, while his face had gone a pasty shade of white. Him, John Forsyth, a strike breaker!

'We've been duped, lied to it seems,' Hamish continued, 'brought down to Atherton under false pretences.'

'Oh my God!' Mary McIntyre husked, putting a hand to her mouth. 'I knew it, we should never have come. We should have stayed in Glasgow.'

'What exactly was said, man?' Wally Killock demanded a second time.

Things in Madge's mind now began to click horribly into place. The carters who hadn't made a move to help them with their luggage, the chill atmosphere in the shop where she and Jane had been cold-shouldered by the other customers, the stone thrown at Jennie. They now all made sense.

Hamish flapped his hands, requesting the uproar to subside. When he could once more be heard properly he replied to Wally.

'The story, as I understand it, is this. The Wheal Tempest workers came out in the General Strike but, like the coal miners, didn't go back again when everyone else did. Over and above a wage claim they are demanding better working conditions and that the management, Sir Reginald, recognizes the National Union of Mine Workers, which he adamantly refuses to do.

'Matters have been at an impasse between Sir Reginald and the strikers all these months, until he came up with the idea of advertising for labour in Glasgow.'

'We're here to break the strike and get the mine operational again.'

Steve Campbell swore which earned him a rebuke from his wife.

'That's what he thinks,' a grim-faced Wally declared, to various shouts of approval.

Alarm flared in Madge.

'He can count me out because I'll be damned if I'll break his strike for him,' Wally proclaimed hotly.

'I'm with you!' Barry Riddell shouted.

'And me!' said Drew McIntyre.

'It's the first train home to Glasgow!' yelled Wally, shaking a clenched fist.

'The first one,' agreed John.

'I think we should talk this through,' Madge said. Then, when that was ignored, she repeated it more loudly.

Jane nodded approvingly at her.

'What's to talk through?' Wally queried. 'It all seems simple enough to me. We've been brought down here as strike breakers whom I, for one, consider to be the scum of the earth.'

Madge felt the happiness she'd experienced since John

73

had landed this life-saving job melting away within her. Her heart was filled with black despair.

'Working men don't take advantage of other working men,' Wally went on. 'A principle is at stake here. A great and noble principle. We're a band of brothers after all. One class, united.'

'Principle doesn't put bread on the table,' Madge retorted.

He regarded her scornfully. 'Meanly said.'

'Only a man who's never had the hardship of making ends meet would come out with such drivel. For drivel is what it is.'

'Madge!' John whispered, wanting her to shut up.

Wally levelled an accusing finger at her. 'Are you telling us you'd strike-break? Or encourage your husband to do so?'

When she didn't reply, he sneered, 'Your silence answers the question loudly enough.'

Wally turned his attention back to Hamish, and was about to speak again when Madge said, 'Jumping on trains and going back to where we came from is all very fine. But I'd like to hear from you what we do when we get there. What do we do then?'

A murmur ran through those listening.

'Good point,' Jane said in support. 'What would we do then, Mr Killock?'

'Do? Does that matter?'

'It does to me and mine,' Madge stated.

'And for me and my family,' Nell James said, for which she received a foul look from her husband Duncan.

'And us,' Jane added.

'We search for other work,' Wally replied.

'Well, I know before we came down here my husband searched high and low for a job, and this was the only one he could find,' Madge said.

'That's irrelevant,' Wally pouted, waving dismissively at her.

'It sure as hell isn't irrelevant to me, or wasn't. Not when I had starving children to contend with.'

'She's right about the work situation in Glasgow. It's chronic,' Gina Campbell said.

'It's worse than chronic,' her husband muttered.

'Besides which,' Madge said, 'how many here have the price of a train ticket home? I know we certainly don't.'

Wally opened his mouth, then closed it again. He hadn't thought of that.

'Do you, Mr Killock?' Madge asked.

He glared at her.

'I thought so,' she said quietly.

'I'll find it!' he blustered.

'How?'

'By getting a job locally,' he replied, and grunted.

'That's right,' his wife Glenda nodded.

'You might do,' Madge said. 'But that would take time. And in the meanwhile where would you stay? Not in Sir Reginald's tied house, that's for certain.'

'I, eh . . . I . . .' He trailed off, looking furious.

'As I said,' Madge went on, 'this needs thinking through. What I suggest is we sleep on it, then get together in the morning and confront those people in the field.'

'To say what?' Barry Riddell queried.

'To explain our situation to them. And see if between us we can't come up with a solution to this mess we've been landed in.'

'I agree with that,' Beattie McDonald said.

'And so do I,' added Jane.

A silence followed during which Madge became acutely aware that every adult eye in the room was fastened on her.

'Shall we say nine thirty?' she suggested.

'That's fine by me,' stated Beattie. She glanced up at Bobby who nodded.

'And us,' said Steve Campbell.

Other voices spoke up, and it was agreed. They'd

meet in front of number three, the Forsyths' house, from where they'd go to the field.

If looks could kill the one Wally gave Madge as she left the room would have laid her out stone dead.

'I don't like it. I don't like it at all,' John said.

Madge and John were in bed, her mind whirling as a result of the night's events. 'It's not a case of like, but necessity,' she replied. 'High falutin' principles go out the window in my book when it gets down to the basics of putting food in our children's mouths and a roof over their heads.'

'How can I be a strike breaker? It's against everything I stand for,' John argued.

She didn't reply to that.

'I won't do it you hear. I won't.'

'You'd rather go back to watching Jennie and Graham starve?'

This time he didn't reply.

'Go to sleep, John. Get some rest.'

'I'll not do it,' he declared defiantly, and turned away from Madge, on to his side.

He would, she thought. She'd make him. They hadn't come all this long way to Atherton, Devon, just to go straight back home again. That would be ridiculous.

Chapter Three

Wally Killock, his wife Glenda and their son Ian were the first to arrive outside the Forsyths' house. Jennie spotted them through the window and told her parents they were there.

'Trust it to be them,' Madge said.

'Can I come?' Jennie asked.

Madge thought about that. 'Yes, all right. And what about you Graham?'

'I'd like to come as well.'

'Fine then.'

The four of them went outside to where the Killocks had been joined by the Cooks and McDonalds.

'Hello again,' Christine Cook smiled at Jennie. 'How's your cheek?'

Jennie gingerly touched the cut. 'Sore, and swollen as you can see. But it might have been worse. How did you sleep?'

Christine pulled a face. 'It wasn't exactly the most comfortable night I've ever had. What about you?'

'I'm stiff all over.'

For some reason both girls thought that funny, and laughed.

'Thanks for the antiseptic. I'll return the bottle later,' Madge said to Pat Cook.

'I'm only glad we could help. It was an unfortunate incident,' Pat replied, sympathetically.

Madge nodded her agreement.

'It's going to be another cracking day,' James Cook commented to John, peering up at the sky.

'Let's hope so.'

There was a loud 'coooeee!' and when Madge looked down the road there was Jane Scott waving at her.

The Riddells were the last to put in an appearance.

'Let's go then,' said Wally, and strode off with Glenda, carrying Ian, by his side.

'Does he know where he's going?' Jane asked Madge, who shrugged.

'Do you know where you're going, Mr Killock?' Jane called out.

Wally hesitated. 'I thought Mr Law would show us the way,' he replied, and indicated for Hamish Law to come forward.

'The man's an idiot,' Jane whispered to Madge, making her smile.

It wasn't a long walk, and soon they were approaching the field Hamish Law had mentioned the previous evening where an assortment of tents, all shapes and sizes, could be seen.

'I hope this isn't going to get nasty,' Jane said to Madge.

'Me too. That's why I think it's a good idea to bring the children with us. Less likelihood of anything physical happening with them about.'

Wally was now deep in conversation with Hamish Law, waving his arms about and repeatedly stabbing the air with a finger as he made point after point.

As they entered the field people around the tents stopped to stare at their approach, while others who'd been hastily summoned appeared from inside the tents.

'Bloody strike breakers!' a male voice shouted.

'Go home, you're not wanted here!' another voice, this time a female, screamed.

'Go back to Scotland where you came from!' a male voice yelled.

Madge spotted the latter speaker, a small man with a red, angry face who shook a fist at them.

The Devonians gathered into a knot to glare at the advancing Glaswegians who stopped about a dozen feet away, as Wally held up a hand. Madge could feel the resentment emanating from the Devonians washing over her.

Graham moved to stand beside his sister, to protect her if anything did blow up.

'We're here to talk,' Wally announced.

'There's nothing to be said,' a man replied from the other side.

'We want you to know we had no idea we were coming down here as strike breakers. We swear that's so.'

Mutterings went through the ranks of Devonians who glanced from one to the other.

'Don't believe you,' a man answered.

'It's so,' Wally stated.

'We swear it,' Drew McIntyre piped up.

'You're in our houses,' a woman accused.

'We only learned so last night. We were all appalled to hear that.'

'Well, now you can leave them,' the same woman went on.

'We came down here in good faith. We've been misled,' Hamish explained.

'Aye, misled,' Duncan James repeated.

'We wanted you to know our side of the story,' Wally declared.

'Your side of the story is that you're here to take our jobs and live in our houses. That's the truth of the matter,' one of the previous male speakers thundered.

Wally looked wretched. 'God, this is awful,' he said quietly.

Madge noted that several other villagers had now come into the field to watch what was going on, one of whom was the elderly man with the dog who'd been in the shop the previous day. She recalled that his name was Les.

'Go home!' a Devonian male repeated.

'You're quite right, I will!' Wally declared, which earned him applause from the Devonians.

79

Wally went on. 'I will have no part in this . . . conspiracy on the part of management. For that's what it is, a conspiracy. We must stand firm, as one, be solid between both groups.'

Madge bit her lip when she heard that.

'Now you're talking, brother,' a balding man said. He came forward and grasped Wally's hand. 'My name's Pete Besley, what's yours?'

'Wally Killock.'

'Pleased to meet you, Wally brother.'

'And to meet you, Pete.'

Wally turned to the other Glaswegians, his face flushed, eyes shining brightly. 'Who's with me for a return to Glasgow?'

'What about the train tickets?' Beattie McDonald queried.

'That's a problem we'll have to sort out, but sort out we shall,' Wally cried in reply.

'Sir Reginald will throw us out the houses,' Gina Campbell said.

'Then you can stay here in the field with us,' a red-haired Devonian woman declared.

A cheer went up from the Devonians.

'Shit,' Jane whispered to Madge.

'I'm going back to Glasgow too,' Barry Riddell stated, which brought forth another ringing cheer.

Agnes Riddell shook her head, but said nothing.

'And me!' declared John.

'No, you're not!' Madge shouted.

There was a hiatus while everyone turned to look at her. 'No, you're not,' she repeated emphatically. 'You're staying here and going to work at the mine Monday morning, and that's that.'

'Bitch!' the red-haired woman snarled, glowering at Madge.

'Right then,' said Madge, and elbowed her way to the front of the Glaswegians to stand beside Wally.

'Madge, be quiet,' urged John, joining her.

'No, you be quiet. For I'm going to speak.'

'Management toady,' Wally sneered.

She felt like slapping him, but didn't. Instead she said in a loud, clear voice, 'If Mr Killock decides to return to Glasgow, that's his decision. And the same for anyone else in our party who chooses to do likewise, good luck to them. But my family won't be going back, and I'll tell you why.'

She paused for breath, and to put her thoughts in order. 'As I pointed out to Mr Killock when we discussed this matter last evening, our family doesn't even have the price of the train tickets needed to get us home.'

'That can be remedied,' Wally interjected sharply.

'Maybe so,' Madge went on. 'But again, taking my family in particular, even if we did get the tickets, what are we going back to? John's firm went under as a result of the General Strike and he's tramped the streets of Glasgow ever since looking for other work. This job at Wheal Tempest is the one and only offer he's had in all that time. So going home for us would mean his tramping the streets again looking for employment that simply isn't there.'

'It's true,' commented Jane, while several other Glaswegian women nodded their agreement.

'What I say is—' Wally began.

'Be quiet for a moment,' Madge cut in fiercely, silencing him. His lips thinned and curled downwards, while his eyes sparked with malice.

Madge continued, 'And where would my family stay if we did return? We don't have a house any more. Not only that, we sold off, and got rid of, our furniture and other furnishings as well.'

'That's not our fault,' a Devonian man said in a surly voice.

'I accept that,' Madge replied. 'I'm only explaining our situation to you so you can understand. As far as I'm concerned, sorry as I am for you and your troubles, we

81

can't go home. It's impossible. It's a case of having been tricked into coming, we're here for good.'

'Our position is exactly the same,' stated Jane.

'And ours,' added Beattie McDonald.

'I'm sure it's the same for all of us. Is that correct?' Madge glanced round the Glaswegians, but there were no dissenters.

'Even you, Mr Killock?' she asked.

He didn't reply.

'I take it that means yes,' she said, a trace of sarcasm in her voice.

'But what about us?' Pete Besley queried.

She stared him straight in the eye. 'You've quite simply been outmanoeuvred by management,' she informed him.

Pete swore.

'Clever that Sir Reginald. Slippery as a bagful of eels,' a Devonian woman muttered.

'You're right there, my lover,' said a chap standing beside her.

'But he wouldn't win if we also refused to work!' Wally declared desperately. 'There's a great principle at stake here.'

Madge focused her attention again on him. 'If Sir Reginald can trick us into coming to Atherton he can go on doing the same to others until eventually he finds those who will strike-break. By employing the tactics he has it is inevitable that Sir Reginald will win. And I believe it to be stupid, no matter what great principles are involved, to fight the inevitable. Which is why my John will be reporting on Monday as instructed.'

A silence fell over all those present while they cogitated that.

'There are people in this country today who would murder for a job, far less strike-break,' commented Emma Law.

'What Mrs Forsyth says makes sense. I'm sorry for you Atherton people but come Monday I'll be reporting also.

I don't like doing it, and don't want to, but will,' said the giant Bobby McDonald.

Jane gave her husband a hard look, followed by a nod. 'Me too,' declared Tam. 'To follow any other course would be cutting off my nose to spite my face.' He addressed the Devonians directly. 'I'm sorry too, truly I am.'

'But you can't do this!' Wally protested.

'You come and camp in the field. That's your prerogative,' Madge told him.

'I will!'

'Then do.'

'I'll be there on Monday also,' stated James Cook. 'It goes totally against the grain I admit, but I'll be there.'

'Are any of you miners?' a Devonian man asked.

Duncan James and Drew McIntyre held up their hands. 'I am,' they said in unison.

'But not copper miners, eh?'

'That doesn't matter, Gideon,' Pete Besley said. 'Mining is mining, whatever. Staddon will soon show them the ropes, and the mine will be producing again before you know where you are. Maybe not the amount of ore it produces when we're there, but producing none the less.' He sighed deeply. 'Much as I hate to admit it, this woman has the rights of it. We're beaten.'

'Don't give in!' Glenda Killock cried. 'You must fight, fight and keep fighting.'

'That's so,' urged Wally.

'Outmanoeuvred,' Madge repeated to the Devonians. 'And us tricked. If you continue to stay out, and we join you, it could well be that none of us have jobs in the end.'

'Slippery as a bagful of eels,' repeated the same Devonian woman.

'Do we go back then, Pete?' Gideon asked.

Pete rasped a hand over his chin. 'It looks that way. Sir Reginald has got the better of us.'

'But after all this time!' another Devonian man exclaimed in despair.

'Wasted,' Pete muttered, and swore again.

'Come on,' said Madge, plucking at John's sleeve. 'This is finished.'

The Forsyths, Scotts and Cooks banded together for the walk back. 'You were marvellous,' Jane whispered to Madge.

'Well, someone had to make them see sense. People like that Wally Killock are a menace. Big mouth and little brain.'

Jane nodded her agreement.

Madge felt greatly relieved that the meeting was over, and that her points had won the day. Maybe now they could get on with starting their new life in Atherton.

'Les Pack to see you, sir,' Jones the butler announced.

Sir Reginald glanced up from his *Times*. 'Where is he?'

'In the kitchen, sir.'

Sir Reginald laid his *Times* aside and rose. He checked he had some money in his pockets before going downstairs.

Les, cap in hand, stood just inside the kitchen door. The dog was tied up outside.

'So Pack, what have you got to tell me?' Sir Reginald enquired. He listened intently as Les reported all that had happened in the field between the Glaswegians and Devonians.

Sir Reginald chuckled when Les came to the end of his story. 'Very good, very good indeed. This Mrs Forsyth sounds a woman of intelligence and wisdom.'

Les had made his day. The strike was broken, and come Monday the ringleaders would pay the penalty for causing him so much inconvenience, not to mention loss of income. He couldn't wait to go back upstairs and break the news to Lady Tempest.

'Here you are, Pack,' he said, handing Les a shilling.

'Thank you, Sir Reginald. Thank you,' Les replied obsequiously.

Sir Reginald was so delighted he added, 'When Christmas comes round I'll see you have a fat chicken for the oven. How's that?'

'Thank you again, Sir Reginald.' Les bobbed his head and shoulders, then repeated the action.

And after speaking to Lady Tempest he'd telephone Staddon at the mine, Sir Reginald thought, turning round and walking away.

Les, clutching his shilling, returned to untie his dog. From there he went straight to the shop to buy more tobacco.

Madge looked up when there was a loud rap on the front door. Jane? she wondered. Or perhaps Pat Cook from next door.

'I'll get it,' said Jennie.

She returned with a man Madge recollected from that morning's meeting. 'Can I help you?' Madge asked pleasantly.

The man glanced sadly round the room. 'This was our kitchen,' he said.

'You lived here?'

'Me and the missus and children.'

Madge took a deep breath. 'I really don't know what to say.'

'Nothing to be said,' the man replied. 'Sir Reginald won't give it back to us, that's for sure. Not with you in it, he won't.'

The man looked at Jennie, and smiled. 'This your daughter?'

'Jennie,' Madge explained.

'A fair maid. We have a maid about the same age. Her name is Patience.'

'A pretty name,' Madge acknowledged.

'Your Jennie will meet my Patience at school no doubt. It's a grand school. The headmaster, Mr Gidley, has been very supportive of our strike. He's been a good friend and brother.'

John entered the room. 'I thought I heard a strange voice.'

'John, this is Mr . . .'

'Zelly,' the man said. 'Tom Zelly.'

'He and his family used to live here,' Madge explained.

'Sixteen year,' Tom stated. 'That's how long.'

John extended his hand and, after a moment's hesitation on Tom's part, the two men shook. 'Being evicted must have been awful for you,' John said. 'When I lost my job in Glasgow we came close to it ourselves. You have my sympathy.'

'And mine,' Madge added.

'It was a shock, I can tell you. One minute here, the next in the field. My Daisy cried for days.'

'How can we help you?' John asked softly.

'I've come to ask for some of my vegetables. The vegetables I planted and tended out back. For today's meal, see.'

'Of course,' smiled John. 'Help yourself. I'm afraid we've used a few, but now I understand what's what, you have my word we won't use any more.'

'You just come round any time you want and help yourself,' Madge said.

'Can't get no fairer than that,' Tom acknowledged. 'We do need them, you understand.'

'We understand,' John replied. 'And there's no need to explain. They're yours by right. I'm sure the other Glasgow families will feel the same way about vegetables they've inherited.'

'Perhaps if you'd speak to them?'

'I will. Right away,' John promised.

'That's kind of you.'

'The very least I can do in the circumstances.'

Tom gazed sadly round the room again. 'Oh well!' he sighed. 'Better get on. Mother's waiting for they veges.'

Madge and John watched Tom make his way up the garden. 'Seemed a nice enough chap,' commented John. Then added, 'I wonder what he did with the stair carpet he took away with him?'

Later, when Madge opened the back door, she found a small pile of vegetables stacked up. She was touched by that.

'Don't fuss woman, I'm all right!' John said tetchily. Truth was he was both nervous and apprehensive and trying not to let it show.

'There's your dinner,' said Madge, thrusting a brown paper bag into his hands. 'And your flask.'

He slid the flask into a jacket pocket. 'That's me then. Wish me luck?'

'Of course.' She pecked him on the cheek.

'A mining we will go,' he sang. 'A mining we will go. Hey ho my daddy o, a mining we will go!'

'Get on with you,' she smiled, and smacked him on the shoulder.

'See you tonight then.'

'Be careful.'

'I will. Don't worry about that.'

He opened the front door and stepped out. It was ten past seven on Monday morning, in twenty minutes' time he would start his first day at Wheal Tempest.

Several other men were emerging, including James Cook. He and John fell into step as they headed for the mine.

Madge watched them go, smiling to herself when Wally Killock went past. Tam Scott gave her a cheery wave as he went by, which she returned.

At Atherton Manor, overlooking Wheal Tempest, Sir Reginald Tempest stood at a window watching the men go into work, his expression one of grim satisfaction.

He reached for his stick, put on his hat, then left to join them.

*　　*　　*

Sir Reginald concluded his speech to the workforce and stared at the shocked faces gazing back at him. If they were going to strike again, now would be the moment.

The moment ticked by. And another. There would be no second strike, Sir Reginald thought, smiling inwardly. They were all too scared to do so in the light of the examples he'd made.

He signalled Staddon to carry on and strolled over to where his car was waiting. He had business in Exeter, but would return to the mine later to see how things were progressing.

'I'm going to assign you new men to an experienced partner, so you will be working in pairs for the time being,' Staddon announced. 'Campbell!'

John stepped forward when his name was called. 'You'll be working with Zelly,' he was told.

Tom came over and nodded to John. 'There's a coincidence,' said John.

''Tis that.'

'There are no hard feelings I hope. Otherwise maybe I should partner someone else?'

'There will be hard feelings whoever you and your mates partner with. So it's best we stay as we are.'

'Right,' agreed John.

'We need to get your gear first. Then we'll go on in.'

When John was kitted out Tom took him to a small tramway where others were already waiting aboard the partially caged cars.

A few minutes later, the tram rattled into life and they entered a large hole in the hillside. John turned round and watched the space with daylight streaming in grow smaller and smaller until, going round a bend, it vanished altogether.

The darkness was absolute, until further along someone turned on his hat lamp. After that others turned on theirs, creating flickering lights in the gloom.

John listened to the trickle of water as it ran and dripped from the surrounding walls and rock overhead.

A dark place, John thought, recalling again Mrs Moore's prediction. Well she was right about that. It couldn't have been darker.

'Know anything about dynamite?' Tom queried.

'Not a thing.'

'I'll have to teach you then.'

The tram continued to rattle on into the bowels of the hill.

'So, how was it?' Madge asked as John came into the kitchen.

Wearily he ran a hand over his face. 'It's hard graft and no mistake. I'm going to be as sore as hell tomorrow morning.'

'That bad, eh?'

'I'll get used to it. Shouldn't take more than a week or two.' He paused, then said, 'Remember that Pete Besley you spoke to in the field? Well, he got the sack. Him and nine others.'

'No!' Madge exclaimed softly.

'Aye, Sir Reginald put in an appearance and did it personally. Ten men out, us ten Glaswegians in as their replacements.'

'What about Tom Zelly, the chap whose house this was?'

'He's all right. He's been allocated a cottage that had been occupied by one of those given the sack. Carrot Cottages, the row is apparently called, all of them Sir Reginald's. Funny thing is I've been made Tom's partner. He's teaching me the job.'

'What are the sacked ten men going to do?'

John shook his head. 'Continue camping I suppose and look for work elsewhere. Poor bastards.'

'All with wives and children, I suppose?'

'I suppose,' John said.

God, it could be a hard life, Madge thought. She pitied the ten men and their families with all her heart.

'Are you hungry?' she asked.

'Starving. And cold. It's very cold down there. Cold and damp that seeps into you.'

'A hot meal and an early night for you, I think,' she suggested.

'Sounds great.'

'It won't be long till I dish up.'

The tea was mince and mashed potatoes, a favourite of John's. When it was ready she called the children and began to serve.

When she went to hand John his plate she found he'd fallen asleep, slumped against the wall.

After he'd eaten he had a good wash, then hauled himself up to bed where he was soon fast asleep again.

John arrived home wearing a huge smile. 'Here you are, lass,' he said, and threw Madge an already opened, buff-coloured envelope which she deftly caught. It was Friday night, his first pay day at Wheal Tempest.

Madge tipped the envelope's contents into the palm of her hand, and counted it. 'You've already taken out some,' she said quietly.

'Of course! You get your bit and I get mine. Fair's fair.'

This was something to which she'd already given some thought. 'I know this is how we've done it in the past, but I feel, because of our new circumstances, it should now be changed,' she said.

He frowned. 'Changed? How do you mean, changed?'

'We have so much to buy, John, and heaven knows, little enough to buy it with. I'll need every penny I can get to help furnish this house.'

'You mean you think I should give you everything!' he exclaimed incredulously.

'Until we get on our feet again, yes.'

'But . . . the pub! I always have a drink at the weekends.'

'You'll simply have to do without that for a while.'

John swore.

'We haven't even got a chair to sit on!' she reminded him. 'All we have is the empty crate we brought a few things down in. We need a table, chair, beds . . .' She trailed off, and made an appealing gesture to him.

She was right, he told himself. He hadn't thought, been selfish. Of course the old ways would have to change, at least for a time, that made sense. But to do without his Friday night at the pub! It had been one thing doing without it when he was on strike, but now he was working again, to go without hurt even more. Looking forward to his weekend drink got him through the week, as it got many a Glaswegian working man through his week. For many of them it was straight from work into the boozer and remain there till closing time.

He dug in his trousers pocket and pulled out the money he'd kept for himself. 'There,' he said, and gave it to her.

'You'll be ready for your tea then?'

He nodded, feeling miserable.

'I'll get it.'

When the tea was finished Madge and Jennie set about washing and drying the dishes. They were in the middle of it when there was a knock on the outside door.

'I'll get it,' Graham volunteered. When he returned he had James Cook with him.

'I wondered if you fancied going out for a pint later?' James said to John.

'No, not for me I'm afraid.'

'Don't you like a drink?'

'I do, it's just that . . .' John shrugged. 'Well, not tonight.'

Madge couldn't help but feel sorry for him. He looked so down in the mouth, like a child who's just been told he's not to have a promised treat after all. The price of a single pint wouldn't make that amount of difference, she thought.

'Why don't you go, John. Just for one.'

He brightened immediately. 'If that's what you want, Madge, then why not?'

'Just the one,' she said.

As she'd relented he thought he'd try and push her that little bit further. 'It'll have to be two, Madge. Would be impolite otherwise.'

'How's that?'

'James will buy me a pint so I'll have to puy him one back.'

She knew full well he was chancing his arm, but didn't want to argue in front of James. 'Two then,' she reluctantly agreed.

John brightened even more, positively beaming now. 'That's settled then,' he said to James.

He saw James out, the pair of them making arrangements *en route* to the door.

Coming back into the kitchen he went straight to Madge and kissed her on the mouth. 'Thanks darling.'

'Two and no more mind,' she stated, handing him a shilling. 'Promise?'

'Cross my heart and hope to die,' he assured her, crossing his heart the way children do.

When he left the house he was humming, 'I Belong To Glasgow'.

John and James paused outside the Atherton Arms which was buzzing with conversation. Through the dimpled glass panel inset in the black painted door, John could make out a number of bodies.

'Let's go in then,' said James, and led the way.

The conversation in the pub stilled as they made their way to the bar. What had been a warm, friendly atmosphere suddenly became distinctly hostile.

John spotted Tom Zelly and nodded. Tom gave him an almost imperceptible nod in return.

The conversation restarted, but was now muted, with a whispering element to it. Every so often someone would glance in their direction, then look away quickly again.

The landlord made sure he'd served everyone else

before approaching them. 'What will it be?' he asked in a neutral tone.

James placed their order and the pair of them watched while their pints were pulled.

'Lovely night out,' John remarked to a man beside him.

The man didn't answer. Instead he turned his back on John.

Tom Zelly laid his now empty glass on the bar and left via a rear door, people calling out and wishing him well as he went.

'I think we'd better sit down,' suggested John.

The table they chose gave them an excellent view of the dartboard where a game was in progress. Several others from the bar drifted round to watch the game, giving good-humoured advice and making comments as the game went on.

Duncan James came into the pub, waved, and indicated he'd be over.

'A hundred and eighty!' a man at the ocke yelled, punching the air. The ocke was the line drawn on the floor from which the darts were thrown.

Several of the onlookers clapped, while the man's opponent muttered darkly about luck.

'You play?' James asked John.

'I've been known to.'

'I like a game myself.'

'We'll maybe have one then sometime.'

'Sometime,' James agreed.

Duncan sat down beside them. 'I've been in friendlier pubs,' he said quietly.

'I suppose we should have expected it,' James replied.

John had a sip of his pint. Good beer, he thought, even if different to what he was used to. He wouldn't have any trouble drinking this.

A dart bounced off the board and flew backwards to land at Duncan's feet. He automatically bent and picked it up.

93

The thrower hesitated when he saw Duncan holding the dart. He glanced at some of his companions, then went over to Duncan who handed it back to him.

'Ta,' the man uttered grudgingly, and returned to his game.

'Another half of cider,' a man at the bar called out.

'I'm certainly glad you mill folk are back at work. It's been somewhat thin here all this while,' the landlord said to a customer.

'And not very profitable,' the customer replied.

'You can say that again!'

'You could afford it,' another customer, who was also a mine worker, said jocularly to the landlord. 'You must have pots of money from what you've taken off us in the past.'

'Oh, pots!' the landlord responded drily. 'Me and the missus keeps it under the bed and counts it every night before we gets in.'

'I believe you,' said the same customer, and laughed.

The door opened and several men entered who were very clearly farm labourers. They were greeted warmly, as they declared in a loud voice how good it was to see those from Wheal Tempest using the pub again.

A dart thudded home, followed by a victory shout from the thrower.

'Proper job! Proper job!' an onlooker said, and clapped him on the back.

John drained his glass, apologized to Duncan for not being able to buy him one also, and went up to the bar to get his round in. He tried not to show any impatience when he was kept waiting.

'Night everyone!' a man shouted at the door.

'Night Norman!' was the concerted reply.

A man and woman were next to leave.

'Night all!' the man said.

'Night Dave! Night Fran!' rang out in answer.

John took the drinks back to their table where they sat watching a new darts game in progress.

Time passed, and eventually John finished his second pint. 'I must be off now, I'm afraid,' he declared.

'Me too,' nodded James.

'I'll walk with you,' said Duncan.

The three of them rose and went to the door. 'Good night!' John called out to those remaining.

There wasn't a single good night in answer.

'All right?' John asked Madge.

'Fine. And you?'

'Looking forward to it.' It was Sunday morning and they were about to go to church, their first visit as they hadn't gone the previous week.

'There's the collection,' said Madge, slipping him a coin which he pocketed.

'I know the Scotts will be there. Jane told me they were going. We might as well sit with them,' Madge said.

John thought that a good idea.

Madge shouted to Graham and Jennie. Jennie ran down from her room and Graham came in from the garden where he'd been idly daydreaming.

'Let's go then,' smiled Madge.

'I adore the sound of church bells, don't you?' Madge commented as they made their way along the road.

John grunted in reply.

Madge wondered if they rang the bells every Sunday morning, and hoped they did. The sound got louder the closer they got to church.

Madge glanced behind her when they were about half-way there and saw they were being followed by the McIntyres and McDonalds, the latter looking as incongruous a couple as they always did when walking side by side.

An elderly couple emerged from a lane, both white haired and stooping. The woman smiled at Madge and John, who smiled back.

'Beautiful day again,' the woman nodded.

'Beautiful,' Madge agreed.

'At least someone's talking to us,' John said as they continued.

They arrived at the church and went inside where they were handed a hymn book and the Book of Common Prayer, the latter quite new to them.

'There's Jane and Tam,' said Madge, having recognized them from behind.

As they made their way up the aisle they were gazed at curiously by some, ignored by others.

'Are you sure it's all right to sit here?' John asked Tam on reaching the Scotts, for the last thing he wanted was for them to take up someone else's regular seats.

'It is. We checked.'

The McIntyres and McDonalds entered the church, looked around, saw the Forsyths and Scotts, and made their way towards them.

'Safety in numbers,' John joked to Tam as the McIntyres and McDonalds filed into the pew behind them.

Shortly after that, the Laws turned up and then the Cooks. They, too, joined the Glaswegian group, Christine coming in to sit alongside Jennie.

John opened the Book of Common Prayer and began reading the Holy Communion Service. He was engrossed in a section of it when the organist began playing.

They sang a hymn, then the minister, or the vicar as John had learned he was called down here, said, 'The Collect for today is—'

John wondered what a collect was? It transpired to be a prayer.

They had a reading after that, followed by another hymn and then a second reading from the Gospels.

'There,' whispered Madge, pointing to a place in the Holy Communion Service when it was obvious to her that John was lost. He muttered to himself under his breath, thinking this far more convoluted than the simpler, Scottish service.

When it was time for communion he wondered

whether or not they should go forward. They were Church of Scotland after all, not Church of England.

'What do you think?' he asked Madge.

'I don't know.'

Behind them the McDonalds rose to their feet, and stepped out into the aisle. John looked at Bobbie, and raised a questioning eyebrow.

Bobbie, realizing what John was trying to ask, bent to him and said quietly, 'We went up last week and no-one said anything. So I presume it's in order.'

Went up last week! John thought. Did they take communion every week? They didn't in Scotland.

'Come on,' he instructed Madge, and rose also.

John knelt at the altar rail, thinking this was another strange departure, in Scotland communion was taken where you sat. He accepted the wafer offered to him, and listened while the vicar blessed Jennie.

When the service was finally over the Scots made their way to the door where there was a queue to leave.

'It's very nice to see you here. Thank you for coming,' the vicar said sincerely to John, shaking his hand.

'A very different service to what we're used to. But I enjoyed it all the same,' John replied.

'Of course! Church of Scotland. You must tell me about their service sometime. I'd be interested to hear.'

'I will.'

John moved away and it was Madge's turn to talk to the vicar whose name was the Reverend Royal.

'I was impressed with the vicar. He struck me as a true Christian man,' John said as he and Madge headed home.

'I was too. We'll be going again then, I take it?'

'I don't see why we should change our habits, do you?'

'No. He did make us feel welcome.'

'There you are then.'

'Did you really enjoy the service?' Madge queried.

John put his hand to the side of his mouth, then said conspiratorially, 'There were bits when I thought I was in chapel with a bunch of left footers.' Left footers was a Scottish slang term for Catholics.

Madge laughed. 'It was rather like that in places.'

'I was half-expecting incense to be used at any moment.'

Madge laughed again, knowing exactly what John meant. The service they'd just attended was in complete contrast to the austerity they were used to.

Tam and Jane Scott came alongside, and the two women fell into conversation about Jane's pregnancy.

'Now pay attention, class,' said Mr Tremlett, Jennie's teacher, and began writing on the blackboard. His chalk squeaked as it moved across the surface.

Jennie grimaced as her hair was suddenly pulled from behind. 'Strike breaker!' a boy's voice whispered in her ear. 'Rotten strike breaker.'

'Here you see . . .' went on Mr Tremlett.

Tears of pain sprang into Jennie's eyes as her hair was pulled again. Then the flesh of her upper arm was nipped hard.

She glanced at Christine sitting several places to her right, but Christine was engrossed in the lesson.

'Stop it!' she whispered over her shoulder.

The reply to that was another nip to the same arm.

The torture continued throughout the morning, stopping for spells, then starting up again. When the bell rang for break the boy behind her dashed out of the door like a flash, but not before she'd identified him.

'What's wrong?' queried Christine as she joined her. Jennie explained.

'Are you going to tell the teacher?'

Jennie thought about it, and shook her head. That was the wrong solution. 'I'll speak to the boy myself,' she announced.

'Are you sure? Maybe you should simply ignore him.'

'No, I'll speak to him.'

They found the boy with a gang of others gathered

outside the toilets. Jennie strode over to stand about a foot away from him and stared him straight in the face.

'Well, if it isn't two of the Scotchies,' the boy smirked.

Another of the boys did a vocal imitation of bagpipes playing, and jigged on the spot.

'Do you think it makes you big to bully a girl?' Jennie said to the boy who'd tormented her. 'Well, it doesn't. All it shows is how pathetic you are.'

One of the gang sniggered, while the one who'd been making the bagpipe noise and dancing, stopped.

'Pathetic,' Jennie repeated.

'Strike breaker,' her tormentor sneered.

Jennie moved closer to him. 'Touch me again in class and I'll turn round and slap you silly. Have you got that?'

His face creased into a frown, for he could see she meant it. And furthermore she wasn't afraid of him one little bit.

'That's you told, Andy!' a boy said, and they all laughed, with the exception of Andy who realized the laughter was directed at him.

Christine was full of admiration for Jennie; she could never have faced up to the boy, and a boy surrounded by his pals, as Jennie was doing.

'Let's go,' Jennie said to Christine, and the two of them walked away.

Behind them the laughter grew in volume and derision.

Madge was pegging out some washing, pleased that at least they had a copper in the house, if no mangle. Perhaps John could find her an old second-hand one somewhere, she thought, and made a mental note to mention it to him when he came in from work that night.

The kitchen window slid open and Graham smiled out at her. 'How are you doing, Ma?'

'As you can see. Any luck with a job yet?'

He shook his head. 'But I haven't come home empty handed. Come in and have a look.'

'When I'm finished here.'

She entered the kitchen to discover Graham arranging a number of wooden boxes. 'What are these?' she demanded.

'Table and chairs. Until we get the real thing, that is. What do you think?'

She laughed. 'Your idea?'

'Saw the boxes being chucked out at the back of the shop and asked if I could have them. Mr Yendell said that was all right.'

'Wait a minute,' Madge said, and vanished upstairs.

When she returned she had a table-cloth with her, one of a pair she'd brought from Glasgow. She flicked it open, then placed it over the two boxes, making do as the table.

'Definitely an improvement,' she stated, eyes shining brightly. Going to Graham she kissed him on the cheek. 'You're a bright boy. Thank you.'

'Well, at least we don't have to sit on the floor to eat tonight's tea,' he smiled.

Suddenly, she was almost overwhelmed with emotion. She turned away so that he didn't see the wetness that had risen into her eyes. Life could be so good, in so many surprising ways, she thought.

'Wish I could find a job though,' Graham said disconsolately.

'You will,' she assured him. 'Something will come up in time. You'll see.'

John had been reading his Bible for only a few minutes when his mind started to wander. The printed words blurred, and were replaced by a picture of a smiling Anne Moore.

He swallowed hard. Anne was in the past, he told himself. He must put her out of his mind, forget about her. Anne was lost to him for ever.

What had happened between them had been so unexpected, totally out of the blue, something to keep as a treasured memory.

He wondered how she was, and what she was doing? Was she at home, or perhaps out with someone else, nearer her own age?

Jealousy rose in him at that thought. He wanted to say her name aloud, but couldn't because Madge and Jennie were in the room. He said it mentally, Anne, Anne!

'Pardon,' he queried, rousing himself from his reverie, realizing he'd been spoken to.

'I said, would you like a cup of tea?' Madge repeated.

'Please.'

He concentrated and the words before him reformed themselves. Anne's image slowly faded, but not before a cold sweat had formed on his brow.

'What's he up to?' Christine whispered to Jennie. The two of them were out walking by the river that flowed through the fields surrounding Atherton.

Jennie studied the boy who was lying on his front apparently staring at something. 'Search me,' she whispered in reply.

Christine giggled. 'His bottom's sticking up.'

Jennie laughed softly, for it was a funny sight. 'Let's go and investigate,' she suggested.

They skirted round some black-faced sheep who were grazing, and approached the boy from his rear.

'He's staring into the river,' Christine said.

At what? Jennie wondered.

When they were about a dozen feet away the boy sensed their presence and twisted round to look at them. He frowned in annoyance, and held up a finger to his lips.

Jennie stopped, for it was the boy called Andy who sat behind her in class, who'd pulled her hair and nipped her arm. She considered walking away without speaking, leaving him to his own devices.

Andy crooked the same finger he'd placed over his mouth, and beckoned them to him. He gestured they were to be as quiet as possible.

The girls bent low, and went the rest of the way on tiptoe. When they reached him they lay down beside him, one on either side.

'Otter,' he whispered, pointing.

Jennie followed the direction of his finger to see a brown, snakelike figure moving through the gently flowing water. It twisted and dived, then resurfaced again to race off in the opposite direction.

'I think it's just playing,' Andy said.

The otter climbed on to the opposite bank where it shook itself, and then stared around, its beady black eyes glittering alertness. It disappeared into some tall pinkish plants only to reappear suddenly down the river bank.

'He's gorgeous,' Jennie enthused.

'There haven't been otters round here for a while. This one's new,' Andy explained.

'There he goes again!' Christine exclaimed quietly as the otter slid back into the water.

'Is he alone?' Jennie queried.

'I believe so. I haven't seen any sign of a mate.'

They watched the otter for a few more minutes, then it returned to the bank and scampered away.

Andy sat up and the girls followed suit.

'Thank you for showing us that,' Jennie said.

'There's lots I could show you.'

'I'm sure.'

'We come from a big city so know nothing about the country,' Christine said.

'I'd hate to live in a big city. Must be dreadful.'

'It's not that bad!' Christine answered defensively.

'Well, I'd hate it.'

Silence fell between them. 'Do you think the otter will come back?' Jennie asked eventually.

'Oh, he won't have gone far. My guess is he'll stay around for a bit, so you'll be able to see him again. If you sneaks up quietly on him, that is. They's shy is otters. Very shy.'

They rose to their feet and Andy stuck his hands deep in his trousers pockets. 'What are you doing out this way anyway?'

'Just walking,' Jennie smiled.

'I come to the water meadows a lot myself. I like it here,' he said.

'Water meadows?' Jennie queried.

'Sure. All these fields are. Don't you know what a water meadow is?'

Jennie and Christine both shook their heads.

'Well, this river here is fed from Exmoor. When it rains heavily in the winter the river bursts its banks and floods all these fields. As far as the eye can see in that direction gets covered in water, like a huge lake.'

'Never!' Jennie exclaimed, thinking he might be teasing her.

'It's true I tell you. You'll see for yourself come January and February.'

Jennie looked out over the fields and tried to imagine them covered in water. 'Does it flood in the village?' she asked.

'Been known to. My dad says he once rowed a boat up the High Street when he was a lad.'

'Up the High Street!' Christine exclaimed, eyes wide.

'Don't worry, your houses have never been known to flood. Though ones near by have.'

'Water meadows,' Jennie murmured, thinking it a lovely name.

'Have you ever seen bullrushes like they speak about in the Bible?' Andy asked.

'No,' Jennie replied, while Christine shook her head.

'There are some further along. I'll show you if you like?'

'Please,' Jennie smiled.

'I'm Andy Alford by the way,' he stated.

'And I'm Jennie, and this is Christine.' She paused, then said, 'Does this mean we're friends now?'

'I suppose so,' he replied awkwardly.

'Then let's shake on it.'

She shook hands with Andy, who then did the same with Christine. He told them more about the water meadows and life in Atherton as he led them to the bullrushes.

John sat on the floor of the mine and opened the brown paper bag containing his dinner. James Cook sat beside him, as did Tam Scott. The other Glaswegians grouped themselves round about.

'What have you got today?' James enquired.

'Egg and tomato. You?'

'Paste of some kind.'

John grunted and poured himself some tea from his flask.

Further along the mineshaft were the Devonians. The two groups worked together, but when it was break-time the Devonians gathered on their own, making it clear that the Glaswegians were to do the same. The Glaswegians had made overtures during various breaks, trying to integrate the two groups, but every gesture had been rebuffed.

John glanced over at Tom Zelly. He and Tom got on extremely well during their work spells, but when a break came Tom distanced himself, joining his Devon mates.

John was thankful for the break, still finding the work extremely hard going. It was always a great relief to him when it was time to go home.

One of the Devonians cracked a joke, causing his companions to laugh. The Glaswegians watched with mixed feelings, all of them wishing that the situation was different.

All too soon John was back loading the heavy ore-stone into trucks which then transported it out of the mine.

*　　*　　*

Madge and Jennie strode across the water meadows *en route* to the river where Jennie was hoping to show Madge the otter and the bullrushes further along.

Madge stopped and picked a small blue flower that she thought looked beautiful. It had a divine scent she discovered, smelling it. There were other wild flowers dotted about which gave her the idea of picking some on the way home. She didn't have a vase for them so an empty bottle would have to suffice.

'Quiet now,' Jennie warned as they neared the river. 'From here on we go on tiptoe.'

Weed waved underneath the water's surface, long green strands of it that streamed with the current. In other places a different type of weed had grown tiny white buds that resembled a white carpet.

Jennie came up short. 'Oh!' she gasped.

Madge saw the little girl a moment later, totally submerged, trapped beneath the weed.

Madge burst into a run and shot off the river bank into the shallow water. She splashed her way towards the girl whom she grasped by the shoulders and yanked out of the weed.

The girl's eyes were closed, her face a waxy yellow. Madge didn't know whether she was alive or dead.

Jennie was beside Madge now. Together they carried the little girl to the bank, and then up on to it.

'Dash to the shop and tell Mr Yendell we need the doctor. Go now!' Madge instructed.

Jennie was galvanized into action, and raced away.

Madge flipped the little girl on to her front. She began working on the girl's back, trying to get her lungs to restart. A trickle of water oozed from the girl's mouth and slipped off into the grass.

Madge continued massaging the girl's back, but that didn't seem to be having any effect. She swore, and swore again.

Then she had an inspiration. She gripped hold of the little girl's ankles and hoisted them aloft, dangling

105

the little girl just off the ground. In that position she shook her.

The girl suddenly coughed, and vomited. As she was doing so, her eyes opened.

Enormous relief surged through Madge. Carefully she laid the girl on the ground again and, using the sleeve of her dress, wiped the girl's mouth.

'Can you talk?' she asked her.

The girl's chest heaved up and down. Already the waxy yellowness of her face had begun to change, her skin reverting to its normal colour.

The girl began to sob.

'There, there,' consoled Madge, gathering the girl into her arms. 'There, there, it's all over now.'

'I fell in,' the girl bubbled.

'Yes.'

'I fell in,' the little girl repeated, and shook all over.

'What's your name?'

'Doreen.'

'Well, it seems you did fall in, Doreen.'

'I'm cold.'

'Where do you live in the village?'

The girl told her.

'Right. Let's get you on to your feet.'

When the girl had scrambled up, Madge lifted her, cradling her close so that she'd get the benefit of her own body heat, and started back to the village.

She was just leaving the water meadows when Jennie reappeared to say the doctor had been sent for. As she was speaking Mr Yendell came hurrying up.

'You take her now,' Madge said to him, handing over Doreen who'd proved heavier than she looked. 'She needs to go straight home and into bed.'

'I'll see to it,' Mr Yendell replied. He walked swiftly away carrying Doreen as Madge had done.

Madge wiped a wisp of hair away from her face. That had been a near thing, she thought. If she and Jennie had happened along any later it would have been too late for the lass.

She suddenly felt done in, drained. What she needed more than anything was a good strong cup of tea. 'Is the doctor going to the river or what?' she asked.

'To the river.'

'Then you stay here and redirect him to Doreen's home.' She gave Jennie the address.

From there Madge went home where she had the cup of tea she so desperately craved.

Graham answered the front door to find a man standing there, cap in hand.

'Is Mrs Forsyth in?' the man asked.

Graham nodded.

'Do you think I could have a word?'

'Certainly. Follow me.'

Graham closed the door behind the man, then led him through to the kitchen where the family were sitting. Madge and John looked up in surprise when he entered the room.

John, who recognized the man as Dick Horrell who also worked at the mine, got to his feet. The two of them had never spoken.

'It's your wife I'm here to see,' Dick Horrell told him. He turned and faced Madge. 'I want to thank you personal for what you did today. Doc says we would have lost Doreen if it hadn't been for you.'

Madge smiled. 'So you're Doreen's father.' She could see the resemblance now. 'How is she?'

'Right as rain, I'm happy to say. Hasn't half had a fright mind, as have me and the missus. We've told her a thousand times to stay away from that river, but today she disobeyed. And we know what happened as a result.'

He twisted his cap in his hands. 'I can't thank you enough. We would have been heart broke if we'd lost the maid. She's dear to us as dear.'

'I'm only thankful I was there.'

'Doc says she would have died for sure if you hadn't made her sick up. He said by the time he would have got to her she would have been gone.'

Madge rose. 'It's kind of you to come round like this . . .'

He held up a hand. 'Nothing kind about it. Least I can do after what you did for us. We'll always be indebted to you. Mightily.'

'I was about to put the kettle on. Would you care to join us?'

He shook his head. 'Don't want to put you out none. Having spoke my piece I'll be on my way.'

'I'll see you out,' volunteered John.

'Thank you.'

At the front door Dick Horrell shook with John. 'I'll see you at work tomorrow.'

John didn't quite know how to reply to that, so said nothing.

Dick Horrell put on his cap, nodded at John, then strode off into the night.

John quietly closed the door again.

That Friday night John and James Cook decided to go to the Atherton Arms for a drink, though John was still restricted to two pints because of the family's financial situation.

On entering the pub they found it to be crowded but had no trouble getting to the bar. Nor did they have long to wait before being served.

'What will it be?' the landlord enquired.

John gave him their order.

The landlord placed a pint in front of James and another in front of John. Beside John's he also placed a large Scotch.

'I didn't ask for that,' John said.

'It's from Dick Horrell over there,' the landlord explained, gesturing to where Dick was standing.

John saluted his thanks, then he and James went over

to sit close to the darts area so they could watch the game in progress.

A short while after that Dick and several of his friends sauntered across. 'Interested in darts are you, then?' Dick smiled.

'I've played a bit in the past,' John replied.

'Me too,' said James.

Dick rubbed his chin. 'Tell you what. We occasionally have a Saturday night competition with a couple of bottles as prizes. A bottle of spirits for the winning man, and sherry for the woman. What about you organizing a team from your Glasgow people to play us locals? Think they'd be interested?'

John saw this for what it was, a conciliatory hand of friendship. 'I'm sure they would,' he answered.

'Then you speak to them, and you and I will talk again sometime next week.'

'So are you suggesting a week tomorrow?'

Dick nodded. 'Men and women.'

'Well, well,' John commented after Dick and his friends had moved off.

'Because of the little girl Madge saved?' James mused.

'What else?'

When John returned home and told Madge she was delighted, and promised that she, for one, would be there the following Saturday.

'A mining we will go, my boys, a mining we will go.
With picks and shovels in our hands, a mining we will go!'

Those miners singing the song gave a great roar at the end of it. One of them raised his pint pot so abruptly into the air that some of the contents splashed out over the rim to splatter on the floor.

'Enjoying yourself?' John asked Madge.

'Thoroughly. It's a terrific evening.'

The pub was jammed to bursting with every last Glaswegian adult present for the darts match that had been arranged. All of them had been made to feel most welcome the moment they had stepped inside. The folk of Atherton had gone out of their way to be friendly.

Beattie McDonald, she of the inturned eye, threw a dart and missed the board altogether. She exploded with laughter thinking it was hilariously funny.

'There you are,' said Dick Horrell, and put another large Scotch in front of John. John hadn't been able to buy a single drink all evening. He and Madge had been drinking for free.

'Thank you,' John beamed.

Dick squatted beside Madge. 'My missus came up with an idea. As you're new to the area you don't know the best and cheapest places for second-hand furniture. The wife says she'll happily take you into Exeter and show you where to go. There is one warehouse in particular where you can often find genuine bargains.'

'That would be very helpful,' Madge enthused.

Dick winked at her. 'Proper job!'

'That was nice of him and his wife,' Madge said to John as Dick walked away.

John nodded and took a sip of the Scotch that Dick had brought over. He'd lost count of how many pints and doubles he'd had. It would be murder getting up in the morning for church, but get up he would. He burped, and giggled. He was having a whale of a time.

'I'd like you to meet the Pugsleys, Norman and Bess,' said Tom Zelly, arriving at their table with a middle-aged couple in tow. The Pugsleys it transpired lived on a nearby farm where Norman was a farm labourer.

'How are you for apples?' Bess Pugsley asked Madge.

Lots of houses and cottages in the village had apple and other fruit trees in their gardens, but the Forsyths didn't. 'We don't have a tree if that's what you mean,' Madge replied.

Bess, a stout woman with a red face, clucked and shook her head. 'I'll drop a few by to you. And how about swedes, could you use a sackful of those?'

110

Madge had already found out that swedes were what the Scots called turnips, and that what the English called turnips was something else again. 'We're very fond of swedes.'

'Then I'll see you get a sackful. Norman here will deliver it hisself, won't ee, Norman?'

'I will that,' he confirmed.

'This is very kind of you both,' Madge said.

'Think nothing of it,' Norman replied.

'And when he brings they swedes there will be a few caulis as well. We got stacks of they this year on the farm,' Bess went on.

Bess hooked an arm round one of her husband's. 'Speak to you both again,' she said.

John half rose out of his seat as they left.

'Madge! Where are you, Madge?' Jane shouted from the ocke. 'It's your turn, Madge.'

When Madge hit a double with her first throw she got a round of applause and piercing whistling from those watching.

As she said to John later, as they were getting into bed, it was one of the best nights out she'd ever had.

From there onwards, despite the ten men who'd been sacked, all of whom had now found some sort of alternative employment and accommodation, including two who'd joined the Army, the Glaswegians were fully accepted into the community, past rancour and ill-feeling completely forgotten.

'It didn't half rain last night,' Jennie said to Christine as they met outside their houses to go to school.

'I woke up at one point and heard it battering on the roof.'

Jennie nodded. 'Me too.'

'And there was a lot of wind.'

Jennie turned up the collar of her coat. It wasn't cold by Glasgow January standards, but chilly none the less.

And there was still a wind about which made it even chillier when it caught you.

They walked to school and went into the playground where they'd wait till the bell was rung.

Jennie stared through the wire fencing at the rear of the playground, and her mouth fell open in astonishment.

'Look at that!' she exclaimed, pointing.

Christine's eyes opened wide. Where the fields had been was now a huge lake.

They went to the fencing and gazed through it. In parts the water was relatively still, in others a raging torrent that swirled and eddied along. The river itself had vanished.

'It's even more amazing than I imagined,' Jennie stated in awe.

Christine nodded her agreement.

As Jennie watched a fallen tree was swept by, followed by an old car tyre that bobbed along as though being bounced.

The landscape was totally transformed, Jennie thought. Majestic was a word that leapt to her mind. That, and frightening too.

They stood at the fencing staring in wonder at the water meadows until the bell was rung, summoning them and the rest of the pupils to lessons.

Chapter Four

Goal!

Graham clapped with the rest of the Atherton supporters. The village team were playing a team from Sanford Barton, a village just over a mile away. The two teams were playing on the same field that the mill strikers had occupied four years previously.

Graham, now nineteen, worked as a driver for a local haulier. He had had several jobs before this, one on a farm, another above ground at Wheal Tempest.

'Hello, Graham.'

He turned to find Ethel Yeo smiling at him. Ethel was the wife of a pal of his.

'Hello, Ethel. How are you?'

'I'm fine, but Mark isn't. Have you heard?'

Graham shook his head. 'What's up?'

'He was rushed to hospital this morning with appendicitis.'

'No!'

'When we arrived they took him straight into theatre and operated.'

'He's going to be all right, isn't he?' Graham queried, full of concern.

'Oh yes. It's simply a case of recuperation and convalescence now.'

'I'll go and see him when I can,' Graham promised.

'Actually, I came looking for you.' She glanced about, then said in a hushed tone, 'Can we move back from the crowd and walk round? I want to talk to you in private.'

'Sure,' replied Graham, wondering what this was all about.

'This is strictly between you and me. Do I have your word on that?' Ethel said as they began to stroll.

'Of course.'

'It was Mark's idea I approach you. We discussed it before the ambulance arrived, and he suggested that you would be able to help him. Do him a favour.'

'Anything,' Graham responded.

She gave him a thin smile. 'You'd better hear me out first before you commit yourself. For what he wants you to do isn't exactly one hundred per cent honest. Well paid yes, but not one hundred per cent honest.'

Graham was intrigued, and fascinated too. Mark had always seemed straight as the proverbial die to him.

Ethel took a deep breath, hoping she and Mark weren't making a mistake here. 'Mark was due to drive to Culmouth tonight to pick up a cargo of contraband which he was then to deliver to Exeter. Of course he can't now and doesn't want to let down those he was getting the contraband from, and wondered if you'd do it for him?'

Graham stopped suddenly and stared at her. 'Contraband?' he queried quietly.

She nodded.

'You mean goods that have been smuggled into the country?'

She nodded again.

'I thought that stuff belonged to the days of pirates and cutlasses?'

'Oh no,' she assured him. 'There's still a lot of it goes on. Once upon a time it was tea, coffee, spirits and tobacco. Tea and coffee are now off the list, but spirits and tobacco aren't.'

Graham was intrigued. 'And that's what this load would be, spirits and tobacco?'

'That's right.'

They resumed walking, a bemused Graham thinking about what she'd told him. How about Mark! he thought. What a sly old devil. 'So how did Mark get involved with smugglers?'

'He comes from Culmouth, and still has family there.' Culmouth was a small port on the coast not all that far away.

'Are the smugglers family?'

'His uncle and two cousins.'

'Goal!' the cry went up from those still watching the football. Graham glanced over and saw that it had been scored by the Sanford Barton team, which meant the teams were now level at one all.

'Well?' she demanded.

'I don't know. You have eh . . . rather caught me on the hop.'

She put a hand on his arm and gazed into his eyes. 'Please. You're one of the few people who can actually drive in Atherton, and someone Mark says he can trust implicitly.' She paused, then added, 'And don't forget the many favours he's done you.'

What she was referring to was the fact that Mark had taught Graham to drive in his car, and had allowed Graham to borrow that self-same car many times since.

Graham sighed. 'He's saying I owe him?'

'He's asking for a return favour.'

Graham didn't see how he could refuse in the circumstances. Besides which he rather liked the idea of being mixed up with smugglers. It appealed to him.

'And you'll get paid,' Ethel stated. 'Fair's fair after all. You'll get exactly the same as Mark would've.'

She then named a figure which caused Graham to raise his eyebrows for it equalled his weekly wages at the hauliers. Extra money like this would certainly come in handy.

'So what do you say?'

'What time am I due there tonight?'

She smiled, and squeezed his arm. They fell to discussing the details.

*   *   *

Madge went into the church where she found John working on a light fitting in a room at the rear under the bell-tower. He spent a lot of time in the church helping out; he enjoyed it and felt it spiritually rewarding.

'You won't be late for tea, will you?' she said. She knew that when he worked in the church he sometimes forgot the time.

'I'll be there. Don't worry. What's for tea anyway?'

'Kippers. The fish man came today.'

He brightened to hear that. He liked kippers. He liked smokies even more, but you couldn't get those in Devon.

'I wish you did as much in our house as you did in God's,' Madge said waspishly.

'That's an awful thing to say in church,' he admonished, stopping what he was doing and staring at her.

'Awful perhaps, but true. We've lots needs fixing at home.'

'I'll get round to it all. I promise.'

'Promise!' she exclaimed, then added tartly, 'We all know what your promises are worth.'

He wished she'd go away and leave him alone. What was she coming nosing round the church for anyway? This was his place. 'Since when did I ever break a promise?' he countered.

'Often.'

'Name me an instance.'

She did.

'Well, that was only the once.'

She named another.

He glared at her, filled with exasperation and blossoming anger. 'I'll never get this finished if you keep on bothering me,' he complained.

What had she ever seen in him? she asked herself. Heaven alone knew. If only . . . She smiled inwardly at the memory of Billy Gunn. What a mistake she'd made in letting him go. The biggest mistake of her life. Or maybe the second biggest, depending upon how you viewed it.

Billy had gone on to become a commercial traveller, at which he'd proved to be very successful. He and his pretty wife lived, at least they had the last she'd heard, in a new house in Croftfoot, a middle-class suburb inhabited to a large extent by professional people. Billy had made something of himself. She admired that.

'The longer you stay the longer I'll be,' John said.

'Don't be late, mind,' Madge warned him, then swung on her heel and left the church.

John returned to his task, swearing volubly when his screwdriver slipped to take a nick out of a finger.

He sucked the finger, and was grateful the vicar hadn't been about to hear him swear like that.

Still sucking his finger he crossed to where he'd earlier hidden a flagon bottle of scrumpy, something he'd developed a taste for since coming to Devon.

He opened the bottle of cider and had a draught. That was better, he thought. You could get just as merry on scrumpy as you could on beer and whisky, for far less money. Especially if you bought it direct from the farmer as he did.

He had another deep swig, and burped. He drank off half the flagon before returning it to its hiding place.

When he was done with the light fitting he retrieved the bottle and finished it off.

He felt quite rosy and glowing inside as he made his way home for tea.

'Any problem getting away?' Ethel Yeo asked Graham as he joined her at the lock-up where Mark garaged his car and an old van. Graham also rented one of the lock-ups where he kept his motor bike.

He shook his head. 'I told them it was a special job for my firm and they accepted that without question.'

'Good,' Ethel smiled.

She'd already opened the lock-up, so they went inside and climbed into the van.

'Key,' Ethel said, handing it to him.

He drove the van out of the garage, then got out and relocked the doors.

'I take it you know the way?' Ethel queried as he climbed back into the van.

He grinned at her in the darkness. 'I drive for a living remember? I know the way.'

The van might have been old but it ran immaculately. Mark was an excellent mechanic who was forever tinkering with his car and van.

'I was thinking . . .' Graham mused as they left the village behind them.

'What?'

'Well, I've often wondered how Mark could afford to own two vehicles. Now I know.'

'I dropped by the hospital again after I'd spoken to you earlier. He sends his thanks for helping out.'

'How is he?'

'Still a bit groggy, and tired. These anaesthetics take a lot out of you it seems.'

'How long will they keep him in?'

'Nine, ten days altogether. Then he'll have a while off before returning to work. Taking things easy.'

'He won't enjoy that,' Graham said. Mark was someone who liked to keep himself busy.

'He won't have much choice. Doctor's orders.'

'Was he in much pain this morning?'

Ethel nodded. 'He said it was excruciating.'

'Poor bugger,' Graham commiserated.

'At least it's over now. The worst of it anyway.'

They drove for a few miles in silence. Then Graham said, 'Tell me about this uncle and two cousins of his? If you're allowed, that is.'

'Uncle Bert is a real sweetie. A nicer man you'd go far to meet. So too are Reg and Alan.'

'Have they been doing this for long?'

'Smuggling? A number of years now. Ever since Reg and Alan gave up deep-sea fishing.'

'And why did they do that?'

118

'They went through an exceptionally lean period at one point. And both wives were forever moaning about them being away so much. Anyway, the upshot was they gave up the sea, sold their drifter and bought a schooner.

'The schooner was Uncle Bert's idea. During the summer they take the tourists out, short trips, fishing trips, excursions, that sort of thing. But in the off-season the trade's dead of course, no tourists. And that's when they do their trips to Sark in the Channel Islands.'

Graham thought all this fascinating.

Ethel went on. 'They also have a small business in Culmouth, a newsagent's. So between one thing and another they do very nicely thank you.'

'Is there an Auntie Bert?' Graham asked.

Ethel laughed softly. 'Aunt Madeleine died years ago. She was never a strong woman, and even less so after having Reg and Alan.'

'Would you like children?'

Ethel didn't reply for a few seconds. When she finally did her voice was tight and strained. 'Naturally. We just haven't been blessed so far, that's all.'

He felt he'd somehow put his foot in it. 'I simply wondered . . . Sorry, I shouldn't have asked.'

'No, that's all right. Why shouldn't you? It's a reasonable enough question, after all.'

How vulnerable she sounded, Graham thought. He realized then that although he'd known Ethel for quite some while he didn't really know her at all. Their relationship had been all 'hello', 'good day', 'how are you?' He further realized this was the first occasion, he discounted that afternoon at the football pitch, that he'd been alone in her company.

'I wanted to go to the doctor about it, but Mark won't hear of that. He laughs every time I bring it up,' she said quietly.

He could easily have been embarrassed by this conversation, Graham thought, but surprisingly he wasn't. Ethel was older than him after all. He knew she

119

was twenty-five because Mark had mentioned it only recently, and she was the wife of a good friend.

He glanced at her in the darkness, thinking how attractive she was. He'd never thought of her in that light before. As a woman yes, but not from the physical, sexual point of view.

'Where are we going to in Exeter?' he queried.

'The Blackboy Hotel.'

'I know it but have never been inside,' he replied.

'It has a nice lounge bar. Mark and I go there sometimes of a Saturday night. Or if we don't go there we might go to the Merrie Harriers out Compton way. They do lovely food there.'

'That's what I want next, a car,' Graham said. 'A motor bike is all very well, but has its limitations.'

'You mean for courting?' she giggled.

'I didn't say that!' he exclaimed, pretending outraged innocence and indignation.

'Maybe not, but it's what you meant. Go out with many maids then, do you?'

'A few,' he answered casually.

'More than that I should think. You have a wicked look in your eye, I've noticed that before now.'

'Have I?' he queried, delighted.

'Most definitely. I should imagine you're highly popular with the ladies.'

He was enjoying this. Wicked look in his eye, popular with the girls! Oh yes, he was enjoying this all right.

'What sort of car do you have in mind?' she asked.

'For the moment any car would do. But for the future, something large and expensive.'

'Oohh! You have got big ideas.'

'I'm ambitious, if that's what you mean. Which I get from my mother. She's a great believer in people pushing themselves to get on, making the most of themselves.'

'Do you have plans then?'

Graham shook his head. 'Not yet. But I'll come up

with some. It's a matter of finding the key to open that first important door. And I'll find it, or bust a gut trying.'

There was something very exciting about Graham, Ethel decided. He had sparkle and fizz.

'When Mark's home you must come round to tea. You've never been,' she said.

'Never been asked.'

'Well, you're being asked now.'

'I accept. I shall be delighted to come.'

He was looking forward to it already.

'There!' she said, pointing to their left.

Graham stopped the van in front of two large gates, across which was painted the legend, PEPPERELL'S BOATYARD.

'Who's Pepperell?' Graham queried.

'Friend of Uncle Bert, Reg and Alan. Wait here.'

She slipped from the van and swung open the gates which weren't locked. She beckoned Graham to drive inside, closing the gates again after he'd done so. She then indicated where he was to park.

Culmouth itself was off to their right. They were now on the outskirts of the small port.

Graham glanced out to sea but couldn't make out a sail. The crescent moon overhead was a shining silver arc piercing a starless sky.

Ethel fumbled in her coat pocket for a torch which she shone on her wrist-watch. 'Well, we're here on time. All we can do now is sit tight and wait for them to show.'

Ethel produced a packet of cigarettes and offered it to Graham, who shook his head.

'Don't smoke,' he informed her.

'Wise man. Filthy habit really.'

'Here, let me.' He took the box of matches from her, and slid it open. The match flared when he struck it. And in the sudden, harsh light they found themselves staring into one another's eyes. She broke that contact first.

'Funny way to spend a Sunday night, waiting for contraband to come ashore,' Graham mused.

'It isn't Sunday night. It's Monday morning.'

'Only just!'

'But Monday morning none the less. You'll be tired when you go into work.'

'I'll manage.' He paused, then said, 'Have you done this with Mark?'

'No. But naturally I know all concerned, and the procedure.'

He was curious, wanting to know more about her personally. 'Are you from Atherton?'

'Stoke Bradley. Born and brought up there.' Stoke Bradley was a large village roughly five miles from Atherton whose main source of employment was a paper mill.

'So how did you meet Mark?'

'He came to work at Stoke Bradley, and we met at a social.'

Was it a happy marriage? Graham wanted to ask, but didn't. He'd always got the impression from Mark that it was.

Ethel drew in a deep breath. 'I love the smell of the sea. There's nothing like it.'

'I like it too.'

'Something we have in common then.'

A strange thing to say, he thought. There was something odd about Ethel Yeo, he was learning, which disturbed him, but he couldn't quite put his finger on it.

'Maybe you'll own your own haulier business one day,' she said.

'Maybe.'

'Would you be a good boss, or a hard one?' she asked, her tone teasing, yet at the same time, serious.

He considered the question. 'Good? I'd certainly try to be. As for hard? Let's put it this way, if I was hard I'd also try to be fair. How's that?'

'Mark thinks highly of you, you know,' she said.

'And I of him.'

Graham was about to elaborate further when he suddenly saw a shape or shadow move upon the sea. Peering into the night he was able to distinguish a two-masted, rigged boat ghosting its way towards one of the several jetties jutting out into the water.

'They're here,' he said softly.

The ship didn't stop at the jetty however, but turned into an area that had been three quarters built round.

'Drive as close to where the boat is and stop,' Ethel instructed.

Graham did so. Then the two of them got out of the van.

Lights winked on and the schooner *Sweet May* was revealed. She was a trim craft with clean lines. Graham thought she was beautiful.

He saw now that the schooner was in a dry dock which was currently flooded. He also noted that *Sweet May* was screened from the road.

'Uncle Bert?' Ethel called out.

A small, barrel-chested man came striding towards them. 'Ethel? That you girl?' He came up short in surprise when he saw that Graham wasn't Mark.

Ethel introduced Graham, then quickly explained about Mark and that Graham was taking Mark's place. Uncle Bert listened intently as she spoke, nodding from time to time, and occasionally glancing at Graham.

'Pleased to meet you, lad,' Uncle Bert said when Ethel came to the end of her story.

They shook hands.

'Good of you to help out,' Uncle Bert went on. 'The last thing I would want is for this stuff to be left lying about. And unfortunately, none of us lot drive.'

Graham met Reg and Alan next. He judged them both to be in their forties – considerably older than their cousin Mark who was in his late twenties – small men like their father, all three bearing a distinct family resemblance.

'How was the trip?' Ethel enquired.

'Smooth as silk,' Uncle Bert replied. 'We took ourselves over and brought ourselves back without a spot of bother. That right, boys?'

'That's right,' Alan corroborated.

'Let's load up the van and then we'll have a tot,' Uncle Bert said.

The brandy was in two- and four-gallon kegs, easy to lift and move, Graham discovered. The cigarettes were in sealed cardboard boxes.

'There we are then,' said Reg, placing the final keg inside the van.

'We'll have that tot now,' enthused Uncle Bert, rubbing his hands together. He led them to a sparsely furnished office where he lit a hurricane lamp.

Reg placed two bottles of brandy on top of a desk and Uncle Bert opened one of them. Cups appeared into which Uncle Bert splashed liberal measures.

'Here's to the next journey, may it be as safe and incident free as this one,' Uncle Bert toasted.

A murmur of agreement went round, after which they all drank.

'Good gear, eh lad?' Uncle Bert said to Graham.

'Good indeed.'

They chatted, and had another drink. Then it was time for Graham and Ethel to leave. Reg checked the road, and having ascertained that it was clear he and his brother opened the gates to let the van out.

Ethel gave a wave as she and Graham started back the way they'd come.

'Nice folk,' Graham commented.

'I think so.'

'Uncle Bert seems quite a character.'

'He is! A natural storyteller who can have you in stitches one moment, crying your eyes out the next.'

'He was a fisherman too I take it?'

'Oh yes, but has been retired for a long time now. He was already getting on when Reg and Alan were born.'

They continued to talk, and as they did the miles sped by. Soon they were entering Exeter and heading for the Blackboy Hotel.

'What's the drill when we arrive?' Graham asked when they were only minutes away from their destination.

'You go into the car park where you back up to a door I'll show you. Then we unload.'

This was precisely how it happened. The owner quickly answered Ethel's knock, then they set to carrying the contraband from the van to a room in the cellar.

When they were finished Ethel told Graham to wait in the van while she had a final word with the owner.

'All right?' he asked when she rejoined him in the van.

'Everything's fine. We can go home now.'

'I rather enjoyed that,' he said as they neared Atherton.

'I'm pleased, for there's another consignment next weekend which Mark won't be able to pick up and deliver either. Are you on?'

'Of course.'

'That's settled then.'

He thought of the extra cash that would bring him, and smiled. 'Will you be coming with me?'

Ethel paused before answering. 'I can if you want. Is it necessary?'

'Not really. If everything's a repeat of tonight.'

'It is.'

'Then there's no need for you to come. But tell me, what about money?'

'You mean yours?'

'No, the money for the delivery.'

'That's taken care of directly between the hotel owner and the Yeos in Culmouth. You won't have to worry about it if that's what you're thinking.'

He pulled up outside the lock-ups and waited while Ethel opened Mark's. He drove inside and parked the van. 'What time is it?' he asked as she secured the door again.

He nodded when she informed him.

'Would you like to stop by the house for a cup of tea?' she asked.

He was sorely tempted. 'No thanks,' he replied after a few moments' deliberation. 'I'd better get all the sleep I can.'

She tried to hide her disappointment, having thoroughly enjoyed his company. 'Drop round Wednesday evening and I'll give you what you're due. That all right?'

'Fine.'

'See you then.'

He watched her walk off into the darkness. It had been an interesting night in many ways. He was sorry she wouldn't be accompanying him the following week. She was fun to be with.

He headed for home, and bed.

'My mother's still living in the dark ages. She's positively medieval. She won't let me wear any make-up,' Jennie complained to Christine. The two of them were in the female toilet of the village hall, the latter where the dance was being held. From outside came the strains of music.

'Mine does let me wear some, but she isn't all that keen, I have to admit,' Christine replied.

Jennie stared at her face in the mirror, and softly swore. 'I might have managed to smuggle some of my make-up out, but *she*, the old cow, put it all on the fire.'

Christine giggled. 'She didn't!'

'She damn well did. Just picked it up and chucked it on the fire. I was furious.'

'I'll bet you were.'

Jennie swung on Christine. 'You wouldn't happen to have . . .'

'I'm away ahead of you,' Christine interjected, already opening the small, sequined, clutch bag she'd brought with her. She pulled out a compact, a tube of lipstick and various other items.

'Terrific!' Jennie enthused. 'I can put it on here and then take it off before I go home again. That way she'll be none the wiser.'

'Well hurry up, I'm itching to get on to the dance floor.'

'You go on and I'll catch you up.'

'Do you mind?'

'Not in the least. Scram.'

As her friend left the toilet Jennie began making up her face. She hummed to the dance music as she worked.

Graham thought Mark looked positively ghastly. His cheeks were sunken, his colour a whitey grey. The last time he'd visited Mark, he had been well on the road to recovery.

'They don't know what's wrong,' Mark said in a raspy voice. 'They've done a number of tests to try and find out.'

Ethel glanced in concern at Graham, then back again at Mark. 'Is it a relapse of some sort?'

'I said, they've no idea. What they have told me is that I'll have to stay in until I'm better.'

'Tough luck pal,' Graham commiserated.

'How do you feel generally?' Ethel asked.

'Weak as a new-born babe. It's as though whatever strength I had has just drained out of me.'

'Is your temperature up?'

'Apparently not. That's normal.'

Ethel made a mental note to speak to the ward sister before she left. This was worrying. She'd never seen Mark look so awful. 'Is there anything I can do?'

'Just keep coming to see me,' Mark replied, attempting a smile. 'That's always a good tonic.'

'I'll be here every day. I promise.'

'It must be connected in some way with your operation, surely?' Graham queried.

'I would have thought so too. But they were evasive when I put that to them.'

Puzzling, Graham thought.

'Can you keep on doing the Culmouth thing for me in the mean time?' Mark asked.

'Of course.'

'Thanks.'

'No need for that. I'm being well paid for my troubles.'

'That's true,' Mark replied, and coughed. A deep, hacking cough that made his shoulders heave.

Positively ghastly, Graham thought again.

They talked until the handbell was rung, signalling the end of visiting time. After saying their goodbyes Graham and Ethel made their way back up the ward, Ethel asking Graham to wait outside in the corridor while she spoke to sister.

'Well?' Graham queried when she later emerged from the ward.

'It's as Mark says, they don't know what's wrong with him. The sister was at pains to assure me that all that can be done for him is being done. But, in the mean time, his condition remains a mystery.'

'Worrying, eh?'

Ethel bit her lower lip, and nodded.

'Would you like a drink?'

She smiled at him. 'Love one.'

'Are there any decent pubs round here?'

'I don't want to go into a pub,' she said. 'Let's go back to my house. I have some brandy in the cupboard.'

Now it was his turn to smile. 'Brandy that came via Culmouth?'

'Of course.'

They went to where Graham had parked Mark's car, and motored back to Atherton in silence. Ethel was lost in thought throughout the trip.

As they went up the drive Graham spotted Les Pack, who had a new dog, as the old one had died, staring at them from down the road. Before the day was out it would be all round the village that he and Ethel had been seen going into her house together, with insinuations attached. He would ask Jennie, who worked in the shop, to let it be known that he'd driven Ethel to the hospital.

Ethel took Graham into their parlour, then left him to fetch the brandy and glasses.

'You pour,' she instructed when she returned.

Ethel lit a cigarette, and inhaled deeply. 'It gave me a shock seeing Mark like that,' she said as she accepted the glass Graham handed her.

'He was doing so well too.'

Ethel shook her head. 'Perhaps it's a complication of some kind.'

Graham tasted the brandy which coldly burned its way down his throat. For his money it was even better than that he'd been given at the boatyard.

Ethel sank into a chair and leant her head back against the antimacassar. 'It's funny not having him at home. Very strange,' she said.

'Only natural you miss him.'

'I was madly in love with Mark when we married, you know. Head over heels.'

'I'm sure,' Graham said quietly, wondering why she'd suddenly come out with that.

'And he with me. We were besotted with one another. Like a couple of rab . . .' She stopped, then said, 'No, perhaps I shouldn't say that.'

He could guess what she'd been about to tell him – all about the physical side of their relationship. Again it was a situation where he might have been embarrassed, but wasn't.

'But that was then,' Ethel mused quietly to herself. 'Strange how things change, isn't it? Nothing ever seems to remain static. It's all a constant state of flux. Or at least it is for me.'

Graham wasn't at all sure what that meant.

Ethel had a swallow of brandy, and closed her eyes.

129

'You know what I thought when I walked in there and saw him? I thought he looked like death warmed up.'

An apt description, Graham mentally agreed.

'Death warmed up,' Ethel repeated, her voice tight and hollow.

'I'd better not stay too long. Les Pack saw me coming in here,' Graham said.

'Sod the old bugger!'

Graham laughed. 'You know the way he gossips.'

'The Atherton Mouth,' Ethel said, her mood suddenly changing to one of jocularity. 'Him and that Mrs Clapp. You can hardly change your knickers in this village without either of them knowing.'

'My mother says they're a menace.'

'Your mother's right. The pair of them should be taken out and shot.'

'There would be plenty of volunteers for the firing party.'

Ethel finished off her brandy. 'I don't know how you've done it but you've cheered me up. Thank you.' She extended her glass. 'Can I have another?'

'It's your bottle.'

He refilled her glass, but didn't bother with his own as he'd hardly touched his first tot.

'You can borrow Mark's car while he's in hospital if you want,' Ethel said. 'I mean on a full-time basis.'

'Are you sure?' Graham exclaimed, delighted.

'Completely. Take a run out on to the moors. They're gorgeous this time of year.'

'My father says Dartmoor reminds him of parts of Scotland. He says he gets quite homesick when he's there.'

Ethel regarded him curiously. 'Do you remember much about Scotland?'

'Oh yes. I was fifteen when we left, after all. I have some extremely vivid memories.'

'Any wish to go back?'

He considered that. 'Not to live. I'm much too settled

here now. But I'd like to go back one day to visit. Look up people I used to know. Chums I grew up and went to school with. Go to the grocery shop where I used to work as a delivery boy. Speak to Mr Baird the owner. He was very good to us when my dad was on strike, and afterwards when Dad was unemployed.'

'I'd like to see Scotland sometime,' Ethel mused. 'But the countryside, not the towns.'

'They say Edinburgh is beautiful,' Graham stated.

'Unlike Glasgow?' she teased.

'Glasgow is an industrial city, and looks exactly what it is. I remember it with great fondness.'

Graham found himself staring at Ethel, who blinked and glanced away.

'I wonder how long it will be before Mark does get home?' she said.

'Maybe whatever ails him will disappear just as quickly as it appeared?'

'Maybe,' she said, but didn't think so. And neither did Graham.

'Anyway, I'd better go. Les Pack is probably outside timing us to see how long I stay.'

Ethel laughed. 'I wouldn't put it past him.'

Graham drained his glass. 'I'll see myself out.'

'No, I'll come with you. Manners after all.'

At the front door they halted. 'When shall I see you again?' she asked.

'Wednesday next I suppose. When I pop in to collect my money. But if you need anything in the mean time don't hesitate to let me know.'

'I won't,' she promised.

'And I'll hang on to the key to the car for now. To use it like you said.'

She reached out and grasped his upper arm. 'Thank you again. For everything.'

To Graham's amusement Les Pack was still loitering on the opposite pavement. He gave him a wave as he went by.

*   *   *

John went up to the bar and ordered another pint of cider. It was Tuesday night, not one of his usual weekend drinking nights, but passing the Atherton Arms on the way home from work he'd come in on impulse for a quickie before tea.

Madge was going to be furious, he thought blearily. It was gone eight o'clock and he was well sloshed. His tea would be ruined by now.

Two farm labourers came in from the rear and joined him at the bar. One was Peter Coffin, the other George Rattenbury. 'Evening,' he slurred.

'Evening John,' Peter and George replied in unison.

John picked up his pint and had a sip. He found himself reeling slightly and decided it was best he return to his seat.

From there he focused on George Rattenbury, and smiled to himself. George was a tall, well-built man who had a terrible reputation for the ladies. Couldn't be on account of his looks, John thought, for George was no oil painting. There again, he wasn't ugly either.

George had something of a belly on him, which was the result of his prodigious appetite. It was rumoured that he ate half a dozen eggs and half a pound of bacon, plus innumerable slices of bread, for his breakfast every morning. It was also said that when he sat down to his evening meal he liked the plate heaped high, twice, if not more, than what an ordinary man would eat.

John wondered if it were true what they said about George. Was he really such a successful womanizer? Well, good luck to him if he was.

Then his thoughts drifted back to Madge, and the smile that was hovering round his lips vanished.

Why couldn't Madge like him more? She despised him, he knew that. She'd done so for years. Despised him for not getting on, improving his lot. But you needed drive for that which he just didn't have.

There had been a time when he'd thought he had, but

he'd been wrong. He'd been kidding himself. He was what he was and nothing, or no-one, not even Madge, was going to change that.

He downed some of his pint, and sighed with pleasure. There was nothing he enjoyed more than a good drink. A good bevvy as they'd called it in Glasgow.

He put his hand in front of his mouth, and burped. This would have to be his last pint as he'd run out of money. Damn! he thought, just when he'd got the taste. He didn't want to stop drinking, he wanted to continue.

He looked again at George Rattenbury and saw that George had gone all fuzzy at the edges. And what was George saying? He couldn't hear properly. It certainly wouldn't be about the women George was seeing, for George was said to be nothing if not discreet.

Mind you, he'd have to be running five women at the same time, that was the figure last quoted to John. Five! The man must be a lion in that department, John thought enviously.

John stared at the table and Madge's face stared back at him. Bloody Madge! he inwardly raged. Why, oh why, had he married her and not someone more like himself? But then, he reminded himself drunkenly, that's what he'd believed he was doing when he'd married her.

Of course he'd lied to her a wee bit at the time, telling her he was going places and all that sort of thing. But Glasgow men were like that, big talkers all. She should have recognized it for what it was. Patter. Pub talk. Chatting-up-a-lassie talk. Trying-to-impress talk.

Christ! he thought, as depression settled on him like a shroud. It always somehow came back to Madge.

His pint was finished, he noted in surprise. He couldn't recall polishing it off.

Then he remembered something which brought a beaming smile to his face. He had two flagons hidden in the church. He'd drink those before going home. If he was to be hung it might as well be for a sheep as a lamb.

The church would be closed but he knew where a key

133

was. It would be no trouble to get those flagons and go on with his bevvying.

'See you,' he mumbled as he passed the bar.

'Mind yourself now!' the landlord called after him.

Outside, he weaved his way churchwards.

'Come on, it's time to get up for work,' Madge said to John, shaking him vigorously by the shoulder.

'Go away,' he muttered.

He stank of cider, Madge thought. The smell wafted off him in waves. He'd been so drunk the previous night it had been murder getting him upstairs and into bed.

'I said it's time for work, John,' she repeated. 'Now get up!'

'Away to hell!'

Anger flared in her. Grasping the top of the bed-clothes she ripped them away exposing John in his pyjamas. 'I don't want any argument,' she stated. 'And if you leave it much longer there won't be time for breakfast.'

He sat up and glared at her through red-rimmed eyes. Normally Madge never noticed his morning growth, but that morning it was sticking out from his face like hedgehog spines.

'Now get up,' she said and stamped from the room.

He scratched an armpit, then shivered. His head was thudding, his mouth and throat Sahara dry. He swung a leg off the bed and immediately regretted it.

'Oohhh!' he groaned.

He drew in a deep breath, and regretted that too because of the effect it had on his throat and lungs. All he wanted to do was lie down again and peacefully expire.

He crawled down the length of the bed, moaning repeatedly as he went, grasped hold of the bedclothes and tugged them back into place. He then stretched out and closed his eyes.

Despite all her efforts Madge couldn't get John up. He remained in bed till early afternoon.

Graham convulsed with laughter, tears streaming down his face. Uncle Bert had just told him a joke that must rank as the funniest, and filthiest, he'd ever heard. It was a Sunday night and he was collecting another shipment of contraband to be delivered to the Blackboy Hotel in Exeter.

'Have some more brandy,' said Reg, topping up Graham's cup.

'That's the finish for me,' spluttered Graham, indicating his cup. 'I have to drive after all.'

'Tell me about yourself, lad,' said Uncle Bert. 'We're interested.'

'We wondered about your accent. There's something there that isn't Devon,' Alan smiled.

This was true. Graham no longer spoke with a broad Glasgow accent, it was overlaid by the softer Devon speech, but an essence of Glasgow remained.

When Graham had caught his breath again he told them how his family, and other Glasgow families, had unknowingly come down to Atherton as strike breakers, and how that had resolved itself. He also spoke of their reasons for moving south in the first place.

'Interesting. Very interesting,' Uncle Bert declared when the story was concluded.

'Glasgow, eh?' Reg mused. 'I thought you might have originally come from Newcastle myself.'

Graham stared through the office window to where *Sweet May* was tied up. 'She's a beautiful ship,' he said. 'I thought so the first time I saw her.'

'Know anything about boats?' Uncle Bert queried.

Graham shook his head. 'Only that they have a sharp end and a blunt end.'

The three Yeos laughed at that.

'When the summer comes I'm going to drive down here and go out with you on one of your trips,' Graham stated.

Uncle Bert struck a match and put it to his old

battered briar. As he sucked he regarded Graham thoughtfully over the flame.

'Fancy a sea trip, do you?' he asked, and flicked out the match.

'On *Sweet May* I do. That's a treat I've promised myself.'

Uncle Bert glanced at Reg and Alan, then brought his attention back to Graham. 'Tell you what lad. When Mark is better, why don't you come over to Sark with us one weekend?'

Graham stared at him in astonishment. 'You mean a smuggling trip?'

Uncle Bert nodded.

Graham didn't know what to think, this offer was so unexpected. He accompany them on a smuggling trip! 'That would be . . . tremendous,' he replied at last.

Uncle Bert misunderstood Graham's hesitancy. 'If you change your mind you can always say.'

'I won't change my mind,' Graham said quickly. 'I was a bit bemused for a moment, that's all.'

'We leaves early Saturday morning and you knows when we arrives back.'

Early Saturday morning, he had to work then, Graham thought. He'd get out of it somehow on the day in question. This was too good an opportunity to miss. He was already excited at the prospect.

'And we'll teach 'ee a little about sailing on the way there and back,' Alan promised.

Wow! Graham thought. 'I can hardly wait,' he declared, and meant it.

'Bugger!' swore Bob Yendell who owned the post office-cum-general shop. He waved his hand up and down, then gazed at his thumb.

'What have you done?' Jennie asked. She'd been working at the shop since leaving school two years previously and thought it an enjoyable, if not particularly rewarding, job. She and Bob got on extremely well, as she did with Bob's wife April.

'Splinter,' Bob explained. 'From that wooden box I just put on the floor.'

'Here, let me see.'

Jennie grimaced when she saw how deep the splinter had gone. 'That must be painful,' she sympathized.

'It is. And April's gone round to her mother's so she can't help.' He picked ineffectually at the tip of the splinter with the thumb and forefinger nails from his opposite hand.

'Well, that won't do any good,' Jennie informed him. 'What I need is a needle.'

'Plenty there,' said Bob, indicating where packets of needles were kept.

Jennie selected a packet, opened it and chose a needle. At that point the door tinged and Bess Pugsley entered the shop.

'I'll serve Mrs Pugsley first,' Jennie said. For once Mrs Pugsley didn't stop to chatter as she normally did. It was a common problem with most of the customers, male and female, who used the shop.

'Right then,' said Jennie, when Mrs Pugsley was gone. 'Now I need a match.'

She heated the tip of the needle until it was glowing red, then allowed it to cool again before attacking the splinter.

Bob's face tightened in anticipation when the needle touched his skin. He bit his lower lip and held his breath.

Being as gentle and careful as she could, Jennie opened up the flesh around the head of the splinter. Using the tip of the needle she tried to impale the splinter and hook it out.

Bob slowly exhaled, and began to relax. This wasn't hurting at all. He even started showing an interest in the procedure.

'It's certainly in deep,' Jennie muttered. 'Awkwardly so.'

She probed and sliced, her brow furrowed in concentration. She shifted positions several times in order to adopt a different angle of approach.

How cool her fingers were, Bob marvelled. And sensitive. An artist's fingers he couldn't help but think.

'Now we're getting somewhere,' Jennie murmured, teasing the splinter towards the surface. When the head of the splinter was protruding above the skin she told Bob to remain exactly as he was, she'd be right back.

She went to her bag where she kept her tweezers, having recently taken to plucking her eyebrows. 'This will make things easier,' she said as she again took Bob's hand in her own.

Delicately she pinched the head of the splinter, then slowly, carefully, drew it out.

'There, all over,' she smiled, gazing at the splinter. It really was a whopper.

'Thank you,' Bob smiled back.

'All part of the service. Do you want me to put anything on it for you?'

He thought about that for a moment. 'I don't think it's necessary, do you?'

She shook her head.

'You did that expertly, Jennie. The doctor himself couldn't have done better.'

Bob gazed at his thumb, then up again at Jennie who was replacing the tweezers in her bag. 'You had a marvellous, sympathetic way about you when you were doing that. Maybe you should consider being a nurse?'

'A nurse!' Jennie exclaimed, and laughed. 'That idea's never entered my head.'

'Well, maybe it should. You really have a caring touch about you.'

Jennie was about to reply to that when the door tinged and more customers came in. These customers were the start of a small rush, at the end of which Jennie had forgotten all about Bob's suggestion.

*　　*　　*

'And they never did find out what the problem was?' Graham asked Mark who'd returned home from hospital that morning.

Mark, sitting on a fireside chair with a rug covering his legs, shook his head. 'Nope.'

'It must have been something you picked up while there,' Graham went on.

'That's what I believe. And they too, although you'd never get them to admit the fact.'

'Well, you're home now, that's the main thing,' Ethel said.

'When will you go back to work?' Graham asked.

'Not for a while yet, I'm afraid.'

Graham pulled a sympathetic face.

'So you'll have to continue with the pick-up and delivery,' Mark added.

'That's fine by me.' It certainly was, Graham thought. The extra money he was earning was piling up. He'd soon have enough for that car he'd promised himself.

'I'll put the kettle on,' Ethel stated, and left the room.

Graham spoke to Mark for a few more minutes, then excused himself to go to the toilet. As he returned he went into the kitchen where Ethel was busy setting out some cups and saucers.

'As Mark will continue to be off work, how are you going to manage?' he asked bluntly.

'Oh, we'll get by. We've got savings, and if we got to the stage where they ran out, then the Yeos in Culmouth would help, as would other members of both families. We wouldn't want.'

'I'm glad to hear it,' Graham replied. 'I was worried for you.'

'That's kind,' she smiled.

'And if there's anything I can do, you only have to say. You know that, don't you?'

She came to him and placed a hand on his arm. 'I do. Thank you.'

'I'll get back to Mark,' he said.

He hesitated for a moment, then broke away and left the kitchen. As he went he could feel her eyes watching him.

'Is it true?' a furious Madge demanded of John.

'Is what true?'

'About you and Wally Killock being hauled up before Sir Reginald? I had it from Jane who had it from Glenda.'

John shifted uneasily in his chair and didn't reply.

'Well?'

'Sir Reginald did send for us, yes.'

'And came within an ace of firing you?'

Again John didn't answer.

'You stupid, stupid man! You and your bloody unions and workers' rights. As for that Wally Killock, he's nothing but a born troublemaker whom anyone with any sense would stay well clear of.'

'He's got good ideas,' John said defensively.

'Good ideas my backside! That clown would start an argument in a mortuary.'

A stubborn look came over John's face. 'The mine should be unionized. Sir Reginald is taking advantage of us because it isn't, as he well knows. Anyway,' John went on huffily, 'you don't have to worry about Wally from here on in. He's going back to Glasgow.'

'Glenda didn't tell Jane that.'

'Maybe she doesn't know yet. But they are.'

Madge took a deep breath. 'Then good riddance to bad rubbish. That's all I have to say.'

John threw his newspaper on to the floor and lurched to his feet. 'I don't have to listen to this. I'm going out.'

'That's right, run away. That's about par for the course for you,' she taunted.

'God, you're a bitch at times!' he accused.

'Better a bitch than a mug. Which is precisely what you are. A fool and a mug.'

It was done before he realized what he was doing. His

hand lashed out to crack against her cheek. With a cry Madge went sprawling across the floor.

'That's enough,' he panted.

Madge started to weep as he strode from the house.

'Another pint,' slurred John, handing the landlord his empty glass.

'You sure John?'

He attempted to focus on the landlord's face, which was difficult as he was seeing it in triplicate. 'Sure I'm sure.'

'All right then,' the landlord said, and refilled the glass.

John leant against the bar and gazed round the pub. There were several strangers in which was unusual, and some men from the mine playing euchre.

He paid the landlord, slowly counting out the correct money, then drank a little of his pint. How many was that? he wondered. He tried to tot up the number, but got lost somewhere in the middle of it.

Good old cider, nothing like it he thought, having another mouthful. If he had nothing else to thank Devon for it was the discovery of that. Scrumpy, a man's drink.

What time was it? He peered at the wall clock, but couldn't make out the figures. Not closing time anyway, the bell hadn't been rung yet.

He thought of Madge. She'd deserved to be hit, he told himself. She shouldn't have called him a fool and a mug. What the hell did she know? He and Wally were right to try and do what they had. Now Wally was going back to Glasgow with his family having declared that he wouldn't, couldn't, work at the mine any longer.

Maybe he should follow suit and go home? He considered doing so, but knew in his heart of hearts he wouldn't. It was one thing for Wally who had a small child, but his children were grown up and working. Returning to Glasgow wouldn't just mean finding one job but three. Unless he left Graham and Jennie behind that was, except if he did Madge would also stay on. He knew that for certain.

No, no, Glasgow was out of the question for him. He was stuck with Atherton and Wheal Tempest.

'Rotten old bastard,' he mumbled, referring to Sir Reginald Tempest.

'Say something John?' the landlord asked.

'I said Sir Reginald's a rotten old bastard.'

The landlord's face creased with anxiety. 'That's enough now, John. I can't have you speaking like that in here. Just won't do.'

John leered at him. 'A friend of the high and mighty Sir Reginald are you?'

'I repeat, that's enough, John. Another word and you're out, barred. And I mean it.'

John swayed where he stood. He used his free hand to hold on to the bar and steady himself.

'Understand?' the landlord said.

John opened his mouth, then closed it again. He gave the landlord an almost imperceptible nod.

He would try and read his Bible before he went to bed he promised himself. He'd derive some comfort from that.

'Now I'm in the chair. What do you want?' Mark demanded. It was his first night out since coming home from hospital, and he and Ethel had decided to make an occasion of it by doubling up with Graham and Betty Sowden, Betty a girl Graham had dated several times before. They were in the lounge at the Blackboy Hotel.

'Betty?' Graham smiled.

'Can I have a gin and orange?'

'Coming up,' stated Mark. 'And what about you Ethel?'

'A port and lemon please.'

'And you Graham?'

'A pint of best will do me.'

'Right then,' said Mark, and went up to the bar where he waited to place his order.

'If you'll excuse me I'll only be a minute,' Betty apologized, and headed for the toilet.

Ethel lit a cigarette. 'It's good to see him his old self again,' she declared, nodding at Mark.

'Yes.'

'He's still not completely right, mind you. But not far off it.'

'There's a huge improvement from when he came home.'

'A huge improvement,' Ethel agreed.

'I suppose he'll be taking over the Culmouth thing shortly,' Graham said, thinking what a loss that was going to be.

'I should imagine so.'

She smiled at him, which he returned. And as they were smiling he saw a sudden look come into her eyes which caused her expression to waver, then slowly fade. She broke eye contact to stare down at the table.

'What is it?' he queried.

'Nothing.'

'Ethel?'

She glanced up again, the smile back on her face. But this time her grin had a fixed, false quality about it. 'I said it was nothing,' she repeated.

'Is there a problem?'

'A sudden headache, that's all,' she lied. 'But don't mention it to Mark. It might upset his evening.'

Graham knew she was lying. And she knew he knew.

Ethel changed the subject.

'There she is. A beauty, eh!' Graham said proudly, indicating the car he'd bought in Exeter that very afternoon.

'What sort is it?' asked a delighted John.

'A Lanchester.'

'I think it's gorgeous,' Jennie said. She went to Graham and kissed him on the cheek. 'Congratulations. Aren't you the clever one!'

'All get inside and I'll take you for a spin. Mum, you sit in the front with me.'

'Lovely comfortable seats,' Madge commented when she was settled.

'Lots of leg room at the back,' John added.

Graham started the engine, and listened with pleasure for a few seconds to the contented hum coming from underneath the bonnet. She was a real find and buy. He'd been lucky.

'Here we go,' he announced, and eased the car away from the kerb.

They passed Jane and her daughter Vicky, who both laughed and waved as they went by. Gina Campbell, out washing the front windows, also gave them a wave when they passed her house.

'I feel like Lady Muck herself,' Madge declared. Then, leaning across and patting Graham on the leg, added, 'You've done well, son. I couldn't be more pleased for you. A smart car is a fine thing to own. A fine thing.'

And he still had some money put by, Graham thought. How loath he'd been to give up the Culmouth run, but of course he'd had to when Mark had proclaimed himself fit enough to take over again.

In the rear John was staring at Madge, thinking that he could almost see the pride oozing out of her. He was thrilled for Graham, of course, but at the same time felt somewhat deflated. In all his working life he'd never been able to afford a car, something he'd have given his eye teeth for. His previous good spirits had now completely deserted him and he sat sunk in gloom and dejection.

They drove on up the High Street, and past the water meadows. It had been a miserable day up until then, but now the clouds parted and the sun shone through lighting up the road and surrounding countryside.

'A real treat,' Madge stated with laughter in her voice. 'That's what this is, a real treat.'

The sun continued to shine throughout the rest of their spin.

A pale-faced Ethel answered Graham's knock. 'I came as soon as I heard,' he said.

She ushered him inside, and shut the door behind him.

'What exactly happened?' Graham demanded.

'Mark said he wasn't feeling too well when he got up this morning. Then when he was at work he collapsed and they had to call an ambulance. He's in the same ward as before. It's a recurrence of whatever it was he had previously.'

'Damn!' Graham swore.

Tears welled in Ethel's eyes. 'Oh Graham!' she said softly.

It was clear how distraught she was, so he took her into his arms with the intention of comforting her. She sobbed into his shoulder.

'There, there, it's going to be all right,' he whispered, stroking her hair.

She looked up at him, her face awash with tears. 'I want you so much it hurts,' she said.

He stared at her, thinking he'd heard incorrectly.

'Kiss me.'

In a daze he bent his lips, and the next moment their mouths were fiercely joined. Her arms snaked round him, hugging him tight.

'Oh God, I wanted that,' she breathed when the kiss was finally over. She smiled through her tears. 'You must have known how I feel about you? That I'm in love with you?'

Had he known? Perhaps he had. He'd certainly never admitted it to himself though.

'It happened that night we all went to the Blackboy Hotel,' she went on. 'In the space of a moment, a heartbeat, I fell hopelessly and madly in love with you.'

'I knew there was something that night . . .' He trailed off. Ethel in love with him!

She took his face in her hands, and kissed him lightly on the lips. Then she kissed him more deeply, her tongue moving sensuously and sinuously inside his mouth.

'What about Mark?' he asked.

'I don't love him any more. Haven't for a long time. I'm still fond of him of course, and concerned for his welfare. But that's as far as it goes.'

She paused, and smiled. 'How do you feel about me?'

He decided to be honest. 'I really don't know, Ethel.'

Her smile faltered, and turned to a frown. 'You do like me though?'

'You know I do.'

She stared into his eyes, her own wide and melting. 'You'll come to love me. I'll make you.'

He thought of Mark, and felt guilty. Mark was a good friend after all, who'd done a lot for him in the past. Maybe he should end this before it started, that would be the sensible thing to do. Then he looked again at Ethel's figure, and felt the blood race in his veins.

'Why don't you come back later tonight when it's dark?' she suggested. 'I'll leave the door unlocked so you can just slip inside.'

'But Mark . . . him being in hospital. Doesn't that bother you?'

'No,' she stated firmly.

His resistance melted in the face of such temptation. 'I'll come round,' he told her.

She kissed him again. 'I'll be waiting.'

Outside he took a deep breath, then shook his head. This was the last thing he'd thought would happen when he'd come charging round to ask about Mark.

He'd thought she was crying because of Mark, but there had been a lot more to it than that. She'd also been crying because of him, and her feelings towards him.

His guilt returned, but not as strongly as before.

The door was unlocked as she'd promised. He slipped inside and closed it behind him. Then he bolted it.

When he turned round she was standing in the hallway dressed in a candlewick dressing-gown. He could smell the scent she'd put on.

Ethel took his hand. 'Come on,' she said, and led him towards the stairs.

There was a single bedside lamp aglow in her bedroom, the bedclothes thrown back. A cosy fire burned in the small grate.

They stopped by the side of the bed and she kissed him. 'What's wrong?' she asked when the kiss was over, for she'd detected a reticence, a block, between them.

'The truth?'

She tensed. 'The truth.'

'You'll laugh.'

'No, I won't.'

'I hope you don't. You see the thing is . . .' He hesitated. 'This is awful!'

'Tell me,' she urged.

'The truth is I've never . . .' He stopped, looking uncertain.

She smiled, knowing now what was bothering him. 'Your first time,' she said.

He nodded.

'Well, that's all right. We all have to have a first time. And I'm only pleased that yours is with me. I'll consider it a great honour.'

His anxiety began to subside.

'I've already been in bed to warm it up. Take off your clothes and join me there.' And with that she slipped out of her dressing-gown, allowing it to drop to the floor, and climbed on to the bed where she lay invitingly outside the bedclothes.

She was even more beautiful undressed than Graham had imagined she'd be. He literally stopped breathing as he stared at her nakedness.

'I'm waiting,' she said.

When he, too, was naked he got on to the bed. Then,

at her suggestion, the two of them pulled the bedclothes over themselves.

'Just hold me for a little while,' Ethel said wisely.

'Hmm!' she murmured when she was in his arms. 'That's nice.'

He thought so too. Soon his hands were straying, touching, feeling, caressing.

She didn't force it in any way, but allowed it to happen naturally, one thing leading to another.

'I love you,' she said when they were finally done.

She closed her eyes and smiled as he moved vigorously within her.

'The men of Culmouth and around those parts have always been smugglers, but never wreckers,' Uncle Bert said to Graham as *Sweet May* carved her way through a choppy sea. He shook his head. 'The wreckers were evil men, and many of them got what they justly deserved, the hangman's noose.'

Graham felt the boat rise and roll beneath him. He had a strange sensation in his stomach, but did not feel the urge to be sick. At least not yet.

Mark had come out of the hospital some weeks previously and was now back at work again, and doing the Culmouth run. His second absence had given Graham the opportunity to earn a considerable amount more money.

Uncle Bert struck a match and puffed his briar alight. This was their last trip before the holiday season started. The following week they would be back to doing business with the tourists.

Graham watched Reg and Alan go about their duties, thinking how nimble and skilful they were. Reg grinned at him, and he grinned back.

'Was it difficult getting time off from work?' Uncle Bert enquired.

'Sent a message in that I was ill, which they believed readily enough. But tell me, what's a lee shore? I heard Reg mention it earlier.'

Uncle Bert went on to explain it and a great many other sailing terms and expressions besides.

Shortly after that the weather worsened slightly, and he and Uncle Bert set to on deck helping Reg and Alan.

Graham thought it all great fun.

Reg flashed a light once. Then in reply, out of the darkness, an answering light flashed twice.

'Now we go in on the tender,' Uncle Bert explained to Graham.

It was just after ten o'clock at night when *Sweet May* had crept into the small, secluded Sark bay where their rendezvous was to be kept.

The anchor chain rattled, followed by a splash. Then the four of them manoeuvred the tender overboard, and got into it. Reg and Alan took the oars, and pulled towards the shore.

Graham was filled with excitement and exhilaration, thinking this was like something out of an adventure story. He fought back the silly impulse to say, 'Yo, ho, ho and a bottle of rum!'

A wave carried the tender on to the strand where they heaved it further up the beach and secured it. A figure emerged from shadow to greet them.

'Hello, L'Corbin,' Uncle Bert said, and shook the man by the hand.

Words were exchanged, then Graham was introduced. Now it was his turn to shake with L'Corbin who said, 'Welcome to Ser, man pôvre ami.'

With Uncle Bert and L'Corbin in the lead they made their way up the beach to where the ground became grassy and firmer underfoot. There a horse and cart were waiting for them, the horse feeding from a nosebag.

'L'Corbin is his local nickname. It means The Crow,' Alan whispered to Graham *en route*.

'Let's get to,' said Reg, and picked up one of the two- and four-gallon kegs piled high on the cart.

It took several journeys for the contraband to be

transferred on to *Sweet May*. Finally the tender was filled for the last time.

Uncle Bert and L'Corbin spoke further then, during the course of which money was exchanged.

After that goodbyes were said, and L'Corbin returned to his horse and cart, while the four Englishmen did the same to their ship.

'It all seems very simple and straightforward,' Graham commented to Uncle Bert later when *Sweet May* was under way again.

'Oh, it is! That's the beauty of it.'

'Have you known L'Corbin long?'

'Many years. He was once a fisherman like myself.'

'And now this is how he makes his living?'

Uncle Bert nodded. 'Nor are we the only people he deals with from our country. He has regular dealings with a number I understand.'

'How about some tea?' Alan called out.

Uncle Bert came to his feet. 'I'll make it. Will you have a cup lad?'

'Please,' Graham replied. 'Would you like me to help?'

'No, you stay where you are. The galley's cramped enough as it is.'

'Put a tot of brandy in mine,' Alan said.

'Good thinking. Will we all have that?' When there was no disagreement Uncle Bert added, 'Right,' and went below.

'Give me a hand here, Graham,' Reg requested. Graham hurried to obey.

'Are you enjoying yourself?' Reg asked conversationally.

'I'm having a marvellous time. Loving every minute of it.'

'Think you'd like to be a sailor?'

Graham opened his mouth to reply, but before he could do so the boat went into a peculiar screwing motion which knocked him from his feet. He took hold of the offered hand, and hauled himself upright again.

'Well?' Reg asked.

'Despite little surprises and upsets like that, yes I would,' Graham replied. 'Now explain to me, what does changing tack mean?'

When Uncle Bert brought up the brandy-laced tea he and Graham sat aft to drink theirs. They talked for a little while, then fell silent, Uncle Bert to puff on his pipe, Graham to think about Ethel and the affair they were having, and then about the additional money he'd been forced to give up when Mark had recovered enough to take over the Culmouth run again.

If only that extra income had continued, he thought morosely, there were all sorts of things he could have accomplished. The car was only the beginning.

Suddenly the idea struck him, an idea so startling it made him sit up straight, and furrow his brow as he considered it.

The worst they could do was say no, he told himself after a while. And where was the harm in asking? It would mean certain adjustments regarding work on his part, but that was something he could worry about if they agreed.

'Uncle Bert?'

'Yes lad?'

'I was wondering . . . I don't suppose you, Reg and Alan would be interested in taking on another hand? A fourth partner so to speak.'

Uncle Bert regarded Graham thoughtfully. 'I take it you mean yourself?'

'That's right,' Graham nodded.

Uncle Bert remained silent for a few moments, puffing on his pipe. 'And why would 'ee want to join us?'

'In a word, money. And the use I could put that money to.'

Uncle Bert drank some more of his tea. 'For various reasons we've always loaded well below capacity, so there's that in your favour. But there's the distribution at the other end which might be a problem, though I doubt it.'

'So it all boils down to you, Reg and Alan,' Graham said, smiling tightly. The more he thought about this opportunity, the more he wanted it.

'I suppose it does,' Uncle Bert mused. 'I'll say this, you're a personable lad. We all like you.'

'And I like the three of you. That must be obvious.'

'You needs cash to buy in, as we pays L'Corbin on the nail.'

'I have cash put by. I'm sure that wouldn't be a problem for me.'

'Hmm!' Uncle Bert murmured, and gazed out to sea. 'I've sailed these waters countless times in my life. There's many a tale I can tell about them.'

Graham waited patiently.

'How about your work situation?'

'Leave that to me.'

'And what about your parents?'

'Again leave that to me. What they don't know won't harm them.'

'Are you someone to be trusted never to open his mouth on the subject lad? More smugglers have been caught through loose talk than was ever taken on the sea by revenue men.'

'I can keep my mouth shut. I assure you.'

Uncle Bert gazed hard at Graham, then slowly nodded his head. 'And what if we are taken one fine night? There's always the possibility you know. Are you prepared for the consequences?'

'I understand the risk.'

'Are 'ee sure?'

'Positive.'

'You'd be expected to pull your weight aboard. Which means literally learning the ropes.'

'I learn quickly,' Graham replied.

'I know you do. I've noticed that. And you're intelligent with it, asking questions the way you do.'

'I'm keen to join you,' Graham said. 'Very keen.'

Uncle Bert puffed on his pipe, and another silence ensued during which Graham, with a sinking heart thought, he's going to turn me down. Damn!

'Wait here,' Uncle Bert commanded, and went over to Reg and Alan. The three of them fell into a confab.

Reg looked at Graham, then Alan did.

Spume spattered against Graham's face. He wiped the wet away with his hand, tasting its saltiness. The moon was up, but there were few stars to be seen. Ribbons and larger areas of cloud crept across the sky.

Graham glanced again at the Yeos, but they were still deep in conversation. Now it was Uncle Bert's turn to look at him.

At last the three of them broke apart, and Uncle Bert returned to Graham who couldn't tell from his expression what the outcome was.

'You're absolutely certain about all this?' Uncle Bert asked softly.

'Absolutely. No doubts whatsoever.'

'Then we'll accept you as an equal partner. You'll start with us next autumn.'

Graham felt like whooping, but didn't.

Uncle Bert extended a horny, calloused hand. 'Welcome,' he said.

They began discussing the practical details.

Chapter Five

'Love your dress,' said Christine Cook as Jennie hung up her coat. It was October 1931 and they'd both come to the village hall for a Hallowe'en dance.

'My mum made it from a pattern.'

'She's clever. It looks a real bought-from-a-smart-shop job.'

Jennie smoothed down the front of her dress which was of a pink, floral material. It had a gently scooped neckline, piping, and two rows of covered buttons. Tucks gave shape to the long sleeves.

'Wish mine was as pretty,' Christine sniffed.

'Yours is lovely too,' Jennie said, confident in the fact hers was far prettier.

On this occasion there was no need for Jennie to put make-up on in the toilet. That battle had long been won by her, although she had compromised by agreeing to keep to a light application. So it hadn't been a total victory.

They went into the hall itself where a number of dancers were on the floor, while a great many others were crowded round the sides. Suspended from, and pinned to, the ceiling and walls were decorations on the Hallowe'en theme.

At least it wasn't fancy dress, Jennie thought. She would have hated that.

'Hello you two,' said Sandra Coffin, joining them. Sandra was a little younger than they.

'What's it like?' Christine asked.

Sandra shrugged. 'I've just arrived myself. The usual crowd as far as I can see.'

'So no movie stars have wandered in?' Christine joked.

Sandra laughed. 'Not to my knowledge. Some of the lads from Sanford Barton are here. I spotted them a moment ago.'

'And one of them is giving you the eye,' Christine whispered to Jennie. 'The big chap they call Tiny.'

Jennie groaned. 'I've danced with him before. Or should I say I've had him tread on my feet before. He's a hopeless dancer, with about as much conversation as a brick wall.'

'Not bad looking though,' commented Sandra.

'If you like them gormless that is.'

'He's coming over,' said Christine.

Would she or wouldn't she? Jennie wondered. But she wasn't asked. It was Christine he requested to dance.

'He must have known what my answer would be,' Jennie said to Sandra.

Jennie spotted an unfamiliar face. 'Who's that?' she said to Sandra, and explained whom she was referring to.

'Dunno. Never seen him before. T'ain't local, that's for sure.'

'Dishy,' Jennie murmured.

Shortly after that the band stopped for a short break, and Christine rejoined them.

'You were right about his dancing,' Christine said to Jennie, and rolled her eyes.

It was beginning to get hot in the hall, Jennie thought, as some new arrivals put in an appearance. Before long it would be sweltering.

'Anyone for an orange or whatever?' Sandra queried.

Jennie shook her head, as did Christine. Sandra went off to join the queue for soft drinks.

It was several dances later that a young man came over to Jennie and smiled. For a moment Jennie didn't recognize him, then the penny dropped. 'You've changed your hair style,' she said.

Andy Alford ran a hand over his hair which was now swept straight back from his forehead. 'Felt like a change. What do you think?'

'Suits you.'

'That seems to be the general opinion.'

'Haven't seen you for ages,' Jennie said.

'That's because I moved to Tiverton. Landed a job at Heathcoat's there.' Heathcoat's was a large textile manufacturer, and the biggest single employer in the small town of Tiverton.

'Good job?'

'All right. But I've left it and am back in Atherton again. I've got a new job at the mine.'

'And what's brought you back?'

'My mother hasn't been too well,' he explained. 'Anyway, I wasn't really enjoying living in Tiverton. I think I'm just a village lad at heart.'

Christine, who'd been excluded from this exchange, was asked up to dance, an offer she accepted.

'Would you like a trot round the floor?' Andy suggested.

'I don't know about trot,' Jennie answered, 'but a dance, yes.'

He laughed. 'You're on!' Taking her by the elbow he steered her on to the floor where they began to waltz.

He'd certainly improved since leaving school, Jennie thought. He'd become quite fanciable.

'Remember how you pulled my hair and nipped my arm that day?' she teased.

'Horrible little swine, wasn't I?'

'Horrible,' she agreed.

'But that was long ago,' he said. 'I'm different now.'

He was too, she thought. What gorgeous eyes he had. She'd never noticed his eyes before. They had a most appealing twinkle.

The dance ended, and they clapped. 'Stay up?' he asked.

'Why not?'

'Good,' he smiled, and took her in his arms again.

When that dance ended a ladies' choice was announced. She tapped him on the shoulder. 'How about it?'

'I'm all yours.'

He laughed when she grasped him, assuming the lead position. 'I know it's a ladies' choice but let's not get ridiculous,' he said.

She was enjoying herself, Andy was fun. 'All right then, you lead,' she replied, and reversed the positions.

They danced for a good half-hour together. Then he said, 'Fancy going outside for a breather?'

'It's cold out there,' she reminded him.

'What I have in mind will warm us both up.'

She raised an eyebrow.

'I've got a hip flask,' he confided to her in a whisper.

'You had me worried there for a second. I thought your intentions were strictly dishonourable.'

'That's later,' he said, taking her by the hand.

The flask he produced outside was a very old silver one with dents in it. 'Family heirloom,' he explained, unscrewing the cap. He handed the flask to her. 'You first.'

She had a mouthful, making a face as she swallowed the whisky. She sucked in a deep breath when it had gone down.

Andy had a swig, then another. 'Good stuff, eh?'

She shook her head when he proffered the flask again. 'I've had enough.'

He took another swallow, then recapped the flask and put it back in his pocket.

Jennie shivered when they returned inside, so Andy led her straight back on to the floor, and into his arms.

She realized she'd become a little lightheaded. The whisky or the company? she wondered. A combination of both, she decided.

'Best dance I've been to in years,' he declared.

'You can't have been to many.'

'Lots. Oodles and oodles. But this is the best by far.' And having said that he pulled her even closer to him.

They danced every dance after that until the last one, and then it was time to leave.

'Can I walk you home?' Andy asked.

'If you want.'

'That's settled then.'

Jennie looked round for Christine, but could see no sign of her. She then realized it was quite some while since she'd last seen her. Christine had in fact left earlier.

Outside it was a crisp night that had turned even colder. Jennie buried her hands deep in her coat pockets.

'Here we are,' she said when they arrived in front of her house. Suddenly she was nervous.

'I was wondering . . .' He hesitated, then said, 'Would you like to go to the cinema with me next Saturday evening? We could take the train into Exeter.'

'What's on?' Not that it mattered, she thought, she was going to accept whatever was playing.

He shrugged. 'No idea.'

'I'd love to go with you,' she said.

'I'll meet you at the station then.' And he suggested a time.

'Fine.'

He kissed her quickly on the lips. 'See you next Saturday.'

'I'll be there.'

'Bye then.'

'Bye.'

He kissed her again, then retraced his steps back the way he'd come.

Andy Alford and her! What a turn up that was for the books, Jennie thought as she went indoors.

Graham leapt on to the dock as *Sweet May* bumped alongside. He tied the boat up while Mark, who'd been waiting for them, did the same with the rope Alan had thrown him.

'How was the trip?' Mark asked Graham, coming over.

'No problems.'

'Good,' Mark nodded.

Graham felt it was a strain to be with Mark since his affair with Ethel had started. He'd never quite lost the guilt he felt towards him

'Haven't seen much of you lately,' Mark commented.

'I've been busy. You know how it is.'

'Busy with Betty Sowden you mean?' Mark said, and winked salaciously.

Graham smiled thinly, but didn't reply. The evening at the Blackboy Hotel was the last time he'd been out with Betty, but if Mark thought he was still seeing her then that was fine by him.

'Will you two stop chatting and lend us a hand,' Uncle Bert chided from the boat.

Graham hurried to obey.

Graham drove the Lanchester through the night, heading for Atherton. Somewhere on the road behind him in the van, a far slower vehicle, was Mark *en route* to the Blackboy Hotel.

Another successful run over and done with, he thought with satisfaction. More money to add to his ever-growing pile. Ethel, the car, the extra money, his cup was truly overflowing.

He yawned, dead tired. The arrangements he'd made at work to get Saturday off made the weekend particularly long and arduous. Still, it was worth it. Well worth it.

As there wasn't a run the following weekend he decided he'd go into Exeter and treat himself to a haircut. He badly needed one. And while he was there he'd have himself fitted for a new suit. His present suit was well past its best. He may as well spend some of the money he was making, there was no point in holding on to it like a miser. A new suit and topcoat, he'd really splash out.

He thought of Ethel, and smiled. He'd buy something for her as well. Something small though which would be easily explained.

Gloves? Underwear? Scent? Earrings? Earrings he decided. She had a fondness for those. He'd buy her some earrings.

'How's that, Graham?' Tommy Tripp asked, holding up a mirror so that Graham could view the back of his head. Tommy had been born and brought up in Atherton but had moved away several years previously. He was a barber by trade, but had only recently come to work in this particular shop which Graham patronized.

'Very nice,' Graham replied, nodding his approval.

Tommy put the mirror away, then removed the cloth draped round Graham's neck. He made a few whisking movements with a brush that suddenly, as though by magic, appeared in his hand.

It was a good haircut, Graham thought, peering into a wall-mirror. Tommy certainly knew his business.

Graham went to the till where he paid, Tommy thanking him profusely as he was handed a tip.

Tommy's eyes flicked to the large windows at the front of the shop, checking if anyone was about to come in. He and Graham were the only ones present.

'Fancy a blue book?' Tommy asked.

Graham, not understanding what he meant, regarded him blankly.

'A blue book. You know,' Tommy went on, and made a pumping motion with one arm.

It dawned on Graham what Tommy was driving at. 'Dunno. I've never seen one, let alone read one.'

'You don't know what you're missing, me old son,' Tommy said, and delved into a cupboard beneath the till. The magazine he handed Graham was a cheap, shoddy affair that was extremely badly printed and put together.

'All the way from Paris, France. The genuine article,' Tommy enthused.

Good God! Graham thought, glancing inside. He'd never seen a picture of a naked woman before, and in such a position.

'What do you think? Terrific, eh?' Tommy said.

'Do you sell much of this stuff?'

'People can't get enough of it. If I could only get the supply I could sell ten times what I do. In fact demand is such that I often have to limit copies to special customers. I'm doing you a favour offering you that.'

Graham read several paragraphs from an article on spanking. It made him grin from ear to ear.

Tommy peered over Graham's shoulder, and laughed. 'I thought that very funny. Had me in stitches.'

'Where do these come from?' Graham asked, genuinely curious.

'A chap I play snooker with every Wednesday night. I've never asked how he lays his hands on them. I don't want to know, that's the best way.'

'And you sell them at a profit presumably?'

'Damn right! What would be the point otherwise?'

'And how much is this?'

'How much!' Graham exclaimed aghast when Tommy told him.

'Expensive I appreciate, but that's the going rate. Take it or leave it.'

Graham returned the magazine. 'It's not for me I'm afraid.'

'Fine. That's all right.' And having said that Tommy tossed the magazine back in the cupboard underneath the till.

'Thanks for the offer anyway.'

'Don't mention it.'

Graham was about to discuss the matter further when the door opened and another customer entered.

'See you again,' Graham said, and left the shop.

Throughout the rest of the day he would occasionally chuckle to himself on remembering the magazine, Tommy's so-called 'blue book'.

The film was *Mr Wu* and starred Lon Chaney and Louise Dresser. It was the story of a Chinese villain who kills his daughter because she wants to marry an Englishman. It was pretty turgid fare, but Jennie was enjoying it none the less.

She glanced at Andy sitting beside her in the back row of the stalls, and smiled. He smiled back.

Jennie returned her attention to the silver screen where the silent, flickering images again caught her attention.

Shortly after that she felt Andy's arm move, and she knew instantly what he was going to do. She kept a straight face as his arm inched up and up till it was resting on the back of his seat. Then the arm began to move sideways.

When his hand clasped her shoulder furthest from him she turned to him and smiled again, wanting him to know it was all right with her.

He bent his head and their lips met in a kiss, a far different, and better kiss than those he'd given her outside her house.

Her heart began to beat rapidly as the kiss went on and on. She felt quite elated, and dreamy.

She murmured when the kiss was over. He could repeat that as often as he liked, he'd get no argument from her.

She snuggled closer to him, then dropped her head sideways so that it was resting on his shoulder.

The pair of them relaxed into one another. Jennie was certain that this was the start of a serious friendship. Which was precisely what it transpired to be.

John yelled in agony, and fell to the tunnel floor. The pick he'd been using clattered alongside.

'What is it?' Tom Zelly demanded anxiously.

'Done something to my back,' John replied and groaned with pain.

Barry Riddell came over. 'What's going on?'

'Hurt myself,' John replied through gritted teeth. Beads of sweat that hadn't been there previously stood out on his forehead.

Tom knelt beside the stricken John. 'Maybe it'll go off,' he said hopefully.

'Perhaps he's torn a muscle. It happens,' Barry stated.

'Whatever I've done it's sodding painful,' John mumbled.

Drew McIntyre joined them and the situation was explained to him by Barry.

'Maybe we should try and get him back on to his feet?' Drew suggested.

The three miners attempted to get John upright again, and quickly realized that was a mistake.

'It's the doctor for him,' Barry said and the others, including John, agreed.

John found it excruciating, but eventually he was manhandled into one of the partially caged tramway cars and was whisked out of the mine.

On the surface a stretcher was fetched and he was carried home to his bed where the doctor later attended him.

'Where have you told Mark you've gone?' Graham asked as he and Ethel drove up a narrow lane that would take them to the outskirts of a forest.

'To my friend Joy's house.'

'He won't go round there, will he?'

Ethel laughed. 'Not a chance. He can't bear Joy.'

As they had arranged the previous day, Graham had picked Ethel up outside Atherton. The procedure was that she kept well down in the car till they were a reasonable distance from the village. This was something they'd done a number of times in the past.

A few minutes later Graham drew off the road, and killed the engine. The forest loomed all around them, tall, dark and strangely menacing. The wind whistled, causing the trees to sway and rustle.

'Spooky here this time of night,' Graham commented.

'Not scared are you?'

'Who, me?' he replied in mock surprise.

'Yes you.'

'Scared rigid, and that's the truth.'

She laughed again. 'Am I madly in love with a big baby?'

'The biggest.'

'Then baby had better come to mama.'

She kissed him, and as they kissed her hand moved into his lap to begin undoing his buttons.

Eventually she lowered her head, and he closed his eyes in ecstasy.

When it was all over he drove back to Atherton and dropped her at the spot where he'd picked her up.

'I could eat you,' were her parting words to him.

He later laughed, thinking how appropriate they'd been.

'Here are you,' said Madge, and placed a tray, on which were a cup of tea and chocolate biscuit, in front of John.

He beamed at her. 'Thank you very much.'

'Is there anything else I can get for you?'

He thought about that. 'I don't think so. At least not for the moment. Except . . .' He trailed off.

'What?'

'I wouldn't mind a drink.'

'That you can do without,' she declared, and swept from the bedroom.

He had just finished his tea and biscuit when Madge returned with a surprise visitor.

'How are you, John?' Staddon, the mine manager, asked.

'Still in a lot of pain, I'm afraid. The doctor says I'm to have complete bed rest until further notice.'

'That's what I'd heard.'

'And I've no idea how long that will be.'

Staddon fumbled in his pocket to produce a buff-coloured envelope which he laid beside John. 'Those are your wages. I've spoken to Sir Reginald about you and his instructions are that you've to remain on full pay until your return. A generous gesture on his part I would say.'

John was delighted, as was Madge. 'Please thank him from me,' John said.

'And from me,' Madge added.

'When is the doctor coming again?' Staddon enquired.

'Tomorrow,' John replied.

'And has he diagnosed exactly what the problem is?'

John shook his head. 'He thinks it might be a torn muscle, but isn't one hundred per cent sure. All he can tell me for certain is that I haven't broken anything.'

'He's given John strong pain killers,' Madge said.

'Which I've to take when I feel the need,' John explained.

'Well, I'm sorry this has happened and hope you get better soon,' Staddon said, and cleared his throat indicating that his visit was over.

'I'll show you out, Mr Staddon,' Madge said, and together they left the bedroom, Staddon saying goodbye to John at the door.

John rubbed his hands in glee. Full pay to lie in bed! He wouldn't be returning to work in a hurry. Not bloody likely. This was a situation to be milked to the fullest.

The following evening there was a ring at the doorbell. Madge answered it to find Andy Alford standing there. 'I'm Andy, Jennie's friend,' he explained.

'Come in. She's upstairs. I'll give her a shout.'

Madge took Andy into the sitting-room, and left him

there while she called Jennie. She then went and put the kettle on.

'Hello,' said a surprised, and slightly flushed, Jennie, as she entered the sitting-room where she discovered Andy staring at photographs on the mantelpiece.

'I know I'm not supposed to see you again till Friday, but having heard about your father I thought it polite to enquire after him.'

'That's kind of you.'

'I've seen him at the mine obviously, but we've never spoken.'

'Sit down,' instructed Jennie, gesturing to the most comfortable chair.

'If you're sure that's all right?'

'Of course it is.'

She sat, and he followed suit. She then talked about her father, telling Andy what the doctor had said and that Staddon had been round.

Andy wasn't really interested in John. Although he was sympathetic, his visit was simply an excuse to spend some time with Jennie. They were chatting when Madge returned to ask if Andy would care for a cup of tea or coffee. He replied quickly that coffee would be lovely, and she went off to make some.

Graham popped his head round the door. 'Thought we had company,' he smiled.

Andy rose to his feet, and shook hands with Graham after Jennie introduced him.

Graham left them and went to speak to John who was sitting up in bed reading his Bible.

'How are you this evening then, Dad?' he asked.

John grimaced. 'If anything the pain's worse. Was that a strange voice I heard a few minutes ago?'

Graham told him about Andy.

'Nice of him to think of me,' John nodded. 'But listen, I wanted a word with you. I need you to do me a wee favour.'

'Whatever.'

John wagged a finger at him. 'But your ma's not to know. This is strictly between the pair of us. Understand?'

Graham, never slow on the uptake, guessed what was coming next. 'Go on,' he said.

'Will you go and get me a half-bottle? There's money in my jacket hanging up in the wardrobe.'

'I'll do it tomorrow.'

'Tonight,' John pleaded. 'Please? It won't take you any time at all in that car of yours.'

Why not! He wasn't doing anything else anyway. But it was a bit of an inconvenience.

'Please, son?' John pleaded again.

'All right then. I'll go now.'

'Thanks Graham. I appreciate it.'

'And I'll buy it for you myself.'

John's face lit up. 'You're a toff, son. A real toff. But only a half-bottle mind, that's a lot easier to hide than a full one.'

When Graham later came back with the whisky John drank some, then secreted the bottle under his side of the mattress where it was out of sight and easy to get at.

'Greyhounds!' Graham exclaimed in astonishment, staring at the two large wicker baskets containing the animals in question.

Uncle Bert chuckled. 'Funny contraband, eh?'

'I'll say.'

'There's a handsome profit in taking greyhounds over which we does three or four times a year.'

Graham squatted and peered at one of the dogs which gazed amicably back at him. 'They don't appear to be doped.'

'Don't have to be. They're never a problem.'

Graham laughed softly. Greyhounds! He'd never have thought of smuggling greyhounds. 'Do you have a particular client?'

'Oh yes. A chap out of Taunton. He'll call at my house the day after tomorrow and pick them up.'

'Smuggled to get round the quarantine laws, I presume?'

'That and other things.'

L'Corbin came over and spoke to Uncle Bert. And while they were conversing Graham, Reg and Alan began loading the tender.

'It would be marvellous to have a child by you,' Ethel said.

Graham, who'd been lying with his face buried in her breasts, raised himself and looked at her.

'Don't you think so?'

His nervousness at being in her house and bed increased. He'd broached the subject of using protection early on in their relationship but she'd insisted he didn't.

'I don't know,' he replied unenthusiastically. 'What if it looked like me? Surely Mark would realize.'

'I doubt it.'

Graham swung himself round and sat up. Ethel smiled at him for all the world like a cat who'd just scoffed a jug of cream.

'I still think it's a risk me being here,' he said.

'Why? Mark's on night-shift. He won't be back till eight o'clock tomorrow morning.'

'There's always the unexpected.'

She reached over and stroked his thigh. 'You worry too much.'

'Maybe you don't worry enough. You are a married woman, after all.'

'He won't suddenly appear. I promise you. So relax.'

Graham took a deep breath. 'I'd better go. The time is getting on.'

'Stay a while longer? There's no rush.'

He tensed when there was a noise at the door. Then he realized he'd only imagined it.

'A few more minutes only,' he said.

Another hour passed before he left.

Graham was humming as he left the bank he used in Exeter. He couldn't have been happier or more satisfied. His account was growing nicely, increasing steadily after every run to Sark and back.

If only he could think of what to do with the money other than letting it gather interest. An idea hadn't come to him yct, but it would.

He turned up the collar of his coat as it started to rain.

Uncle Bert crossed to Graham at the helm. 'I was just thinking to myself that you look a propcr sailor standing there.'

Graham grinned at him. 'Thank you very much. That's quite a compliment coming from you.'

He gazed out over the water. 'You know, I've really come to love the sea.'

'You have a feel for it. I mentioned that to Reg and Alan only t'other day and they agreed. You're a natural sailor.'

Graham checked the compass, and fractionally corrected his course. 'I've still a lot to learn though.'

'True. But you've come a long way in a relatively short time. And you'll always be still learning. Even I am after a lifetime at sea.'

The boat yawed, and pitched. 'There's a storm coming up,' Graham commented.

'There be,' agreed Uncle Bert. 'But we'll be back in Culmouth before it breaks proper.'

A few moments' silence passed between them. Then Graham said, 'Have you always stuck to spirits, tobacco and the occasional greyhound?'

Uncle Bert nodded. 'That's what we knows.'

'You're not tempted to enlarge that field?'

Uncle Bert banged out his pipe in the palm of his hand, then proceeded to refill it. 'What did you have in mind?'

'I don't know. Perfume for instance. Or cameras. Or binoculars, those sort of things.'

'Not really,' answered Uncle Bert. 'The operation we has at the moment runs smoothly. So why change it?'

It was a valid point, Graham thought.

'Why make matters more complicated than they have to be?' Uncle Bert continued.

'You might make a larger profit?'

'There is that,' Uncle Bert mused. 'But me and the lads are satisfied with the profit we're already making. Neither of us is big time, tycoons so to speak.'

Graham laughed, the idea of Uncle Bert as a tycoon was hilarious.

'No, no,' Uncle Bert went on. 'We're happy with our present set-up. It pays us handsome.'

'Fair enough.'

'Why, would you like to bring in some of the items you named?'

'Me!'

Uncle Bert finished tamping down his tobacco, and put the pipe into his mouth.

'I couldn't do that if you didn't agree, could I?' Graham answered.

'But the notion has crossed your mind?'

'Only idly. That's all.'

Uncle Bert struck a match which flared brightly. He regarded Graham keenly as he sucked on the stem of his pipe.

'Only idly,' Graham repeated.

'Baccy and brandy, that's our game,' Uncle Bert said.

'And the occasional greyhound.'

'And the occasional greyhound,' Uncle Bert agreed with a smile.

Uncle Bert was proved right. They made Culmouth before the storm broke properly.

'No!' exclaimed Jennie, tugging Andy's hand out from underneath her skirt.

'Oh, come on!'

'I said no and mean it. I'm not like that.'

'You're human, aren't you?'

'Human enough. But that doesn't mean I'm going all the way.'

Andy swore.

Jennie crossed to the mantelpiece and peered into the mirror hanging above it. She patted her hair back into place, as it had become disarrayed.

It was a Friday night which she and Andy were spending alone at his house, as his parents had gone out to a whist drive in the village hall.

'Lots of the other girls do,' Andy said sulkily.

'I don't care what the other girls do,' she retorted.

He swore again, then jumped to his feet and paced up and down.

'God, you get me so worked up,' he said.

She sympathized with that, but didn't say so. She could get pretty worked up herself.

'There wouldn't be a risk, I swear,' he said. 'Just trust me.'

'No,' she stated emphatically.

'Jennie!' he cried out in anguish, his face contorted.

'Maybe I should go home.'

He rushed to her and swept her into his arms. 'Don't go, please. I want you here. I want to be with you.'

He gazed deeply into her eyes, and sighed. 'I'm crazy for you. Stark raving bonkers. You've really got under my skin. What I feel for you is eating me alive.'

Jennie reached up and gently touched his cheek. She chose her words carefully before replying. 'I'm flattered, Andy, truly I am. And I feel a lot for you too. More than I've ever admitted. But I won't . . . can't . . . It's just not right. For me anyway.'

'You're sure it isn't me?'

'I assure you it's not. I think you're lovely. Gorgeous. But if I did what you want I'd regret it. I'm simply not ready yet.'

'I can wait. If it's only a matter of time.'

'I don't wish to run into anything, Andy. Certainly not that. There's so much going round in my head that I don't fully comprehend yet. Things about me, and how I am.'

He didn't quite understand that. But then there were many things about Jennie he didn't understand. She was a very complicated person who totally mystified him at times.

His gaze dropped from her eyes to rest on her gently rising and falling bosom. He groaned with desire.

'I think I had better go home,' she said.

'No, please!'

'Then why don't I make us both a cup of tea? And while I'm doing so you can sit here and calm down.'

He knew further argument was useless which made him feel wretched. He was positively aching for her, his young blood afire.

Jennie disentangled herself. 'I'll put the kettle on.'

He swore again as she left the room.

'And how's John?' the vicar asked at the church door. Madge and Jennie were leaving the Sunday morning service.

'Much the same, I'm afraid.'

The vicar pulled a sympathetic face. 'This is dragging on, isn't it?'

'The doctor says there's nothing we can do except be patient and wait for nature to take its course.'

'I'll tell you what. I'll pop round later this afternoon after lunch and sit with him for a while.'

'He'd like that,' Madge replied.

'We have some very interesting theological conversations, John and I. Most knowledgeable on the Bible.'

'That's how he was brought up. And how we've brought up our children.'

'You're a credit,' the vicar smiled.

'It was a lovely service,' Madge said, shaking his hand.

She and Jennie then moved off so that he could speak to those behind.

Often they lingered outside chatting to neighbours and friends but that morning Madge didn't. She and Jennie made their way directly home.

John's face was a picture when they walked into the kitchen to find him there. He opened his mouth, but couldn't think of a thing to say.

'You're up and about,' Madge stated, eyes blazing with anger.

John swallowed hard.

She nodded, understanding now. 'You forgot it was a family service today which is why we're home a lot earlier than we would normally be.'

She advanced on John who hastily back-pedalled. 'How long have you been better?' she demanded. 'How long?'

'Days only. Honest.'

'Liar!' she hissed.

'And I still have twinges.'

'Liar!' she again accused. 'How I allowed myself to be taken in by you I don't know. I should have smelt a rat ages ago.'

Jennie went to a chair and sat down. It wasn't her place to comment on this. In one way she felt the whole thing very comical, in another she was saddened by her father's deceit. Madge had done her utmost to be kind and understanding.

'I'll get back to bed,' said John, edging past Madge and making for the door.

'You'll do nothing of the sort. You'll go upstairs and get dressed. And tomorrow morning you return to work.'

'Oh Madge!'

'To think Sir Reginald has been paying you full wages all this while! You make me thoroughly ashamed of you.'

John fled the room.

'I should have known,' Madge said softly.

'Is there anything I can do?' Jennie queried.

Madge shook her head.

'I'll go and get changed then.'

'Jennie!'

Jennie stopped in her tracks.

'No-one outside this house gets to know of this. I'd never hold my head up again if they did.'

'They won't from me, Mum. You have my word.'

'Damnation!' Madge muttered when she was alone. She knew she'd never trust John again. Not about anything. To think how she'd run after him, danced attention. Would you care for another cup of tea? And how about a slice of cake? The evening newspaper? I'll go to the shop and get it for you. How he must have laughed up his sleeve at her, thinking her a fool.

'Damnation!' she swore again.

'Forsyth, I want to speak to you.'

John experienced an awful sinking feeling, and for a moment panicked that somehow Staddon knew he'd been malingering. He can't do, John reassured himself. Madge had been adamant that it remained a family secret.

'Yes Mr Staddon, sir?' John smiled, joining the mine manager.

'You're back then.'

'Fully recovered, sir. Whatever the problem it just suddenly cleared up. I'm right as rain now.'

'Good. We've been concerned about you.'

'Thank you,' John said. 'I'll get on with it then.'

Staddon laid a restraining hand on John's shoulder. 'I don't want a recurrence of this, Forsyth. And wondered, in your own best interests that is, if you shouldn't be assigned to lighter duties.'

John stared at the mine manager. He liked the sound of this. 'What sort of lighter duties?'

'A maintenance job. The one snag is that the wage would be less.'

Maintenance! That would be dead easy after the

back-breaking toil he'd been used to. And so what if it meant a little less money coming in. Graham and Jennie were both earning.

'I accept, Mr Staddon, this is extremely kind of you.'

'Not at all, Forsyth. We try to be an enlightened management, despite what you and the others might think.'

John dropped his gaze.

'So that's settled. You'll start your new duties right away. Come with me and I'll make the necessary arrangements.'

A maintenance job! John couldn't believe his luck.

'A lower wage,' Madge said softly.

'He was insistent. I had no choice in the matter,' John lied.

'Exactly how much lower?'

She frowned when John told her. It was a considerable drop.

'I genuinely did hurt myself. And could easily do so again,' John argued. 'There's bound to be a weakness from an injury like I had.'

Madge's lips thinned in scorn. 'I wouldn't go on too much about that if I was you.'

John looked away.

'I suppose we'll manage,' Madge said.

'That shouldn't be a problem if you take Graham and Jennie into account.'

'They won't stay at home for ever you know. What then?'

He hadn't thought about that. 'I had no choice,' he repeated dully.

Madge picked up a basket and went outside to take down the washing she'd pegged out earlier.

John, singing softly and jauntily to himself, strolled through to the sitting-room to read his newspaper.

It had been a terrific day as far as he was concerned. An absolutely memorable one.

'Of course I'll contribute more to the house, Mum,' Graham said. 'And gladly do so.'

She patted him on the cheek. 'You're a good son. A mother couldn't have a better.'

'I just wish . . . Well, that things had been happier between you and Dad over the years.'

'It's that apparent, eh?'

Graham shrugged. 'I'm not a fool. I've got two eyes and a pair of ears.'

Madge stared at Graham. This was a subject that had never been broached between them before. It pained her that her relationship with John was so obvious. But she supposed it must have been evident to Graham and Jennie.

'Did Staddon really insist?' Graham asked.

Madge shrugged. 'Who knows. I suppose I could find out if I wanted to, but what's the point?'

'He's a lazy sod. Inconsiderate too. I have . . .' Graham halted in mid-sentence.

'What?'

'No respect for him,' Graham went on softly.

'You and me both. But none the less, he remains my husband and your dad. We'll just have to put up with him the way he is, faults and all.'

'You should have chosen someone else, Mum.'

'I've often thought that. Then I remind myself if I had I wouldn't have you and Jennie which makes me think I did the right thing after all.'

She couldn't have said anything that would have touched Graham more. The love he had for Madge swelled within him. 'I'd better go now. I'm off out.'

'Enjoy yourself.'

He shrugged himself into his jacket, and took out his wallet. 'In the mean time, here's a fiver to be spent on yourself next time you get into Exeter,' he said, pressing the large white note into her hand.

'You can't afford this!' she protested, knowing

nothing at all about his smuggling activities.

'Oh yes I can, so I don't want any argument.
Something strictly for yourself, mind. A treat.'

A hint of tears appeared in her eyes. 'Thank you son.'

'And I'll start giving you the extra this coming Friday.
All right?'

'Fine.'

A good son, she repeated to herself. The best.

John fumbled in his trousers pocket for some money
only to discover, with a frown, that there wasn't any. He
tried his other pocket, then the pockets of his jacket with
the same result. He'd spent everything he'd had on him.

He balefully regarded his empty glass, studying it
intently as though he could refill it through the power of
concentration alone.

He took a deep breath, then another. Borrow? From
whom? He glanced about. He knew everyone present of
course, but who to approach?

His gaze lit on Jane Scott sitting in a corner with her
husband Tam, the two of them having a night out while
their daughter Vicky was looked after by Emma Law.

Jane was beautiful, he thought with envy, remembering how he'd noticed her on the train down from
Glasgow. How he would have loved to get his hands on
her. He wondered what she was like stripped, and
smiled. Tam was a lucky man, a truly lucky man.

Lurching to his feet he went over to the bar and placed
his empty glass on it.

'Another?' the landlord asked.

'I have a small problem.'

'What's that?'

'The wherewithal.'

The landlord adjusted his spectacles. 'I see.'

'You know me, where I live and work. It's not as if I'm
going to run away or anything.'

'Just what are you driving at, John?'

'How about opening a slate for me and I'll square with

177

you pay night.' He waved a hand in front of his chest. 'Cross my heart and hope to die. Honest injun.'

The landlord considered John's request. It wasn't completely unknown for him to give tick, but he didn't like doing it. Tick could easily lead to bad feeling and trouble. There again, John was a good customer whom he'd never had any problems with.

'You'll square pay night?' he said, repeating John's promise.

'I will.'

'You're certain about that?'

'Certain as can be. I give you my word as a believing, practising Christian. Now you can't get better than that, can you?'

John's faith was well known in the village. A strange anomaly when you considered his drinking habits.

'OK, dokey, it's a deal,' the landlord said.

John beamed at him. 'And buy yourself one for being such an excellent chap.'

'I will. I'll take a half.'

'A pint,' John corrected him. 'I don't do things by halves.' And, having made what he considered to be a hilarious joke, he laughed loudly.

Madge sang the offertory hymn while at the same time watching a solemn-faced John performing his duties as sidesman. When he'd finished gathering the collection from his side of the church he and Tim Lovers, also a sidesman, took the collection up to the altar rail and gave it to the vicar.

The three of them whispered together, then John returned to take his place beside Madge.

She sometimes found it difficult to reconcile this facet of his character with the others she knew only too well. But John's commitment to, and belief in, the church were genuine enough.

Hypocritical? There were those who might accuse him of that. But in John's mind there wasn't any hypocrisy.

178

He didn't come to church to be seen or because he thought it the right thing to do, but because he truly believed.

Madge glanced at her husband, thinking if he could only always be as he was at that moment, things might have been very different between them.

'I'll have to stay behind,' he said to her when the service was over. 'I have a meeting with the vicar and the churchwardens about repairs that are needed.'

'Will you be long?'

'No more than half an hour I shouldn't think.'

'I'll see you later then.'

After lunch he returned to the church where he worked solidly by himself on the repairs that had been under discussion until almost eight o'clock when he called it a day.

If asked, John would have said he found peace inside a church, a peace he'd never found anywhere else.

'Palm trees. I've never seen palm trees before. Only read about them,' Madge said in delight. It was a Saturday and she and Graham had motored down to Torquay for a walk along the sea front.

Graham, who never worked Saturdays any more, was free that weekend as there wasn't a trip to Sark.

'It's very tropical here,' Graham explained.

'It would have to be for there to be palm trees!' Madge exclaimed sarcastically.

He regarded her with fond amusement. 'Enjoying yourself?'

'Thoroughly.'

'Fancy an ice-cream?'

She shook her head. 'But I wouldn't mind some fish and chips later.'

'Then that's what we'll have.'

She hooked an arm through his. 'You're spoiling me.'

'And why not! You deserve to be spoiled.'

'It's a wonderful feeling,' she said.

That pleased him.

They made their way to the promenade which they strolled along till they came to the harbour where boats of all types and sizes rode at anchor. It was a fine sailing day, Graham thought, with a moderate wind blowing. The sea itself was a dull grey colour, as was the sky, filled with scudding clouds.

He stopped to stare at a splendid looking motor cruiser tied to the harbour wall. A thirty footer, Graham estimated, and powerful he rightly guessed. Then he noticed the sign attached to the side of the cabin: FOR SALE.

He wondered what the asking price was, for she'd be a fine craft to own. While he stood gazing at her a man appeared on deck.

Graham explained to Madge that he wished to speak to the man, and the two of them moved closer. The motor cruiser was called *Waterwitch*, Graham now saw.

'Hello,' he smiled to the man.

'Hello.'

'She's for sale then.'

'She is.'

'And why's that?'

The man fixed him with an honest, steady stare. 'I've bought a bigger boat.'

That was a reasonable enough explanation. 'How much?'

The man named a figure that seemed fair to Graham. 'Can I come aboard?'

'Of course.'

'Do you want to come with me, Mum?'

Madge shook her head. 'I'll stay here thank you very much.'

'I'll only be a few minutes.'

'The name's Powels,' the man stated when Graham joined him on deck.

'And I'm Graham Forsyth.'

They shook hands. 'Well, look away. Help yourself.

I'll try and answer any questions you might have,' Powels said.

It didn't take Graham long to give *Waterwitch* the once-over. He asked Powels to start the engine, which he did. He then requested some details which Powels readily gave him.

'What do you think?' Powels queried.

'She's a sweet enough vessel, no denying that. Has a lovely "feel" to her.'

Powels nodded. 'I know exactly what you mean. That was something I noticed when I bought her, and have been aware of ever since. I'm sorry to lose *Waterwitch*, but I'm afraid my purposes have outgrown her.'

'Thank you for letting me have a nose around then.'

Powels handed Graham his card. 'If you want to talk further or look her over again I can be reached there most evenings, or leave a message.'

Graham pocketed the card. 'Thank you.'

'I didn't know you were interested in boats?' Madge said when Graham rejoined her and they started to move away.

'I'm not really. That one just caught my eye,' he lied. 'Now what about those fish and chips?'

'Oh, yes please! This air has made me ravenous.'

That evening, back in Atherton, Graham went up to his bedroom and lay on the bed. There he reflected on *Waterwitch* which he'd established from Powels was easily run by one man.

'Hello, me old son. Dropped in for a game, have you?' Tommy Tripp said to Graham. It was a Wednesday night, the night Graham recalled Tommy telling him he played snooker, and he'd scoured the snooker halls in Exeter till he'd finally found the one Tommy frequented.

Graham shook his head. 'Wanted a chat, that's all. When you've finished playing.'

Graham then crossed to a bench where he sat, and was soon lost in thought. He could afford *Waterwitch*, so that wasn't a problem. What was was selling the contraband he would bring in. And then there were the Yeos to speak to, and L'Corbin if they agreed.

He started when a hand was waved in front of his face. 'That's the most serious look I've seen in years,' Tommy joked.

Graham rose. 'Can we go somewhere quiet for our natter?'

Tommy regarded him curiously. 'There's a pub just round the corner that's never very busy.'

'Sounds ideal. I'll buy you a drink.'

When they got to the pub Tommy sat at an out-of-the-way table while Graham went up to the bar for two pints.

'Now, what's this all about?' Tommy queried when Graham placed his drink in front of him.

Graham sat facing Tommy. He glanced about, checking again that they couldn't be overheard. 'This is in confidence, right?'

Tommy nodded.

'You know all sorts, including various shady characters. Would there be among your acquaintances someone who'd be in the market for cheap, but new, luxury items such as watches, binoculars, etc.?'

'Stolen?'

Graham shook his head.

'Then how come they'd be cheap?'

'That's my secret.'

Tommy pulled out a packet of cigarettes, and lit one. 'Are they fakes of some sort, is that it?'

'No, they'd be the genuine article.'

'What sort of quantity are we talking about?'

'Enough. And it'll be a regular supply.'

Tommy blew a perfect smoke ring that floated ceiling-ward. The ceiling had once been white but was now a horrid streaked yellow from age and cigarette smoke.

'I might know someone. But what's in it for me?'

Graham thought about that. 'How about an introductory fee?'

Tommy gazed quizzically at Graham. 'This isn't like you at all, me old son. You're a nice lad, not a spiv.'

Graham didn't reply to that.

'Twenty nicker. How does that sound?'

'Twenty pounds providing the man you introduce me to and I do business together.'

Tommy laughed. 'I like that. You're not as green as you're cabbage looking.'

'Is it a deal?'

'A deal.'

'Right,' said Graham, and drank off some of his pint.

'What are you up to?' Tommy queried.

'Making money. Simple as that.'

'And this stuff won't be bent?'

'It will not be stolen,' Graham answered truthfully.

'Well, well,' Tommy mused.

'When can I meet your man?' Graham asked.

'Tomorrow night. Half-past eight. Here.'

Graham nodded.

'Ring me at the shop late afternoon to confirm though, in case he's otherwise tied up.'

'Will do,' Graham agreed.

Tommy had a sudden thought. 'Talking about making money, I don't suppose you can lay your hands on any pornography? There's a lot in that.'

Graham recalled the previous conversation he'd had with Tommy on the subject. 'If I could would the same man be interested?'

'Bugger him. I'd be interested! I can sell or sell on just as much as I can get hold of. And the mark-up is incredible.'

Porn, Graham thought. Was he morally against dealing in that? He considered it, and decided he wasn't. 'And it's a big profit margin, you say?'

'Huge.'

'More than watches and binoculars?'

'Far more. Unless you were getting the watches and bins for free, which according to you you're not.'

'Hmm!' Graham mused.

Tommy was really excited now. 'Can you get hold of some?'

Graham pulled a face. 'It's possible.'

'A lot?'

'I don't know yet. I'll have to make enquiries. Listen, forget this man I was going to meet for now. When I come back to you I'll have the answer about the porn.'

'If you can do it in bulk I can sell it on to Plymouth, Bristol, Bath and even the "Smoke". The potential is enormous.'

'I'll speak to you again when I know what's what. All right?'

Tommy's eyes were shining. 'You're a beauty, Graham. What are you?'

'I haven't promised anything,' Graham warned him. 'Only that the possibility is there.'

'Let me get you a drink,' Tommy said.

When Tommy returned from the bar he brought two large whiskies with him.

He tried to pump Graham further, but Graham kept his own counsel. Whether he dealt with Tommy or this man he wouldn't divulge the source of his supply.

'Would you be offended if I struck out on my own?'

Uncle Bert's eyes narrowed. 'How would you do that?'

'There's a motor cruiser for sale that I'm thinking of buying.'

'To smuggle?'

'If you have no objections. The last thing I want is any upset or ill-feeling between us. You, Reg and Alan have been extremely good to me after all. You've helped me make a considerable amount of money.'

'Enough to buy a motor cruiser,' Uncle Bert jibed.

'Exactly. And a car.'

'Mustn't forget the car,' Uncle Bert said drily.

Uncle Bert glanced up at the sails crackling in the

wind. They were making particularly good time this trip.
'And what type of contraband do you have in mind?'

'Not brandy and baccy. That's strictly your province.'

'I see.'

'I won't interfere in your set-up in any way.'

'So you won't be using the Blackboy?'

'Nope. But I do need L'Corbin. Whom I will only approach with your permission.'

Graham could see from Uncle Bert's expression that he'd said the right things, gone about this the right way.

'Well?' he queried softly.

Uncle Bert crossed to Reg and Alan and the three of them fell into a huddle in exactly the same way they'd done when Graham originally asked to join them. This time the answer was quicker forthcoming.

'That's all right by us,' Uncle Bert announced, coming back to Graham's side.

'I appreciate this.'

'Why shouldn't you strike out on your own? You're the ambitious type who'll do well for yourself. We wish you all the luck in the world. What cargo were you thinking of?'

'That depends on L'Corbin. But I'm going to enquire about pornography.'

Uncle Bert frowned. 'You mean dirty books?'

Graham nodded.

'I'm not so sure about that. Still . . .' He shrugged. 'It's your conscience, lad.'

'I'll speak to L'Corbin when we go ashore.'

It turned out L'Corbin had never been requested to supply pornography before. He told Graham he'd consult his contacts on the French mainland on the matter.

Powels handed Graham two sets of keys, one a spare. 'She's now officially yours,' he said. 'I hope you'll be as happy with her as I've been.'

'I'm sure I will.'

Graham gazed around *Waterwitch*, delighted and

thrilled to be her owner. He knew she was a good buy. Uncle Bert and his friend Pepperell, the boat builder, had given her a thorough inspection and pronounced *Waterwitch* to be in first-class condition.

Graham said goodbye to Powels, then started up the engine and took *Waterwitch* out of the harbour. On rounding Hope's Nose he set a course for Culmouth.

The light winked once in reply to Graham's two flashes. Then lanterns were lit illuminating the interior of the cave.

Graham eased *Waterwitch* forward, taking her towards the cave where L'Corbin was waiting.

The moon was up, casting pale shadows over the water. The entrance to the cave loomed ahead like some great mouth. He felt like Jonah about to be swallowed by the whale.

Waterwitch entered the cave, the growl of her engine suddenly much louder due to the cave's acoustics.

'Stop now,' L'Corbin said.

Graham did as he was bid.

'Catch hold and make fast,' L'Corbin instructed, and a rope snaked through the air to land on *Waterwitch*'s deck.

When Graham had done that L'Corbin and another man pulled *Waterwitch* to the side of the natural pool that filled the cave where it bumped gently against a flat area of rock.

L'Corbin came aboard and smiled at Graham. 'How was your trip over?'

'No problems.'

L'Corbin nodded. 'Good.'

The other man came aboard to join L'Corbin and Graham. 'This is Majohn, an associate of mine,' L'Corbin said, introducing his companion.

Graham judged Majohn to be in his early to mid-thirties. He had large soulful eyes and a droopy moustache. They shook hands.

186

'I will not always be here to meet you, in which case Majohn will take my place. You will pay him and make future arrangements as though you were dealing with me personally, understand?'

'I understand,' Graham replied.

L'Corbin made a gesture that took in the entire cave. 'A better rendezvous than the beach for a boat like yours, eh?'

Graham gazed round the cave, the roof of which was very high, out of sight. 'It's certainly an impressive rendezvous,' he answered.

'I hope you're not scared of ghosts,' Majohn said with a twinkle in his eye.

'Why? Is the cave haunted?'

'Vied'à. Yes. Many years ago a witch drowned herself here after being whipped and having her ear cut off for practising the black arts. She is often seen on this very spot. And then there is Tchi-co, who is also sometimes seen prowling around down here.'

'Tchi-co?'

'The phantom black dog of the dead. Whoever sees him will lose a loved one shortly afterwards,' Majohn breathed.

Graham felt the hairs on the nape of his neck stand upright, while gooscpimples stood out on his shoulders, back and upper arms.

L'Corbin laughed. 'Stop it, Majohn. I don't want you frightening my client away with your nonsense.' To Graham he said, 'Old wives' tales, nothing more. Take no notice. Let's start loading, shall we?'

Graham leapt on to the flat area of rock and went over to where some cardboard boxes were stacked. He didn't bother checking the merchandise knowing there wouldn't be any duplicity from L'Corbin who was totally trustworthy in these matters.

He and Majohn, each carrying a box, arrived back at the boat together. 'Aprie teu,' said Majohn, indicating that Graham should go first.

When the consignment was fully loaded Graham settled with L'Corbin, and then made arrangements to repeat the procedure at the same time the following week.

'À buèto,' said Majohn, shaking Graham again by the hand.

Graham knew what that meant as L'Corbin had used it in the past. 'Goodbye to you too,' he replied.

'Ghosts, witches and phantom dogs of the dead!' Graham laughed to himself as he headed home. It seemed Majohn was a character in the mould of Uncle Bert.

Graham started up the River Parry which was situated several miles down the coast from Culmouth. Half a mile along the narrow river brought him to the boathouse that Uncle Bert had arranged for him to rent.

On arriving at the boathouse, he took *Waterwitch* inside, then closed the river doors.

That done he lit several lamps similar to those used in the cave, and in their light unloaded *Waterwitch*, transferring the cardboard boxes to the van he had parked outside. He had sold the Lanchester to buy the van as unfortunately he hadn't been able to afford both.

When that job was completed he locked the boat-house, got into the van and began the journey to Exeter where Tommy Tripp would be waiting for him.

As he drove along he congratulated himself on the success of his first solo trip. If Tommy was able to keep up his end of the bargain, which Tommy assured him he could, from now on, he would be making a fortune.

Chapter Six

It had become a tradition in Atherton that every old year's night, as the Devonians called it, a Hogmanay dance was held in the village hall. Hogmanay was the greatest of all Scottish celebrations.

The dance was always organized by the Scots, and that year by John and James Cook in particular. A piper had been found and hired in Exeter, and so far he had already played several sets, and would be playing more later. There were also two accordionists playing Scottish reels and jigs which, as always, were proving tremendously popular with the Devonians as well as the Scots.

Later there was to be a No Talent Contest with a prize for the winner. There were six entries, none of whom knew what the others were going to do.

'It's a tremendous evening,' declared Andy Alford to Jennie. His top shirt button was undone, his tie pulled down.

'I'm certainly enjoying it.'

'Another drink?'

She considered it, then shook her head.

'Well, don't run away while I get one for myself.'

When he was gone, Christine Cook and Henry Down came over, the pair of them having been going out together for some months now.

'How are you?' Christine asked, face shining with excitement.

'Fine. Yourself?'

Christine nodded.

'Andy's gone up to the bar, eh?' Henry said, having

189

spotted Andy in the bar queue. The customers were served through a hatch that led to the kitchen.

'You've had enough!' Christine warned.

'Did I say I wanted any more?' Henry replied in mock surprise.

'Just don't get any ideas, that's all.'

Women, Henry thought, they could put a right dampner on things.

The accordionists, who'd been taking a break, struck up again. A middle-aged man and his wife, he was something to do with the electricity people, were first on to the floor.

'How about it?' Henry asked Christine.

'So charming, eh?' Christine said to Jennie, who smiled.

'We don't have to get up,' he frowned.

'Oh, come on!' And with that Christine dragged him on to the floor.

'It's going well, I think,' John slurred to Madge; they were sitting at a table not far from where Jennie was.

'Very well.'

'Can't wait for the No Talent Contest. That should be a hoot.'

Madge agreed.

Beattie and Bobby McDonald got up to dance, as incongruous looking together as ever. She might have been a child in his bearlike embrace.

John sat back in his chair and closed his eyes. His senses were whirling and he kept forgetting what he'd just said a moment before.

'You all right?' Madge asked anxiously.

'Never better,' he replied with a lop-sided grin.

He fixed his gaze on Jane Scott sitting close by. He'd have a dance with her, he thought. No harm in that. Just being neighbourly.

'Why, of course,' she replied to his invitation.

Jane fitted snugly into his arms.

'I hope you haven't got two left feet,' she teased.

'Nope. I can honestly say I haven't. I dance like I've got three.'

Jane laughed.

'But in my defence it has to be said I try hard.'

'Oh, you're very trying,' she jibed back instantly.

'Your patter's like watter,' he retorted, which was an old Glasgow saying.

'I haven't heard that in years,' she smiled.

'Bring back memories?'

She nodded.

'Dear old Glasgow town. There's nothing the matter with Glasgow except . . .'

'It's going round and round,' she finished for him.

'You and I get on well together,' he said.

She frowned, not quite sure what he meant by that.

He dropped a hand till it rested on the swell of her bottom. 'Going round and round,' he repeated.

Jane got the message, and disentangled herself the instant the dance finished. 'Thank you very much, John,' she said.

'How about another?'

'I'd rather sit down if you don't mind. My feet are hurting.'

They returned to their respective tables; he was disappointed she hadn't stayed up with him.

Ethel Yeo lit a cigarette, and gazed about her. She wasn't enjoying this at all. She wanted to be with Graham who was talking to some folk on the other side of the hall. Mark said something to which she replied without really taking in what he'd said. God, he was boring! Boring and becoming more so with every passing day.

She decided there and then she was going to mention divorce to Graham; it was a subject she'd avoided until now hoping he'd broach it. Divorced from Mark and married to Graham, that made her feel aglow inside and brought a smile to her lips. Marriage to Graham would be heaven on earth. Then she could have him in her bed every night, and wake with him every morning. Sheer bliss!

Who was he speaking to now? That Mayberry woman. Cow! She'd never liked Roz Mayberry, thinking her vulgar and common. And everyone knew her hair wasn't naturally that colour, that the colour came out of a bottle.

Obvious was another word to describe Roz Mayberry. Why, look at the way she was flirting outrageously with Graham, almost throwing herself at him. She could have scratched the bitch's eyes out.

'What?' she snapped to Mark who'd addressed her again.

'I said, do you want to dance?'

'No.'

'How about another drink then?'

'No.'

He regarded her curiously. There were times when he just didn't understand Ethel. One minute she was nice as pie, the next biting your head off. And she'd become so moody.

'Is there anything I can get you?'

'Nothing.'

Sorry for asking, he thought to himself, and picked up his pint.

Graham caught sight of Ethel glaring at him, and realized right away what was wrong. Damn her, she was becoming more and more possessive, not to mention demanding. If she kept up her present behaviour she might blow the gaff to Mark and then where would they all be!

Then he thought of being in bed with her and what they got up to in the back of his van. How could he ever give that up? Certainly not lightly. But he had to admit, Ethel was beginning to pall. Perhaps the time had come to think about breaking things off between them.

He smiled across the hall at her, and that mollified her a little. A few minutes later he casually strolled over and joined her and Mark. And then, of course, it was the most natural thing in the world to ask his friend's wife up to dance.

'What were you talking about with that awful Roz Mayberry?' she demanded in a hiss.

'Relax,' he replied. 'We were only chatting, that's all.'

'Jesus, I want you. Right here and now if I could.'

The idea of that amused him. In his mind he could picture he and Ethel at it on the floor with everyone else present, including John, Madge and Jennie, gazing on.

'Why are you grinning like some demented idiot?' she queried.

'I was just visualizing what you suggested. The two of us doing it in front of all these onlookers.'

Her mood changed abruptly, and she laughed. 'That would be some sight, eh?'

'Some sight,' he agreed.

A little later those involved in the No Talent Contest began disappearing backstage to get ready. Andy's father was one of them; he intended singing a comic, bawdy song full of *double entendres* called 'To Be a Farmer's Boy'. Andy saw his dad go, and had an idea.

He turned to Jennie, his face flushed. Bending close to her ear he said, 'Dad's in this contest and Mum will be watching. Why don't we pop back to my house for a while?'

'Don't be silly,' she whispered, in reply.

He became belligerent, not realizing just how drunk he was. 'Why the hell not? It's a perfect opportunity.'

'For what?' she demanded coldly.

'For us to . . . you know?'

Here it was, the same old suggestion. You'd think he'd learn! 'The answer's no,' she stated.

'Oh Jennie!'

'No,' she repeated.

He glanced about, making sure they weren't being overheard. 'We've been going out together long enough.'

'The length of time has nothing to do with it,' she answered, beginning to get annoyed.

'Well, it has to me.'

Her annoyance started to turn to anger. 'Just drop it, will you!'

'Is that all you can say?' When she didn't reply he went on, 'It is your Scottish Hogmanay after all. Out with the old and in with the new.'

'I am not going to sleep with you and that's that.'

'Bitch,' he muttered, and swayed on the spot.

Her anger increased. 'What was that?'

He eyed her balefully. 'You heard me.'

'Did you call me a bitch?'

He nodded.

She fought back the urge to slap him. How dare he? Her anger blossomed.

'You've no heart, Jennie,' he accused. 'You can't have to treat me as you do.'

'I have a heart all right. And right now it's not all that kindly disposed to you, Andy Alford.'

'I sometimes wonder if it ever is,' he riposted huffily.

'Stupid!' she exclaimed.

'I am not.'

'But what you just said was.'

'Sod you,' he answered.

That was it. She knew this had escalated out of all proportion, but she wasn't going to let him speak to her like that. 'Bitch' was bad enough, but 'sod you' was unforgivable. She made a decision.

'I'm going home,' she announced.

He shrugged. 'Suit yourself.'

'Right.' And with that she swept from the hall, only pausing momentarily to pick up her coat.

'Shit,' said Andy. How had all that come about? He drained his glass and decided to get another. He and Jennie Forsyth were through. Finished. There were plenty of other fish in the sea, he told himself. Fish that would treat him a damn sight better than she'd done.

Little miss virgin, he thought. Well, she could stay one as far as he was concerned.

Christine came over. 'What's happened to Jennie?' she queried.

Andy glared at her. 'She buggered off.'

'Off? Off where?'

'Home she said.'

'Have you two had a fight?'

'And what if we have? It's no bloody business of yours.'

'Here, steady on,' said Henry Down, materializing at Christine's side. He put a protective arm round Christine.

'I'm going to get another drink,' Andy stated, and stamped his way over to the bar queue.

'I wonder if I should go after Jennie?' Christine mused.

'Do you want to?'

Christine thought about that. 'No, probably best to leave things as they are.'

'Unpleasant lout,' Henry said, staring over at Andy.

'He's not usually like that at all. As you well know.'

Jennie's departure had also been noticed by Poppy Dewdney. Poppy was a plainish girl who made the best of herself.

'Hello,' she said a little later, coming over to Andy who was standing morosely in a corner.

'Hello yourself,' he retorted sourly.

Poppy lowered her face slightly, and blinked up at Andy through heavily made-up eyelashes, a trick she'd picked up from a friend of hers.

A good figure, Andy noted, quite busty.

'What happened to Jennie Forsyth? I saw her go storming out of here.'

'We had a row,' Andy stated.

'Looked serious.'

He shrugged.

Poppy had fancied Andy for a long time. But there had been Jennie, and before that he'd hardly noticed her even though she'd made it clear she was interested and available.

'Can I buy you a drink?' she offered.

'That's very kind of you.'

'What'll it be?'

'A short. Whisky.'

'I'll make it a double, my lover.' And having said that, she sauntered off, purposefully accentuating the waggle of her hips as she made her way to the bar.

When Poppy returned the No Talent Show was announced, which they proceeded to watch together. The show was a great success, won by six village men who, dressed in black tights, tops and wearing pink tutus, danced a piece from Swan Lake. They were so good, by being so abominably awful and outrageous, that they won by a mile.

'Like to dance?' Andy asked when the accordionists started up again.

'Love to.'

They danced for the next half-hour, he talking about all sorts, she listening intently and giving the responses she thought he wanted.

They took a break for another drink, then danced again till midnight was proclaimed, and things went wild. All too soon it was the last waltz.

By now Andy knew just how drunk he was, but didn't care. 'Shall I walk you home?' he asked when the last waltz was over.

This was precisely what Poppy had been hoping he'd do. 'If you want to.'

He thought of Jennie, then put Jennie out of his mind. She could go to hell as far as he was concerned. She was nothing but a tease. 'Let's get our coats,' he said.

People were spilling from the hall, going in all directions, some laughing, others calling out to friends.

'A smashing night,' declared Andy.

Poppy shivered, for it was cold out.

'It is a bit nippy, isn't it?'

'I should have brought my gloves,' she said.

'I'll warm one for you,' he replied, and took a hand in his.

At her door they stopped and turned to face each other. She smiled, and he smiled back.

'I didn't see your folks there tonight,' he said.

'They didn't go. They like the quiet life. They'll have been tucked up for hours.'

'They don't bring in the New Year?'

'Haven't done for years.'

Poppy moved closer to Andy. 'Thank you for walking me home. It was very kind of you.'

'My pleasure.'

She kissed him, her lips lingering on his.

He put a hand on her neck, the other on her back. The kiss changed to one of fierce passion as they clung to one another.

They kissed and kissed, their tongues darting and twining. Andy's hand that had been on her back came round to slide inside her coat and encircle a breast.

Poppy broke off, panting. She wanted more of this. 'Not here, round behind,' she said. She then grasped his hand and almost dragged him after her.

They came to a shed which she opened, and pulled him inside. She closed the door and leant up against it.

'This is better. More private,' she husked.

She groaned as his mouth fell again on hers. How she'd dreamt of being in this situation with Andy Alford.

He undid her dress, and freed her breasts. She closed her eyes and smiled as he took a nipple into his mouth.

Andy was on fire, his body aching for release. She made no effort to stop him when he pulled her dress up to her waist.

Moments later, after a little fumbling on his part, they were joined. She moaned as he plunged in and out of her.

And then it was all over. He drew in huge breaths from his exertions.

'That was beautiful,' she crooned, stroking his hair.

When he'd caught his breath he readjusted his clothing, and she did the same. When they were both ready they returned to the front door where he kissed her again.

Before leaving he promised he'd contact her before the weekend to make an arrangement.

Andy woke with an incredibly sore head and a totally parched mouth. He felt dreadful.

Slowly it all came back to him. His fight with Jennie, her going off and leaving him. Poppy Dewdney. Their dancing together. Him walking her home. What had happened in the shed. Him promising to see her again.

'Ooohhh!' he sighed. What had he done! Not that he regretted Poppy, that had been most pleasurable, but how could he have fought with Jennie like that. How stupid of him. How utterly stupid.

Of course he wasn't finished with Jennie, that idea was absurd, out of the question. It was the drink that had made him think like that. And the drink that had made him act as he had.

He'd go and speak to Jennie right away and make up. As for Poppy, that was a one-off, no more. He'd simply fail to get in touch as he'd promised. She'd get the message.

Jennie, he thought, getting out of bed. He'd have some tea, he couldn't face any breakfast, and go straight over.

They went for a walk in the water meadows, each bundled up against the biting wind that was blowing.

'There's snow in the air. I can smell it,' Jennie said.

'Look, I really am sorry. Truly I am. Please forgive me.'

She glanced sideways at him. 'You were frightfully rude.'

'I know. I apologize. I'll even go down on my knees and beg forgiveness if you demand it.'

She laughed. 'Don't be silly.'

He caught hold of her hand, and gazed deeply into her eyes. 'I love you, Jennie. You know that.'

'Do I?' she teased.

'Yes, you do. You're the only girl for me.'

She pulled her hand from his. She wasn't going to let him off that lightly. 'Last night you thought I was a bitch.'

'I was drunk.'

'You were certainly that.'

'God alone knows why I called you that. Frustration I suppose.'

'I wish you wouldn't keep on about us sleeping together. You're well aware of my feelings on the subject.'

'There are occasions when you drive me mad. It's as simple as that.'

'With lust?' she further teased.

'No. Love.'

A pair of swans flapped overhead. Jennie halted and stared up at them, listening to that strange, asthmatic wheezing sound they made when in flight. She adored swans; there were a lot of them in the area. The pair she was watching were no doubt mates, she thought.

'Am I forgiven?' he pleaded.

'Bitch is bad enough but what about "sod you"?'

He took hold of her hand again. 'I regretted it the instant I said it.'

That was a lie, she thought. But one with the best of intentions behind it. He was certainly contrite this morning. And so he should be.

'I was furious,' she said. 'Boiling with anger.'

'It was all so . . . ridiculous really.'

They walked a little way in silence, then he said, 'About us going all the way. I'll wait as long as that takes. Honest I will.'

He was now sounding like a little boy. But he was sincere enough, of that she had no doubt. He was genuinely sorry for what he'd done.

'All right, you're forgiven,' she said.

With a cry of delight he swept her into his arms and kissed her. Then they continued with their walk, he babbling on from sheer relief and happiness.

'Say that again?' Madge demanded.

John nervously licked his lips. 'There's no money this week,' he repeated in a small, chastened voice. It was the Friday night of the first week back at Wheal Tempest after the New Year holiday.

'And why not?'

'Because I . . .' He took a deep breath, and swallowed hard. 'Because I've had to pay off my slate in the pub.'

Madge regarded him venomously. 'What slate?'

'I've had one for ages. Only, over Christmas and the New Year it sort of got out of hand.'

'You've drunk an entire week's wages?'

'Well, it was the festive season and things, rounds . . . I suppose you might say I got carried away.'

Madge sprang forward and hit him with the flat of her hand as hard as she could. A loud crack rent the air and John went reeling backwards.

'Is the slate clean now or do we still owe something?'

John muttered inaudibly.

'Speak up!' she shouted.

'Three bob only. I'll pay that next week.'

Madge picked up her handbag and stalked from the kitchen. She threw on her coat and left the house to go striding up the street.

'I want a word,' she declared to the landlord of the Atherton Arms whom she found behind his bar.

He adjusted his spectacles. 'I've a good idea what you've come about.'

'I'll bet you do!'

'To be honest it's partially my fault. I didn't realize how much he'd chalked up till I came to do my figures. It's the most hectic period of the year after all, things go unnoticed that otherwise wouldn't. But he paid on the nail, which is the rule. The same rule for everyone.'

Madge was curious. 'And if he hadn't?'

'I'd have come round to see you. Or Staddon at the mine if I'd had to,' the landlord replied softly.

So John had had no option but to pay up fully and then confess to her. 'We're still three shillings outstanding I believe,' she said.

Madge opened her handbag and took out her purse. She counted three shillings on to the bar while the landlord watched. When she'd laid out the right amount she pushed the money across to him.

'From here on in no more slate for John,' she stated.

The landlord nodded. 'If that's how you want it, Madge.'

'I do.'

'He'll have no more tick in here then. I promise you.'

'Good.'

Madge returned her purse to her bag, snapped the bag shut, wheeled about and left the pub.

The landlord shook his head. Tick was a double-edged sword upon which some people, like John, became horribly impaled.

He promptly forgot about Madge and John when a customer beckoned him over.

Madge entered the house and slammed the door shut behind her. She went through to the kitchen where she found John slumped in a chair before the fire. At least he hadn't fled to bed which she'd half expected him to do.

'What a face. Like fizz!' Jennie joked, referring to her mother.

Madge rounded on her. 'Just who do you think you're speaking to young lady?' she retorted.

Jennie bristled. 'I didn't mean anything by . . .'

'You never do mean anything. The trouble with you is you speak before you think.'

John shrank into his chair.

'That's unfair! And just not true,' Jennie answered.

201

'Anyway, how dare you speak to your mother like that? Shows no respect whatsoever.'

Jennie took a deep breath, and started to leave.

'Just where do you think you're going?' Madge demanded.

'To my room. Any objections?'

'That's cheek!'

'It's not meant to be,' Jennie replied, staring her mother straight in the eye.

'It's your tone that's unacceptable and cheeky.'

'Then I'm sorry. I'll try and watch my tone in future.'

'Do that!' Madge snapped.

A fuming Jennie left the kitchen, went upstairs and threw herself on her bed. There were times when she wanted to run away from home and never see either of her parents again – and this was one of them.

Andy was dog tired; for some reason it had been a particularly hard shift. He couldn't wait to get home, have a wash, something to eat and then put his feet up for half an hour. He was with a group of his mates on their way home from Wheal Tempest.

He thought of Jennie, and smiled, a smile that was quickly wiped from his face when he saw Poppy Dewdney walking towards them with a girlfriend named Sandra.

This was his first encounter with Poppy since old year's night. He went cold all over.

Poppy's gaze hardened when she caught sight of him. If looks could kill he'd have died on the spot.

'Christ!' he muttered, and dropped his own gaze to stare at the pavement.

Would she stop and insist on talking? He prayed she wouldn't.

One of his mates called out to Sandra, who answered jocularly.

Then they were passing one another, the men moving slightly aside to let the girls pass.

He watched Poppy's legs go by, his heart in his mouth, waiting for them to stop suddenly.

But they didn't. They kept on walking.

He sighed with relief. If she'd been going to say anything, surely she would have done so there and then? He was off the hook as far as Poppy Dewdney was concerned. She was history.

He grinned at the memory of what they'd done in the shed. It was an incident to remember – as a secret.

Graham was sunk in thought as *Waterwitch* cut through the water *en route* to Sark. He was mentally going over a recent conversation he'd had with Tommy Tripp. Their venture couldn't be going better; Tommy was arranging all the business behind shifting the porn he was given. In conversation Tommy had complained that he'd only wished there was more for him to sell.

Why not? Graham asked himself. If this goose could lay a golden egg once a week then why not twice? That was if L'Corbin could supply a second consignment. He decided to speak to either him or Majohn, whoever was there to meet him, about it later.

He'd have to give up his job of course, which would be a loss of revenue, but a second run per week would more than make up for that.

What would he tell Madge and John though? He considered that issue, and came up with the idea of telling them he'd found a better job in Culmouth which he would travel up and down to on a daily basis.

Twice a week, twice as risky. But the profits were tremendous and made the risk, at least in his eyes, worth while.

He laughed out loud. Mark had really put him on to a winner when he'd suggested he drove the van for the Yeos while he was laid up.

Andy and his parents were listening to the wireless one

evening when there was a rap on the front door. 'I'll get it,' said Connie Alford, rising.

'Good programme this,' stated Rafe Alford.

Andy was enjoying it as well, he liked big band music.

A frowning Connie returned with Ken Dewdney and his daughter Poppy. Andy's mouth fell open when he saw who it was. He went rigid from head to toe, while his heart felt as though it had suddenly stopped.

'Good evening,' said Ken Dewdney in a stern voice.

Poppy was red eyed and appeared to have been crying. Her hands were clasped tightly in front of her, shaking.

Although irritated at being interrupted, Rafe Alford did the polite thing and got up and switched off the wireless. 'This is an unexpected pleasure,' he lied.

'No pleasure when you hear what I've come about,' Ken Dewdney answered grimly.

Fear clutched at Andy's insides. Disaster was about to strike. He just knew it. Surely the stupid cow hadn't gone and said something!

'I'll put the kettle on, shall I?' offered Connie.

'Not for me, thank you,' Ken Dewdney replied, and cleared his throat.

There was a few moments' hiatus, then Ken Dewdney said, 'Our Poppy's pregnant by your lad.'

Andy sat pole-axed, his expression one of stunned incredulity. He couldn't believe this was happening.

Rafe looked at Andy, then back again at Ken. 'I, eh . . .' He trailed off, lost for words.

'Are you certain she's pregnant?' Connie asked quietly.

'There's no doubt about it,' Ken answered.

Rafe turned to Andy. 'Well?'

Andy didn't reply.

'So it's a possibility?'

Andy closed his eyes. Should he deny it? He could he supposed. But in his heart of hearts he knew the truth would out. 'Yes,' he admitted in a small voice.

'Old year's night. After the dance,' Poppy said, speaking for the first time.

'Don't be offended, but I have to ask. Are you sure it's Andy's baby?' Connie queried.

'There's been no-one else,' Poppy told her, which wasn't exactly true, but there hadn't been anyone else within that period. The baby was Andy's all right.

What was Jennie going to think? Andy wondered. What a nightmare. He wanted to disappear, or run, screaming, from the room. Once in a garden shed! How bloody unlucky could you get?

'I'll sit down now if I may,' Ken Dewdney said.

'Please,' responded Rafe, gesturing to an empty chair. Ken sat, as did Poppy.

'The question is,' said Ken Dewdney, 'will Andy do the honourable thing by Poppy?'

Honourable thing! Those words seared themselves into Andy's brain.

Ken went on. 'He's had his fun. Now the piper has to be paid.'

'You're talking marriage,' Rafe stated dully.

'I am. And quickly. Do that and we can get away with telling the world the baby, when it arrives, is premature.'

Connie worked out Poppy's dates. Ken Dewdney was right, they could get away with it, but only just. 'Who else knows about this?' she asked.

'Those in this room, the wife and doctor. That's it.'

Connie nodded.

I don't want to marry Poppy, Andy wanted to protest. *I want to marry Jennie*.

Connie turned to her son. 'I agree, Andy, you have to face up to your responsibility. You're old enough to marry, and earning.'

'They can stay with us till they find a place of their own,' Ken declared.

'Andy?' Rafe prompted.

'I could use a drink,' Andy croaked.

'Good idea,' Rafe acknowledged. 'I think we all could. What do we have, Mother?'

'There's some Scotch at the back of the cupboard. I'll get it.'

Andy stared at Poppy who stared pleadingly back. He could almost hear her begging 'please?'.

When Connie handed Andy a glass of Scotch he found his hands were shaking, just as Poppy's were.

He had a gulp, and tasted nothing. 'What if I say no?'

Poppy sobbed, and stuffed a hand into her mouth. Tears glistened in her eyes.

'You can't say no,' Rafe stated quietly. 'You can't let the girl down. It's not the done thing.'

'But I don't love her.'

'You should have thought of that on old year's night,' Connie admonished.

'But that . . .' He shut up. How could he explain about falling out with Jennie and then Poppy letting him do what he'd wanted to do in the first place with Jennie?

'I'll make you a good wife. There won't be a better one in Atherton. I swear to that,' Poppy said in a tremulous voice.

'This sort of thing has happened before and will happen again. Many successful marriages come out of these situations,' Connie declared.

Rafe muttered in agreement.

'Poppy's life will be ruined if you don't marry her,' Ken said to Andy.

'There are people . . . places where something can be done,' Andy argued.

Ken's face clouded, and for a moment Andy thought Ken was going to come over and hit him.

'No,' Ken stated flatly. 'I won't have my maid going to those "people" as you call them. I've heard stories that would turn your stomach. Girls in agony afterwards, some dying. No, there will be none of that where Poppy is concerned. She's having the baby, and that's that.'

'I totally agree,' said Connie, and shot Andy a withering look for suggesting such a thing.

Andy drank off the rest of his Scotch, rose, crossed to the bottle and poured himself another, splashing some on the table in the process.

Rafe went over to Andy and put an arm round his son's shoulders. 'I'll have a word with the vicar tonight and have the banns called, beginning Sunday. All right?'

He felt trapped, and sick. This had all happened so quickly, so completely out of the blue. He'd been happily listening to the wireless, then there had been a knock on the front door, and with that knock his entire world had turned upside down.

'All right?' Rafe repeated, this time more firmly.

Andy sighed, a sigh that came from the very depths of his being. Jennie was lost to him for ever. He wanted to cry. If only he could turn the clock back. If only . . .

'All right,' he replied.

It was settled.

When he woke up next morning he was still shaking, and he shook for the rest of the day. After supper he went round to Jennie's house with the intention of telling her that he would be marrying Poppy, but he just couldn't bring himself to do so.

He went to the pub instead where he got blind drunk.

'And this is for the first time of asking,' the vicar said.

Madge turned in surprise to Jennie, and so, too, did John. It had to be some kind of joke, Jennie thought. I mean . . . her Andy and Poppy Dewdney!

But vicars didn't make jokes like that, she told herself. So it must be true. Andy and Poppy were to be married. But how? Why?

Andy had said he loved her. Swore he did. And now this.

When the congregation left the church Andy and Poppy went out together, Poppy smiling fit to bust.

A red-faced Andy refused to meet Jennie's gaze.

Jennie sat on her bed weeping her eyes out. She was angry, confused, hurt beyond belief. How could Andy have done this to her without a word of explanation? He hadn't even had the decency to tell her what he was going to do.

She balled a hand into a fist and beat her thigh. Above all she felt stupid, stupid to have believed his lies. How long had he been carrying on with Poppy while he'd been seeing her? God, it made her want to throw up.

'Andy!' she sobbed.

There was a tap on the door, which then opened to reveal John. He had been on the wagon since the day he'd had to pay over his entire week's wages to the landlord in the pub.

'Can I come in?' he asked quietly.

Jennie replied with a sob.

John crossed over and sat beside her. 'That bad, eh?'

'Worse.'

'What a rotten, lousy thing to do.'

'He's a pig!' she hissed.

'You could have knocked me down with a feather when the Reverend Royal made the announcement.' He put a hand in his pocket and pulled out a large, clean, white handkerchief. 'Here, I brought you this.'

Jennie gratefully accepted the hanky and wiped the tears from her cheeks.

'Is there anything I can do, lass? Anything I can get you?'

Jennie shook her head.

'I've a good mind to go to his house and have it out with him. Thump him for what he's done.'

'No, Dad, don't do that. It would only make matters worse.'

'Are you sure?'

She nodded.

'It breaks my heart to see you like this. I might not be the best of fathers, but I do love my children. I'd do anything for you and Graham.'

She managed to smile through her tears. 'I know that, Dad.'

He patted her on the knee. 'You'll get over him. Time's a great healer. Someone else will happen along eventually. You'll see.'

She thought of Poppy Dewdney who wasn't a patch on her. Why? That was the question that screamed in her mind. Why?

'Your mother's got the kettle on. How about a nice cup of tea or cocoa?'

'I couldn't eat or drink anything, Dad.'

'Oh lass!' he muttered sympathetically.

'I think I'd like to be alone now if you don't mind,' she said.

'Aye, of course. Whatever you want. Just remember your mother and I are downstairs if you need us.'

'Thanks Dad.'

He kissed her on the cheek, then left the room as quietly as he'd entered it.

Children, he thought outside, if only you could take their pain on to yourself. But that, of course, was impossible.

'Damn Andy Alford,' he muttered. For two pins he'd have knocked the bugger's block off. But Jennie was right, that wasn't the solution – though it would have made him feel a lot better.

Jennie didn't go to work next day. Madge went over and told Bob Yendell at the shop that she wasn't feeling well. Bob understood.

Jennie lay late in bed, as she was desperately tired, having been awake for most of the night. Eventually she got up and dressed, then went downstairs where Madge tried to tempt her with a special breakfast. Jennie said she had no appetite whatsoever, but did manage to force

209

down a cup of tea. She then decided to go for a walk.

She went to the water meadows where she strolled along the river bank. She stopped to watch some moorhens fussing in and out the tangled undergrowth where their nests clearly were, and then gazed at a flight of Canada geese who landed near by.

'Jennie!'

She turned round and saw Graham hurrying towards her.

'I had to go out earlier and then when I got home Mum said I'd probably find you here.'

'You're not at work today, either?'

'Took the day off as well,' he lied. He hooked an arm through hers. 'So, how are you?'

'How do you think?'

'Bloody, eh?'

'That's one way of putting it.'

He stared into her face which was white and strained. 'I'll tell you something, which you might not want to hear, but if Andy could do this to you then you're well rid of him.'

She knew Graham was right, but that didn't make matters any easier.

'Anyway, I've a suggestion,' Graham went on. 'Why don't I take you into Exeter and treat you to a whole new wardrobe?'

She couldn't help but smile.

'Clothes, shoes and perfume perhaps. What do you say?'

It was absolutely perfect. 'Can you afford—?'

'Money's no problem,' he cut in, thinking, if only she knew!

She took a deep breath, then another. 'You know, I feel better already.'

He laughed. 'That's my favourite girl!'

They walked back to the house where his car was parked. He still had the van which he used to transport his imported pornography from Sark to Exeter, but he had managed to buy another Lanchester to replace the one he'd had to sell.

Jennie insisted on tidying herself up first, and putting on some make-up. Then she and Graham were off, he gunning the Lanchester in the direction of Exeter, giving her the thrill of her life by driving far too fast.

They went to Colson's, a large department store, where Graham gave her *carte blanche* to buy whatever she liked.

She was looking at dresses when she had a sudden inspiration that brought a grim smile to her face. She knew exactly what she wanted, and where she was going to wear it.

When they'd completed their purchases Graham insisted on taking her to Tinley's for a cream tea, where she positively gorged herself on cakes which left her feeling absolutely wonderful.

'You're going to the church ceremony then?' Madge said in surprise.

'I am,' Jennie replied.

'I would have thought . . . well, I don't know. I just wouldn't have imagined you'd have wanted to, that's all.'

'I most definitely want to be there,' Jennie stated. 'I have my reasons.'

'Suit yourself. I'll go with you.'

A gleam came into Jennie's eyes. She knew the pew where she'd sit, a pew where Andy couldn't fail to notice her when he walked back up the aisle with his bride.

Jennie was taking great care over her make-up, determined to get it exactly right. She frowned in concentration as she stared into her vanity mirror, wondering if the shade of lipstick she'd chosen created the desired effect.

'Almost ready?' Madge queried, popping her head round Jennie's bedroom door.

211

'Shortly.'

Jennie paused to think momentarily of Andy. A strange flicker passed over her face, and then was gone.

When she'd finally finished her make-up she put on the suit she'd bought with this occasion in mind. It was black, rather severe in cut, with a pencil skirt. It made her look older than her eighteen years, which was deliberate. She then slipped on some plain, black shoes.

She recombed her hair which hung straight to her shoulders. And then she gazed at herself in the mirror, pleased with the result. She looked mature, sophisticated and quite stunning. She could have walked down Bond Street and given the impression of belonging there.

Her last act was to dab on a little of the French perfume Graham had bought her.

She went downstairs where she found Madge drinking a cup of tea, waiting for her.

Madge was raising the cup to her mouth when Jennie entered the kitchen. The cup stopped in mid-air as Madge caught sight of her daughter.

Madge smiled. Now she knew why Jennie wanted to go to the wedding. And she approved.

'Well?' Jennie asked.

'You don't need me to tell you.'

Jennie nodded. 'Shall we go? I want to be there early so we can get a good seat.'

Madge finished her tea, and they left the house and headed for the church. There would be many villagers there which was the custom with all village weddings and funerals. Invitations weren't required.

The church seating was in two sections, front and rear. By tradition, family or families connected with the ceremony occupied the front pews, villagers and others those at the rear.

On entering the church, Jennie went straight to the front pew of the rear section, selecting a seat close to the aisle. She and Madge sat down, waiting for the ceremony to begin.

The church filled rapidly, and buzzed with muted conversation. The Yendells were there and the Coffins. Then came the Zellys, Besleys, Pugsleys, the latter followed by Les Pack who was to be seen for once without a dog by his side.

John wouldn't be there, having refused point blank to attend. He had gone out earlier on a private errand.

Andy arrived in a hired morning suit, and with him his best man, another miner from Wheal Tempest. Jennie lowered her head and withdrew into herself as much as possible. She didn't want Andy to notice her yet.

Soon after that the organ struck up: the bride had arrived.

As always, Poppy had made the best of herself. But none the less underneath it all she remained what she was, plain. The dress, Jennie thought with grim satisfaction, was far too fussy. Above all it looked cheap.

Rafe Alford walked Poppy down the aisle to where Andy was waiting, and the service began.

The appropriate words were uttered, vows exchanged, and the ring placed on Poppy's finger. When all was said and done, the bridegroom kissed the bride.

Then the bridegroom and bride, arm in arm, were walking back up the aisle. About three-quarters of the way up, everything happened exactly as Jennie had planned. Andy caught sight of her.

Something inside him crumbled and fell apart as he realized afresh just what he'd lost. Jennie and Poppy, it was like comparing a thoroughbred to a cart-horse. And Jennie had never looked more thoroughbred than she did at that moment.

Jennie smiled thinly, knowing she'd made her point. From now on she'd start to get over Andy Alford.

'Feel better?' Madge asked when they were outside.

'Lots.'

As they began making their way home, to the pealing of bells, Jennie was aware that she was getting many

213

admiring glances from the men about. She was also aware that she'd just gone through a watershed in her life.

Hate Andy Alford? No. If anything she pitied him.

Andy rolled off Poppy and stared at the ceiling. It was the first night of their four-day honeymoon.

Poppy sighed. 'That was beautiful,' she crooned.

She couldn't have said anything that would have jarred against him more. He remembered with crystal clarity those were the exact words she'd spoken after they'd done it in the garden shed.

'How was it for you, darling?' she asked.

'Terrific.'

'I'm pleased.'

She twisted round in bed and stroked his flank. 'It's lovely being in bed together like this, isn't it?'

He grunted.

'And we'll sleep all night together, and then wake up together.'

He wished she'd shut up.

'You're not very talkative?' she said.

'I suppose I'm tired,' he lied. 'It's been a long day.'

'The day of our marriage. One I'll remember for the rest of my life.'

He groaned inwardly. The rest of her life. The rest of *his* life, what was that going to be like. He contemplated it with dread. To think what he'd had and thrown away. Madness!

He pictured Jennie as she'd been in the church. God! He'd have given anything for it to have been her on his arm and not Poppy.

Poppy talked, and then a little while later whispered, 'Let's do it again, Andy.'

He kissed and caressed her, then remounted her. As he moved he stared down at her face. Only it wasn't Poppy's he saw, but Jennie's.

And when he slept he dreamt of Jennie.

* * *

Madge was darning, John reading the evening newspaper, while Jennie was ironing. 'I hear Poppy Alford is
expecting,' Madge said.

John glanced up from his paper. 'That was quick.'

Madge shrugged, but didn't comment.

'When is she due?' Jennie asked.

'End of the year.'

Jennie set down the iron and folded the sheet she'd
been pressing. Poppy expecting, well, that was natural
enough. When she'd folded the sheet she laid it to one
side, picked up a shirt and started on that.

How did she feel about it? she asked herself. Nothing
really. Certainly no resentment or jealousy. Andy was
very rapidly becoming a thing of the past. She decided if
she felt anything it was happiness for them.

'Have they found a place of their own yet?' John
queried.

'Not that I know of,' Madge replied. 'Still, something
suitable will come up in the village eventually.'

'They definitely want to stay here then?'

'So I believe.'

Whether they stayed on or moved away didn't bother
her one way or the other, Jennie thought. What did
bother her was this restlessness she'd been experiencing
of late. It was like having an itch you couldn't scratch.

Maybe she should take up a hobby. That might be the
answer.

Jennie was slicing ham when Bob Yendell said, 'Poppy
Alford's just had a little girl. Both are doing fine
apparently.'

Jennie paused at his news. 'A little girl?'

'She arrived prematurely. The midwife was called late
last night, then the doctor.'

'And you say both are fine?'

'That's what Barbara Lockyer told me, and she's a
great friend of the family.'

215

Jennie continued slicing ham. Premature? Could be. It did happen, after all.

She began working out dates. Say the baby wasn't premature, and that Poppy had actually gone to her full term. That would mean she'd become pregnant . . .

Jennie stopped, and sucked in a breath. That could explain why Andy had suddenly married Poppy. It was all speculation on her part, mind, but it fitted.

The night of the Hogmanay dance when she'd left him? Poppy had been there, she remembered seeing her.

Yes, it did make sense. Particularly when you took into account what they'd quarrelled about. Andy had gone with Poppy that night and paid a terrible penalty as a result.

Now she understood. And the more she thought about it the more convinced she became she was right.

Premature, that was a good excuse.

Christine nudged Jennie, and giggled. The two young men in the train compartment sitting opposite them were clearly giving them the eye.

Would the young men speak or not? Jennie wondered. And would they reply if the young men did? They were a couple of farm hands by the look of them, she thought.

Then the train pulled into Exeter St David's, and the opportunity for the young men to speak was over. The four young people left the train and went their separate ways.

'The red-haired chap was quite fanciable,' Christine said; she and Henry Down had broken up the previous month.

'Did you think so?'

'Yours wasn't so nice though.' And having said that, Christine laughed, as did Jennie.

They strolled down to the picture house where they paid their money and went inside. The main feature was an American film set in a New York hospital, showing the trials and tribulations of a young doctor.

Jennie found herself absorbed by the film, and was sorry when it was finally over. She could easily have sat through a rerun.

'I really enjoyed that,' she declared as they left.

'Wasn't bad,' commented Christine. 'Do you want some fish and chips?'

'I don't think so,' Jennie replied. 'What about you?'

Christine shook her head.

'Back to the train then.'

Jennie talked enthusiastically about the film as they returned to the station, it had caught her imagination.

When they reached their platform Christine glanced about, wondering if the two young men they'd travelled in with would put in a reappearance. But they, somewhat to her disappointment, were nowhere to be seen.

They left the train at Atherton and walked back to the Forsyths' where they had a cup of tea.

John, still on the wagon, asked them if they'd had a good Saturday night out. Jennie enthused about the main feature, saying how taken she'd been by it.

Later, in bed, she found it hard to get to sleep. Scenes from the hospital film kept flitting through her mind. The film had definitely struck a chord deep within her, whatever that chord was.

The customer Jennie loathed most came into the shop, the awful Les Pack. If possible Les never bought anything in a hurry, liking to drag the process, and conversation, on as long as possible. And he was always probing, prying, trying to find out about people.

'Hello, my lover,' he smiled to Jennie in that sly way of his, while his dog stretched itself out on the floor.

Jennie was alone in the shop, he the sole customer. This transaction would most certainly take time. 'What can I get you, Mr Pack?' she asked.

'Let me see,' he mused.

Twenty minutes later he left having bought some

tobacco, grumbling about its price as he nearly always did, and two ounces of boiled sweets.

She was bored, Jennie thought, bored witless with her job at the shop. The real question was, she told herself, what did she want out of life? Marriage, babies, being a housewife? Admirable enough, but she considered herself capable of more than that.

The trouble was she had limited education, having left school at fourteen. She wished now she'd stayed on and got better qualifications. Then who knows what she might have done?

The door tinged open and another customer entered. This one wanted a pork pie, a pound of butter and some vegetables.

Jennie did her best to be pleasant, but her heart wasn't in it.

'You what!' John exclaimed in astonishment.

'I've applied to attend night school in Exeter and have been accepted,' Jennie repeated.

'Night school for what?' John queried.

'I'm going to take up where I left off at ordinary school. I want to get some better qualifications.'

'For what?'

'I don't know. I haven't decided yet.'

'Well, I think it's a splendid idea,' enthused Graham. 'If that's what Jennie wants to do, then why shouldn't she?'

'I don't know what to think,' Madge muttered.

'My mind's made up,' Jennie stated. 'And it was before I applied.'

'Why didn't you say?' Madge asked.

'Because I wanted to get accepted first.'

'I can understand that,' Graham nodded.

'And this night school is in Exeter?' a bemused John said.

'That's right. I'll go after work. Take the train in and back.'

'It certainly shows initiative,' John declared, not quite sure what to make of this. Why on earth should Jennie suddenly decide she wanted to get better educated? Seemed a queer notion to him.

'Tell you what,' smiled Graham. 'Forget about the train. I'm going to make it easy for you and buy you a car of your own.'

Now it was Jennie's turn to be astonished. 'You will?'

'And teach you to drive myself. How's that?'

She squealed with delight, then ran to her brother and threw her arms round him. 'That's wonderful. Thank you! Thank you!'

'A car of her own? Bloody Nora,' John said quietly.

'Can you afford that, son?' Madge queried with a frown. She sometimes wondered how Graham could be so well off with only an ordinary job.

'I wouldn't have offered if I couldn't,' Graham answered.

'A two-car, one-van family. We're certainly coming up in the world,' John mused.

'Thanks to Graham,' Madge told him.

John glowered at her, knowing it was a dig at him. He'd never owned a car, nor was he ever likely to.

'So when do you start at night school?' Graham asked.

While Jennie spoke he thought of cars, and one in particular he knew to be up for sale. He'd talk to the owner the following day.

'I'm going to the church to do some repair work,' John announced to Madge.

'All right.'

'See you later then.'

Outside he turned his coat lapels up against the soft, drizzling rain. He'd had no intention of doing what he did next. Instead of going to the church he went to the pub.

'Hello, John,' the landlord said in surprise. 'Haven't seen you for quite a while.'

'No. No, you haven't,' John replied, suddenly desperate for a drink. He gazed about the pub, loving the sight and smell of its interior. In a way coming back was like coming home.

'So what will it be?'

'A pint of cider, I think.'

'Proper job,' the landlord smiled, and pulled the pint which he set in front of John.

John paid, then raised the glass to his lips. It was like mother's milk going down, he thought, and saw off half the pint before putting the pint back on the bar.

My God, that was good! He felt a new man already. He quickly drank the rest of the pint and ordered a refill.

Dick Horrell came into the pub and stood beside him. John said he'd pay for whatever Dick wanted, for which Dick thanked him.

John and Dick started having a good old chinwag which was interrupted by the appearance of Barry Riddell and Hamish Law who joined in the conversation.

I haven't enjoyed myself so much in a long time, John thought later. How he'd missed the pub, and his cider. He was glowing inside as though lit and heated by his own little internal sun.

Madge was aghast, and furious. 'You're drunk!' she accused.

'Steamboats,' John laughed in reply. It was an old Glasgow expression.

He went to her and wrapped her in his arms. 'I feel absolutely marvellous,' he declared.

She averted her face from his breath.

'How about a kiss, eh?'

'Let me go,' she said, trying to push herself free.

'Just a kiss. Where's the harm in that?'

'I said, let me go!' she exclaimed.

'Not until I get that kiss. And then how about we go to bed for a bit of the other?' He dropped a hand and fondled her bottom.

Madge succeeded in breaking free. She was so cross she could have spat. 'I thought you were going to the church?'

'So I was, but I changed my mind.'

John lurched over to a chair which he grabbed hold of to keep himself steady. He belched, then belched again.

'Pissed as a newt,' he muttered with a silly, fatuous grin on his face.

'It's bed for you,' she said.

'Exactly what I suggested,' he slurred in reply.

'Alone,' she stated angrily.

He winked salaciously at her. 'Are you sure about that, my wee dumpling?'

'I couldn't be more so. Now get upstairs this instant.'

'Only if you help me. Can't manage it on my own,' he lied.

She took a deep breath. 'All right then.'

She put an arm round him, and they started for the kitchen door.

'Talking of dumplings,' he said, and squeezed her breasts.

'Stop that!'

'You used to like it once.'

A long time ago, she thought grimly, and smacked his hand away.

They were half-way up the stairs when Jennie appeared, emerging from her bedroom where she'd been studying. 'What's going on?' she asked.

'Your dad's been to the pub,' Madge explained.

'Oh!' Jennie exclaimed in a small voice.

'And I'm afraid he's very much the worse for wear.'

Jennie came down the stairs to assist, and between them they soon got John into his bedroom.

He was far drunker than he'd realized. Sitting on the bed he now saw multiple Madges and Jennies. But no pink elephants he thought, and giggled.

'Let's get him out of his clothes,' Madge said.

She and Jennie started pulling off his trousers when,

with a long, drawn-out sigh, John fell backwards and began to snore.

Jennie came out of night school, said goodbye to a friend, and headed for her car. A bright red Wolsley Hornet, it was her pride and joy which she adored driving.

Soon she'd left Exeter behind and was motoring through the night, the Exe River on her left, woods on her right. She thought back over the maths class she'd been in, and was contemplating the lesson when suddenly, out of nowhere, it dawned on her what she really wanted to do with her life.

It was a stunning revelation, and one which set her heart racing. She could feel it pounding away inside her chest.

An audacious ambition, yes. But was it possible? That was the question.

She'd have to make some enquiries, talk to people, find out what was required.

She smiled, thinking it was as though a veil had suddenly dropped from her eyes allowing her to see the promised land.

It was what she wanted to do in life all right, of that she was certain.

But again, was it possible?

The Hornet purred through the night towards Atherton.

'I don't love you and never will. You'll simply have to accept that,' Graham said. He and Ethel were in her bed, Mark doing another stint on night-shift.

'It's you I want to be married to, not Mark,' Ethel said wretchedly.

'That will never be. I've told you often enough.'

'I keep hoping . . .' She trailed off, and bit her lip. Then she swore in a most unladylike fashion.

'I've been thinking for some time. Maybe we should call it a day?'

She stared at him, appalled. 'You don't mean that?'

He nodded.

'But why?'

'You're getting in deeper and deeper, Ethel, whereas I'm not. It's simply not fair on you.'

'I'm not complaining,' she replied quickly.

'Yes, you are, that's just what you've been doing. You're forever on about divorce and marrying me.'

She picked up her cigarettes from the bedside table and lit one. 'What if I was to divorce Mark anyway?' she said.

'That wouldn't alter matters.'

She gazed at him through a curl of smoke. 'Don't you love me even a little bit?'

'I like you a lot, Ethel. You're great fun. We have terrific times together. I enjoy your company. It's tremendous going to bed with you. But I don't, and never will, love you. That's a fact, and something I can't change.'

She swore again, while her eyes filled with tears. 'I'm being stupid, aren't I?'

He gently took hold of her arm. 'No, you're not. You can't help what you feel, just as I can't help what I don't.'

'The times with you are . . . everything to me,' she said.

He didn't attempt to reply to that.

'I desperately wanted a child by you. I thought that might make a difference. But that's not to be. I'm a barren woman married to someone I don't love, in love with someone who doesn't love me.'

There was a silence between them. Then he said, 'So, what do you think?'

'About what?'

'Maybe we *should* finish it.'

She shook her head. 'Please don't.'

'I don't want to hurt you any further, Ethel.'

'That's what you'd be doing if you broke it off between us.'

He thought about that. 'But it might be for the best in the long run.'

'Don't Graham,' she pleaded, voice riven with emotion. 'I'll do anything for you. Anything you want. Anything at all.'

Her abject, pathetic expression tore at his heart strings. He was extremely fond of her, after all.

'Anything,' she repeated in a small, lost voice.

He took her into his arms and held her tight, feeling possibly closer to her at that moment than he'd ever been.

Tears splashed on to his arm as he rocked her back and forth.

Madge stepped down on to the railway platform and, using a foot, slammed the compartment door shut behind her. She was laden with two crammed shopping bags plus various paper parcels. She'd been into Exeter to buy items you couldn't get in the Post Office stores.

She was heading towards the exit when one of her parcels crashed to the platform. 'Blast!' she exclaimed.

'Here, let me,' a male voice said.

It was George Rattenbury dressed in a pair of cavalry twill trousers, a hacking jacket and a smart cloth cap. He looked quite the country gentleman.

'Thank you,' she replied, smiling.

He picked up the fallen parcel, then regarded her thoughtfully. 'Some balancing act,' he commented.

'I have bought rather a lot,' she confessed.

'Still, no trouble. I'll help you home.'

'That's all right!' she protested.

'No, I insist. Can't see a woman struggling like you are.' And with that he took the paper parcels from her.

'Now which be heaviest. These here parcels or they shopping bags?'

'The shopping bags,' she replied.

'Then we'll switch.' Which is what they did.

'This is very kind of you,' she told him as they continued on towards the exit.

'Don't mention it. I'm George Rattenbury, by the way.'

'And I'm Madge Forsyth.'

'I knows that. Seen you about but never been introduced.'

'I'm pleased to meet you, George.'

'Likewise,' he answered affably.

At the exit they had to hand in their tickets, and from there went on their way. Madge glanced sideways at George, she was aware of his reputation with the ladies, of course. Everyone was.

'I been into Exeter on business,' George explained. 'Nice to get a break.'

'I've been shopping as you can see.'

'Spending money, eh? Never known a woman didn't enjoy doing that.'

Madge smiled to herself, neither did she.

As they walked George talked about all sorts, the weather, the land, crops, animals, the farmer he worked for, and a variety of other topics including philately about which he waxed lyrically.

The normal trudge home from the station became a delightful stroll that ended all too quickly.

'Thank you again George. As I said, this was very kind of you.'

He raised his cap to her. 'Pleased to have been of service, Madge.' He hesitated. 'Or do you prefer Mrs Forsyth?'

'Madge is just fine,' she smiled.

'Then pleased to have been of service, Madge,' he repeated. Placing his cap back on his head he strode away.

What a nice man, she thought. Not at all as she'd expected. And imagine him interested in philately! That had surprised her.

Laughing, she went inside.

Chapter Seven

Graham pressed the starter, but *Waterwitch*'s engine remained silent. Something was obviously wrong.

Half an hour later he gave up. Whatever the fault with the engine it was beyond his ability to detect it. He needed professional help, which meant a visit to the Pepperell boatyard. It was the first time *Waterwitch* had ever let him down.

Just before noon he turned up in Atherton to tell Madge that due to unforeseen circumstances at work he'd been given the weekend off. Madge was delighted and immediately said she hoped he'd attend the church fête that afternoon, which he agreed to do.

Madge left early as she was helping out on the cake stall. John followed shortly after her to go to the pub. John asked Graham if he'd like to accompany him, but Graham declined. Jennie spent the time until the fête studying in her room where she now had a proper desk and chair that Graham had bought her.

Although it was August, and the night school had closed for the summer holidays, Jennie was maintaining her studies with work set her by her tutors. She was making excellent progress and had received glowing reports from all her tutors at the end of the previous term.

Graham and Jennie left the house together, calling at the pub *en route* to pick up John as Madge would expect them to arrive as a group. John planned to stay only a short while, then sneak back to the pub.

Graham went over to the cake stall, a trestle table groaning with home-made cakes of all varieties.

'The Battenberg's very nice,' Madge said.

'Who made it?'

'Bess Pugsley.'

'Do you want me to buy it?'

'I do like Battenberg,' Madge confessed.

'Then put it aside and bring it home with you.' And having said that, Graham paid for the cake.

He then crossed to the white elephant stall which he perused with interest. You never knew what you might find. But in this instance there was nothing he wanted or could use.

Children were running around everywhere, all of them having great fun.

And there was the Reverend Royal with his wife, Cynthia, by his side; they were both holding cups of tea as they chatted with a couple of parishioners.

Graham spotted Sir Reginald Tempest there with Lady Tempest. They always turned up at the fêtes, but never stayed long. They were renowned for 'putting in an appearance'.

'Didn't expect to see you here,' said James Cook, stopping beside Graham.

Graham repeated his story about unforeseen circumstances at work.

Pat Cook joined them. 'The plant stall has excelled itself this year. I've just been looking at it.'

As the three of them talked Graham noted Mark and Ethel arrive. James and Pat moved on, and he went to the plant stall to see if it was as good as Pat claimed. She hadn't been exaggerating.

'Very impressive,' he said to Mrs Bending who was behind the stall and its chief organizer. Mrs Bending was an enthusiastic and accomplished gardener.

'Thank you. How about buying something?'

'Possibly later,' he prevaricated.

He was leaving the plant stall when a gorgeous blonde walked past. She was late teens, early twenties, he judged. And what a figure!

He found himself following her, wondering who she was, for he'd never seen her before.

He was stopped by John. 'I'm just going to slip off now, son. Should your mother ask if you know where I am, say I'm around somewhere, that you saw me only minutes previously. Not a word about the pub, eh?'

'I won't let on.'

'Good lad.' John squeezed Graham's arm, then sauntered off to dodge behind the ice-cream cart from where he could leave the fête unobserved by Madge.

'Come on, Graham, have a go,' urged Mrs Zelly. She was in charge of a game where you had to manoeuvre a small metal ring on the end of a handle over a wire that bent and twisted. If the hoop made contact with the wire a bell rang.

Graham got half-way along the wire before the bell rang. On his second attempt it rang almost straight away.

'Too difficult for me,' he acknowledged.

Mrs Zelly shouted out to someone else, exhorting them to play the game.

'How about a tea cosy?' asked Mrs Horrell, from behind the knitwear stall.

'Just what I need,' Graham replied, tongue in cheek.

'Here's a lovely one you could wear as a hat,' Mrs Horrell joked, and sat the cosy referred to on her head.

Graham laughed. 'Suits you.'

'Want to try it?'

'No, thanks, those aren't my colours.'

Now it was Mrs Horrell's turn to laugh.

'How are you doing, mate?'

Graham turned to find Mark and Ethel behind him. 'Fine, enjoying myself.'

'They've certainly got a marvellous day for it,' Mark commented.

Graham glanced up at the azure blue, cloudless sky. A gentle breeze was blowing, and birds were singing.

'Lovely and warm,' Ethel smiled. She was wearing a short-sleeved dress revealing arms tanned by the summer sun.

Mark indicated they should move a little way off, which they did. 'So, why aren't you on the way over?' he asked quietly.

Graham explained about the trouble he'd had with *Waterwitch*, and that he'd be driving down to Culmouth on Monday morning and hoped to find the engine fixed

'A lost run, too bad,' Mark commiserated.

'Let's look on the bright side, it gives me a chance to come to the fête.'

'You wouldn't want to miss that,' Mark said drily, pulling a face.

'We're going to the pub later. Want to join us?' Ethel queried.

'I might look in,' Graham replied, leaving his options open. Ethel's expression told him she'd be disappointed if he didn't.

'We'll leave here in about half an hour,' Ethel went on, pursuing the subject.

Graham nodded. 'Right.'

Shortly after that he was browsing at the book stall when he caught sight of the blonde he'd noticed earlier. Gorgeous, he thought again, a real glamour puss.

She joined the queue waiting for teas, and on impulse he joined it as well. Who was she? He supposed that she could be a friend of one of the villagers.

She asked for a cream tea; he ordered the same. She then sat at the only empty table.

'Do you mind if I sit with you?' he asked politely. 'All the other seats seem to be taken.'

'Please do.'

He sat next to her. 'I'm Graham Forsyth. My family live in the village.'

'I'm Kerensa Sturt. My father and I live in Poltiham.' Poltiham was a hamlet about a mile and a half from Atherton.

'Kerensa?' Graham queried. 'Unusual name. I've never heard it before.'

'It's Cornish, means peace and love,' she explained.

Peace and love, Graham liked that. 'Is your family Cornish then?'

'My mother was. But my father's Devon born and bred.'

She spoke extremely well, Graham thought. Posh, without being too much so. 'You know what Devonians say about themselves. "Devon born, Devon bred. Strong in the arm, thick in the head".'

Kerensa laughed. 'Yes, I have heard that and always thought it rather amusing.'

'I'm Scots, from Glasgow originally. We moved down here eight years ago.'

'Really? Why was that?'

He told her his story, which she listened to attentively. 'I never heard anything about that,' she said when he was finished. 'But then I was young and away at school most of the time. And if I wasn't at school, I was often up in London.'

'Away at school?' he queried.

'Sherborne Girls, in Dorset. I was a boarder there. And when I left I went to live in London where I worked as a secretary.'

'Worked? Past tense?'

'I've come home to stay with my father. He hasn't been well, I'm afraid.'

Sturt, he had heard of someone with that name out Poltiham way. 'You said stay with your father, what about your mother?'

'She died when I was ten,' Kerensa answered sadly.

'I'm sorry.'

'Cancer. A rather horrible death which devastated my father. He's never been the same since.'

Graham spooned strawberry jam on to a scone, and spread it. He then put a dollop of cream on top of the jam.

'Terribly fattening these cream teas. I only allow myself one as a special treat,' Kerensa said.

'I adore them.'

'Me too, that's the problem.'

He munched on his scone, then asked, 'Whereabouts in Poltiham do you live?'

'The house is called Corfe Mullen. You know the crossroads?'

He nodded.

She then explained how to get to Corfe Mullen from there.

'Corfe Mullen,' he mused. 'Sounds very grand.'

She smiled, and didn't reply.

'So, what brings you to our fête today?' Graham asked.

She regarded him curiously. Clearly he didn't know. 'This is a combined fête, Atherton and Poltiham. Half the proceeds are going to the Poltiham Church roof fund. The roof was badly damaged in last year's storms.'

'Oh!' Graham exclaimed. 'Nobody told me.'

'It's very kind of the Reverend Royal whose idea it was. And it's why the Poltiham congregation will be joining the Atherton congregation tomorrow morning in a joint service.'

'You'll be there then?' he asked quietly.

'Most certainly.'

In which case so, too, would he. Wild horses wouldn't keep him away.

They continued to chat.

'That chocolate cake looks like it would melt in the mouth,' George Rattenbury said to Madge.

'Very nicely decorated, don't you think?' The cake had been intricately decorated with chocolate piping.

'How much is it?'

Madge told him.

'And what if I buys two cakes. Do I get a discount?'

Madge laughed. 'A small one perhaps.' Typical

farming person, she thought, they always had to haggle.

'And what about three?'

'You do have a sweet tooth,' she said.

'Very. And a large appetite.'

She didn't know why, but found herself blushing at that comment.

'Very large,' George added.

'So is it one, two or three?' she enquired.

'The chocolate cake plus they two,' he replied, indicating. 'How much?'

She named a combined price.

'Is that with discount?'

She named a lower price.

'Hmm!' he mused, rubbing his chin.

There was a great deal of strength in him, she thought. Mental as well as physical. And he had charm, something she had noticed on their first meeting. There was also a slightly roguish quality about him which she found appealing. Yes, she could understand why he was so successful with the ladies.

'Can't you come lower still?' he asked slowly.

'The proceeds are for a worthy cause,' she reminded him.

'That's so, have to admit. Still, it's a lot for three cakes.'

Was he now teasing her or not? She wasn't sure. It was probably that and a combination of him paying what he considered a fair amount. She decided to tease him in return.

'You're not mean are you, George?'

A smile curled his lips upwards. 'Careful's the word I'd use.'

'Oh, so you are!'

'I'm only a humble farm hand, Madge. I has to watch me pennies.'

Humble indeed! Now she knew he was teasing her. 'Well, I can't go any lower I'm afraid.'

'Can't or won't?'

She stared him straight in the eyes. 'Won't, George, *won't.*'

'Then maybe I'll come back later and try again?'

'Maybe they'll not be here later,' she countered, thinking she was enjoying this.

'True enough,' he nodded.

'We have sold quite a few already,' she informed him.

He could see that was so.

'I'm sure the chocolate cake won't hang around much longer. It's a real bargain at the original price I quoted you.'

'You're a hard woman,' he said.

She laughed. 'Rubbish! You're the hard one.'

'Hard? Me? I be soft as putty.'

'That'll be right,' she mocked.

He stared at the chocolate cake, then at the other two. 'Well . . . I suppose you've got me beat. I'll pay your price.'

'For the three?'

'For the three,' he confirmed. He took out a leather purse and counted the money into her outstretched hand.

'Now, how do you want to take them?' she asked.

'Stack 'em, with the chocolate one on top.'

She did that, and gave them to him. 'Pleasure doing business with you, George.'

'I'll see you again, Madge.'

She watched him walk away with his three cakes. Charismatic wasn't a word Madge knew, but if she had she would have applied it to George Rattenbury. She found it interesting that when he talked to you, you felt the focus of his attention. You felt that during the course of your conversation only the pair of you existed.

Her thoughts were interrupted by the arrival of another customer who bought a sultana cake.

Graham was already sitting in church when the Sturts came in, Kerensa every bit as beautiful – no, even more so – than he remembered. A line from a nursery rhyme leapt into his mind, '*wasn't that a dainty dish to set before a king*'. Well, in this case, the dish was Kerensa.

Mr Sturt was small and dapper, sporting a thin moustache. Kerensa didn't look at all like him which meant she must have taken after her mother.

Kerensa saw Graham, and smiled. He instantly smiled in return. He hoped they would sit close to him in a seat where he could see Kerensa, but they went and sat at the rear.

To Graham the service seemed to drag on and on. But finally it was over and time to leave.

'I'm staying on for a while. I'll be back later,' John informed Madge.

'I'm dying for a cup of tea,' Jennie said to Graham, who replied vaguely that he could use one too.

They went outside where Graham told Madge and Jennie to go on, he'd catch them up. There was someone he wanted to have a word with.

Finally the Sturts emerged, Kerensa smiling again when she saw him hovering. He crossed over to her and her father.

'Good morning. Enjoyable service, wasn't it?'

'Most enjoyable.' She turned to her father. 'Daddy, I'd like you to meet Graham Forsyth. He lives in Atherton.'

The two men shook hands.

'I met Kerensa at the fête yesterday. We shared a table together when we had cream teas,' Graham explained.

'Oh!' Mr Sturt said.

'The fête did well, I thought,' Graham stated, for the vicar had announced the takings during the service.

'Very well,' Mr Sturt acknowledged.

'And it was such a lovely day for it,' Kerensa said.

Not half as lovely as you, Graham thought. 'Yes, wasn't it.'

'Unfortunately I couldn't attend the fête, had

something else on,' Mr Sturt declared. Then to Kerensa, 'Well, we'd better be getting along.'

'Nice to meet you,' Graham said to Mr Sturt, who nodded.

Graham didn't want Kerensa to go, but there was nothing he could do to stop her. If she'd been on her own he'd have suggested he walk her home.

'See you again sometime,' Kerensa smiled.

'Goodbye,' said Mr Sturt.

'Goodbye.'

Graham watched the Sturts walk away. 'Kerensa,' he muttered softly. A beautiful name for a beautiful creature.

'Kerensa,' he repeated. He was quite smitten.

Graham couldn't get Kerensa out of his mind. He kept visualizing her as she'd been in, and outside, church. And how she'd looked the previous day.

'You're very quiet,' Madge said to him over lunch.

He roused himself from his reverie. 'Am I?'

'Very. Most unlike you.'

'Sorry,' Graham said.

'Are you feeling all right?' Madge queried.

'Fine. On top of the world.'

'Good piece of pork this,' John stated, looking forward to the crackling he was keeping for last.

Graham returned to day-dreaming about Kerensa.

Graham drew up in front of Corfe Mullen which he'd easily found from the directions Kerensa had given him. It was later that afternoon.

Nothing ventured, nothing gained, he thought, getting out of the car.

Corfe Mullen was a large, imposing stone house built in the middle of the nineteenth century. It was even grander, and larger, than he'd expected.

It wasn't all that well maintained though, he noted. The woodwork could do with painting. It was badly flaking in places, and one section round a window looked decidedly rotten.

Going to the door he pulled a brass knob, and a bell reverberated inside. Servants? he wondered. It transpired to be Kerensa herself who answered the door.

'Hello!' she exclaimed in surprise.

'I was out driving this way,' he lied. 'And suddenly wondered if you'd care to go for a spin? I have my own car.'

'So I see,' she replied, glancing over his shoulder.

'I know it's rather forward of me. But there we are.'

She hesitated for a second, then said, 'Come in. I'll have to speak to Daddy.'

Mr Sturt was in a somewhat shabby drawing-room reading a quality Sunday newspaper. He looked up, and frowned, when Graham entered the room.

'Good afternoon, sir,' Graham said politely.

Kerensa explained the reason for Graham's calling at the house.

'You have your own car?' Mr Sturt said with interest.

'Yes, sir. A Lanchester.'

Mr Sturt considered both Graham and that statement for a moment, then folded his newspaper and laid it aside. 'I usually take a glass of sherry round about this time on a Sunday. Would you care to join me?'

'That would be very nice.'

'Excellent. Kerensa, would you mind organizing that?'

'Of course, Daddy.'

'Sit down, young man,' Mr Sturt said, indicating a chair.

'What was the name again?' he asked when Graham was seated.

'Graham Forsyth. I live in Atherton.'

'Forsyth,' Mr Sturt mused. 'I don't think I know the family.'

'We're Scots, sir, came down eight years ago.'

Mr Sturt's eyes suddenly went beady. 'That so? Your

father wouldn't happen to work for Sir Reginald by any chance?'

'Yes, sir. At Wheal Tempest.'

Mr Sturt slowly nodded. 'A miner?'

'He was, but hurt himself a while ago. He's now on maintenance duties.'

'I see,' Mr Sturt stated very quietly.

Kerensa returned carrying a silver tray on which were a decanter and three glasses.

'Mr Forsyth has been telling me about his family,' Mr Sturt smiled thinly at her.

'Graham, please,' Graham said.

The beady eyes focused themselves back on Graham. 'And how do you earn your living, Graham?'

'I have a job in Culmouth, sir.'

Mr Sturt stared at Graham, waiting.

'For a firm of hauliers,' Graham lied.

'And what exactly is your position with them?'

'I'm a driver.'

Graham accepted the glass Kerensa handed him. 'Thank you.' To Mr Sturt he said, 'This really is most kind.'

'Don't mention it,' Mr Sturt replied.

Kerensa gave her father a glass, took the last one from the tray and settled herself down on a sofa that had seen better days.

'A driver, my, my,' Mr Sturt said.

Kerensa's gaze flickered from her father to Graham, then back to her father.

'Kerensa went to Sherborne School for Girls,' Mr Sturt stated.

'Yes I know, she mentioned it yesterday at the fête.'

'Did she?' Mr Sturt said in that same quiet tone. 'And what about yourself?'

'The local school in Glasgow,' Graham answered, and had a sip of sherry.

'So what about this spin, Daddy. Is it all right if I go with Graham?' Kerensa asked.

'It must have slipped your mind, darling, but we're due at the Horton-Thompsons later. So I'm afraid a spin with Graham is out of the question.'

'The Horton-Thompsons? I knew nothing about that,' Kerensa replied softly.

'I mentioned it yesterday. You must have forgotten.' Turning his attention again to Graham he said, 'The Horton-Thompsons live in Stockwell Manor. I've known him all my life. Has the most charming wife called Anne.'

Graham felt his neck stain with embarrassment. He'd made an awful mistake in coming here. What a fool he'd been. When he'd seen the house he should have swung his car round and gone straight back to Atherton.

'I'm terribly sorry, Graham,' Kerensa said to him, eyes filled with sympathy.

'Not to bother. It was just a thought.'

Graham drained his glass, it was best he got out of there as soon as possible. 'Thank you very much for the sherry, but I've already taken up too much of your time.'

'I'll see you out,' Kerensa said.

'No, you get ready for the Horton-Thompsons. I'll escort Graham to the door,' Mr Sturt said. He rose, laid his glass on a nearby table, and smiled at Graham.

'Bye,' Graham said to Kerensa, who'd risen also.

She extended a hand. 'Goodbye, Graham. Thank you for calling in.'

Graham and Mr Sturt walked in silence to the front door which Mr Sturt opened.

'Nice to have met you, young man,' Mr Sturt said affably.

'And for me to have met you, sir.'

'I think we understand one another. Isn't that so?'

'I believe we do,' Graham replied.

The door closed firmly behind Graham as he turned to his car. His neck and face were flaming when he drove away.

*   *   *

238

Madge paused to stare at George Rattenbury and several others busily engaged in corn harvesting. It was a good corn harvest that year, the farmers were pleased. Haymaking had also gone well, and there was a bumper apple crop.

George glanced up to see Madge gazing at him. He waved and she waved back before hurrying on her way.

'I was watching them corn harvesting today,' Madge said to John. They were alone in the house, as both Graham and Jennie had gone out.

'Oh aye?'

'George Rattenbury was in the field.'

'Was he indeed!' John chuckled.

Madge waited a few seconds, then asked casually, 'Is what they say about him true?'

'You mean the women?'

She nodded.

'He's got a reputation a mile long where they're concerned.'

'I know that, but is it deserved?'

John shrugged. 'I suppose so. I mean, he's well known for the ladies.'

'Any names in particular?' Madge persisted.

'He's very discreet is George. Even in his cups he's tight lipped where that's concerned. At least so I'm told, I don't really know the man.'

'Strange he's never married,' Madge mused.

'Yes, it is,' John nodded.

'Must be a reason for it.'

'Must be,' John agreed. 'Anyway, what's this sudden interest in George Rattenbury?'

'No interest,' she replied quickly. 'It's just that I saw him today and got to wondering about him.'

'I wouldn't mind a spot of tea,' John said.

'How about coffee? I've some in.'

He beamed at her. 'Better still.'

Madge got up, put the kettle on and changed the subject.

It's a relief to get Vicky back to school. She's been under my feet all summer long,' Jane Scott said to Madge, *en route* to the Post Office stores.

Madge nodded. 'I remember well what it was like when Graham and Jennie were young. School holidays were always difficult from that point of view.'

'Has Jennie restarted night school?'

'Next Monday. She's looking forward to it. She's a good lass is our Jennie, if difficult at times.'

'Oh! How so?'

'She's very stubborn, which is a good and bad thing. And she can be wilful. Strong-minded too. But it's not only that, I suppose she and I just have the ability to rub one another up the wrong way.'

'Has she decided what's she going to do when she completes her studies?'

'Not that I'm aware of.'

They reached and turned into the High Street where a man was coming towards them leading a pair of shire-horses. The man, Madge now saw, was George Rattenbury.

'Whooah me beauties!' George said, stopping beside Madge and Jane.

'Hello, Madge. How are you today?'

'All right thank you, George. Have you met Mrs Scott?'

'Never had that pleasure. How do, Mrs Scott.'

'Hello, Mr Rattenbury.'

'And how are things with you, Madge?'

'Fine,' she smiled in reply. 'This is your busiest time, isn't it?'

''Tis that. Dawn till dusk, and then some this past while. Still, I enjoys me work, that's the main thing.'

'We're off to the shop,' Madge explained.

He patted one of the shires on the side of the face. 'Do

you like rabbit?' he asked, the question directed at Madge.

'I do. We all do at home.'

He winked at her. 'I'll leave a couple on your doorstep later. They'll have to be skinned though, can you manage that?'

'I've done it before often enough.'

'Proper job. Now I'd best be on my way. Farmer be waiting for these horses.'

'I didn't know you were friendly with George Rattenbury?' Jane said quietly when George had left them.

They continued towards the shop. 'I'm not exactly friendly,' Madge replied. 'We merely speak when we bump into one another, that's all.'

'He fancies you,' Jane teased.

'Never! Get on!'

'He does. I noticed the gleam in his eye. He fancies you all right.'

'Nonsense,' Madge further protested. 'Absolute tosh.'

Jane suddenly giggled. 'I wonder what he's like in bed? He looks strong as those horses he had.'

Madge thought about that, and found herself covered in goosebumps. She tried to block out an image that popped into her mind.

'I'll bet he's terrific,' Jane went on. 'The sort to put a smile on a girl's face.'

'Well, we're not girls, far from it,' Madge replied somewhat primly. 'And married don't forget. We shouldn't be talking like this. It's not nice.'

'What's marriage or age got to do with it? It's only chat after all, it's not as if either of us is ever going to find out.'

'Quite so,' Madge said, tone still prim.

Jane giggled again. 'He does fancy you though. That was clear.'

Madge's stern expression belied how she actually felt, which was elated. It was lovely to think that a man found her attractive at her age, and she with two grown-up children.

241

They walked a little way in silence. Forty-four wasn't that old, Madge told herself. She was middle-aged, that's what she was. But then so, too, was George. And with a tummy that didn't do him any favours. Mind you, she was the last one to pass comment about carrying too much weight. She was carrying too much herself and could easily have done with losing half a stone.

Forty-four, she thought. God, there were times living with John when she felt twice that. If ever a man could drag you down within yourself he could.

'Are you going to the WI tonight?' Jane asked.

'I am.'

'Then we'll go together. Will I knock for you or you for me?'

'Whoever's ready first knock for the other. I believe there's to be a demonstration.'

'Oh good!'

They were still chatting about the WI when they reached the shop.

'Hello.'

Graham turned round to find Kerensa. He immediately coloured. 'Hello,' he replied.

'I spotted you from across the road and thought I'd come over.'

'I've just been to the bank,' he explained. 'What brings you into Exeter?'

'I had to pick up a few things I'd ordered last week.'

There was a pregnant pause between them.

'About that Sunday . . .' she started to say.

'That's all right,' he cut in.

'It's not all right. My father was . . . well, very much my father I'm afraid.' She hesitated, then said, 'I was on my way to Tinley's for tea. Would you care to join me?'

That threw him. There was nothing he'd have liked more, but there again . . .

'Please?' she smiled, placing a hand on his arm.

242

'I'd love to, but only if it's my treat.'

She removed her hand. 'We'll discuss that later.'

She started in the direction of Tinley's, and he fell into step beside her. He felt suddenly shy in her presence, which surprised him. He hadn't felt shy at the fête. But that had been before his disastrous visit to Corfe Mullen. He still cringed when he remembered it.

They entered Tinley's and found a table for two. When a pretty, young waitress asked them what they'd like, they ordered a pot of tea and some cucumber sandwiches.

'The last time I was here was with my sister,' Graham commented.

'What's her name?'

'Jennie. She'd just broken up with her boyfriend and I brought her here to try and cheer her up.'

'That was thoughtful of you.'

Graham shrugged. 'We're very close, Jennie and I. Have you any brothers or sisters?'

'No, I'm an only child.'

'I always think that's rather sad. I would have hated not to have a sister.'

'Perhaps if my mother had lived . . .' Kerensa trailed off.

'I'm sorry. I forgot.'

'That's all right. But getting back to my father, I must apologize for that Sunday. I love him dearly, he's a sweetie, but he really is the most frightful snob.'

'I shouldn't have called in. It was stupid of me.'

'It wasn't stupid at all. I was thrilled.'

She'd been thrilled! That pleased him enormously. 'Tell me, did you go to the Horton-Thompsons?'

Kerensa laughed. 'No, that was a story that Daddy made up to stop me going out with you.'

'The Horton-Thompsons,' Graham mused. They were one of the most well-known families in Devon, the wife forever in the newspapers in connection with charity work.

'I thought he was a bit heavy-handed saying we were going to visit them,' Kerensa said.

'It made his point though, which of course was what he intended. Do you really know them?'

'Oh yes! Daddy and he have been great chums all their lives. Daddy wasn't fibbing about that.'

'And here was me a miner's son asking you out. How presumptious!'

'It wasn't that at all,' Kerensa replied. 'I would happily have gone if Daddy hadn't objected. I was quite taken with you at the fête.'

'You were!'

'You were very pleasant company.'

'I thought the same of you,' he said softly.

They were interrupted at that point by the arrival of their tea and sandwiches.

'Shall I pour?' Kerensa offered.

'Please.'

She had exquisite hands, he noted. Long and tapering, her nails white and gleaming.

'What's wrong with your father?' he asked. 'You said you returned home from London because he hasn't been well.'

'Trouble with his heart. It's very worrying.'

'That serious?'

'Possibly,' she said.

'And so you've come back to look after him.'

She nodded.

'Lucky man, in that respect anyway.'

She smiled at Graham and passed him his cup.

'You've got green eyes the same shade as my sister's,' he said.

'Really!'

'But her hair is auburn, not blonde like yours.'

He waited till she'd helped herself to a sandwich, then did likewise. 'Does your father work?' he asked.

'He used to, but stopped when Mummy died. As I told you at the fête that devastated him.'

Graham thought of Corfe Mullen and its run-down appearance. 'So, what does he do, live off invested capital? Or am I being too nosey?'

'No, that's all right. I don't mind. He did have a considerable amount of capital when he stopped work, but subsequently lost a lot of it in railway and mining shares that went horribly wrong. We get by now, but it's a squeeze.'

That explained the house and interior, Graham thought. 'And yet he put you through boarding school?'

'He managed that somehow. But money is something he and I rarely discuss. He doesn't like to.'

Her nose had an arch to it, Graham noted with fascination. Quite a distinct arch now he came to study it. It gave her a somewhat regal appearance.

'Will you find yourself a job down here?' he asked.

'That's a bone of contention between us. I want to, for the money if nothing else, but Daddy is completely against it. It was one thing me working in London, that's considered acceptable, but for me to do so locally would involve a certain loss of face on his part. Or at least so he believes.'

'Proud, eh?'

'Extremely.'

She picked up another sandwich. 'These are delicious.'

Delicious and tiny, Graham thought. One decent bite and the sandwich was gone. 'Will you insist?'

'On getting a job? Let's just say, if I decide to, he'll eventually come round to my way of thinking.'

Graham laughed softly. 'Very female.'

'Of course. I am after all.'

He wouldn't argue with that. 'Will you go for a secretarial position?'

'That's what I'd prefer. But we'll have to see what's on offer at the time.'

'If I needed a secretary I'd employ you,' he said.

'Would you indeed!' she teased.

'Oh yes. Any day.'

'Pity drivers don't need secretaries.'

'Pity,' he agreed. He was thoroughly enjoying himself, the pair of them had natural empathy.

'You haven't touched your tea,' she said.

He looked down at his cup, then back at her. 'I'd forgotten all about it.'

'You are daft!' she admonished lightly.

'You bring out the best in me,' he retorted.

She regarded him strangely, then picked up her own cup and took a sip.

Graham experienced a sudden overwhelming impulse to rush out and buy her an expensive present – anything that would make those green eyes light up with pleasure.

'Why aren't you working today?' she enquired. It was a Tuesday afternoon.

'I have peculiar hours.'

'Oh?'

'I work long periods when I do, then have days off at a time.'

'You're a long-distance driver then?'

He thought of Sark. 'Yes,' he replied truthfully. He did drive *Waterwitch* after all, and Sark was a long way away.

'Have you always done that?'

They talked about him for a while. He told her in further detail about his family and his life in Glasgow before coming down to Devon.

All too soon she said, 'I'm afraid I have to go.'

His stomach sank when he heard that. A glance at the wall clock informed him they'd been there a lot longer than he'd imagined. The time had simply flown by.

She reached for the bill that had arrived during the course of their conversation. He quickly placed a hand over hers, stopping her from picking it up.

'My treat,' he declared.

'I asked you.'

Her hand was cool and silky to the touch. He wanted

246

to take it in his own and hold it for ever. 'And I said it would be my treat.'

Using his other hand he removed the bill from underneath hers.

'Very well, your treat,' she agreed, liking his being so firm.

Reluctantly he pulled the hand away that had been covering hers. He stared at her, drinking her in.

'Goodbye then. Thank you,' Kerensa said, starting to rise.

'Wait!'

She hesitated, then sat down.

'Is there any chance that we might meet again?'

She thought of her father. The last thing she wanted was to upset him in his condition. And he would certainly be cross if he found out she was seeing Graham. It was so difficult.

Graham took a deep breath, exhaled, and said, 'Tell you what. Rather than make a decision now, think about it. I'll be here, in Tinley's, at the same time next Tuesday. And I'll be at this table if it's free. It would be marvellous if you joined me. If you don't, I'll understand.'

She didn't reply to that. Instead she rose and walked out of the tea-room.

A whole week, Graham thought, going up to pay the bill. Every minute of it was going to be excruciating.

Poppy Alford hummed quietly to herself as she pushed the pram along the street. She was going to visit another married friend of hers in the village. They'd have tea, biscuits, and a good old chinwag. She was looking forward to it.

'My, how the baby's grown. She was only tiny when I saw her last.'

The speaker was Ethel Yeo who'd come up beside Poppy.

'Well, she is a year old now,' Poppy replied.

Ethel stared down longingly at the child tucked up in the pram. 'What's her name again? Awful of me, but I've forgotten.'

'Ruth.'

Ruth sucked her thumb and gazed back at Ethel who would have adored to pick her up and cuddle her. 'Is she much trouble?'

'Not really. No more than any other baby.'

'I see her father in her,' Ethel said.

'A lot of people say that.'

'There's something of you there too, of course.'

Ethel reached into the pram and tickled Ruth's cheek which made Ruth smile. What she would have given for Ruth to be hers.

When Ethel finally parted from Poppy and Ruth she did so with a heavy heart, and a feeling of quiet despair.

Graham stared at the wall clock for the umpteenth time. He was in Tinley's waiting for Kerensa as he'd promised.

She wasn't going to come, he thought. Since their last meeting he'd hoped, and prayed, that she would. His mood had swung from wild elation at the prospect of seeing her again, to total wretchedness at the thought that she wouldn't turn up.

'Damn!' he muttered quietly to himself.

He looked through the window at the cathedral beyond. When he left Tinley's he'd go in there, he decided. The peace and serenity he'd find inside might help.

'Damn!' he muttered again through clenched teeth.

His gaze flicked once more to the clock. She wasn't going to come, he knew it. She'd have been there by now if she'd intended to.

He stirred his tea, something he'd done a number of times already. The plate of cucumber sandwiches in the middle of the table – he'd been lucky in securing the same one they'd sat at the previous week – remained untouched.

He remembered the way she'd eaten those other sandwiches. How they'd slipped past those fabulous lips of her. Lips he'd found sensuous, and inviting in the extreme.

He recalled touching her hand. How cool and silky it had felt, her nails white and gleaming.

He swallowed hard, and took a deep breath. Well, it just wasn't to be. No matter how difficult it was, he was going to have to accept that.

'Damn!' he muttered again.

He replaced the spoon in his saucer, and stared at the cathedral. People were coming and going as they always were – locals, tourists, folk from all walks of life.

He looked yet again at the clock, wishing he could somehow make the hands go backwards so that there might still be a chance, that he could wait in hope.

He shivered. Perhaps he had a cold coming on? Perhaps . . . perhaps nothing. The only thing wrong with him was that Kerensa hadn't showed.

'Hello, sorry I'm late.'

There she was, standing before him. It was as though the sun had suddenly burst through a grey sky, a sky rapidly turning to brightest blue.

He hastily rose. 'I didn't see you come in. I was lost in thought. I'd, er . . .' he smiled weakly, 'given you up actually.'

'Well, I'm here now.'

'Yes,' he said softly. 'So you are.'

They sat, and began to talk.

'So what did you tell your father?' Graham asked Kerensa. They were in his Lanchester *en route* for Dartmoor where they intended eating a picnic lunch Madge had made up for them.

'That I was going to visit a girlfriend in Topsham.' Topsham was a charming little port, and sailing centre, on the Exe estuary.

'Is there such a girlfriend?'

249

'Oh yes! Her name's Vanessa.'

Graham shifted gear.

'You drive extremely well,' Kerensa commented.

'I should hope so, doing it for a living. Do you drive yourself?'

'Yes. But rather badly I'm afraid.'

'Then maybe I can help you improve your technique. I taught my sister, she drives well too.'

He thought for a few moments, then said, 'In fact we can start on the return journey. You can drive back.'

They entered an area of high, overhanging trees on either side of the road, the light which shone through the branches creating a dappled effect.

'Where did you live in London?' he asked.

'In St John's Wood with my Aunt Charlotte, my mother's sister.'

'Older or younger?'

'Older sister. I often stayed with her during the holidays when I was at school.'

'Is she married?'

'With two grown-up children, Gerald and Amy. He's in the Army now.'

'So, in a way, you did have a brother and sister. Or is that not the case?'

She smiled at him. 'You're quite right. I suppose I do see them as the brother and sister I never had.'

'So you're not such a bad case after all,' he joked, harking back to the first conversation he'd had with her in Tinley's.

'Cheeky!'

He sighed with contentment. Being with Kerensa was sheer bliss. 'I presume you've been to Dartmoor before?'

'Often. But not for quite a while now. We've got a lovely day for it.'

'Not too chilly considering it's November.'

She glanced at him sideways, studying him. There was a lot of character in his face, that and kindness. She was very attracted to him.

'There's something I haven't asked you yet,' he said. 'How old are you?'

'Twenty.'

'Same age as Jennie. I'm twenty-three.'

'You've done well to own a car like this,' she said.

'You mean because I've had to work for it and not had it handed to me on a plate by some doting, wealthy parent?'

'Do I detect a note of sarcasm there?' she replied.

'No, I'm not the envious sort. If people get born to wealth and privilege then good for them. Though my father would have a fit if he heard me say that.'

'Why?' she queried.

'Because he's a socialist through and through. Used to be very active in the trade unions, but isn't any more. He's still a dyed-in-the-wool socialist though. I think if he had his way the entire upper class would be shot at dawn.'

'Bit drastic,' Kerensa commented drily.

'His views are.'

'And what about your mother?'

'She's more practical about life. She believes in working hard and doing your best. If she's told me that once in my life she's told me a million times. Do your best in life and that way you'll succeed, which I fully intend happening to me.'

Kerensa could hear the steel in his voice as he finished speaking. 'What do you have in mind?' she queried with interest.

'I'm not sure yet.'

'Well, you've certainly succeeded in buying yourself a nice car,' she said.

'And boat.'

Her eyebrows went up. 'You own a boat?'

'A thirty-foot motor cruiser called *Waterwitch* which I keep at Culmouth. But she's a secret. You're the only one outside Culmouth, and that includes my family, who knows about her.'

251

'I am honoured.'

He smiled at Kerensa. 'I'm sure my secret is safe with you.'

'But why is your boat a secret?' she queried, intrigued.

'Let's just say I have my reasons, and leave it at that.'

A motor cruiser, she thought. How exciting!

'Perhaps I can take you out on *Waterwitch* one day?' he said.

'I'd like that very much. I adore the sea.'

'You do!' he exclaimed in delight. 'So do I.'

'That's something we have in common then.'

'Have you done much sailing?'

'Some, with Vanessa whom I mentioned earlier. She's a real addict.'

'A motor cruiser isn't the same as real sailing,' he said. 'But fun none the less.'

'So why a motor cruiser?' she asked.

'It suits my purposes,' he replied vaguely.

They drove into Postbridge, and past the clapper bridge spanning the East Dart River. The non-sided bridge was constructed of slabs of granite, known as moorstone because it wasn't quarried or worked but simply picked off the moor. The bridge itself was part of the old packhorse route between Plymouth and Moretonhampstead.

Soon after that Graham pulled the Lanchester off the road, and killed the engine. 'We're here,' he announced.

Kerensa gazed out over the moor. 'I haven't been to this part before,' she said.

'Good.'

They got out of the car, and she tied a scarf round her head.

'Shall we have a walk, then eat the picnic in the car?' he suggested.

'Fine by me.'

He wanted to take her hand, but resisted, thinking that was too forward at this stage.

There were tall standing stones all around, and many

tors in the distance. The ground underfoot was spongy in places.

'It's wild country,' Kerensa said.

'Amazing to think people used to live here.' He pointed to stones embedded in the ground. 'You do know these used to be Bronze Age homes?'

She was surprised. 'No, I didn't.'

'The walls of the huts consisted of two circles of stones, the space between which was filled with earth. At the centre of the hut was a stout pole supporting a roof formed from branches covered with turves.'

'I'm impressed,' she admitted. 'You are knowledgeable on the subject.'

He shrugged. 'I read a lot, and read a book about Dartmoor recently. It was actually thinking about that book which gave me the idea for us to come here today.'

'I didn't know you were a bookworm?' she teased.

He laughed. 'Hardly that! But I do read quite a bit. And have done since I was young.'

'Anything in particular?'

'Novels in the main, but all sorts really.'

This was a side to Graham she wouldn't have guessed at.

'Now these,' he said, pointing to a tall standing stone, 'are called Menhirs. While over here' – he led the way and she followed – 'is a kist in which one of the élite would have been buried. It's believed that the ordinary folk were buried out in the open.'

A covering stone still lay atop the kist, but it had been broken, and the resulting two sections slid partially back, to reveal the tomb beneath.

'There have been people hunting on what is now the moor since the early Stone Age,' Graham went on. 'But the standing stones and stone circle kists belonged to the Bronze Age when the Beaker Folk lived here.'

'You should have been a history teacher,' she gently mocked.

'Sorry. Am I being boring?'

'Not at all. Quite the opposite.'

'I wouldn't have minded being a history teacher,' he mused. 'History fascinates me. It's not just words on a page for me, but something alive and exciting.'

She stared down in the kist, wondering what sort of person had been buried there. Man or woman? There were no bones to be seen, the kist was quite empty.

'In those days the climate here was completely different to what it is now. It was far warmer, more like a Mediterranean country. And I believe at least part of the area was covered in forest,' Graham said.

He gazed out over the rugged bleakness that was so totally unlike the rest of Devon, with the exception of Exmoor.

'Look, there's a hawk!' Graham exclaimed, pointing skywards.

The black shape cut through the air, then hovered. With a cry it wheeled and flew away.

They walked towards a squat, granite-topped tor and had to cross several meandering streams.

Some ponies came into view, and then a little further on some sheep. And as they walked Graham and Kerensa talked about all manner of things.

How good it was to be with her, Graham thought. It felt so right when the pair of them were together. Somehow they fitted, like two interlocking pieces in a jigsaw.

A wind sprang up which reddened their cheeks. Kerensa's scarf couldn't have been tied properly for it fluttered from her head and twisted away.

'I'll get it!' Graham cried, racing after the scarf.

He tried to snatch it from the ground, only to lose his balance and tumble over as it moved again a second before he could grasp it.

Kerensa laughed to see him lying sprawled on the ground, for it was a comical sight. He made a face at her before jumping to his feet and chasing the scarf.

Eventually he managed to catch it, and paused for a moment to draw breath. Then he strolled back to her.

She was standing with her hair blowing in the wind. God, she was heartachingly beautiful, he thought.

Her eyes locked on to his, and the smile that had been creasing her face faded and died altogether. 'Thank you,' she said in a small voice when he reached her.

'My pleasure.'

Their eyes continued to bore into one another. Then somehow she was in his arms and they were kissing, a kiss, that for Graham, was far better than any he'd ever experienced before. He felt totally transported.

They broke off, and again their eyes locked. He kissed her a second time, after which he took her by the hand.

'Hungry?' he whispered.

'Ravenous.'

'Then let's go and eat, shall we?'

She nodded in agreement.

He held her hand tightly all the way back to the car.

'I have an announcement to make,' Christine Cook informed Jennie and Madge, when the three of them were sitting in the Forsyths' kitchen.

'Da ra!' she sang, thrusting out her left hand which she'd been holding behind her back.

'An engagement ring!' Jennie squealed.

Christine waggled her hand so that the diamond sparkled in the light. 'It's now official between Henry and me,' she declared. She and Henry Down had got back together again some while previously.

'Congratulations!' Madge beamed.

Jennie hugged Christine. 'I couldn't be more pleased for you. Really I couldn't. You're marrying a smashing chap.'

'There are worse about than Henry,' Christine acknowledged.

'Let's see the ring properly then,' said Madge.

Madge took hold of Christine's hand and stared down at the ring. It was a single rectangular stone in a gold setting. 'Very nice,' she commented.

255

'It's lovely,' Jennie enthused.

'It cost him, I can tell you,' Christine stated proudly

For a few moments a sudden sadness invaded Jennie. She didn't have a boyfriend, and there seemed no prospect of getting engaged. There had been no-one since Andy Alford, she simply hadn't been interested. She'd had offers, including one from a very pleasant chap at night school, but she'd turned them all down. The only interest she had at the moment were her studies, and hopefully what lay ahead.

As suddenly as it had come her sadness vanished. 'So, when is the wedding?' she asked.

'Next July. And I want you to be a bridesmaid. Will you?'

'Of course. I'll be happy to.'

'The reception is to be a big one in the village hall. We intend hiring a band for the occasion.'

'Are there to be other bridesmaids? And what sort of dresses will you want us to wear?' Jennie queried.

'Just two bridesmaids. You and Patience Zelly if she'll agree. As for dresses, I haven't thought that far ahead yet.'

'And what about a house?' Madge asked.

They were still chattering away like magpies when John arrived home over an hour later.

Madge woke with a start, having been dozing in front of the fire. She came to her feet when there was another loud rap on the front door.

Who could it be at this time of night? she wondered, glancing at the clock on top of the mantelpiece. She was alone in the house; John was at the pub, Graham and Jennie both out.

She opened the door to discover George Rattenbury supporting a drunken John.

'I found him slumped on the pavement in the High Street,' George explained.

Madge was mortified. 'Bring him in, will you.'

John grinned inanely at her. 'Mouth . . . mouth won't work,' he slurred.

'Neither do his feet,' added George.

'Will you help me take him upstairs to bed?' Madge asked.

'Lead on, we'll follow.'

'He's in a terrible state,' Madge said apologetically, as they mounted the stairs.

'Couldn't leave him where he was. Anything could have happened to him,' George replied.

'I'm very grateful. This really is most kind.'

'Don't mention it,' George said.

When they reached the bedroom Madge snapped on the light. 'If you'll just put him on the bed,' she requested.

John hiccuped, and hiccuped again.

'I'd better get something in case he's sick,' Madge said, and flew back downstairs.

When she returned she found George had removed John's shoes, socks and trousers. She placed the bowl she'd brought up on the floor below John's pillows. Then, with George's assistance, she got the bedclothes out from underneath John, and laid them over him.

'He'll be all right now,' George proclaimed.

'Just wait till the morning. He'll be sorry for this,' Madge declared angrily.

'Glad tain't me in his boots tomorrow,' George smiled.

'I'm embarrassed beyond belief,' she said to George as she flicked off the bedroom light.

'No need to be that.'

'But I am.'

'Have you been in the pub?' she asked as they walked downstairs. It was Saturday night, the pub's busiest night of the week.

'No, I haven't.'

She wondered where he'd been, or was going to at such a late hour, and immediately assumed a woman must be involved.

257

As though guessing what she was thinking, George said, 'I was on my way home from visiting Dave Hannaford whom you probably know has been right poorly.' Dave was another farm labourer who lived in a cottage on the outskirts of the village.

'I had heard he wasn't well,' Madge replied.

'Suffering something awful with his stomach. Doctor has given him some pills he has to take three times daily.'

'And are they helping?'

'A bit, Dave says.'

They halted by the front door. 'Would you like a cup of tea?' she asked. Then, remembering his fondness for cake, she added, 'There's also a nice sponge that I made earlier.'

His eyes twinkled mischievously. 'Are you sure about that, Madge? What if I was seen coming in here, what then? Your good name would be mud if I stayed even a short time.'

His teasing tone made her smile. 'You do have a terrible reputation,' she said.

'Terrible,' he agreed, smiling also.

'They all talk about you, you know.'

'I know. I'm a living legend.'

She laughed. 'Living legend indeed! Come through and I'll put the kettle on.'

He followed her into the kitchen to stand in front of the fire. 'Nippy out,' he said.

'Sit down and don't clutter up the place,' she instructed him, waving at a chair.

He sat and gazed about him. 'Nice kitchen. Real homey feel to it,' he commented.

'Seeing you're not married I take it you cook for yourself?'

'I do. And a dab hand at cooking I be.'

She wondered if she dare ask him. It was a very personal question after all. But he could aways refuse to answer if he didn't want to.

'How come you never married, George? I mean, I

258

would have thought someone like you would have married years ago.'

His good-humoured expression disappeared, and he turned to stare into the fire.

'Sorry, I've offended you,' she apologized.

'No, I tain't offended.' He paused, then said slowly, 'There was a lass once, long time ago now. Pretty little thing. We were going to get married, 'cept she changed her mind. Truth of the matter is I've never met anyone since whom I'd want to marry.'

Madge bit her lip.

George shrugged. 'That's life for you.'

'Did she marry another?' Madge enquired quietly.

'She did. Several years later. And happy they've been together too.'

He must have been very much in love, Madge thought, her heart going out to George. It was clear that to think about his 'pretty little thing' still distressed him.

Madge roused herself, and got on with making tea. When she'd attended to the kettle she took the sponge cake from a cupboard and cut it into generous slices. As she did this she was aware that George was watching her.

'I suppose you like your tea good and strong?' she said.

'Strong enough to stand a spoon in,' he replied, and laughed.

'Same with John.'

'Your fire could do with some coal on. Shall I?'

'Please,' she smiled at him, putting out cups and saucers.

'It isn't true what they say,' George said as he dug into the scuttle.

'What isn't true, George?'

'About me and women. Most of it is nothing more than village gossip.'

She wasn't sure whether to believe that or not. 'There are some vicious tongues in the village. Can't deny that,' she replied.

'Oh, I'm not pretending I haven't had the occasional female friend from time to time. Boys will be boys after all. But I'm not the Lothario they makes me out to be.'

His tone was certainly sincere, she thought. And his expression of 'boys will be boys' made her smile. 'So why don't you do something about the gossip?' she queried.

He replaced the small shovel he'd been using and returned to his chair. 'The truth, Madge? The truth is I rather likes it. It appeals to my sense of humour. It makes me laugh.'

She regarded him quizzically. 'Makes you laugh?'

'Sure. My reputation is like a snowball running downhill. It's just got bigger and bigger. If you believed the amount of women I'm supposed to have carried on with, then I'd have slept with every female in the village three times over.'

'So you're innocent then?'

He shrugged. 'I said, there have been a few females over the years. But only a few. I swear to that.'

She got out the tea caddy and opened it. She'd have to buy more tea on Monday, she noted vaguely, her mind on George and what he'd said. 'So, why are you telling me this?' she asked.

'Dunno,' he replied. He hesitated, then said, 'Maybe cause I didn't want you to think bad of me.'

'And does it matter what I think?' she queried.

He considered that. 'Must do, otherwise I wouldn't have spoke.'

'So, who are these females you've been friendly with?' she asked as she warmed the teapot.

He gave her a pained look. 'Madge, that tain't a fair question. And certainly one I'll never answer.'

She approved of that. 'You're right, I shouldn't have asked,' she said.

She put a slice of sponge on to a plate, and handed it to him. 'Hope you like it,' she said.

'I'm sure I will.'

George took a mouthful, and rolled his eyes

heavenwards. 'Truly delicious,' he pronounced. 'You could take up baking as a living.'

She laughed. 'There's no need to go overboard!'

'I mean it Madge, this is first class. And when it comes to food, any sort of food, I knows what I'm talking about. I have a discerning palate, I has.'

He could be a scream at times, she thought. Some of the expressions he used were so funny. What was also nice was that he often adopted a self-mocking tone. George evidently didn't take himself too seriously which was lovely.

She made the tea, and put the pot by to mask, as they say in Glasgow, mash as the English call it. When she glanced again at George the slice of sponge was gone.

'Another piece?'

'Ta.'

'That's something else you've got a reputation for,' she said, taking his plate, 'a prodigious appetite.'

'Be true. I loves eating. But then most folk who do hard graft out of doors has hearty appetites.'

'But from what I hear yours is more than hearty?'

He smiled boyishly at her. 'Prodigious was the word you used, and I reckon that be the right word. Prodigious,' he repeated. 'Has a fine ring to it.'

'Milk and sugar?'

'Lots of milk. Four sugar.'

'You do have a sweet tooth!' she exclaimed.

'A terrible failing of mine, Madge. I has to admit it.'

She poured his tea and handed it to him. 'Another piece?' she asked, for the second slice had also vanished.

'I'm making a pig of myself I know, but that sponge would tempt an angel into sin.'

'The sin of gluttony?'

Now he laughed while she reddened.

'Sorry, that was a dreadful thing to say,' she apologized. 'It just sort of slipped out.'

'Awful but true, Madge. I'm well aware of my faults. And that's one of them.'

She gave him a third slice of sponge, and helped herself to one. She then sat facing him.

'Are you from Atherton?' she asked.

'No, Newton Abbot way. I moved here sixteen year ago when I got my present job.'

They continued to chat until Jennie suddenly appeared. 'Oh!' she exclaimed, surprised at finding George there.

Madge introduced them, and explained that George had brought John home the worse for wear.

'Again!' Jennie said, and shook her head.

George went over to the table and placed his cup, saucer and plate on it. 'Thank you very much for that, Madge. It was real enjoyable. Now I'd best be going.'

'I'll see you out,' Madge said.

They halted at the front door. 'Thank you once more for what you did,' she smiled.

'Glad to have been of help.'

'He really does drink far too much. Something that seems to have got steadily worse over the years. Just don't think too harshly of him.'

'Tain't for me to criticize or judge,' George said. 'As we mentioned earlier, I got faults of my own.'

'You're a very understanding person, aren't you?'

'I try to be.'

'You're a good man, George Rattenbury.'

'And you're a fine, upstanding woman, Madge,' he replied softly.

She blushed at the compliment.

He opened the door. 'I'll see you about.'

'Yes,' she smiled.

He strode off into the night, and she closed the door behind him.

She shouldn't have such thoughts at her age, she told herself. It wasn't decent.

Then she giggled, just like a young girl.

* * *

262

'That's the last time you have scrumpy. It's back on beer for you, John Forsyth!' Madge stormed. 'Imagine having to be brought home in that condition! I couldn't have been more ashamed.'

John hung his head. 'Scrumpy's cheaper than beer,' he replied in a small voice.

'I don't care. It isn't doing you any favours, and that's a fact. So if you have to drink then it's back on the beer. Agreed?'

'Agreed,' he mumbled.

'And you limit yourself. No going over the top with the beer either.'

'I'll try,' he said.

'You won't try, you'll do it!'

John took a deep breath. He felt like death. His head was pounding, his throat red raw. He was also cold and shivery.

'Are you fit enough for church?'

He nodded.

'Then go wash and get ready.' She screwed up her face in disgust. 'God, you stink!'

He rasped a hand over his stubbly chin. He knew he stank, he could smell himself. It was too early to have a bath though, as their hot water came from a back boiler, so he'd just have to make do with an all-over flannel. He'd have a bath later when the fire had been on for a while.

'You say it was George Rattenbury who brought me home?'

'Found you slumped in the High Street.'

'I don't remember a thing,' he confessed.

'I'm not surprised.' She glared at him. 'I wish you knew what you're like to sleep with when in that state. You snore, you thrash about, you throw your arms around, often hitting me in the process, and you keep wrapping yourself in the bedclothes.'

'I'm sorry,' he muttered.

'Don't be sorry. Just don't drink so much.'

'I never intend to. I simply sort of . . . well, get carried away. I enjoy the company.'

He might enjoy the company, she thought grimly, but he didn't fool her. The booze was the main thing.

'The kettle's boiling,' she said. 'Your shaving water's ready.'

'Do you want any breakfast, Dad?' Jennie asked quietly from where she was sitting at the table.

'Breakfast!' Madge exclaimed sharply. 'If he wants any of that he can make it himself. I won't.'

'I'll get you some if you want it, Dad.'

'You'll do no such thing!' Madge retorted, waving a finger at her daughter. 'He'll get it himself.'

'But Mum . . .'

'That's the end of it,' Madge interjected, and folded her arms across her chest.

'Thanks Jennie,' John said, picking up the kettle.

'He's not capable of getting his own breakfast the way he is, and food would help him,' Jennie said to Madge when John had left the room.

'If you must know I prefer that he suffers,' Madge declared angrily.

'That's cruel.'

'Cruel! What do you think he does to me? Don't you think that's cruel?'

'All the same . . .'

'All the same, my eye!' Madge exclaimed, cutting Jennie off.

Jennie stared at her mother who was tired and wan after having spent an awful night with John. Madge had had little sleep, and had come downstairs that morning in a real fluster.

'I don't think that being cruel in retaliation is the answer,' Jennie replied softly.

'And what is the answer?' Madge demanded.

'I honestly don't know. But that isn't.'

'Hmm!' Madge sneered.

'I'll get ready too,' Jennie said, rising from the table.

'Put your plate in the sink before you go!'

'I was going to.'

'It didn't look like that.'

Jennie felt her own anger mounting. 'Well, I was. That's the trouble with you, you jump the gun far too often.'

'Oh, I do, do I?'

'Yes, you do.'

'You're turning into a proper little madam, know that?'

'And you're turning into a monster.'

With a cry of rage Madge rushed across the room and smacked Jennie on the cheek. 'I don't have to take that from you.'

'And I don't have to take that from you!' Jennie shouted in reply.

'Get upstairs,' Madge commanded.

'I don't want to go to church now.'

'Suit yourself.'

'Right then, I will,' Jennie retorted, and stamped out of the room.

Madge stood rigid for a few seconds, then gave a long drawn-out sigh. How had that come about? She hadn't meant . . . She'd just been so cross that was all.

She ran a hand disconsolately through her hair. She would have to ready herself for church as well. Time was getting on.

Ethel's eyes were shining when Graham picked her up in the car. 'I've got some news,' she declared excitedly.

'So have I. But let's keep both till we get there.'

She put a hand on his crotch, and rubbed.

'Don't,' he said.

'You sound sour?'

He didn't reply to that.

Ethel frowned as she gazed at him. He looked quite out of sorts, maybe there were problems connected with his smuggling, she thought. Or at home perhaps.

Graham was dreading what he had to do next, but do it he must. He couldn't wait for the next half-hour or so to be over.

They drove through the series of lanes that surrounded Atherton, and interlaced all of Devon, till eventually they arrived at a forest where Graham pulled off the road into a small clearing. This was a place they had often come to. He killed the engine.

'I can't wait to tell you my news. But you first,' Ethel said.

He'd planned to stare her straight in the face, but now found he couldn't. He studied his lap instead.

'Well?' Ethel prompted.

'This is going to hurt.'

Her smile vanished to be replaced by a look of apprehension. She didn't like the sound of this at all, not one little bit. She waited for him to go on.

'I want to end it,' he stated.

It was as though a red hot dagger had been plunged into her. 'Why?'

'It's finished between us, Ethel.'

'Why?' she repeated.

'It just is.'

Oh Graham, no! she wailed inside her head. Aloud, she said, 'I don't believe that. There must be a reason?'

'You're a married woman, Ethel, and I'm getting older.'

'There's someone else, isn't there?' she accused in a wounded tone.

He hadn't intended telling her, but now he realized he had to. He was very fond of Ethel after all, he owed her a full explanation. 'Yes,' he whispered in reply.

Ethel made an animal type sound at the back of her throat, and slumped in on herself. Her nightmare had finally become reality.

Graham started to reach out to comfort her, then decided not to. 'You always knew I didn't love you. I never pretended otherwise.'

Which was true enough, she thought. But that didn't alter how she felt. She loved him so much it went beyond words.

She realized tears were streaming down her face, and rummaged in her handbag for a handkerchief. When she found one she dabbed at her eyes and cheeks.

'You must have known this would happen one day,' he said, filled with pity for her.

Ethel fumbled for her cigarettes, stuck one in her mouth and lit it. She dragged smoke deep into her lungs, which helped a little. 'Is she a lot younger than me?' she husked.

'Age has got nothing to do with it.'

'I know, but is she?'

'She's twenty.'

Ethel laughed bitterly. 'And . . .' She had to force herself to ask this. 'Do you love her?'

Graham didn't answer.

'Do you love her?' Ethel persisted.

'To be honest I don't know. But I think I'm on the verge of it.'

'And what about her?'

This was proving difficult in the extreme, but then he'd known it would. 'She certainly likes me a lot.'

'But does she love you?'

'If she doesn't now I feel she could in time. It's very early days between us yet.' He was about to add that it might still come to nothing, then thought better of doing so in case it gave Ethel hope.

'Have you slept with her?'

'No,' he answered truthfully.

That was something Ethel told herself. 'So you don't know what she's like in bed? She could be useless.'

At the moment that wasn't a consideration, Graham thought, but didn't say so.

'Is she a virgin?'

Graham shrugged. 'Probably. But whether she is or not has nothing to do with it.'

267

Ethel puffed on her cigarette. 'I'm pregnant,' she stated. Then, after a few seconds pause, added, 'By you.'

Graham was aghast. 'Are you certain?' he asked in a suddenly trembling voice.

'Quite. On both counts. That was my news. After all these years I'm expecting.'

'And it's mine?'

She nodded.

What a bloody mess! he thought. He'd given up worrying about her conceiving, believing her barren as she herself believed. 'How far er . . . ?'

'Four months. I'm pregnant all right, no doubt about it.'

He was stunned by this bombshell. But it didn't alter matters, he reminded himself, unless Kerensa found out about it. That was a chilling thought, for he had been with Ethel since meeting Kerensa.

'What are you going to do?' he asked.

'Do! Have it of course. What else would I do?' She dabbed away more tears, and sniffed. She felt as if she was coming apart, and at any moment would disintegrate into a million pieces. She placed a hand on her stomach where the baby was, Graham's baby.

'It's going to be a boy,' she said.

'You can't possibly know that.'

'Call it female intuition, but it's going to be a boy.'

After all this time, with Mark and him, to become pregnant. It was unbelievable!

'What's the girl's name?'

'I don't think I should say.'

'Anyone from the village?'

'No.'

'But from the area?'

'Yes.'

Ethel drew heavily on her cigarette. 'I don't mind you seeing her as long as you continue seeing me. I wouldn't exactly like it, but would put up with it if I had to.'

'That's not on,' he answered.

'Don't make me beg, Graham. But I'll go down on my knees and beg if I have to.'

'No begging, Ethel. I wouldn't let you do that.'

She stared at him, eyes glittering with pain and anguish. 'You're a bastard, Graham, a fucking bastard,' she said.

He averted his gaze.

She suddenly launched an attack on him with the hand not holding her cigarette. A balled fist hammered again and again into his shoulder and upper arm. 'A bastard! A bastard! A bastard!' she repeated over and over again.

Graham sat there, taking it, letting her vent her fury. The attack ended when she collapsed blubbering back into her seat.

'I love you,' she moaned.

After a while they returned to Atherton; he dropped her at the same spot where he'd picked her up.

It had been even worse than he'd anticipated – Ethel carrying his baby!

He drove a little further on, then hastily stopped the car, got out, and vomited.

Chapter Eight

'There's an old friend here to see you,' Anthony Sturt said to Kerensa when she breezed into the drawing-room, back from a shopping expedition in Exeter.

'Rupert!' she exclaimed.

The handsome blond-haired young man rose and smiled at her. 'Hello, Kerensa. How are you?'

She crossed and kissed him affectionately on the cheek. 'I'm fine. How are *you*?'

'Fit as a fiddle. Never better.'

'It's been absolutely ages!'

'Well, I was up at Oxford, you in London. Then after Oxford I travelled a lot. Our paths just haven't crossed for a while.'

'Would you care for a drink, Kerensa? Rupert and I are having some whisky.'

She shook her head. 'Not for me, Daddy.'

'Refill, Rupert?'

'Please, sir.'

Anthony took Rupert's glass and went over to a crystal and silver tantalus from which he refilled both Rupert's glass and his own.

Kerensa sat and gazed at Rupert who was an old friend and admirer. 'Are you home for good?' she asked.

'I am. To help manage the family estate.' The Poundsberry Estate consisted of a little over nine hundred acres, large sections of which were grade one land. They grew crops, kept a dairy herd, bullocks and pigs. Adrian Poundsberry, Rupert's father, was a very successful landowner and farmer.

'Super!' Kerensa exclaimed, clapping her hands.

Anthony gave Rupert his recharged glass. 'Rupert has just been telling me about his travels. Sounds wonderful,' Anthony enthused to Kerensa. He liked Rupert, and had always thought he and Kerensa would make an ideal match.

'Where have you been?' Kerensa enquired.

'Just about everywhere on the continent really. France, Germany, Italy, Spain, you name it.'

'How exciting,' Kerensa breathed.

'But I'll tell you this, there's nowhere like Devon. I'm pleased to be home, I can tell you.'

'When did you get back?'

'Three days ago. And only heard yesterday that you were home as well.'

'Daddy hasn't been well,' she explained.

'Oh, I am sorry!'

'So Kerensa came to my aid as a sort of ministering angel,' Anthony said.

'I can't think of anything nicer.'

Anthony nodded his approval, Rupert had been sweet on Kerensa since childhood.

'And how were the gels at Oxford?' Kerensa asked, tongue in cheek.

'A mixed bag,' Rupert replied.

'Any of them take your fancy?'

Rupert knew he was being teased, and decided to go along with it. 'Let's say I had my moments.'

'Really? Sounds interesting.'

'It was,' Rupert answerd enigmatically. 'And what about you since we last met? Any ardent swains in the offing?'

She couldn't tell him about Graham, that was right out of the question. 'None at the moment,' she lied.

'Good. Then you're free to go with me.'

She frowned. 'Go where?'

'The Hunt Ball which is being held next Saturday at Atherton Manor. Short notice I realize, but as I said, I only returned three days ago and heard about your being

271

in residence yesterday. And here I am today to ask if you'll partner me.'

A Hunt Ball, next Saturday. She'd been to a number of Hunt Balls in the past and had always enjoyed them. They were fun. But should she accept Rupert when she was going out with Graham? If she turned Rupert down her father would be furious, and want to know why. And if she did accept should she tell Graham? He'd be around that Saturday, having altered his work rota so that he now had weekends free. (Graham's new schedule consisted of two weekday runs to Sark and back.)

'Should be a jolly evening,' Rupert said.

'Very jolly,' Anthony added, wondering why Kerensa was taking so long to reply.

'I'd love to go,' Kerensa smiled at Rupert. 'What time will you call for me?'

Rupert beamed at her. 'Eight – on the dot?'

'On the dot,' Kerensa agreed.

'That's that then.' He couldn't have been more pleased.

Kerensa decided she wouldn't tell Graham. She'd simply make an excuse, say it was impossible for them to meet that night.

She began quizzing Rupert about his travels, in answer to which he regaled her with highlights.

'What do you think, Daddy?' Kerensa asked, and twirled so that he could get the full benefit of her evening gown which he'd never seen before.

'A vision in red,' he said. 'You'll be the belle of the ball.'

Kerensa laughed with delight. 'I doubt that.'

'Well, I don't. You're quite stunning, my darling. Every man there, young and otherwise, will wish he was your partner.'

Kerensa ran her hands down the sides of her gown which was made of shot silk, and had a large bow of the same material on her left hip.

'So like your mother,' Anthony said, and shook his head at the many happy memories that flashed through his mind. How he missed Rebecca. Even now, after all these years, the pain at times could be almost unendurable.

'Come here,' he instructed, holding out his arms.

He held her close for a few moments, then patted a bare shoulder. 'Thank you my darling,' he said, releasing her.

The doorbell clanged. 'I'll get it. That'll be Rupert,' she declared.

'*I'll* answer it,' Anthony told her. 'You remain here.'

Kerensa was looking forward to the evening, and would, of course, know most of the people there. She certainly knew all the members of the hunt, many of whom were personal friends of her father's.

'I say!' Rupert exclaimed, as he entered the drawing-room.

'Approve?' she asked.

'And how! What a corker.'

'Whisky before you leave?' Anthony offered Rupert.

'Not for me, thank you.'

'Then you'd best be off,' Anthony said.

Kerensa walked over to where she'd laid a Persian lamb coat that had belonged to her mother, which she intended wearing. Rupert, mindful of his manners, rushed over to help her into it.

'Have a good night the pair of you. I'm sure you will,' Anthony said.

Kerensa kissed Anthony on the cheek. 'Bye Daddy.'

'Bye darling.' Then to Rupert, 'Take good care of her now.'

'Oh, I will, sir. Have no fears about that.'

Anthony saw them to the front door, and waited till they'd climbed into Rupert's car before closing it on them. He then returned to the drawing-room where he poured himself out a glass of whisky from the tantalus.

What a splendid couple they made, like a couple of

blond gods, he thought. And Rupert such an upstanding young man. And a young man, as the sole offspring, who would be extremely well off one day.

Rupert was all he could wish for in a son-in-law, and more.

Felicity Horton-Thompson brayed a laugh and threw a bread roll at 'Tiny' Colenut-Davis, laughing again, when she succeeded in hitting him on the head.

'Well aimed that gel!' roared Sir Reginald Tempest, his puce face testimony to the vast amount of champagne he'd consumed.

'Tiny' picked up a cushion and tossed it at Felicity who ducked out of its path.

Pippa Ellicott, 'Tiny''s fiancée, whispered something in his ear, to which he nodded. He then bent, and she jumped on to his back, securing her position there by clamping her legs round his waist and curling an arm round his neck.

Rupert grinned at Kerensa. 'Things are beginning to hot up, eh?'

She nodded her agreement.

'Give me a cushion,' Pippa ordered her cousin Emma, who handed her one.

'A joust! A joust!' 'Tiny' yelled, while Pippa waved the cushion in the air.

'We challenge you,' Pippa shouted to Felicity, whirling the cushion round her head.

Felicity's escort was a chap called Charles. Moments later she was mounted on Charles's back also armed with a cushion. 'Tiny' and Charles charged at one another, the girls bashing each other with their cushions when they clashed.

Sir Reginald thought this great sport, and thumped his thigh in approval. Others of his generation did likewise.

'A guinea on Fliss!' someone cried.

'Taken!' was the immediate reply.

'How's your drink?' Rupert asked Kerensa.

'Fine, thank you.'

He grabbed another from a passing waitress. 'Down the hatch,' he declared, and had a gulp of champagne.

A cheer rang out when Charles fell to one knee, nearly sending Pippa tumbling. But she managed to hang on, and he to regain his feet. The cushion fight went on.

Another bread roll went whizzing through the air, followed by yet another. Pippa issued a telling clout on Felicity who lost her hold round Charles's neck and fell backwards to dangle upside down.

'We win! We win!' proclaimed a triumphant Pippa.

'We challenge you now!' shouted Henry Passmore who had Caroline Mugford on his back.

'And we the pair of you,' yelled Geoffrey Malet who had a girl called Davina on his.

It didn't stop there, and soon a general mêlée developed with over a dozen couples bashing away at one another. And they weren't all young either, some of the couples were middle-aged.

'Want to have a go?' Rupert asked Kerensa.

'No, thank you.'

'Aw, come on!'

'No,' she stated firmly. These sort of high jinks weren't for her.

'Spoilsport,' he teased.

'Ask someone else if you wish.'

'Not likely.'

A couple careered into Sir Reginald who went sprawling. He sat on the carpet, shoulders shaking with laughter. He was having a whale of a time.

A cushion burst and its contents billowed all around. Pippa and 'Tiny' went crashing to the floor, followed almost instantly by Geoffrey and Davina.

It was all rather silly, Kerensa suddenly thought, the smile fading from her face. She'd much rather have been out with Graham, somewhere quiet, just the two of them.

'Top hole ball, eh?' said Joss Sharpin, joining them.

275

Joss, a long standing friend of Rupert's, was currently home on leave from the Royal Navy.

'Top hole,' Rupert agreed.

Rather silly, Kerensa thought again, and wondered what Graham was doing, and where he was.

It would have given her great pleasure to have known that at that exact moment he was thinking of her.

Kerensa sliced a tomato for the salad she was preparing for lunch. Dr Court was with her father in the drawing-room where he was examining Anthony.

She paused when she heard the front door shut, followed shortly by the sound of a car starting. She picked up a tea-towel and wiped her hands, intending to go and speak with her father, but before she could do so he appeared in the kitchen, grinning from ear to ear.

'What did the doctor say?' she asked.

'You're not going to believe this, but I don't have a heart problem at all.'

'Oh Daddy!' she breathed. 'That's marvellous.'

'Indigestion.'

She frowned. 'I beg your pardon?'

'Indigestion, that's what has been wrong with me. Indigestion.'

'You're joking!'

'Far from it. According to Court the symptoms of angina and indigestion are very similar. In my case he thought it was the former, but has now established that it's the latter. There's absolutely nothing wrong with me that a change of diet and eating habits won't cure.'

Tears of joy brimmed in her eyes.

'From now on I must eat light meals only, and never late at night. If I do that then no more chest pains or galloping pulse.'

'I'm so . . . relieved,' she said, as she kissed him on the cheek.

'You and me both girl. You and me both. I really did think it was the beginning of the end.'

'I've been so worried. I can't tell you.'

'It has been a trial. A trial ending in farce.' He laughed drily. 'Indigestion! Of all things to put the wind up me like that.'

Anthony heaved a sigh. 'Tell you what, this calls for a celebration. Shall I open a bottle of claret?'

'Is that allowed?'

'Alcohol in moderation, he said, which is all I ever drink anyway.' He allowed a few seconds to pass, then added, with a twinkle in his eyes, 'Most of the time, that is.'

'When you're paying for it you mean,' she teased.

'Exactly. Now where's that corkscrew?'

Kerensa wiped away her tears, and sniffed. What a load this was off her shoulders. Indigestion, who would have credited it!

'Is fish all right?' she queried. 'That's what I had planned for lunch. But I can always do something else.'

'Fish is fine. We'll discuss food later.'

'So, from now on those late suppers you enjoy so much are taboo?'

'Completely.'

This meant she could return to London, she thought. But did she want to? The answer to that was no. Not now she'd met Graham.

'Would you like me to stay on at Corfe Mullen?' she asked.

Anthony stopped to stare at her. 'I'd prefer it if you did,' he replied, thinking of Rupert. 'But, of course, you're a free agent.'

'I will on one condition, Daddy.'

'What's that?'

'I get a job.'

There was a pop as he pulled the cork from the bottle. 'You know my feelings regarding that.'

'I worked in London . . .'

'London's London,' he interjected. 'It's different here.'

'We need the money,' she stated.

He didn't argue with that, for it was true. A wage coming into the house would be a great help. He found two glasses and filled them.

'And I need the stimulation of a job,' she told him.

'Modern nonsense,' he snorted, handing her a glass.

'It's one or the other,' she bluffed. 'A job or I return to St John's Wood.'

He sniffed the wine in his glass, and tasted it. 'Should really be chambred,' he said.

'Daddy?'

He wanted to encourage her relationship with Rupert in the hope that something would come of it. A relationship couldn't develop if she was in London and Rupert in Devon. So, there was nothing else for it, reluctantly he would have to compromise.

'I've got used to having you back round the house. I'd be lonely if you went again.'

She smiled, realizing she'd won. 'That's agreed then.'

Anthony nodded.

She'd start looking right away, she thought. '*A votre santé!*' she toasted.

'*Salud*,' he responded. Then, darkly to himself, 'Indigestion, quite incredible.'

The baby, its face a miniature replica of his own, leered up at him. And what was that? Women talking, gossiping. Women huddled in groups, heads turning in his direction. And there a finger pointing, straight at him.

Graham woke suddenly, and sat bolt upright in bed. He was covered in sweat, his hair sodden and plastered to his head. It wasn't the first time he'd had this particular nightmare.

He took a deep breath to try and steady himself. He wished to God he'd never started his affair with Ethel. But how could he have known that one day he'd meet Kerensa, and that Ethel would fall pregnant by him at the same time?

What if the baby did look like him and people started talking? What if Kerensa heard and asked him about it? A child by another man's wife, the indisputable proof in the baby's face.

He took another deep breath. He felt sick, his stomach heaving. He lay back on the bed and stared at the ceiling.

Pregnant, by him. The words thundered in his mind. It was a sin to hope that Ethel might lose the child, but he did.

'God,' he groaned.

Guilt was a terrible thing, he thought. It could eat you alive, consume you like some animal devouring its prey.

He couldn't bear the thought of losing Kerensa. And yet, if she found out, he could easily.

He put a hand to his chin and discovered the hand was trembling. He was trembling all over he now realized. And he was so cold.

He wished he smoked. He wished he had a drink there. He wished Kerensa was in bed beside him. Above all, he wished he'd never heard of Ethel Yeo.

Kerensa left the building and waved to Rupert sitting parked at the kerb. He immediately got out of the car as she hurried towards him. Her own vehicle had developed a mechanical fault which was why he'd offered to bring her into town for the interview she'd just attended.

'Well?' he demanded.

'I've got the job. I start next Monday,' she replied, face flushed with excitement.

'Well done!' he cried, and kissed her.

'It's an excellent salary too. I couldn't be more pleased.'

'And I'm pleased that you're pleased. Well done again.'

He helped her into the car, then got into the driver's seat and drove off.

Across the street an incredulous Graham stood rooted

to the spot. Kerensa with another man. A man she was clearly intimate with from the way he'd kissed her on the mouth. Another boyfriend.

Graham was totally and utterly stunned.

Graham pulled the Lanchester off the road and parked overlooking the water meadows which were partially flooded from recent heavy rain on Exmoor.

He went over in his mind what he'd witnessed in Exeter. Kerensa had emerged from a building, a man had been waiting for her in a car – an extremely handsome young man no less – the man had got out the car, words had been exchanged, and then the man had kissed her on the mouth. Not on the cheek as a chum might, but on the mouth.

There could be no other interpretation, Kerensa was seeing someone else. Someone from her own background judging by the chap's appearance.

Graham was bewildered, and profoundly hurt. How could she do that to him? She knew how strongly he felt about her. And he'd thought she felt the same about him.

But she couldn't if she was two-timing him. So what was the true situation? Had she simply been playing with him all this while? Amusing herself with one of the peasants? Was he no more to her than 'a bit of rough'?

Fury erupted inside Graham, making him grind his teeth and ball his hands into tight knots.

Bit of rough! And what did she do after they'd been together, laugh at him? Make jokes to her hoity-toity friends about him?

And to think he'd cared. How he'd cared! And all the time there had been someone else – that blond Adonis wearing a university scarf.

'The bitch!' he muttered to himself, writhing inside. 'The bloody bitch!' Well, she'd get no more laughs at his expense, he'd see to that. She could go and jump off a cliff as far as he was concerned.

'Bitch!' he muttered yet again.

Graham stood with his hands deep in his pockets staring at the light shining from the Yeo's sitting-room window. Ethel was in, and Mark was on night-shift. All he had to do was go and knock on the door to be welcomed into a pair of loving arms. Ethel's arms, and bed.

He was sorely tempted. Why not? he thought. Why the hell not? There would be comfort there, and solace, both of which he badly needed.

Ethel would hold him, caress him, make him feel better. Ethel would take away some of this awful wretchedness and despair that was tearing him apart. Ethel would be a lifebelt to a drowning man.

He started across the road, then stopped on the opposite pavement. To knock or not?

Ethel's arms, Ethel's body, Ethel doing some of the things that had given him such pleasure in the past.

Only it wasn't Ethel he wanted, was it? It was Kerensa. Beautiful, gorgeous Kerensa whom he'd never been to bed with, and now never would.

'Kerensa.' He whispered the name aloud, and in that instant knew it would be wrong for him to knock on the door. Ethel wasn't the answer, not even the partial answer to what ailed him.

With a heart heavy as lead, and a churning stomach, he turned away from the house and, hands still deep in pockets, head drooping, began trudging homewards.

Kerensa glanced again at her watch. Graham was ten minutes late, which was most unlike him. Previously he'd always been early at their rendezvous point.

She stamped her feet to try and warm them, for it was freezing. 'Hurry up Graham,' she grumbled, and shivered.

Perhaps something had happened she speculated a few minutes later. What if he'd crashed his car? It had been reported that black ice lay heavy on some of the roads and lanes. If he had she prayed he hadn't hurt himself.

There again, he might be detained in Culmouth. That was always a possibility. Or he might be motoring back from there and it was taking him longer than he'd anticipated.

Then there was 'flu, there was a lot about at the moment. He could be in bed with no way of contacting her to let her know he wasn't coming.

It could be one of a dozen reasons, she thought. But she'd hang on a little longer yet. He'd be so disappointed if he turned up and she'd gone back to Corfe Mullen.

She waited twenty-five minutes in all before leaving, thinking surely he wouldn't be coming now. He'd no doubt explain what had happened when he left her a note in their special letter-box, a note that would suggest another time for meeting.

As she returned along the lane that would take her to Corfe Mullen it began to snow. Huge flakes fell steadily and thickly. By the time she reached Corfe Mullen the world had been transformed into a magical, white wonderland.

'What's wrong, son?' Madge asked quietly.

Graham, who'd been staring into the fire, turned his head to look at his mother. 'Nothing.'

She crossed over and sat opposite him. Jennie was out at night school, John through in the sitting-room. 'You can talk to me,' she urged.

'Why should anything be wrong?'

'Something obviously is. I've never seen you so withdrawn and . . . well, agitated. Is there some way I can help?'

When she received no reply she went on, 'Is it work? Are you having problems there?'

'No problems at work, Mum.'

She had a sudden alarming thought. 'You haven't been to the doctor's and been diagnosed as having a terminal disease?'

That made him smile. 'No Mum, no doctor or terminal disease.'

'Thank the Lord for that,' she said in relief.

Silence ensued, broken only by the ticking of the clock on the mantelpiece, during which Graham went back to staring into the fire.

'Well, I'm always here if you need me,' Madge said eventually.

'Thanks Mum.'

She rose, went to him and patted his knee. 'Maybe you'd prefer to speak to your da?'

'I'm all right, Mum, honest,' he lied.

'How about a nice cup of tea?'

He shook his head.

'Coffee?'

'No thanks.'

She sighed. 'Suit yourself.'

Graham gazed into the dancing flames. He was filled with grief and self-pity. It was as though he was suffering from an actual bereavement. He would have thought it would have passed, or begun to. But quite the contrary, every day saw his feelings worsen.

Perhaps he should confide in his mother? He considered that, and decided against it. She knew nothing about Kerensa after all, none of the family did. Like *Waterwitch* she'd been a secret. He had a horrible suspicion that if he did talk to Madge, or anyone come to that, about Kerensa he'd break down and cry like a big baby. And how could he possibly tell his mother that he'd been someone's 'bit of rough'. Think of the humiliation!

He rose to his feet. 'I'm going for a walk round the village,' he announced.

Madge shook her head when he'd left the room. You couldn't tell her nothing was wrong. It was plain as a pikestaff that something was.

Children, she thought wryly. Once you had them you never ceased worrying about them, no matter how old they were.

She hoped that whatever was troubling Graham would soon sort itself out.

'I'm off then,' said John, kissing Madge on the cheek. He was going to Exeter Cathedral with a party from the church, headed by the Reverend and Mrs Royal, to hear the *Messiah* sung by a touring German choir.

'Enjoy yourself.'

'I'm sure I will.'

Madge listened to the front door being shut. She could have gone with John but choirs, no matter how excellent, weren't really her.

She put the kettle on. It was lovely having the house to herself, Graham and Jennie having already gone out.

She thought of George Rattenbury whom she'd heard that morning was down with a bad dose of 'flu, and felt sympathy for him. Luckily she and the rest of the family had been spared so far, and hoped they would be spared altogether.

George would be laid up in bed, she thought, and wondered what he was doing about meals? If he had 'flu he could hardly cook for himself.

The farmer's wife would surely take him in something. There again, maybe not. You never knew with farmers, they could be as tight as a midge's bottom. The one George worked for wasn't known for being exactly the well of human kindness. Nor the missus, as his wife was known.

George had been off work for several days now, she'd gathered. It could be that the poor bugger was lying prostrate in bed starving to death, or trying to get by on a diet of biscuits and stale bread.

She worried at a fingernail. Maybe she should do something to help. It would be a Christian act after all.

She glanced at the saucepan containing what remained of the stew they'd had for tea. There was a lot left over. It wouldn't take her long to heat it up on George's cooker.

What was she thinking of? she berated herself. She couldn't go to George Rattenbury's. He was a single man with a reputation a mile long, even if he swore that that reputation for the main part was the result of malicious village gossip.

And what if he had a current lady friend who was even now there attending to him. She'd look a proper fool turning up on his doorstep to be confronted by such a person.

And even if the missus didn't feed him, surely the wives of the other farm labourers would? They'd be aware of his situation and do something about it.

She flushed. All she'd been trying to do was talk herself into going to see George whose company she enjoyed. Even the extra stew, hadn't she really made more than usual because at the back of her mind she'd intended using it as an excuse to visit George? Hadn't she subconsciously been planning such a visit since she'd heard he was ill?

No, no, visiting George was completely out of the question.

She poured some hot water into the teapot and swirled it round. She had plenty to be getting on with at home. There was a pile of ironing, and two shirts that needed their collars turned.

Jennie was doing well at night school, she thought, and smiled. Yes, Jennie would get on in life, which pleased her enormously. Who knew what she might do after she left night school? All sorts would be open to her.

Nor were things all that bad with John at the moment. He wasn't drinking nearly as much, and of late had been quite kind and considerate.

It was only Graham she was concerned about. And wondered what was worrying him. She'd noticed he'd lost some weight, his face was becoming rather thin and gaunt.

The kettle started to boil. She waited till it was

steaming well, then lifted it off the cooker and filled the teapot.

She thought again of George, and laughed. Of course someone would be looking after him. That was bound to be the case. There were probably a dozen women dancing attention on him. Would George like this? Would George like that? Would George like the next thing? He was probably being spoiled and pampered rotten.

She'd like a dog she suddenly thought. She'd never had a dog, and one would be nice. Dogs were very companionable. She made a mental note to mention it to John. If he had no objections she'd look into the matter.

Ironing? she thought, or turning collars? Neither appealed. In fact all she really wanted to do was sit down and put her feet up. Which was precisely what she would do, she decided.

Sitting with her feet up in front of the fire with a cup of tea and piece of cake made her think again of George. She smiled in memory of the banter between them when he'd bought the three cakes from her at the church fête. He'd been taking the michael there, as she'd been well aware.

He had a lovely sense of humour. She liked that in a man. John had flashes of it. Or at least, he had once. Being with John was inhabiting a grey area, whereas with George the area was filled with riotous colour.

'George the rainbow,' she said aloud, and smiled.

She poured herself a cup of tea, then cut a slice of cake. She then crossed over to the fire and sat beside it.

She bit into the cake. 'Hmm!' Even if she said so herself it was delicious. George would have enjoyed it.

When she'd finished eating she wiped crumbs from the corners of her mouth, and considered indulging in a second slice.

Bad for the waistline, she told herself, which had expanded somewhat in recent years. Due to contentment? That was a laugh. How could she ever be content living with John? That man was the bane of her life, a millstone round her neck.

She looked over at the cake tin. Maybe she should take it round to George? She could assess the situation first before knocking at the door. He would certainly appreciate the cake, there was no doubt about that.

If there was anyone with him she'd hear voices and general movement. And if by any chance he should be alone then she'd knock and give him the cake.

But if he was alone he'd be in bed and she didn't want him having to get up to answer the door. She could go right in, she thought. That was common practice in the country where doors were often left unlocked.

Go right in and give him the cake in bed. A treat for an ill chap, and a Christian act on her part as she'd told herself earlier.

She thought about it. Dare she? If she was to be seen who knows what would be said? Well, of course, she knew exactly what would be said. Two and two would make five as the result.

She'd go, she decided, amazed at her audacity. But she'd be extremely careful not to be seen. She wouldn't take any chances.

She put on her coat, then picked up the cake tin. Outside it was bitterly cold with a keen wind blowing that cut like a knife.

She was mad going out on a night like this when she didn't have to, she thought. She should have stayed in front of the fire. But despite these misgivings she continued on her way.

George's cottage stood by itself, and was isolated. As she approached it she saw that a solitary light was lit. The colour of the light told her it was lamplight and not electric.

She stood at the end of the path leading to George's cottage. Everything was quiet. Not a sound could be heard. She went closer, walking warily, ready to turn and bolt should she hear voices.

She stopped in front of his door, and listened. Inside was as quiet as the grave. She'd go round to the lamplit window and listen there.

The curtains were open to reveal George lying in bed.

He was quite alone, she thought jubilantly. Now, there was no reason why she couldn't go on in.

She returned to the door and as she tried its handle, the door swung open.

She closed the door behind her. 'George! It's Madge Forsyth!' she called out. 'Can I come in?' Daft question that, she thought, she already was standing inside.

His reply was muffled.

She walked towards his bedroom. 'Are you decent?' she queried loudly, not wishing him to know she'd peered in his bedroom window.

'In bed,' came the hoarse reply.

As she walked into the room George was struggling to sit up in bed.

'Just lie where you are. There's no need for that,' she said, frowning.

'Madge? What are you doing here?'

'I heard you were ill and decided to bring you a cake I'd made. As a treat.'

'Do you have it there?'

She opened the tin and showed it to him. 'Looks lovely,' he said.

'Would you like a piece?'

He shook his head. 'Haven't eaten since the day before yesterday. And funny thing is, tain't hungry at all. I've completely lost my appetite.'

He looked dreadful, she thought. His face was a pasty shade of white, and he was unshaven.

'My skin feels like she's crawling,' he said. 'It's as if a million ants were marching up and down my body.'

She glanced around the room. 'It's almost as cold in here as it is outside. I'll put a fire on. Is there another lamp?'

'In the kitchen.'

'Right then.'

She used his lamp to light her way through to the kitchen where she found the second lamp, and a box of matches. She lit the second lamp, then returned to the bedroom.

'Hasn't anyone been to see how you are?'

He gave her a wry smile. 'No doubt they all thinks I'm being looked after by my reputed women friends.'

Madge dropped her gaze, remembering her fanciful notion about a dozen women dancing attendance on George. Thank goodness she had come round. He was in a right old state.

She busied herself at the fireplace where there was some old newspaper stacked ready, and a few pieces of kindling lying to one side. Soon a fire was roaring in the grate.

'That's a lot better,' George said, nodding his appreciation.

'How about tea, could you manage a cup?'

'I could. But first I'd like some water. I'm parched.' He indicated an earthenware jug on the floor beside his bed. 'Ran out earlier and haven't had the strength to fill it again.'

'That's easily done,' Madge said, picking up the jug.

She returned to the kitchen where there was a hand pump by the side of the sink. She filled the jug, then searched for a tumbler which she took through with the jug to George.

George greedily drank two tumblerfuls of water, then sank back on to his pillows. 'I needed that,' he said.

'Now for some tea,' she smiled.

'You'll have to put the range on in the kitchen to make some,' he told her.

She eyed the bedroom fire, but there was no hanging facility, or any other device she might have used for a kettle. Back she went to the kitchen where she dealt with the range, after which she filled the kettle at the hand pump.

She rummaged round looking for cups and saucers and finally found them in a cupboard along with a caddy of tea and a half-empty packet of sugar. There was, of course, no milk.

As she waited for the kettle to boil she had the opportunity to take in the kitchen. It was obvious that George was a bachelor, and a pretty messy one at that. The walls were papered, but the paper so old and dirty that the pattern had completely faded away. The linoleum underfoot was worn through in places. It was ancient and should have been replaced long since. A crack traversed the entire breadth of the ceiling.

When the kettle boiled she made the tea good and strong the way he liked it. She put four teaspoons of sugar in his cup, recalling the amount from the night he'd brought John home drunk.

'I be as weak as a new-born babe,' George said when she handed him his cup.

'You certainly don't look too hot.'

'This is a fair old attack of the 'flu, I can tell you. Felled me good and proper.' He sipped his tea. 'Very nice.'

'Four sugar. I remembered.'

He smiled at her and then sighed. 'These lamps need filling too.'

'I'll do it before I go.'

'I'd be obliged.'

'No appetite at all?' she said.

'None. Strange for me, eh?'

She'd make some soup the following day and bring it over in the evening. That might tempt him.

George had a thought. 'I hope you weren't seen coming here?' he queried anxiously.

'I wasn't. I was very, very careful.'

'Don't want you getting a bad name on my account. That would be right hurtful.'

His concern for her touched Madge. He really was a

290

sweet man. 'Are you sure I can't entice you to a slice of that cake?' she asked.

He decided to humour Madge, knowing if he ate it it would please her. 'A very small piece then,' he replied.

She was delighted. 'Even if you've no appetite you should eat something,' she said. She fetched a knife from the kitchen and cut him a thin slice.

'Tastes even better than she looks,' he pronounced when he'd had a mouthful.

When he finished his tea she poured him another cup.

'I feel a lot better now. Thank you,' he declared when he'd drunk that.

'I'll shave you if you want?'

'No, I couldn't bear a razor on me face at the moment. But it's a kind offer.'

They chatted for a little while, during which Madge refilled the lamps, then it was time for her to go. She banked up the bedroom fire before doing so.

'I'll come again tomorrow night,' she informed him.

'Be careful though.'

'Don't worry, I will,' she smiled.

'And Madge,' he said, holding out a hand. She took hold of it and he gently squeezed. 'Thanks for being a friend.'

'Tomorrow then,' she responded.

'I'll be here. You can count on that,' he said drolly.

She laughed, and left him, closing the outside door quietly behind her.

Chicken broth she thought as she hurried home, she'd make it in the morning. And she'd have to think up an excuse to go out the following night.

Something to do with the WI, she decided.

Kerensa shone a torch into the tree cavity she and Graham used as a special personal letter-box. Her letter to him was still there.

She frowned, perplexed. It was a fortnight now and

still no word. What was wrong? *Had* there been an accident? If it had been the 'flu surely he would be over it by now, recovered enough to leave her a letter. But the fact remained, there was no word. It was all most puzzling.

In the mean time she was missing him a gréat deal. It amazed her just how much.

Madge was thinking it was a pity George's cottage didn't have electricity when he appeared in the kitchen. 'What are you doing up?' she demanded.

He swayed, and had to grab hold of the door knob to steady himself. She was instantly by his side to take his arm.

'Light headed,' he mumbled. 'Everything's suddenly going round and round.'

'Come on, back to bed. That's the place for you.'

'Feel guilty lying there with you cooking and cleaning like you are.'

'There's no need to feel guilty,' she gently admonished, steering him in the direction of the bedroom. 'As for the cleaning, well, that badly needed to be done. You're certainly no housewife, George Rattenbury.'

She sat him on the edge of the bed, and helped him get under the covers. She then tucked him in.

'I don't know what I would have done without you,' he confessed.

'Survived somehow,' she smiled.

'I'm not so sure about that.'

She surveyed the bedroom which she'd tidied and cleaned during her last visit. 'I'll have to go shortly,' she said. 'How about another cup of tea before I do?'

'That would be lovely.'

'And I've made you a big plate of sandwiches to get you through the day tomorrow.'

'You're a saint, Madge. You surely be.'

'I wouldn't say that!' she laughed.

'Well, I would. I'll never forget your kindness. You've

been a friend to me, and I'll be one to you till my dying day. I swears I will.'

Madge took a deep breath. She felt gloriously happy. Her visits to George's cottage gave her great pleasure. She would miss them when he was better.

George stared at her, thinking how terrific she was. John was a lucky man. He'd have given anything to be in his shoes. He just wondered if John realized how fortunate he was.

'I'll make that tea,' Madge said, and left the room.

She'd turned his little cottage into a home, George thought. Before it had simply been a house, now it was a home, filled with something she brought with her. A vibrancy and feeling of well-being.

'Now, you be careful and not be seen,' he warned her a short while later as she was about to leave.

'I'm getting quite good at sneaking in and out,' she replied jocularly.

'Take care then.'

On impulse she went to him and kissed him on the forehead. 'I'll be back tomorrow night.'

When she'd gone he touched the spot she'd kissed, and smiled.

Jennie answered a knock at the front door to find a young woman of her own age standing there. She vaguely recognized her face. 'Can I help you?'

'Is Graham in?'

'No, I'm afraid he's not. He's gone to the pictures in Exeter.'

The pictures in Exeter! Kerensa thought numbly. 'Has he had 'flu or been in an accident recently?' she queried.

'He's fine, and he certainly hasn't been in any accident,' Jennie replied, wondering what this was all about. 'Are you a friend of his?'

She thought she'd been and possibly more than that. 'Just tell him Kerensa called by.'

'Of course.'

Kerensa managed a smile. 'Thank you.' And with that she turned and walked swiftly to her car.

How could he just drop her like that, and without even a word! she thought as she drove away. He hadn't only dropped her, but stood her up into the bargain. He might at least have written.

She was angry, confused, and furious with herself for feeling as she did about him. How could she fall for someone who'd do that to her?

What an actor! What a performance! But why? That was the aspect she couldn't understand. Everything had been wonderful between them, or at least so she'd believed, and then suddenly . . . end of story. She was left standing waiting for him.

She felt a real idiot. Gone to the pictures indeed, probably with some other female, too. He was out enjoying himself while she'd been worried sick about him, imagining all sorts of disasters.

Not only did she feel a fool and an idiot, but humiliated beyond belief.

How she wished now she hadn't knocked on his door. Somehow that made matters ten times worse.

She knew what she'd do. She'd go to Rupert's and get him to take her out for a drink somewhere. A nice little pub where the atmosphere was cosy and romantic. And she'd flirt with Rupert, outrageously.

Heavens, she was angry!

'How were the pictures?' John enquired as Graham came into the kitchen, having just returned from Exeter.

'Fine.'

John grunted.

Graham went over and warmed his hands by the fire. 'Where's Mum?'

'Gone to bed with a headache,' John answered, continuing to play patience at the table.

Jennie looked up from the book she was engrossed in.

'By the way, a young woman called Kerensa knocked earlier asking for you.'

Graham went very still. 'Did she indeed?'

'I told her where you'd gone.'

'And what did she say?'

'Just asked me to tell you she'd been round.' A twinkle appeared in Jennie's eyes. 'Who is she, Graham? A secret pash, eh?'

He shrugged. 'Simply someone I know. That's all.'

'She's not a girlfriend then?'

'Most certainly not.'

'I thought she looked nice and extremely pretty.'

Graham didn't answer that.

Jennie studied her brother in amusement, his lack of response told her more than he realized. 'So, who is she?' Jennie persisted.

'I said, just someone I know.'

'From where?'

'Why don't you mind your own business!' he snapped irritably.

'And why are you so defensive?'

'I'm nothing of the sort.'

'Oh yes, you are,' Jennie smiled.

Graham glared at her. 'Just drop it, eh? Just drop it.'

'I was only curious, that's all.'

'I'm going up to my room,' Graham stated, and left the kitchen.

'Touchy,' Jennie mused aloud when he'd gone. 'Interesting.'

'And you're too inquisitive by half,' John admonished.

Jennie returned to her textbook. Kerensa was extremely pretty indeed, she thought, with beautiful hair.

Gradually Jennie became reabsorbed in her book. And soon forgot about Kerensa, and Graham's odd behaviour.

'It is love sickness, I would recognize it anywhere. I tell you, I know about these things,' Majohn smirked.

Graham was seething inside. He'd just about had enough of this teasing which had started two trips previously. Lord alone knew how Majohn had guessed what was troubling him, but the bloody man had.

Majohn stroked his droopy moustache. 'I am right, am I not Graham? Come along, own up. Admit it.'

'You are becoming very annoying,' Graham replied through gritted teeth, picking up another cardboard box, part of the consignment which needed to be loaded.

'Leave him alone,' said L'Corbin; this was one of the rare occasions when both he and Majohn were present. 'I think he's had enough.'

But Majohn wasn't going to let Graham off the hook. He was enjoying himself, thinking this great sport. And the more upset Graham got the more he enjoyed it.

'So what has happened?' queried Majohn hurrying after Graham. 'Has your girlfriend given you the old heave-ho? Is that it?'

Graham didn't answer.

'Perhaps she has met another?' He paused, then went on, 'Or perhaps . . .'

'Shut it. I'm warning you!' Normally Graham would have shrugged off any good-humoured ribbing, but he was still hurting fiendishly over Kerensa. Where she was concerned he had no sense of humour whatsoever.

Majohn glanced at L'Corbin and winked one of his large soulful eyes. Turning his attention again to Graham, he said, 'Or it could be you have fallen head over heels in love with a girl who isn't interested in you?'

Something snapped inside Graham. Majohn had gone too far. He dropped his box and whirled on Majohn.

Graham's fist connected with a solid crack, sending a surprised Majohn tumbling backwards, his box crashing to one side. An infuriated Graham pounced on him, with the intention of hitting him again.

Graham's arm was suddenly grasped and held before he could deliver the second blow.

'Enough!' L'Corbin commanded sternly.

Majohn gazed up at Graham, blood running from his mouth to mingle with his moustache.

A few taut seconds ticked slowly by. Eventually Graham's shoulders slumped. 'It's all right now,' he husked to L'Corbin, who then released him.

Graham came to his feet and drew in deep breath after deep breath.

L'Corbin spoke rapidly to Majohn in Sercqais, who replied using the same language. Majohn wiped blood from his face, stared at the stain on his hand, and then wiped his hand on his trousers. L'Corbin spoke to him again in Sercqais.

Majohn stared at Graham. 'It seems I've been a bit out of order man pôvre ami. I apologize.'

The remaining tension drained out of Graham. 'Apology accepted.'

'The subject is closed now, for ever,' L'Corbin said.

'For ever,' Majohn agreed.

Graham held out a hand to Majohn which, after a moment's hesitation, Majohn grasped. Graham pulled him upright.

'That tongue of yours will get you hung one day,' L'Corbin admonished Majohn.

'Let's continue loading,' Graham said, and picked up the box he'd dropped.

When the loading was complete they all had a large tot of cognac, then Graham went back aboard *Waterwitch*, started her engine, and eased her out of the cave.

It was a dull night with lots of clouds scudding overhead. A pale yellow moon gazed wanly down.

It was stupid of him to have lost his temper like that, Graham berated himself as he set course for Culmouth, but the damn man just wouldn't let up.

He shook his head. Things might not have come to the pass they had if L'Corbin had been present during the last two trips, but unfortunately L'Corbin hadn't. L'Corbin would probably have put a stop to it before he came to the end of his tether.

'Kerensa,' he whispered. How long was it going to take to exorcize the bitch! Erase her from his mind and emotions. If only he'd never met her in the first place. Never gone to that damn fête. That fête certainly had a lot to answer for.

The night passed quietly; he made good time despite the choppy sea. It was shortly after dawn when another motor vessel appeared bearing down on him.

When Graham saw the vessel his heart leapt into his mouth. It was a vessel Uncle Bert had described to him often enough: a revenue cutter.

He swore, and opened *Waterwitch*'s engine to its fullest. *Waterwitch* leapt ahead, its powerful engine throbbing as it knifed through the water.

Graham found he was sweating profusely. He was lost, he knew it. It was only a matter of time before the cutter came alongside.

'Ahoy! Heave to!' cried a voice magnified by a megaphone.

He thought wildly of chucking the boxes of porn overboard, then realized that wouldn't do any good as they'd only float and be picked up later by the cutter.

He was mesmerized by the cutter, fast gaining on him. Again the voice called out instructing him to heave to, which he again ignored.

He thought of his mother, this was going to devastate her. For a son of hers to end up in prison! Well, he had only himself to blame, he'd known the risks involved. Uncle Bert had made sure of that.

And then he spotted it, a thick bank of fog hovering atop the water. He immediately altered course and headed that way. The question was, how big was the bank? Big enough to lose himself in? He prayed fervently that it was.

He entered the fog, and again altered course. A few minutes later he altered course once more.

Stop and wallow or continue to run? He decided on the latter. He could hear the cutter's engine, but couldn't place where the sound was coming from. The fog was distorting things, which was in his favour.

To his delight, and relief, the fog got even thicker. A wet, grey soup that he ploughed through.

He could still hear the cutter, but she was far away now. He crossed two fingers that he was saved.

The fog went on and on. Normally he would have cursed it as an inconvenience, but not that night. That night he positively welcomed it with open arms

He killed his engine, and listened. Nothing. The only sound was that of tiny waves lapping against *Waterwitch*.

He collapsed over the wheel. That had been a close shave. Far too close for comfort. He'd come within an ace of being apprehended.

He kept a bottle of Scotch in the wheel house. He now opened the bottle and had several large swigs. What a trip. First the Majohn incident, then this.

He restarted the engine, and set a new course. He'd been frightened out of his life back there, he thought.

Frightened out of his life.

'It's Mr Rattenbury to see you both,' Graham announced.

George entered the sitting-room carrying a cardboard box, his face wreathed in smiles.

What was he doing here? Madge wondered in alarm. She couldn't think of any reason for him to visit.

'Why, Mr Rattenbury, what a pleasant surprise,' declared John, rising from his chair. He, too, mystified as to why George should visit them.

'I heard it mentioned in the village that Mrs Forsyth be interested in having a dog. Be that so?' George enquired innocently. He hadn't heard anything of the sort. Madge had told him herself when he was down with 'flu.

'Why yes, that's right,' said Madge.

'Then perhaps we're in a position to help one another. I got a nice little pup here looking for a good home. A home maybe you can give him, if you likes the cheeky little beggar.'

'A puppy!' Madge smiled. That explained the cardboard box.

'Here he be,' said George, setting the box on the floor and opening it.

The family crowded round. 'Oh, he's gorgeous!' Madge exclaimed.

'Only a mongrel mind. Nothing fancy.'

Madge delved into the box and scooped out the puppy which she cradled against her bosom. The puppy gazed up at her out of large, liquid brown eyes.

'He's adorable,' said Jennie. 'Can I hold him?'

'In a minute,' replied Madge, not wishing to part with him so soon. 'Does he have a name?' she asked George.

'Not yet. That'll fall to you if you decides to have him.'

'Have him! Nothing would stop me having him. You'd have to fight me if you want him back.'

George laughed. 'That seems to be settled then.'

'Put the kettle on,' Madge instructed Jennie. 'You will stay for a cup of tea, won't you Mr Rattenbury?'

'I'd be delighted to.'

'And a piece of cake?'

'Better still.'

Madge held the puppy above her head, then cradled him again. 'This is wonderful. I couldn't be more pleased.'

Nor could George who'd searched out the puppy as a thank you present to Madge for what she'd done for him. For a moment their eyes met, and she gave an almost imperceptible nod that she understood.

By the end of the evening the puppy had been named Brownie on account of his eyes.

Graham was walking down Exeter High Street, sunk in thought, when suddenly he realized Kerensa was coming towards him from the opposite direction. She saw him at the same time, and stopped dead in her tracks.

What should he do? he wondered. Avoid her by

300

crossing the road? Walk past and ignore her? Say hello in passing?

Much to his annoyance he felt his stomach go all strange, and his legs weaken. Kerensa was even more beautiful than he remembered. He didn't hate her at all, no matter what she'd done to him. Hate her? It was quite the opposite.

He halted when he reached Kerensa, his heart pounding madly inside his chest. He had to fight the impulse to reach out and touch her.

'Hello,' he said.

'Hello. How are you?'

'Fine. And yourself?'

'I'm fine too.'

He attempted a smile which came out all crooked. 'So, what brings you into town?'

'Work. I'm on my lunch break.'

'Work?'

'It turned out that my father didn't have heart trouble after all. Quite funny really. He had indigestion.'

'You're joking!'

'No, true,' she nodded. 'So, with that worry out the way I decided to get a job.'

'And not return to London?'

'No,' she replied softly. 'At least not for now.'

'I see.'

There was a pregnant pause between them. 'I suppose I'd better get on,' he said, although it was the last thing he wanted to do.

'Me too.'

'Well, goodbye then.'

'Goodbye.'

Neither moved.

'There's a little place I sometimes go to for a bite to eat. I'm off there now.' She hesitated, then said, 'Would you like to join me?'

Bit of rough, he thought. Maybe he should join her, and confront her with what he'd seen. 'Yes,' he replied.

Kerensa moved off, and he fell in beside her. They walked in silence, till eventually Kerensa said, 'In here.'

They both elected to have cottage pie which Graham insisted on paying for. The table they chose was by a window overlooking the street. When they sat down it was clear she was as nervous as he.

He toyed with his meal, pushing bits of it around his plate. He had no appetite whatsoever.

'You might at least have written,' she said quietly.

He shrugged. 'I didn't feel obligated to do that.'

She stared at him, frowning. 'You didn't?'

'No. Not after what you'd been doing to me.'

She laid down her fork. 'And what exactly had I been doing to you?'

The words poured from his mouth in a rush. 'I saw you in the street one day, you and some Adonis. You came out of a building, he was waiting for you in his car, and when you got to him he kissed you. Not a peck on the cheek either, a proper kiss. That made me realize I was only some "bit of rough" to you. That you'd probably been two-timing me all along.'

Kerensa was both astonished and appalled.

He rattled on. 'Did you amuse your smart friends by telling them about me? How this peasant was mad for you? Was that your game, eh?'

She opened her mouth, found herself unable to speak, and closed it again.

Graham gazed disconsolately down at his cottage pie. 'You've no idea how much you hurt me.'

'You've got it all wrong,' she said at last, her voice shaking.

'Have I? You mean you didn't kiss that blond chap?'

'The blond chap is Rupert and he kissed me as you yourself said. And I most certainly never thought of you as a peasant or a "bit of rough". Nor did I ever discuss you or our relationship with my friends, none of whom know anything about you.'

'So you say.'

'I'm telling you the truth, Graham, I swear.'

'Maybe about your friends,' he said reluctantly. 'But what about this Rupert?'

She sighed. 'Rupert is an old chum who's only recently returned from university and abroad. And yes, he is attracted to me, very much so. And I like him, but strictly on a platonic level.'

Graham looked at her in disbelief.

'On a platonic level,' she repeated. 'Daddy would have it otherwise, of course. He sees Rupert as a perfect match for me, and would be delighted if Rupert and I were to marry.'

She paused, then went on, 'To be honest, I did agree to go out with Rupert on his return, but only because it pleased Daddy and acted as a sort of cover for you. Besides which, if I hadn't agreed to see Rupert Daddy would have nagged me incessantly to do so. But I assure you there's nothing between us, at least not on my side. As for that kiss, it was his reaction to my news that I'd just landed a job, having been in the building you mentioned for an interview. And the reason Rupert was waiting for me was because my own car had broken down. He was doing me a kindness by giving me a lift to and from Exeter.'

Graham felt sick.

'You weren't the only one hurt by this misunderstanding,' she said.

'Kerensa . . . I am sorry.'

'I was so worried. I thought something must have happened to you. That you'd had an accident, or were ill.'

He reached out and took her hand. 'Can you ever forgive me?'

'How could you believe that I'd think of you as a "bit of rough"?'

He hung his head. 'I was so angry, and confused. I suppose my imagination simply ran away with itself. Love does funny things to a person.'

'Love?' she queried softly.

He looked into her eyes. 'I love you. Very much,' he husked.

She smiled with joy to hear that. 'Know something?'

'What?'

'I love you.'

He was filled with elation. His spirits soared. 'You do?'

She echoed his words, 'Very much.'

'Oh Kerensa, it's been sheer hell since that day I saw you with Rupert.'

'Same for me. I missed you dreadfully.'

'I've never stopped thinking about you. You've been constantly in my thoughts.'

'And I've done a lot of thinking about you.'

He sighed. 'I've never been happier than I am right now. Suddenly the world's a marvellous place again. I love you and you love me. Sheer magic.'

When it was time to go he walked her back to the office. 'Can you meet me tonight?' he asked eagerly.

She nodded.

'Eight o'clock at the rendezvous point?'

'Right.' She took hold of his arm. 'And you will be there this time, won't you?'

'You can bet your life on that.'

She pecked him hastily on the mouth, then went inside.

He was back with Kerensa and she loved him! He couldn't wait till eight.

Graham glanced again at his watch. Another five minutes to go. He was in a fever of impatience waiting for her to arrive.

A figure hurried out of the darkness, opened the front passenger door, and slipped inside.

'I'm early,' said Kerensa.

'Me too.'

They fell into one another's arms, and their mouths met. They kissed and kissed, murmuring endearments as they did.

'God, you feel and smell so good,' Graham declared when they finally stopped.

'Where shall we go?'

'The Bakers' Arms?' It was an out-of-the-way pub they'd often frequented.

He started up the car, but couldn't resist another kiss. He kissed her holding her face between his hands.

'I love you,' he breathed.

'And I love you, Graham.'

He kissed her on her closed lips, then engaged the gears and drove off.

'You're going to have to tell your father about us,' he said.

'I know. But . . . well, not yet. Call it cowardice if you like, he's bound to make such a fuss.'

'You're only putting off the inevitable. For I'll never let you go.'

'I'll never want you to.'

She put a hand on his thigh, and rubbed it.

'Saucy wench,' he teased.

'You like?'

'Stupid question.'

She laughed.

'Tell me about your job,' he said.

While she was doing this, her left hand came into contact with a magazine stuffed into the door pocket. When she'd finished speaking she pulled the magazine out, intending to have a look at it.

'What's this?' she queried.

'What's what?'

'This magazine?'

His heart leapt into his mouth. Bloody Norah! He'd totally forgotten that was in the car. It was from a recent consignment, and obscene in the extreme.

'Here, let me have that,' he said, and snatched it from

her. He hastily pushed it down the side of his seat, and then further underneath the seat.

'What was that all about?' she asked.

'Nothing.'

'You didn't act as if it was nothing.'

How could he explain? He couldn't. It would be awful for her to find him in possession of such a thing, far less her discovering he smuggled such filth for a living. He broke out in a cold sweat at the thought.

Who knew what her reaction to the latter would be? No, smuggling porn was his secret about which she must never find out.

He thought of his recent close shave with the Revenue cutter. Apprehension would have meant not only prison but public exposure, and that would be disaster as far as his personal life was concerned.

Kerensa, he'd lost her once through a misunderstanding. The last thing he wanted was to lose her again. He experienced the acute sense that someone somewhere was trying to tell him to quit while ahead. And there and then he decided that was exactly what he'd do.

There would be one final trip to inform L'Corbin and Majohn that he was finishing. And then that would be it.

'Graham?'

He roused himself from his reverie. 'Sorry. Yes?'

'The magazine?'

He decided to tell her a little of the truth. 'A friend loaned it to me. It has a few naughty pictures inside. Nothing that outrageous, but it would embarrass me for you to see them.'

She laughed. 'You are silly!'

Not too outrageous! That was a whopper if ever there was one.

She continued rubbing his thigh.

Chapter Nine

Graham drove in through the wrought-iron gates belonging to the Stanton Brick Works and parked the Lanchester close to the main door. He was dead on time for his appointment with Mr Gerald Stanton who owned the works.

He got out of the car and locked it. Clutching his brand new attaché case he went inside.

The Stanton Brick Works was situated on the outskirts of Sanford Barton, a village just over a mile away from Atherton. It was a small firm employing fourteen locals and had existed for over a hundred years.

Graham was shown into Gerald Stanton's office. Gerald Stanton was a man in his late sixties. Stanton immediately rose and came round from behind his desk to shake Graham's hand.

'Pleased to meet you, Mr Forsyth,' he said, his expression one of slight puzzlement.

'And I you Mr Stanton.'

'You live in Atherton I believe from our correspondence?'

'That's correct.'

'I'm afraid I've never previously heard of you.'

'Well, I've heard of you, Mr Stanton. You and your firm are well known in the area.'

Stanton took in Graham's expensive suit, shoes, shirt and silk tie. An ensemble that made the statement Graham intended it to.

'Cup of tea?' Stanton offered.

'That would be nice.'

Stanton ordered the tea, then asked Graham to sit

down. 'How did you come to hear that the firm was up for sale?' he enquired.

'It's common knowledge that it's been on the market for some time.'

'But you weren't interested before?'

'To be honest I never considered it. And then recently it suddenly dawned on me it might be what I'm looking for, hence my visit today.'

Stanton cleared his throat. 'I mentioned the asking price in my letter to you. I presume that would be within your financial scope?'

Graham smiled thinly. 'If it wasn't I wouldn't be here wasting your time.'

Stanton cleared his throat again. 'Quite so.'

'You must be sad to sell,' Graham sympathized.

Stanton nodded. 'Unfortunately I'm the last of the line. I had two sons you know, but both were killed in the war. James at the Somme, Simon when *Nestor* went down at Jutland.'

'I'm sorry,' Graham murmured.

Stanton's eyes took on a faraway look. 'They were both good boys, and intelligent. James in particular. He's the one who would've succeeded me in the normal course of events.'

'And Simon?'

'His wish was to go into law.'

'Your wife is also dead, I understand,' Graham said.

'Yes, last year. A stroke. A great loss to me. We were very close.'

'What will you do when you sell?' Graham asked.

'I've promised myself a sea cruise followed by a long holiay in the South of France.'

'Good for you!' Graham enthused.

'Don't want to stop at home and rot like some vegetable, eh?'

'No indeed,' Graham agreed.

The tea arrived along with some biscuits. 'Your secretary I take it?' Graham said after the woman had gone.

'Miss Pritchard. Very efficient.'

If getting on a little now, Graham thought. He judged her to be in her early sixties, the same generation as Stanton himself.

They drank their tea and talked. When they were finished Stanton said, 'Now what would you like to do first? Where shall we start?'

'With your books,' Graham replied. 'I'd like to study those.'

'Of course.' Stanton rose. 'Why don't you sit here and I'll get them for you?'

'I'd like to see everything,' Graham stated. 'Order books, correspondence files and bank statements.'

Stanton crossed to a filing cabinet and soon Graham was lost in piles of facts and figures. He read slowly, cross referring a great deal, and made many notes. Lunch-time found him still engrossed.

Miss Pritchard appeared to ask if he'd care for something to eat, and he replied he could use a sandwich and some more tea. There was no canteen in the works as the employees all went home for their dinner as they called it, so a sandwich was fetched from a nearby pub.

Graham ate it and continued with his task. Shortly after three o'clock he closed the final ledger and pronounced himself satisfied. He now knew what was what regarding the financial side of things.

He spoke to Miss Pritchard who brought Stanton back to the office. 'Well, Mr Forsyth?' Stanton enquired hopefully.

'Very interesting.'

'So do you wish to proceed?'

'Yes, I do,' Graham replied.

He knew nothing about making bricks, but as far as he was concerned that didn't matter. The workforce did, which was what counted.

'Hello Graham!' exclaimed Danny Green as Graham and Stanton began to progress through the plant. Danny

309

was roughly the same age as Graham and someone he'd known for years.

Graham smiled in return, but didn't answer. He was already aware that because he was local, and from the same working-class background as the workforce, over familiarity might be a problem. If he bought the factory that was something he'd have to sort out straight away.

Graham asked question after question which Stanton patiently answered. Before long Graham had a general idea about the manufacture of bricks.

When the tour was completed they returned to Stanton's office where Stanton produced a bottle of sherry.

'Will you join me?' Stanton asked.

'Please.'

Graham was excited, and trying not to show it. The brick works was ideal, and had tremendous potential.

Stanton handed Graham a brimming schooner. 'Well, Mr Forsyth, what's the verdict?'

'I'll sleep on it if you don't mind. And I think I'll take a little professional advice into the bargain.'

Stanton's face lit up. 'You're interested then?'

'I won't pretend that I'm not. But as I say, I want to mull it over.'

'Fair enough!' Stanton declared.

If he did buy he'd knock down the price, Graham decided, eyeing Stanton over the rim of his schooner. The man was bursting to sell and get off on his sea cruise.

When he drove away he was well satisfied with his visit.

Madge gaped at Graham. 'Buy Stanton Brick Works, you?'

'Me,' Graham said.

'But . . . but how? I mean . . . where would you get that sort of money? He must be asking a fortune.'

'It's ridiculous,' stated John emphatically. 'All a load of pie in the sky.'

'It is not ridiculous or pie in the sky. I'm in deadly earnest about this,' Graham retorted.

'As your ma says, it would cost a fortune to buy a firm like Stanton's. Are you trying to tell us you've got a fortune tucked up your sleeve, eh?'

'I'm quite clever financially, and have made certain worthwhile investments over the past years,' Graham replied smoothly. 'If I liquidize my assets I can afford the brick works.'

'Liquidize your assets, what sort of talk is that from a son of mine?' John sneered.

'Business talk,' Graham answered quietly.

'Liquidize his assets,' John said, cruelly mimicking Graham. 'Ptah!'

'Well, I hope it comes off for you,' Jennie smiled, crossing the room and kissing Graham on the cheek.

'Thanks sis.'

'Are you sure you won't be borrowing money?' Madge asked fretfully. 'It would worry me to death if you were.'

'No borrowing, I promise you,' Graham assured her.

'Debt's a terrible thing,' she went on. Then, with a sideways glance at John, 'I should know.'

John had a sudden thought which made him sit bolt upright in his chair. 'Jesus Christ! If you buy this bloody firm that would make you a boss.' He spoke the word *boss* as though it was the foulest thing imaginable.

'That's right,' Graham said.

'Which would be awful. Disgraceful. John Forsyth's son a boss!'

'I'm sure you can live with the stigma, Dad,' Graham teased.

John glowered at him. 'None of your lip now. This is serious. You'll be turning traitor to your class. You'll be one of *them*.'

'True enough, Dad, though I think "traitor" is a bit harsh. But certainly I'll be one of them.'

John had gone white. He now shook with anger. 'I forbid it, you hear. I forbid it!'

311

'I'm sorry, Dad, but it's got nothing to do with you.'

'Oh yes it has!' cried John, jumping to his feet. 'For a start I'll not have a boss staying under my roof.'

'John!' Madge exclaimed in alarm. 'Don't say anything you'll regret later.'

'I'll not, you hear.'

Graham took a deep breath. He'd expected an outburst from his father, knowing John's deep-held beliefs and history, but not this. 'You want me to leave home, is that it?'

'No!' protested Jennie, appalled at that protest.

John wagged a finger at Graham. 'I won't have you shaming me and mine like this. So go you must.'

'Shame!' a livid Madge hissed. 'That's something you're well acquainted with, John Forsyth. And me, I can tell you.'

'Quiet woman.'

'No, you be quiet. How dare you! If anyone leaves this house it'll be you, not Graham.'

John put his hands on his hips. 'Is that so? Well, let me inform you here and now you'll never get me out. And that's a fact.'

'Leave it, Mum, I don't want to be the cause of a fight,' Graham said.

Madge's eyes were sparking with fury. 'Our son does well and all you can do is chuck him out of the house as a result? Then let me put it this way. If you insist on staying you can, but I go with Graham.'

John dropped his hands, and blinked.

'I mean it, I'll go with him.'

'And me,' Jennie added.

John glanced from Madge to Jennie, and saw they meant what they said.

Madge went on, her tone steely with a cutting edge to it, 'You haven't even got the decency to praise your own flesh and blood when he tries to succeed, and you know why? Because you're a born failure who's never amounted to anything in life, and never will.'

Madge went over to Graham and grasped him by the shoulders. 'I'm proud of you, son. Even if this doesn't work and you fall flat on your face, I'm still proud.'

'I won't fall flat on my face, Mum, I promise you.'

Tears came into her eyes. 'The owner of a firm, who would ever have thought that my son would achieve such a thing.'

'And I'm proud of you too,' Jennie stated, coming to stand beside them,

John made a noise at the back of his throat and sat down again. 'I just hope there won't be any redundancies and that it's a union shop,' he declared.

Graham didn't answer that. Instead he said to Madge and Jennie, 'Thanks.'

'You're certain you know what you're doing?' Madge asked in a quiet voice, her worry again coming to the surface.

Graham's reply was to smile and kiss Madge on the forehead, then he did the same to Jennie.

'What's for tea, I'm starving?' he said.

'Bloody capitalist,' John muttered darkly.

Madge felt like kicking John as she stalked past him.

'I'm impressed,' Kerensa said.

'I was rather hoping you'd be.'

They were in Dane's Wood where Graham had brought them for a Sunday afternoon walk.

'But how can you afford it? I thought you were a lorry driver. Has someone died and left you an inheritance?'

Graham laughed. 'No-one's died. I've simply been careful with my money and made some shrewd investments. There's no mystery about it.'

She gave him a sideways glance. 'They must have been very shrewd investments.'

'Oh, they were! You might say I'm talented in that direction.'

He took her hand as they passed under a huge oak that must have been several hundred years old. 'I've already

313

instructed a solicitor on the matter, and prior to that had an accountant go over the figures in case there was something I'd missed. There wasn't.'

'So when does it become yours?'

'Just as soon as the formalities can be completed. I knocked Stanton down on the price too. He wasn't exactly happy about that, but there you are. Business is business.'

'I'm beginning to see you in a new light,' she said.

He smiled. 'I've got big plans for the brick works. It's been ticking over for years, making a profit, but stagnant. Stanton has only been selling locally which is something, in time, I plan to change. I've made a lot of enquiries and it should be possible for me to sell not only county wide but throughout the entire south-west. It'll be a case of motivation and application, both of which I have in plenty.'

Kerensa stopped and turned to him. 'I'm so pleased for you, Graham.'

'Be pleased for *us*.'

She pulled him closer. 'I'm sure you'll make a go of it.'

'You can bet your boots I will. As I told you, one of the ingredients is motivation. And I think you know what mine is.'

'You're lovely,' she said.

'And you're gorgeous. That was what I thought of you the first time I saw you. Simply gorgeous.'

She kissed him lightly on the lips.

'What about friend Rupert, have you been out with him recently?' he asked.

'Not for a while.'

'Still using him as a blind though?'

'It's best that way. Keeps Daddy off my back.'

'I wish you'd tell your father about us.'

She stroked his cheek. 'I think I'll wait till you do own the brick works. That might change his attitude towards you.'

She hesitated, then said, 'I love my father, you do

314

appreciate that. The last thing in the world I want is to hurt him.'

'Maybe so, but at the end of the day you have to put your own happiness first. That's what common sense tells me to do. You might love him, but you also love me. And I most certainly love you. It'll all come right in the end, I promise.'

Kerensa fervently hoped that Graham was right.

John woke with a grunt, but didn't open his eyes. He'd been having such a lovely snooze. He started to drift off again.

'Wakey, wakey, Forsyth,' a voice said.

John was about to mutter to Madge to leave him alone, when it suddenly clicked that the voice wasn't Madge's. He stared up in horror at Staddon, the mine manager.

'Having a crafty doze, are we?' Staddon said quietly.

John scrambled to his feet. 'I, eh . . . I . . .' He trailed off when no plausible explanation sprang to mind.

Staddon took in the pile of sacking John had been stretched out on. Which gave the impression that it had been in that niche for a while. A niche in the rock tucked conveniently out of sight round a corner from a now seldom used side tunnel. Sacking that told him this wasn't a one off, but something John did regularly. His expression became grim in the extreme.

'Please,' John pleaded. 'Don't fire me. It's all a horrible mistake.'

'On your part,' Staddon replied.

'Please?' John further pleaded.

Staddon saw fear in John's face. And something he'd never seen there before, weakness. A great streak of it. He might dislike John personally, but at that moment he also felt sorry for him.

'Don't tell Sir Reginald,' John begged. 'That would certainly be the end for me.'

There was a long hiatus during which Staddon

considered the matter. 'See me at knocking off time,' he said eventually, and strode away.

John slumped where he stood, his mind numb. Knocking off time was hours away. And then what?

'Suspended for a fortnight, without pay,' Madge repeated.

John moved from one foot to the other, and didn't reply.

'Why?' Madge demanded harshly.

John murmured something incomprehensible.

'I said why?'

'A mistake on my part,' he prevaricated.

'What sort of mistake?'

'It's not important.'

'If I've to manage two weeks without your wage coming into the house it's important.'

John shrugged. 'Staddon's got a down on me. Always has had.'

'I don't believe that.'

'It's true!' John protested.

'I repeat, why?'

Damn, she wasn't letting up, John thought. 'It was just something I did, that's all.'

'What did you do?'

'Something he didn't like.' Then, full of bluster, 'You can't please everyone all the time. It's just not possible. And Staddon can be terribly demanding. Particularly if he doesn't like you.'

Madge was determined to get to the bottom of this. 'What was this something?'

'Nothing important.'

'*What*, for heaven's sake!' she shrieked.

John was totally taken aback. 'Sleeping.' The word slipped out before he'd realized it.

'Sleeping?' Madge queried, incredulous.

John recovered his wits. 'I wasn't feeling well, and lay down for a bit,' he lied. 'It was most unfortunate that Staddon found me.'

'Weren't feeling well?'

'Pain in my stomach.'

'So you lay down?'

'Only for a short while, until I felt better. And somehow I fell asleep.'

He was lying, she could read it in his face. 'But you feel all right now?'

He nodded. 'Whatever the problem it's completely disappeared.'

'So it was just unlucky that Staddon came upon you.'

John smiled uncertainly. 'That's right. Anyone else would have got away with a ticking off, but not yours truly. As I said, Staddon doesn't like me.'

'Has it in for you?'

'That's it.'

'Well, if he has,' Madge went on quietly and ominously, 'it's because he knows what you are. A slacker and wastrel. A good for nothing . . .'

'Here, wait a minute!' interjected John.

She fought to control herself. She wanted to fly at him, to pummel him, scratch his eyes out.

'Liar!' she accused. Then, so loudly it caused some cups and saucers on the draining board to rattle, she screamed, 'Liar!'

She rushed past John, grabbed her coat, and fled the house. A fortnight without wages! Graham would come to the rescue, but that wasn't the point. Going to sleep on the job! She could hardly believe it. He was lucky he hadn't been fired straight away.

She went to the Scotts intending to seek solace with Jane, but Jane was out. She'd gone to Exeter and hadn't returned yet.

'Is there anything I can do?' Tam asked, concerned.

She shook her head.

'Do you want to come in?'

'No, I won't bother. Thanks.'

She turned and made her way back up the road. She didn't want to go home yet, so she'd walk she decided.

317

Her mind was in turmoil, a combination of anger, self-pity and bitterness.

She strode through the night, not making for anywhere in particular. Just walking, thinking.

It was a little later that she suddenly realized she was close to George Rattenbury's cottage. And with that realization the heavens opened and rain bucketed down. It was a torrential downpour that would very soon soak her through.

She started to run, heading for the cottage, as that was the closest shelter. George answered almost immediately when she hammered on his door.

'The rain . . .' she began to explain, then George pulled her inside and shut the door behind her.

She fingered her hair which hung down limply. 'I feel like a drowned rat,' she said. 'It must be a cloud burst.'

'You might be right there, Madge,' answered George, glancing through a window. 'It's certainly pelting.'

She was suddenly embarrassed. 'I hope you don't mind me barging in on you like this?'

'No need to apologize,' he replied, holding up a meaty paw. 'You were caught short by the rain. I'm pleased you knocked. Now let's get you out of that wet coat, shall we?'

He helped her with her coat, which he hung on a nail behind the kitchen door. He then disappeared from the room to return with a towel. 'She's a bit rough, I'm afraid,' he said. 'But she'll do the job none the less.'

'Thank you, George,' she smiled, accepting the towel from him.

'Now I'll put the kettle on. I was just about to have a cup of cocoa myself. How about that?'

'Cocoa would be lovely.'

'There be tea if you wants it?'

'No, cocoa will be fine.'

He filled the kettle at the pump, then placed it on the range.

'Go closer to the range,' he urged. 'It's warmer there.'

318

She did, and enjoyed the waves of heat that washed over her. 'You wouldn't have a comb I could borrow?' she enquired.

He disappeared again. 'How be that?' he queried on his reappearance, handing her an old comb with several teeth missing.

'Will you take offence if I clean it first?' she asked with a smile.

'No, none at all.'

She washed it at the sink, as the comb badly needed cleaning. Then she ran it through her hair.

'Do you want a mirror? There's my shaving one.'

'That's unnecessary thank you.'

George had a thought. He took an old wooden chair and placed it before the range. Then he took her coat from behind the door and draped it over the chair. 'That's better,' he declared.

'You're being very kind.'

'Not at all! Nowhere near as kind as you were to me. I told you once you have a friend for life in George Rattenbury.'

Madge peered out the window and saw that the rain was still lashing down. 'If this keeps up there'll be flooding,' she predicted.

'That's a dead certainty if it's the same up Exmoor way,' George said.

'Would you like me to make the cocoa?' she offered when the kettle began to boil.

He studied her for a few moments, then nodded. 'If you care to, Madge. That would be nice.'

She was in the middle of making the cocoa when she thought of John, and the reason for her flying from the house. She trembled all over.

George was instantly by her side. 'Are 'ee cold, Madge? Shall I fetch a blanket for 'ee?'

'No, not cold,' she informed him. 'Just . . . angry I suppose.'

'Angry?'

'Very.' Should she tell him about John, or keep silent on the subject. It would be disloyal of her to speak about John behind his back. But she'd been going to do just that with Jane if Jane had been in, and since when had John ever merited loyalty?

In a faltering voice she told George about the incident at Wheal Tempest, and of her relationship with John in general. George listened in silence.

'I see,' he said when she was finally finished.

'There are times, George, when I totally despair, despair so deep it's a bottomless pit.'

'He certainly appears to have caused you a great deal of unhappiness,' George sympathized.

'You can say that again.'

'But at least he's given you two fine, upstanding children.'

Madge smiled at George. 'That's how I look at it. That's the bright side of our marriage.'

She sipped her cocoa, and suddenly began to cry, overwhelmed by all manner of emotions.

George placed his cup and saucer on the table and hurried from the kitchen. When he came back he was carrying a large, clean white handkerchief.

'Here, try this for thae tears,' he said softly to Madge, handing her the hanky.

'Thank you,' she sobbed.

George remained standing beside her while she dabbed at her eyes. And as she dabbed she became very much aware of his physical presence, the sheer potency of the man. He smelled of the earth, and masculinity, a most attractive sensual combination, she thought.

She gazed at him through misty eyes, and he stared back. She didn't know how it happened, but one moment they were apart, the next she was in his arms, his mouth on hers.

She resisted fractionally, then let herself go, moulding herself against George, kissing him as eagerly, and passionately, as he kissed her.

320

Her insides flamed, and she felt more alive than she'd done in years.

Madge lay listening to the rain drumming against the roof, and spattering against the window. It was over an hour since she'd arrived at George's cottage, and still the downpour continued. Beside her George snored gently.

She wouldn't have believed she would have made love to George, but she had and enjoyed every glorious minute of it. She sighed with contentment, her body satiated.

She smiled at the memory of his hands, rough, calloused hands that could easily have been unpleasant, but had been quite the opposite. Hands that had touched and caressed her as tenderly as a mother would a new-born babe.

Did she feel any guilt? Not a shred of it, she decided. That surprised her somewhat, for she was a married woman after all, and an extremely moral person. She was someone, no matter how the marriage had turned out, who'd taken her marriage vows very seriously indeed.

She stretched, putting her arms above her head, and yawned. Then she snuggled further down under the bedclothes, and turned to face George.

He ceased snoring, and his eyes blinked open. He smiled at her. 'How are 'ee?'

'Couldn't be better.'

'No regrets?'

'None whatever. You?'

'Same.'

'I suppose this makes me one of the infamous George Rattenbury's conquests,' she teased.

His smile vanished. 'Don't say that, Madge, not even in jest. I thinks too highly of you for that.'

She believed him for his voice had rung with sincerity and truth. Reaching out under the clothes she stroked his protruding hairy belly.

'That tickles,' he said.

She continued stroking.

'Torture is it?' he joked.

She laughed.

He became serious again. 'You and I gets on right well together, Madge.'

'I agree.'

He covered her hand with his own. 'Will you be coming back here again?'

'Do you want me to?'

'I does. Very much.'

'Then I'll come back, George.'

'That pleases me greatly, Madge.'

The prospect pleased her too. 'I've got a confession to make.'

'What's that?'

'I've got stretch marks and a droopy bottom.'

Now it was his turn to laugh, a low rumble in his chest. 'Can't say I noticed. Nor do I particularly care. As far as I'm concerned you're absolutely perfect. Perfect as a flower or a golden sunrise.'

'Why George!' she exclaimed. 'That's quite poetic.'

'I has my moments,' he replied.

'Oh, you certainly do that,' she breathed.

He smiled, knowing what she meant. 'Do you have to rush off?'

She thought about that. 'No.'

'Good.'

He drew her to him, enveloping her in his arms, arms she felt she belonged in, arms that weren't strangers, but she might have known all her life.

Her and George Rattenbury, who would have thought!

Graham drove the Lanchester in through the wrought-iron gates of the Stanton Brick Works and parked where Gerald Stanton had parked his car. He'd considered changing the name to the Forsyth Brick Works, but for various reasons had decided against that, although it was a decision he might reverse in the future. It was his first day at the works as owner and boss.

He got out of the car, and locked it. Holding his attaché case he stared at the building before him, and smiled with satisfaction.

He had a great many plans for the firm, but wouldn't implement any of them until he'd found his feet. He didn't want to go rushing in like a bull in a china shop.

Miss Pritchard was waiting for him inside. 'Mr Stanton always had a cup of tea on his arrival. Would you like one?' she asked.

'Not for me,' Graham replied.

She followed him into what was now his office. 'Is there anything I can do for you, Mr Forsyth?'

He considered that. 'Yes, there is. Explain and show to me where everything in the office is located.'

'Of course.'

That took about ten minutes, at the end of which Graham knew where everything was kept. He dismissed Miss Pritchard then who returned to her own office which was no more than a glorified cubbyhole containing a desk, a typewriter and a filing cabinet.

A little later Graham left his office and headed for the plant, determined to talk to the foreman. While making his way through the plant he ran into Danny Green.

'Hello, Graham. Big day for you, eh?'

Graham stopped and looked at Danny, his expression neutral. 'While at work it's *Mr Forsyth* from here on in Danny,' he replied mildly, but authoritatively.

Danny's broad smile vanished. He nodded. 'I understand, Gr . . . Mr Forsyth.'

'You can pass that around the workforce.'

'I'll do that, Mr Forsyth.'

'Fine. Carry on then.'

He gave the same instruction to Norman Butt, the foreman, when they finished their introductory conversation.

That done Graham returned to his office where he began going through the files, drawing up a list of customers he intended to write to, and to visit in person along with the company rep.

It was gone 9 p.m. when the door to Graham's office opened to reveal Kerensa.

He glanced up from some papers he was poring over. 'This is a pleasant surprise,' he smiled.

'You said you'd been working late recently, so I thought I'd stop by, say hello if you were here, and be given a guided tour.'

'I'll enjoy that,' he replied, coming to his feet.

He went towards her and kissed her lightly on the mouth. 'Just what the doctor ordered,' he joked.

'You look tired.'

'I am, dead beat. There's just so much to do and so few hours per day in which to do it.'

'Let's forget the guided tour. I think you should go home to bed. Have you had any food?'

'A couple of sandwiches at lunch-time.'

'Naughty!' she admonished.

'Mum will give me something when I get back. She's good that way, never any complaints. And we won't forget the guided tour, it's well overdue.'

He sat on his desk and took her hands in his. 'How much do you earn?' he asked.

She raised an eyebrow, and named a monthly sum.

'I'll better that if you'll come and work for me.'

'For you!'

'As my secretary. Miss Pritchard is a good soul, but I think she feels that now Stanton's left and I am settled in, she'd like to retire. I know she's a very keen gardener and would enjoy spending some more time developing her patch. And don't forget, I told you once that if I ever needed a secretary I'd employ you. Well, now I do.'

He smiled. 'Just think of the advantages. I'd get to see you all day long, and you me. What could be better?'

324

'I don't know,' Kerensa said slowly.

'What don't you know?'

'There's the adage about familiarity breeding contempt?'

'Nonsense, in our case that is.'

'And what if we were to fall out over something?'

'Married people do that all the time, and get over it. So, what's the difference?'

She could see how keen he was. And truthfully, now it had been mooted wasn't she just as keen? She was only putting up an argument to give herself time to think.

'I'll be devastated if you refuse,' he said. 'So devastated in fact I might well cry. A real boo hoo!'

She laughed. 'Don't be an idiot.'

'That's what I feel like when I'm with you, a raving idiot. Love does that to a man.'

'Fool.'

'It makes him that as well.'

'You're incorrigible!'

'And you're beautiful, and gorgeous, and I still can't believe how lucky I am to have met you and fallen in love with you. And more importantly, you with me.'

'Are there any perks with this job?' she asked.

'Yes, me.'

She laughed again. 'Besides that?'

'What sort of perks would you like?'

'I don't know. Tempt me.'

'Regular lunches with the boss?'

'Sandwiches in the office?' she teased.

'There's always the pub. And I'm sure we can get into Exeter from time to time and go to a restaurant.'

'What else?'

'Whatever you wish, within reason. Now I can't say fairer than that.'

'Then it's a deal,' she agreed.

'When can you start?'

'I'll have to give a month's notice.'

He pulled a face.

'I insist on doing that.'

'All right. So be it.'

'And you are sure about poor Miss Pritchard?'

'Quite sure. We've already had a long conversation about her feelings; she doesn't want to let me down, but feels that now is an opportune time to leave. She's got tremendous plans for her garden, so don't worry.'

Kerensa kissed Graham, and he kissed her back. 'Now the guided tour,' he said.

'You don't have to!' she protested.

'I insist.'

They left his office arm in arm.

'A new job,' Anthony Sturt repeated, nodding his head. 'Interesting.'

'With more money.'

'That's useful.'

'Considerably more,' she spelled out, for Graham had been most generous.

'Better still,' Anthony smiled. 'And who exactly is this company?'

'The Stanton Brick Works in Sanford Barton. I'm to be the owner's secretary.'

'I see,' Anthony replied. 'How did you hear of this job?'

The moment Kerensa had been dreading had finally arrived. She hated having to upset her father, but there was no other way. The truth had to out at last. 'I know the owner very well. In fact, we've been seeing one another for a while now.'

Anthony stared at her in blank astonishment. 'I beg your pardon?'

'I said, I know the owner very well and have been seeing him for some while,' she repeated.

'But I thought . . . What about Rupert?'

'I have gone out with Rupert a number of times also. But there's no romance there.'

'And there is between you and this owner chappie?'

Kerensa nodded. 'You've met him actually. Graham Forsyth, he came to the house once. The day after last summer's church fête which is where we met.'

Anthony's face clouded with anger. 'I remember the fellow. Lorry driver, wasn't he?'

'Then he was. Now he owns the Stanton Brick Works.'

'Owns it? How did he manage that?'

'By saving and investing. He's fairly shrewd at investing apparently.'

'And you've been seeing him?'

'Yes, Daddy.'

'Without my being aware?'

'I knew it would anger you,' she confessed.

Anthony rose to his feet and began pacing up and down. He was furious, having believed everything was going swimmingly between Kerensa and Rupert. This was awful, simply awful.

'Don't you think you've been extremely deceitful, young lady?' he chided.

'I can't deny that,' she replied.

'I'm terribly disappointed. Terribly.'

She didn't answer that.

'Why, that man's father works at Wheal Tempest for Sir Reginald and came down here originally as a strike breaker. The family are as common as muck.'

'Aren't you being a snob, Daddy? And if I may say so, rather pompous.'

'Snob perhaps, pompous never. Dammit all, Kerensa, we have a position in society to uphold. There are certain standards that must be maintained. And that means you can't run around with riff-raff, no matter what misguided reason you might have.'

'Graham is not riff-raff,' Kerensa replied coldly. 'He's a lovely, sweet man whom I've become very fond of. And he of me.'

'I'll bet he has!' Anthony exclaimed. 'Can't you see the chap's a social climber. He's using you to try and advance himself, that's all. Well, it's just not on. I've seen through his little game.'

'He's not a social climber, nor is there any game to see through,' Kerensa retorted.

'He may have pulled the wool over your eyes, but he hasn't mine. Knew the type the moment I saw him. He's trying to take advantage of you. You mark my words, young lady.'

'He's nothing of the sort, Daddy, I can assure you.'

'You may think you know it all at your age, Kerensa, but you don't. You still have a great deal to learn.'

Anthony smacked a fist into the palm of his other hand. 'It's the deceit that hurts more than anything.'

'I knew you wouldn't approve, and there was what was thought to be your heart condition to be considered at the time,' she answered.

'So you were really thinking of *me*,' he replied sarcastically.

Kerensa rose. 'I'd better be getting on now.'

'On no you don't, I'm not finished yet!' Anthony cried. He pointed a finger at her. 'I absolutely forbid you to see this Forsyth chap ever again. Do you hear?'

'But I'm going to work for him.'

'You won't take the job. You can write and inform him of that. But as from this moment you and he are finished. That's my final word on the matter.'

She forced herself to count to three. 'You can't tell me what to do any more, Daddy, or force me to do something against my will. Surely you understand that?'

'Oh yes I can!'

'I shall continue to see Graham, and I shall take the job he's offered me.'

'You will not! And if things aren't working out between you and Rupert as I'd hoped, then we'll simply find someone more suitable, someone of our class and breeding.'

'With money,' she stated. Now she was being sarcastic.

'I can't deny that would be useful,' Anthony acknowledged.

She thought of Graham, and the love she felt for him, then of the love she had for her father. What was it Graham had said? At the end of the day she had to put her own happiness first. Yes, that was it. And he was right, she knew so instinctively. That was what common sense told her to do.

Kerensa drew in a deep breath. 'Don't make me choose between you, Daddy. I'd hate to do that.'

Anthony's eyes narrowed. 'You mean you'd choose him?'

'I love you, Daddy, but I also have my own life to think about. And I will do what I consider right and best, not what I'm ordered to do by a parent.'

She decided on a parting shot. 'I don't have to stay at Corfe Mullen you know. I can always rent accommodation in Exeter if I have to.'

Kerensa then walked from the room, leaving Anthony, upset and contemplative, behind her.

'Do you fancy a pint, son?' John asked Graham.

Graham stared up at his father, it was a rare event for John to propose they go to the pub together. 'You mean you're broke,' he replied, reaching into his pocket.

'No, no!' John protested. 'I've got money. In fact it's my intention to treat you. So, what about it, eh?'

He wouldn't mind a pint, Graham thought.

'You aren't busy, are you?' John queried.

Graham shook his head. 'Not at all.'

'Well, come on then!'

Madge glanced over from the sink where she was washing the dishes. 'On you go,' she urged Graham. 'It will get the pair of you out from under my feet for a spell.'

That settled it. 'All right,' he declared, rising from his chair.

John beamed, and mentally rubbed his hands.

Going into the pub John instructed Graham to take a seat while he went up to the bar. He rejoined Graham carrying a pint of best and another of scrumpy.

Graham frowned. 'I thought Mum had warned you off the cider?'

John gave him a wink. 'It's a lot cheaper than beer. And what your mum doesn't know won't hurt her. You won't let on, will you son?'

'I suppose not,' Graham replied quietly.

'Cheers!' toasted John, lifting his glass.

'Cheers!' Graham responded, and they both had a draught of their respective pints.

'How's the firm doing?' John asked.

'Fine.'

'Everything running smoothly?'

Graham nodded.

'That's good then.'

'And how are things at Wheal Tempest?' Graham enquired politely.

John screwed up his face. 'That man Staddon has it in for me. He makes life very difficult. I never seem to be able to do anything right for the sod.'

Graham didn't comment on that, knowing Staddon to be generally well liked and respected as mine manager. He had a name for being fair. So if he had a down on John there was a reason for it.

'Regarding your foreman, what's your opinion of him?' John asked.

It was a question which surprised Graham. 'Norman Butt? Extremely competent. I've no complaints there.'

John grunted.

'Why do you ask about him in particular?'

'Oh, I was just thinking . . . I could do that job.'

Graham's eyebrows shot up. 'You?'

'I'd make a grand foreman. And being your father I'd be sure to look after your interests. Get the best out of the men. So what do you say?'

Graham now understood why he'd been invited to the

pub. He was flabbergasted. 'I've just told you that I'm pleased with Norman.'

'I heard you. But none the less, what about me replacing him? It would mean more money coming into the house which would go down well with your mother. Maybe that's how you should look at it, doing your mother a favour.'

Graham had another swig of his pint.

'Well?' John prompted.

'The answer's no.'

'Why the hell not?'

Graham regarded his father, thinking John had aged quite a bit of late. Strange he hadn't noticed it before. 'I'd rather not answer that if you don't mind.'

'But I want you to. Why the hell not? I'd make a cracking foreman, and one you could trust implicitly. Surely you must see that?'

'I see nothing of the sort.'

'You owe me,' John stated.

Graham sat back in his seat. 'For what?'

'I'm your father after all. If it hadn't been for me you wouldn't be where you are today.'

Graham wanted to laugh at the absurdity of that. It was too ridiculous for words. 'I'm where I am because of myself and my own efforts. You had absolutely nothing to do with it.'

'There's gratitude for you,' John complained, genuinely miffed.

'Nothing at all,' Graham emphasized.

'I brought you to Devon, didn't I?'

'At Mum's instigation and insistence. As I recall you didn't want to come. You wanted to stay on in Glasgow.'

'Aye, well . . .' John trailed off, and shrugged. 'You still owe me.'

'I owe you nothing, Father. Except for the part you played in helping to bring me into the world, that is.'

John reached over and grasped Graham's hand. 'Please son? The foreman's job would be a big thing for me. Perhaps redeem me a little in your mother's eyes.'

There was that, Graham thought.

'Please.'

Graham moved his hand. 'No, Father. I don't want you working for me. Not as foreman or in any other capacity.'

'But why?'

'I think your record stands for itself, don't you?'

'What record?' John demanded hotly.

'Sleeping during working hours for a start.'

'I wasn't feeling well. I lay down to ease the pain, and somehow fell asleep. I told your mother that. Anyone else would have got away with a ticking off, but not me. Thanks to that swine Staddon.'

Graham didn't want any more beer. He pushed his glass aside. 'I'm going back,' he said.

'I never thought I'd see the day when my own son would turn against me,' John grumbled.

'I'm not turning against you. I'm simply refusing to give you a job, that's all.'

'Same difference.'

Graham went up to the bar and ordered another pint for his father.

'Are you sure you won't reconsider?' John asked, joining him there.

'I'm sure.'

Graham started for the door, only to be stopped by John who grabbed hold of his arm. 'And there'll be no mention of the scrumpy to your ma?'

A real sad case, Graham thought. That's what his old man had turned into, a real sad case. 'No mention, I promise.'

'All right then.'

Graham returned home where he explained to Madge why John had asked him out for a drink.

'Foreman!' Madge exploded. 'That would be the worst mistake of your life.'

'I know that, Mum.'

'He's only after the job because he thinks it's easier than the one he has now. Bossing folk around, getting others to do the work, would be right up your father's street. Of all the cheek!'

'I won't be replacing Norman Butt in a hurry I can tell you.'

'Foreman!' Madge repeated, shaking her head. 'He'd be a total disaster.'

Graham couldn't have agreed more. Neither he nor his mother had any illusions about John.

He wasn't exactly nervous, more apprehensive, Graham thought, as he pulled the brass knob by the side of the Sturt's front door. This was his second visit to Corfe Mullen. He was calling for Kerensa whom he was taking out for the evening.

Kerensa answered. 'Hello,' she smiled.

He pecked her on the cheek. 'Your father home?'

'In the drawing-room,' she replied.

Graham stepped inside, and Kerensa shut the door behind him. 'What's his mood?' Graham asked.

She made a face.

'I see.'

'You don't have to speak to him if you don't wish. But it would be better.'

'Lead on Macduff,' Graham instructed.

She took him into the same shabby drawing-room he remembered from before. Anthony Sturt was sitting reading a book, a glass of whisky on the table beside him. He glanced up at Graham as he walked into the room, and glared at him.

'Good evening, sir.'

'Come to take Kerensa out I'm told,' Anthony replied, his cold tone one of disapproval.

'That's correct, sir.'

'Hmm!'

'I'll fetch my coat. Shan't be a minute,' Kerensa said, and left Graham and Anthony.

'I don't wish to sound rude but you do know I'm dead set against this relationship,' Anthony said.

'So I understand, sir. And I'm sorry about that.'

Anthony stared at Graham. It wouldn't last between them, he told himself, given time it was bound to fall apart. After all, they came from two entirely different worlds. No, Kerensa would see sense eventually, he was certain of that.

'I believe you've bought a brick works,' Anthony said.

'Yes, sir.'

'Admirable achievement,' Anthony grudgingly acknowledged.

'Thank you, sir.'

'Accrued the capital through investments?'

Graham became wary, hoping he wasn't going to be quizzed on the investments supposedly in question. 'That's correct.'

Anthony murmured, 'Played the market myself a while back.'

Graham recalled the railway and mining shares Kerensa had once mentioned, and decided not to reply to that.

'With less success than you've had I have to admit.'

'Bad luck, sir,' Graham commiserated.

Graham watched Anthony sip his glass of whisky. He wasn't offered one.

He glanced about, taking in the room. It really could have done with total refurbishment. The carpet, he noted, was threadbare in places.

Kerensa reappeared wearing a bright smile. 'I'm ready,' she declared.

'We'll be off then,' Graham said.

'Don't be too late,' Anthony warned.

'We won't be,' Graham assured him.

Kerensa went to her father and kissed him on the forehead. 'See you later if you're still up, Daddy.'

'I will be.'

'Good night, sir,' Graham said.

The reply to that was a grunt as Anthony returned to his book.

'Trollope,' Kerensa declared outside, when the door was shut behind them.

'I beg your pardon?'

'Daddy was reading Trollope whom he adores. Have you ever read him?'

'A little, years ago. Not my taste at all.'

Graham assisted Kerensa into the Lanchester, then got in himself. He glanced at Corfe Mullen, wondering if Anthony was watching their departure. As far as he could make out Anthony wasn't.

'How was it?' Kerensa queried.

'Like trying to walk through sticky treacle.'

She laughed. 'Was he nasty to you?'

'Not really. Though he did say he was dead set against our relationship.'

'He'll come round eventually, you'll see.'

Hopefully he would, Graham thought. Not that it mattered for him, but it did for Kerensa.

'Love you,' Graham stated softly, and kissed Kerensa on the lips.

'And I love you.'

He smiled to hear that. He experienced the most incredible feeling every time she declared her love for him. It was as though he was filled with rainbows, and sunshine, and a million birds were singing.

'Where shall we go?' he asked as they drove away, for that hadn't been decided.

As far as he was concerned Graham didn't care in the least where they went. He was happy to do or go anywhere. The important thing was that he was with Kerensa, that was simply everything.

Graham concluded his speech, picked up the gold watch from the table in front of him, turned and presented it to Harry Bury who was retiring that week after thirty-five years with the company.

Graham and the others present clapped when a misty-eyed Harry accepted the watch. Graham then sat down while Harry made a short speech of thanks and recollections.

Norman Butt came up to Graham a little later when refreshments were being taken. 'I thought that passed off very nicely, Mr Forsyth,' he said.

'Yes, I thought so, too.'

'Good man, Harry. I'll be sorry to lose him.'

Graham sipped his tea, and wondered where Kerensa was. She'd been there only a few moments ago.

'So, when are you taking on Harry's replacement?' Norman asked.

'There won't be a replacement,' Graham replied quietly.

Norman frowned. 'I don't understand?'

'There won't be a replacement, Norman,' Graham repeated.

'I see,' Norman mused.

'That's not all,' Graham went on. 'There not only won't be a replacement but I shall still expect the same level of output, which means everyone having to work that bit harder.'

Norman became grim-faced.

'The men are quite capable of it. I'm not asking the impossible,' Graham went on. Far from it, he thought. There was a great deal of slackness in the firm's work practices, a slackness he fully intended to eradicate.

'They won't like it, Mr Forsyth.'

'It doesn't matter whether they do or not. That's my decision. Starting next week productivity per man will have to be increased, and not by overtime either. I was going to speak to you about this later, but now's as good a time as any.' He spotted Kerensa and waved. She waved back.

'Any questions?'

'None, Mr Forsyth. What you've said is quite clear.'

'Good.'

And with that Graham terminated the conversation with his foreman.

Kerensa popped her head round Graham's office door. 'Mr Butt's here to see you,' she said.

'Send him right in.'

Norman Butt entered the office holding his cap in one hand. 'You wanted a word?' he said.

'I do.' Graham indicated a chair,

'I prefer to stand, Mr Forsyth.'

'Fine.'

Graham gazed at the papers before him, then up again at Norman Butt. 'I've been looking over Terry Hepton-stall's attendance record. It isn't good at all.'

'Easily explained, Mr Forsyth. Terry suffers from asthma.'

'Does he now!' Graham affected surprise, but it was something he already knew.

'He's off regular, but more so in the winter when the weather's bad. He's a hostage to his asthma is Terry.'

'He's seen the doctor I take it?'

'Often.'

'And there's no cure?'

'None, Mr Forsyth. When Terry comes down with the asthma all he can do is go to bed and wait for it to pass.'

'During which time we pay him.'

'That's so, Mr Forsyth. Terry always gets his full wage.'

'Well I think the time has come to reassess his position. I'm running a business here, Norman, not a charity for lame ducks. I appreciate Terry has a problem, but I cannot afford to suffer financially because of it. I understand that even when Terry's here he doesn't always pull his weight – he's been caught leaving early and allowing others to cover for him on a number of occasions. I need to turn Stanton's into a viable financial business and I simply cannot carry any dead wood. I want you to give him a month's notice.'

'A month's . . .' Norman whispered, unable to believe his ears.

'That's right.'

'But you can't, Mr Forsyth.'

'Why not?'

'Terry's a married man with a boy and a maid. And his wife is expecting yet again.'

Graham had known all of that also. 'One way or another Terry seems fond of his bed,' he commented drily.

'Oh, he's genuine with the asthma, Mr Forsyth. I can assure you of that.'

'None the less, it's still a month's notice. I feel sorry for him, but it is more than my business is worth to keep him on.'

Norman twisted his cap in his hands. 'If you say so, Mr Forsyth. But it's the most unenviable task I'll have in telling him.'

'I can do that if you wish,' Graham stated.

Norman considered the offer. 'No, it's my position as foreman to do so. So do it I will. Now what about a replacement?'

Graham shook his head. 'No replacement.'

'But that means we'll be short two men!' Norman protested.

'One and a half, as Heptonstall was only ever here half the time. If that.'

'Even so Mr Forsyth.'

Graham gazed at Norman, wondering whether to say what he planned or not. He decided he would. 'In my opinion the workforce at Stanton's can do with slimming down, which I fully intend to see happen. Nine men could easily achieve the output we're currently producing.'

'Nine!' Norman exclaimed.

'*Easily*,' Graham emphasized. 'And you may repeat that to the workforce, it might serve as an incentive to them.'

Norman nodded. 'I'll do that.'

'Stanton's is a good firm, Norman, but a very inefficient one. Something I shall be changing. Now good-day to you.'

Kerensa came into the office when Norman had gone. 'He looked like he'd lost a pound and found a sixpence,' she said.

'I've fired Heptonstall,' Graham informed her.

'So that was what it was all about.'

'And there are a couple more I have my eye on,' he added.

'But I thought you planned to expand?'

'And so I do. But before that happens I want to change the attitude of the men. They're basically a decent bunch, but not the hardest of workers. Stanton let them get away with murder. It's my plan to make the company leaner and fitter by cutting out the dead wood.'

'I see,' Kerensa said.

'Now I wish you to place an advertisement in the *Western Morning News* for me. I need a new sales rep.'

'To join forces with Jack Marsden?' she queried. Marsden was their existing sales rep.

Graham shook his head. 'I'm not at all satisfied with Marsden's performance so I'm sacking him.'

'There's quite a ruthless streak in you, isn't there?' she teased.

'I suppose there is, if you view it that way. I prefer to look on myself as someone who does his best and who expects the same from others in his employ.'

'In other words you want your money's worth.'

Graham laughed. 'That's one way of putting it. It must be the Scotsman in me.'

He was going to make a big success of the brick works, Kerensa thought, she just knew it. 'I'll write out and place that ad for you. Do you want to see it before it goes off to the *News*?'

'Nope. I'm sure it will be satisfactory.'

As she was walking out of the door he stopped her. 'Kerensa!' She turned and faced him.

'I've decided that office of yours is far too small. I'm going to have this one enlarged and sectioned so that your office will be adjacent to mine. What do you think of that?'

'That way I'm even physically closer to you?'

'Exactly,' he smiled.

She, too, was smiling as she closed the door behind her.

'You sacked a man for having asthma!' exclaimed John, incredulous.

Graham was enjoying the fish Madge had served up for tea. It was cod landed that very morning at Brixham. 'That's correct,' he replied.

'But the chap's married with children, his wife expecting another.'

'He's also been costing the company a fortune by his chronic absenteeism.'

'Legitimate illness, Graham!' John protested.

'Legitimate maybe, but I also know that he was using his asthma as an excuse to skive off on occasion. He used to leave early and expect the others to cover for him.'

'Can you prove that?' John queried.

Graham shook his head. 'No, I can't. But that doesn't matter. Even when Heptonstall was at work he wasn't up to scratch. And so I've got rid of him.'

'Well, I think it's disgusting,' John went on. 'Heartless, cruel of you. That poor woman and her children, what will they do now?'

'That's Heptonstall's problem, not mine,' Graham replied quietly.

'You've become hard, Graham, hard as stone, and a typical boss.'

Graham placed his knife and fork together on his plate. He'd suddenly lost his appetite. 'Do you think I did wrong?' he asked Madge.

Madge took her time in replying. 'On the surface it does seem harsh. But there again, it is your firm and you're the one subsidizing the man's illness and supposed malingering.'

'Precisely,' Graham replied. 'Of course I'm sorry about his wife and children, and the fact she's pregnant. But none the less I'm not prepared to continue shelling out for little return. Perhaps I might have taken a different attitude if I hadn't been convinced the man was using his illness to skive off, but I doubt it. His skiving merely made my decision easier.'

'Skiving you can't prove!' John declared hotly.

Graham regarded his father. 'No, neither I nor my foreman have been fortunate enough to find him asleep on the job if that's what you mean.'

John went beetroot red.

'Maybe I should have called in your assistance, after all you're an expert on the subject by all accounts,' Graham further jibed.

Madge wanted to laugh, but didn't. John meanwhile looked as though he was going to explode. Jennie dropped her head and stared at her lap so that no-one saw the smile on her face.

'Lovely fish, Mum,' said Graham, rising.

'There's treacle tart to follow.'

'Not for me thanks, I've had enough.'

Graham went up to his room where he lay on his bed. Sacking Heptonstall hadn't been an easy decision, but he'd thought deeply about it. He was convinced the man was taking advantage, and that was what had sealed Heptonstall's fate.

He did feel for Mrs Heptonstall and her children, but as he'd said to Norman Butt, he wasn't a charity.

He put Heptonstall from his mind and thought about the advertisement Kerensa had placed in the *Western Morning News* which would appear in the following day's edition.

He wondered how many replies he'd get, and hoped

he'd find someone suitable among them. What he wanted was a live wire, a chap with plenty of motivation.

Of one thing he was determined, he was going to put the Stanton Brick Works on the map. His initial enthusiasm might have started out as purely financial, but now it included Kerensa.

He knew she loved him. He also wanted her to be proud of him.

'There's a girl I'd like you to meet, Mum. I thought I might bring her home to tea one night?'

Madge stopped what she was doing to stare at Graham. 'A girl you say?'

He nodded. 'Her name's Kerensa Sturt.'

'I had no idea you were courting?'

'Kerensa and I have been seeing one another for some while now. I met her at the church fête last year. She lives in Poltiham.'

'Sturt?' Madge mused. 'The name isn't familiar.'

'They own a house called Corfe Mullen. She and her father that is, her mother's dead.'

'And what does this Kerensa do?'

'She recently became my secretary.'

Madge raised an eyebrow. 'Your secretary, eh? Who's idea was that?'

'Mine.'

'I take it you're fond of this girl as you've never brought one home before?'

'I am,' he confessed.

'And is she fond of you?'

'Very.'

'I see,' Madge murmured. 'And you've been seeing her for some while. Why no mention of her before this? Why the secrecy?'

'I don't know, all sorts of reasons I suppose. However, I want you to meet her now. Maybe you'll make something special?'

'How about this Friday night?' Madge suggested.

'Fine. I know she's free.'

'I'll expect her Friday then.'

Graham went to his mother and kissed her on the cheek. 'Thanks, Mum.'

This had to be important, Madge thought. As she'd said Graham had never previously brought a lass home. She was intrigued, and couldn't wait to make Kerensa's acquaintance.

Something special? What could she cook to fill that bill, she wondered.

'Have some more wine, Kerensa?' John gushed. Graham had provided the wine which he'd bought from a vintners in Exeter.

'Not for me, thank you,' Kerensa replied, placing a hand over the top of her glass.

Graham was irritated by his father who'd fawned over Kerensa from the moment he'd discovered she was a 'toff'. Graham daren't think what Kerensa was making of John. She probably thought he was a right creep.

'And your father doesn't work,' John went on. 'It's all right for some, eh!' And having said that, he laughed, a laugh that was both raucous and too loud.

Graham winced.

'Are you enjoying being at Stanton's?' Madge asked, deliberately taking the conversation away from John whom she, too, wished would shut up. She considered that he was making a right fool of himself.

'Very much so, Mrs Forsyth.'

'And you lived in London for a while you briefly mentioned earlier?'

The Forsyths listened politely as Kerensa spoke of London, her job and friends there, the places she'd been, sights she'd seen.

'Did you ever get to the palace?' John asked. 'I mean, go inside, that is.'

'No, I'm afraid not.'

'But you must have been to many posh dos. Real glitzy affairs?'

Kerensa smiled. 'A number I suppose, yes.'

'And met lots of lords and ladies?'

Graham silently groaned.

'A few.'

'You look like a lady yourself. You could well be Lady so and so,' John said.

Jennie, who'd recognized Kerensa from when she'd called to enquire about Graham, was thinking how pretty Kerensa was. Nor had she failed to notice how Graham seldom took his eyes off her. It was definitely love, she thought, and was pleased for Graham. An image of Andy Alford momentarily crossed her mind, which caused her to frown. What an upsetting experience that had been. But it was now in the past.

'Graham has told me you're at night school,' Kerensa said to Jennie.

'That's right.'

'I admire you. Are you finding it difficult?'

'Not a bit of it,' John cut in. 'She's got brains, our Jennie. A head full of them.'

'So too has Graham, who's doing well for himself,' Madge stated quietly.

'I just wish . . .' John started to say, then stopped when Madge shot him a withering look. She'd correctly guessed that John was going to make some remark about Graham being an owner and boss. He'd been strictly warned before Kerensa's arrival not to talk about politics or related subjects.

Kerensa finished her main course, and wiped her mouth with a napkin. 'That was delicious. Thank you,' she said to Madge.

Graham was delighted with the meal Madge had prepared; saddle of lamb with vegetables – an English classic.

John drained his glass and reached again for the wine

bottle, earning him another reproving look from Madge who'd also warned him not to get drunk.

John pretended not to notice and refilled his glass. 'Good stuff this,' he declared jocularly. 'Not my usual tipple mind, but it goes down nicely all the same.'

'Do you have a career in mind for when you finish night school?' Kerensa asked Jennie.

'Not yet,' Jennie lied.

Madge rose from the table. 'I'll get the sweet,' she announced.

'Want me to help?' Jennie offered.

'No need for that, thanks.'

When Madge returned she was carrying a chocolate sponge pudding in chocolate sauce and a lemon soufflé.

Kerensa's eyes lit up. 'Yummy!' she exclaimed. 'I'm going to have some of each.'

God, he loved her, Graham thought.

'Have you heard this one?' John said to Kerensa. He then launched into a joke that fell absolutely flat.

Graham silently groaned again.

'I'm sorry about that,' Graham apologized to Kerensa as they drove away.

She laughed. 'It wasn't so bad.'

'Dad was dreadful.'

'I must say I did find him a bit much at times. But your mother was charming, as was your sister. I liked them both a great deal.'

'I'm glad about that.'

'Now it's my turn to invite you to our house for dinner.'

'Won't your father object?'

'He can try,' Kerensa said softly, 'but it won't do him any good.'

'Well, what did you think?' Graham asked Madge when he arrived home.

'A very pleasant lass.'

'I thought she was terrific,' said Jennie. 'And weren't the sparks flying between you two?'

Graham blushed slightly. 'We do get on well together. I can't deny it.'

'I thought her very nice too,' John said from his chair by the fire. 'But quite unsuitable.'

'Dad!' Jennie exclaimed. 'That's tosh.'

'It isn't tosh at all,' John went on. 'She is quite unsuitable. Look at her background, big house, private education. No, no, she's not for such as you, lad. Nor you for her.'

'She and I have discussed that at length,' Graham retorted. 'And the fact that we come from different backgrounds doesn't matter.'

'Then the pair of you are deluding yourselves. Mark my words if you aren't.'

'What about this father of hers? What does he think of the pair of you?' Madge asked hesitantly.

'He's dead set against our relationship.'

'There you are then!' said John. 'Wise man.'

'The difference between you is a consideration,' Madge said quietly.

'Nothing that can't be overcome.'

'Ostrich. Head in the sand,' John declared. 'Lovely girl, mind, was fair taken with her myself. And a beautiful speaker. Where did she say she went to school again?'

'Sherborne School for Girls,' Graham informed him.

'Aye, that was the one. Must have cost a packet to send her there.'

'Her father isn't wealthy by a long chalk,' Graham stated.

'Wealthy enough to send his daughter to a fancy school though.'

'He has had money in the past, but not now.'

'Anyway,' John argued. 'Money's only part of it. It's the social structure, you see. Her friends, relatives and the like. They'd never accept you. And the folk you know would be . . . how shall I put it? Uncomfortable with her.'

'You weren't,' Graham riposted.

'Not in this instance perhaps,' John countered. 'But we were certainly well aware that she was different to us.'

'Your father does have a point,' Madge said.

'I think you're being horrible to Graham!' Jennie exclaimed.

Graham held up his hands for silence. 'No-one is saying anything that Kerensa and I haven't already thought about and discussed. If there's a problem it's ours and we'll work it out. Now, if you don't mind, I'm going to bed.'

He kissed his mother good-night, then Jennie. 'Don't listen to them,' Jennie whispered. 'You do as your heart tells you.'

That was exactly what he intended doing. He left the kitchen and went upstairs where he undressed and got into bed.

He was thinking of Kerensa as he fell asleep, but dreamt of Ethel and her baby, a baby that was the spitting image of him.

347

Chapter Ten

Kerensa pushed Graham away and jumped up from the sofa. She was breathing heavily, her hair awry. 'Enough!' she declared.

Graham leant back and gulped in air. 'I'm sorry,' he said.

'There's nothing to be sorry about. I was enjoying it just as much as you. But none the less, I'm not going all the way until I'm married. I've told you in the past, I'll lose my virginity on my wedding night and not before.'

She paused, then added, 'But, by God, it can be difficult at times – like now.'

'I'll say.'

She smiled at him. 'All right?'

'I'll survive. If only just.'

'Me too.'

She readjusted her clothes, after which she went back to him and kissed him tenderly on the lips. 'How about a nice cup of tea?'

'That's no substitute.'

'I agree. But it's the best I can do.'

He grabbed her and pulled her on to his lap where she struggled. 'Graham!'

'Don't worry, I'm not about to force my evil way on you.'

'I should hope not.'

He took in the curve of her neck, and swell of her breasts. Desire was rampant in him. 'You smell lovely,' he said.

'Thank you, kind sir.'

'Pity about the face though,' he teased.

'Funny, I was just thinking the same about you,' she teased in return.

He nibbled her ear which made her squirm.

'Will you please let me go.'

'*Not* till your wedding night?'

'That's my intention.'

'Then we'd better get on with that as soon as possible.'

She frowned at these words. 'What do you mean?'

'Don't you know a proposal when you hear it?'

Her frown disappeared to be replaced by a soft, beguiling smile. 'Are you serious?'

'Couldn't be more so.'

She'd known it would happen of course, but hadn't been prepared for it quite coming out the blue like this. She'd expected something a little more formal.

Marry Graham? There was nothing she wanted more. He'd come to mean everything to her. She knew their life together would be an extremely full and happy one.

He suddenly became anxious at the ensuing silence. 'You will, won't you?'

'Of course I will,' she answered, and kissed him.

'That's official then, we're engaged. We'll go into town on Saturday and buy the ring, any ring in the shop that takes your fancy.'

'*Shops*,' she corrected him. 'I'm not going to settle for just one shop. This has to be done properly.'

'You mean, make a meal of it,' Graham commented drily.

'No, enjoyed to the fullest extent is how I'd put it.'

'You're gorgeous,' he told her.

'You're fairly scrumptious yourself.'

'I love you, Kerensa. With all my heart, soul, now and for ever.'

'And I you.'

He drew her closer. 'How long till your father gets home?'

'Ages yet.'

'Let's forget that tea, shall we?'

'I meant what I said though. Nothing's altered. Nothing doing until our wedding night.'

'When shall we get married then. Let's set a date.'

They fell to discussing dates till eventually they agreed on one.

'Engaged!' exclaimed Anthony, appalled.

'Marrying next spring.'

'But . . .' He trailed off. He was confused, mentally reeling. He'd convinced himself she'd drop Graham in time, that it wouldn't last.

'You can't,' Anthony croaked.

'I can and will, Daddy.'

'You're making an awful mistake, Kerensa. Surely you can see that?'

'I see nothing of the sort.'

'He's working class, for God's sake!' Anthony protested sharply.

'I'm well aware of that. He's also a natural born gentleman, and one I'm convinced will go far in life. He's only twenty-four and already owns his own firm. Goodness knows what he'll achieve in the years to come.'

'Impressive I admit, Kerensa. But he isn't one of *us*.'

The anguish she was causing her father pained Kerensa, but there was nothing else for it. She intended marrying Graham, and that was that. Anthony would simply have to accept the fact, unpalatable as he might find it.

'And what if I say I forbid it?'

'You'll get the same answer as when you tried to forbid me seeing, and working for, him.'

Anthony crossed to a decanter and poured himself a hefty Scotch. 'This isn't at all what I wanted for you or planned for you,' he said, his voice choking.

'I know,' she replied softly. 'But he's the right man for me, Daddy. I have no doubt about that.'

'I may not be able to stop you marrying him, but the

union will not have my approval. And another thing, I won't contribute financially to the wedding. Not a single brass farthing.'

'If that's how you feel, fine.'

Anthony swung on Kerensa, his eyes blazing. 'You're marrying not only beneath you but far beneath you. Why all you would have to do is snap your fingers and Rupert would come running.'

She smiled. 'The trouble is I love Graham, not Rupert.'

'Love, huh!' Anthony snorted.

'I thought you would have understood that. You loved Mummy after all, didn't you?'

'That was different.'

'No, it wasn't,' Kerensa argued. 'Love is love, no matter who's involved.'

'Your mother. Dear, dear Rebecca,' Anthony sighed. 'I miss her still. Even after all this while, it still hurts as much today as it did on the day of her death.'

Anthony's eyes misted over in memory as he saw again his beloved Rebecca whom he'd worshipped and adored. With a shake of the head he brought himself back to the present.

'It's ridiculous to compare you and Graham to what your mother and I had together,' he snapped.

'I appreciate you and Mummy had something very special together Daddy, but so, too, do Graham and I.'

'I just don't believe that!' he declared vehemently.

'Well, it's true. I've been as blest in love as you were. And I couldn't be more happy.'

Anthony thought about that, then dismissed it with a shrug. 'Not a brass farthing. And don't think I'll be changing my mind either, because I won't.'

Kerensa stared at her father, at that moment feeling only pity for him. What a sad, blinkered creature he was. If only he'd take the trouble to find out what Graham was really like, instead all he saw were Graham's background and origins.

Anthony finished his Scotch and returned to the decanter. 'Not a brass farthing,' he muttered darkly.

Kerensa left him still muttering and drinking.

'You're looking a bit pale, it's all that studying,' Madge said to Jennie. 'Are you all right?'

'Right as rain.'

Madge ran a hand over Jennie's face. 'How's night school coming along?'

'Fine. Couldn't be better. Everyone's pleased with me and my results.'

'Good. I'm delighted,' Madge nodded.

'I'll get on then.'

'Wait,' said Madge. 'I wanted a word.'

Jennie looked expectantly at her mother.

'I don't want you to think I'm interfering or trying to pry,' Madge began hesitantly. 'But it's been over two years since you broke with Andy Alford and there's still no sign of a new boyfriend. It's not natural, Jen.'

Jennie glanced down at the carpet. 'I don't really have time for lads. There's the shop during the day and I'm either at night school in the evenings or studying here at home.'

'Those are simply excuses I think,' Madge said gently. 'You're not still pining for Andy, are you?'

Jennie shook her head. 'No, I'm long over him. And that's true, believe me. I think, being honest, I'm simply not ready for another involvement yet. I don't feel the need to have a chap. If I did I'd probably do something about it.'

'It doesn't have to be anything serious or deep. I'm talking about having some fun.'

'Now that Christine is engaged she isn't available to team up with nowadays.'

'Granted, but there are other girls in the village you could be pals with.'

'I appreciate you've got my best interests at heart, Mum. But really, it's not a problem.'

Madge went over to Jennie and took her by the arm. 'Are you sure, lass? I mean there's no-one more pleased about your studies than me, you know that. But you also know what they say about all work and no play?'

'Maybe I'll meet someone nice and that will change my mind,' Jennie smiled.

'Only to meet someone you have to get out and about. Now there's a dance at Stoke Bradley this Saturday, I saw it advertised. Why don't you go to that?'

'I'll think about it, Mum.'

'Don't think, go,' Madge urged.

Jennie began to get irritated. 'I wish you wouldn't go on. I am quite capable of running my own life, thank you very much.'

'There's no need to take that tone with me,' Madge retorted.

'I'm not taking any tone.'

'Oh yes you are.'

Jennie pulled herself out of Madge's grasp. 'Look, just leave it, eh? I'll think about the dance on Saturday night. And if I want to go when the time comes, then I will. If not I'll stay at home.'

'There are occasions when you can be most aggravating,' Madge replied waspishly.

'Aggravating? Me!' Jennie laughed, finding that funny. If there was anyone in the house who was aggravating it was her mother.

'I'm sorry I spoke now,' Madge said huffily.

Get out before this develops further, Jennie told herself. 'I'm going up to my room. I'll be there if you need me,' she stated, and promptly strode off.

Madge picked up a cushion, plumped it, and returned it to the sofa. 'Damn!' she swore softly.

Then she picked up another cushion and pummelled that.

Madge glanced round when the organist struck up 'Here Comes The Bride'.

There, at the top of the aisle was Christine, radiant in her wedding dress, on the arm of her father, James, beaming fit to bust.

Behind Christine and James were the two brides-maids, Jennie and Patience Zelly. Jennie bent to make a quick adjustment to the hem of Christine's dress, then they began the long, slow walk down the length of the church.

At the bottom of the aisle Henry Down stood nervously waiting with his best man. They were both dressed in rented morning suits, each sporting a red rose in his lapel.

As the bride and her entourage passed Madge and John, Jennie gave them a brief smile.

Shortly after that the ceremony began.

'Your turn next, you caught the bouquet,' Christine said to Jennie. They were at the reception in the village hall.

'I couldn't fail to catch it, you threw it straight at me,' Jennie answered.

'That doesn't matter. It's still you next time round,' Christine persisted.

'We'll see about that.'

Henry came up to them, his face flushed with alcohol. 'How's the missus then?' he said, and giggled.

'Missus indeed!' Christine exclaimed.

'Well, that's what you are, aren't you – Mrs Henry Down.'

'Aaahhhh!' sighed Jennie, tongue firmly in cheek.

'Mrs Henry Down,' Christine mused. 'I like the sound of that. It has a certain ring to it.'

Patience Zelly joined them. 'Talking of rings, let's have another look at that one you got today.'

Christine held up her left hand on which a gold band now lay below her engagement ring.

'Proper job,' breathed Patience.

A little further off Graham was talking to Hamish and Emma Law to whom he'd just introduced Kerensa. Due

354

to work pressure he and Kerensa hadn't made the church, but had been able to come on to the reception.

Graham glanced away from Kerensa and the Laws, his smile fading when he saw Mark and a hugely pregnant Ethel bearing down on them. Panic flared in him when he noted the steely glint in Ethel's eye.

'Graham, how are you my old son? It's been ages,' Mark cried by way of greeting. They, of course, knew the Laws.

Graham shook Mark's hand. 'It has been a while, hasn't it?'

'You've been a right stranger.' He focused his attention on Kerensa. 'And is this who I think it is, I ask myself?'

'Ethel, Mark, I'd like you to meet Kerensa Sturt, my fiancée,' Graham said.

'How do you do,' smiled Mark, and shook hands with Kerensa. Ethel didn't offer her hand.

'We had heard the good news. Hadn't we my lover?' Mark declared, turning to Ethel.

'Yes,' Ethel agreed in a cold voice.

Ethel looked like a snake sizing up its intended prey, Graham thought in alarm. Please God she wasn't going to do or say anything about their past. There was only one person in the world he feared, and that was Ethel. For she could lose him Kerensa.

'When is your baby due?' Kerensa enquired politely.

'Next month.'

'And how has your pregnancy been so far?'

'Fair to middling. Nothing to really complain about. I've been lucky, I suppose.'

'Why don't you both come round one evening and have a drink with us?' Mark suggested. 'You and I have a lot to catch up on Graham.'

'I'm extremely busy just now,' Graham prevaricated. 'But perhaps sometime in the future.'

'How is the brick works doing?' Hamish Law asked.

A few minutes later the Laws moved off. If Ethel was

going to blow the gaff it would be now, Graham thought. To his enormous relief she didn't. She was cold as ice, but her lips remained tightly sealed.

'Enjoying yourself?'

Kerensa turned to find it was Madge who'd spoken.

'Yes I am, thank you.'

'I don't suppose you're used to receptions held in village halls, eh?'

'I've been to my fair share,' Kerensa replied. Though, if pressed, she'd have had to admit she'd been to some rather grand ones also.

'Have you seen your dad?' Madge asked Graham.

'Not for a little while.'

'Me neither.'

'Well, he must be around somewhere,' Graham said.

Madge excused herself and went to look for John. She hadn't progressed far when she stopped to have a word with Doreen Horrell, the girl she'd saved from the river shortly after they'd moved to Atherton. While she was talking to Doreen, Norman and Bess Pugsley joined them, Bess remarking on how grown-up Doreen was becoming.

'And how be 'ee Madge?' Norman enquired.

'Fine thank you. And you.'

He winked at her. 'Feels like a young thing I do. Tain't that so, Bess?'

'That be so,' she confirmed.

Madge suddenly spied John in a corner with some cronies. They were sitting at a table with pint pots in front of them.

'If you'll pardon me,' she said a few moments later. 'I've just seen John whom I must talk to.'

John glanced up at her approach. 'Hello Madge! Come and join us,' he declared.

'Can I get you a drink, Madge?' asked Duncan James, rising from his chair.

'Not for me, Duncan, thank you,' she replied.

The glassiness of John's eyes told Madge what she

wanted to know, he was already well on his way to being drunk, which was exactly what she'd hoped, and expected.

'I'm popping off for a while,' she informed him. 'I'll have to take Brownie for his walk or he may disgrace himself indoors.'

John made a vague gesture. 'Sure.'

'I'll see you later then.'

'I'll be here.'

She was certain of that. As long as there was booze on the premises he'd be there all right.

'Bye then,' she said, and left him and the others.

It was a beautiful day for a wedding, she thought as she hurried home to change. Christine and Henry couldn't have chosen better. She hoped it continued like this for their honeymoon. They were spending a week at Bath.

She changed quickly, put the leash on Brownie, and left the house, heading towards the water meadows. When she arrived there, she began strolling along the bank of the river.

She crossed a stile, and continued on her way. And as she walked she hummed, a jaunty tune she'd heard on the wireless that morning.

She eventually came to a clump of trees by the water's edge, the trees surrounded by tall stinging nettles. There was a hidden path through the nettles, however, which took her into a secluded grassy area surrounded on all four sides by trees. Close by the river gurgled on its way.

She stroked and patted Brownie, then tied his leash to what remained of a broken branch of a fallen tree. That done she lay down on her back and gazed up at the sky.

It was hot, with the lazy ambience of a perfect summer's day. A panting Brownie sat watching Madge as she gradually dozed off.

She woke when a hand closed round her breast, and there was George smiling at her. 'Sorry I'm late,' he apologized.

'That's all right. I fell asleep.'

'And a picture you were. I stood there admiring you for a good minute and more.'

'You did?' she said, delighted.

'I surely did. As pretty a picture it was too as I ever did see. And that's the plain God's honest truth.'

She murmured as he began caressing her.

He glanced round the spot he'd first brought her to weeks previously and where they now met regularly, weather permitting. He referred to it as their love nest.

'How was the wedding?' he enquired.

'The ceremony itself went off well, and the reception was in full swing when I left.'

'What about John?'

'I told him I was taking Brownie for a walk. I doubt he'll even remember.'

'So, there's no rush.'

'None at all.'

'That be good, Madge.'

He started unbuttoning her blouse to reveal her breasts. He dropped his mouth to first one nipple, then the other.

'It feels incredible when you do that,' she said, breathing heavily.

'I likes it too, my girl,' he replied.

Her breathing became even heavier as he explored her body.

It was heaven she thought, sheer, beautiful, heaven.

'Oh my beauty. My darling beauty,' George murmured.

When it was over she lay in his arms where she always felt safe, protected and wondrously happy.

They stayed there for hours, a lot longer than they normally did, neither wanting to part from the other.

Jane Scott took a sip of coffee, then replaced her cup on its saucer. She and Madge were having morning coffee together at her house.

'You've definitely lost weight. You look so trim and sleek!' Jane marvelled.

Madge nodded. 'I've lost over a stone.'

'How have you done it, diet?'

'No, I haven't been doing anything different.'

'And so healthy, your skin is positively glowing.'

Madge thought of George, and smiled. It was as a direct result of her relationship with him that she'd slimmed down and was glowing with . . . not health exactly, though that was part of it, but joy and satisfaction. She felt so good within herself nowadays!

'Are you taking some sort of pills then?' Jane asked.

'No pills, Jane. It's probably walking Brownie that's done this to me. I walk him quite a bit which he and I both enjoy.'

'Well, if that's what a dog does for you I must get one,' Jane quipped.

Walking the dog! Madge thought, and mentally laughed. If Jane only knew! Meeting George, with the exception of her children that is, was the best thing that had ever happened to her. It wasn't just the sex side, though she enjoyed that tremendously, it was his company as well. The two of them talked in a way that she and John never had. She felt so comfortable spending time with George.

'Being slimmer certainly suits you. I envy you,' Jane said.

'You're slim!' Madge protested.

'Putting it on a bit round the old tum of late,' Jane replied, and patted her stomach.

'I can't see it,' Madge retorted. 'If you think you're overweight then it's all in your imagination.'

'I only wish it was,' sighed Jane. 'Anyway, I meant to ask. What's wrong with Jennie?'

'Wrong?' queried Madge. 'How do you mean?'

'I spotted her coming out of the doctor's surgery yesterday.'

This was news to Madge. 'Are you sure it was her?'

'Of course! I know Jennie well enough. It was her all right, I wasn't mistaken.'

Jennie coming out of the doctor's surgery? Now why had she been to see the doctor? She hadn't said anything. Did she have some sort of complaint she didn't want to speak about? 'I've no idea why she was there,' Madge confessed. 'I'll ask her this evening.'

'Oh!' exclaimed Jane, remembering something. 'I heard the most fabulous piece of gossip yesterday afternoon. Want to hear it?'

Madge leant forward in her chair. 'I'm all ears.'

Jane went on to relate the story which Madge listened to wide eyed.

Jennie picked up a plate and started drying it. It was that evening and she and Madge were doing the washing-up after tea. Graham had gone out directly the meal was over while John was at the church replacing several light bulbs that had burnt out.

'So, why were you at the doctor's yesterday?' Madge asked casually.

Jennie hesitated, then carried on with what she was doing. 'Who said I was at the doctor's?'

'Mrs Scott. She saw you coming out of the surgery.'

Jennie's thoughts raced. 'Yes, it was me,' she admitted, putting the dried plate away and picking up another wet one.

'Well?' Madge prompted after a few seconds had ticked by.

'Well, what?'

'Why were you there? Are you ill?'

Jennie laughed. 'I'm perfectly healthy thank you very much. There's nothing whatsoever wrong with me.'

'So, why did you go and see the doctor?' Madge persisted, relieved.

She could say she was on an errand for the shop, Jennie thought. But what if Madge mentioned it to Bob Yendell who said she'd been on no such thing. Trivia like that did get mentioned in villages, it would be quite normal for Madge to bring up the subject as a matter of conversation when next talking to him. So no, she wouldn't take the chance of using the shop as an excuse.

'It was in connection with a project I'm doing for night school,' Jennie said, which was a half-truth rather than a downright lie.

Madge frowned. 'But it's August, night school is closed down?'

'This is a subject I was set to do in the holidays.'

Madge's frown disappeared. 'Ah!'

'There's no mystery. The explanation's quite straight-forward,' Jennie stated.

'I was worried when Jane mentioned seeing you and you hadn't said. You know what mothers are like.'

Jennie pecked Madge on the forehead. 'Thanks for your concern.'

She then talked about something else before Madge thought to quiz her on the project and how the doctor had been able to help with it.

'Where are we going?' Kerensa asked as the Lanchester sped along a quiet Devon lane.

'Wait and find out.'

'Graham!' she exclaimed.

He grinned at her. 'It's a surprise. Don't make me spoil it by telling you in advance what it is.'

'Well, I hope it's a nice surprise.'

'I would hardly spring a nasty one on you, would I?'

That was true enough, she thought, and wondered what the surprise was.

Shortly after that Graham drew up outside a pictur-esque cottage on the outskirts of the village of Tankerton which was a large village boasting a population of almost two thousand.

The cottage was thatched, constructed of cob which consists of natural clay or chalk mixed with straw or hair as a binder. The walls were sparkling white, the door and window frames black. Wistaria grew on either side of the door to trail out towards the corners. There was a tiny garden at the front, with some ground at the sides leading to a reasonably sized garden at the rear.

Kerensa took all this in. 'Quaint and cosy looking,' she declared.

'Has an inglenook fireplace I'm told, and a great many exposed beams.'

He got out of the car, went round to her side and opened her door. 'Shall we go inside?' he suggested.

Kerensa eyed the cottage again, then turned to face Graham. 'Is it for rent?'

'Nope,' he smiled. 'For sale. I thought it might do us. If you like it, that is.'

'I'm certainly taken by the exterior,' she replied. 'The overall effect is . . . sweet.'

'Of course you must see it only as a start. As time goes by, and the family comes along, we'll move to larger and grander things.'

'And how many would you like in this family you've mentioned?' she asked softly.

'I thought a dozen would be a good round figure,' he teased.

'A dozen! Is that all?'

'More if you wish.'

'Half boys half girls, I suppose,' she said drily. 'Nice and neat that way.'

'Exactly. We'll even call one of the boys Anthony after your father.'

She took his hand in hers, raised it to her mouth, and kissed it. 'It's a lovely surprise,' she told him.

'Well, it's time we thought about a place to live in. For one thing's certain, we're not going to stay at Corfe Mullen. With your father feeling as he does about me that would be just asking for trouble.'

'You're right,' she agreed.

Graham produced a key and opened the door. They stepped directly into a sitting-room boasting bilious wallpaper and badly stained floorboards. There were spider webs everywhere.

'Ugh!' said Graham, obviously disappointed.

Kerensa gazed around. 'I like it,' she declared.

'You do?' queried Graham, incredulously.

She nodded. 'It has tremendous potential. The wallpaper would have to go of course, and then . . .'

Graham smiled as she rattled on. Maybe the cottage was a success after all.

She crossed to the inglenook fireplace, and could just imagine it roaring in the winter sending out waves of heat. And there would be evenings when she and Graham could sit in front of it making toast which they would eat with homemade jam and local farm honey.

'Come on, let's see more,' she said, excited.

The kitchen housed an Aga which delighted her. Ideal, she proclaimed it. The room itself would need a substantial amount of work, but nothing structural in her opinion.

'How many bedrooms are there?' she asked.

'Two.'

They climbed up some well-worn stairs to arrive in a passageway with a pair of doors leading off it. The first bedroom they went into was the larger and overlooked the rear garden. Kerensa went straight to the window and stared out.

'Lovely view,' she said.

Graham joined her, and thought so too. There were several apple trees in the garden, and another which was a plum. He also noted several gooseberry bushes.

If anything the wallpaper in the bedroom was even worse than the sitting-room, and Kerensa located a small damp patch. The floorboards creaked loudly when they were walked on.

'You won't recognize the room when I'm finished with it,' she enthused.

'So we're buying?'

'No question about it. That's providing the price is right.'

'The price is right,' Graham confirmed, making a mental note, as so much needed doing inside, to try and knock a bit off the asking price.

The second bedroom was painted a gruesome shade of yellow which Kerensa said made her think of mouldy custard. 'Whoever lived here before had ghastly taste in decoration,' she stated. 'But in a way that's a good thing for it allows me to do over the place completely. I'll enjoy it.'

From there they went into the garden and strolled around. Graham decided to employ a gardener as it hadn't been looked after for some time and would need a considerable amount of attention. He was far too busy with work to do the gardening himself. Anyway, it wasn't something he particularly liked doing.

'Does it have a name?' Kerensa asked. She hadn't noticed one above the door.

Graham nodded. 'Wait for it, it's called Gone To Ground.'

Kerensa laughed. 'Seriously?'

'It's true. We could change it if you want?'

'We'll do nothing of the sort. I think that's a tremendous name. Full of character, same as the cottage itself. No, Gone To Ground it remains.'

He swept her into his arms. 'Love you,' he said.

'And I love you. Thank you for finding this place. It's absolutely perfect.'

'I'm happy you're happy.'

'Which I most certainly am. Couldn't be more so in fact.'

Before they left, Graham picked them both apples, which transpired to be delicious.

As she walked Madge consulted the shopping list she'd drawn up of all the purchases she wanted to make at the Post Office Stores. She ran through the list – was there anything else? Anything she'd forgotten?

'Hello Madge,' said George from the adjacent field.

She stopped and smiled at him across the hedge. 'Hello George.' Then she realized he was standing in front of a stationary machine, which she didn't recognize. 'What's that?' she enquired.

George patted the machine affectionately. 'This here be a tractor, Madge. Farmer took delivery only last week.'

'A tractor!'

'To replace the horses, which I must confess I'm right sad to see go. But there you are, there's no stopping progress, is there?'

The tractor had small metal wheels at the front, and large spiked ones at the rear. 'Fearsome looking brute,' Madge commented.

'Don't half get through the work though. And it's a lot easier sitting on her than walking behind horses I can tell you.'

'You drive it then?'

George puffed out his chest. 'I do. Tain't easy mind, but I've got the knack of it now.'

'Let's see you then.'

'All right.'

He swung himself aboard the tractor, smiled at Madge, then started the engine. The tractor came alive with a loud roar.

'Dear me!' Madge said to herself. Then to George, 'It's very noisy.'

He cupped a hand to his ear. 'What?'

'I said, it's very noisy.'

He shook his head, still unable to understand being deafened by the engine. He engaged the gears and the tractor lurched off.

He was a fine sight on his tractor, Madge thought. And clearly he was extremely proud of it. She certainly approved if it reduced some of the back-breaking graft he had to endure.

George had to get on so didn't return to Madge. Instead he waved his cap at her as the tractor trundled away, and she waved in return.

They weren't due to meet that day, but Madge had said she'd contrive to visit his cottage the following night, as it was now too cold for their love nest by the river.

Treacle! Madge suddenly thought. She needed a tin and it wasn't on her list.

She hurried on her way.

Graham nodded with satisfaction as he went through the figures in front of him. Phil Crane, who'd replaced Jack Marsden as rep, was proving a great find. His results were excellent and far outshone anything Marsden had managed. But then Phil was young, and keen as mustard, with a most engaging personality that he used to devastating effect.

A year from now, Graham thought, would give him time to consolidate his position, after which he could start looking further afield for orders. And as he expanded their territory so he would, eventually, expand their business.

He was still contemplating the future when Kerensa returned from an errand. 'Are you ready for your tea yet?' she asked.

'Please.'

She was about to disappear again when she remembered something. 'By the way, Rupert paid me a visit last night.'

'Oh?'

'He's invited us to a dinner party he's giving. Black tie.'

Graham was momentarily nonplussed. 'When is it?'

'Saturday the twenty-third. He'll be sending us an At Home to Corfe Mullen.'

'Who's going to be there?' Graham queried.

She shrugged. 'I never thought to ask. I could ring him and find out if you wish?'

Dinner with Rupert, Graham thought, and Rupert's friends. Was this some sort of trap? Was he to be mocked because of his humble background? There was always that possibility, he supposed. But surely not with Kerensa present? Rupert, according to Kerensa, held her in very high esteem. Still, you never knew with these types. They could be cruel in the extreme.

There again, perhaps nothing would be done or said overtly, it was merely to point out to him that he didn't fit in at the social level Kerensa had been born and brought up to.

Then a new thought crossed his mind. Had Anthony something to do with this? Had Anthony and Rupert conspired together and the dinner party was the result?

'What do you think?' he asked Kerensa suspiciously.

'It might be fun.'

Or a fiasco, he thought. 'Would you like to go?'

'Only if you were happy to do so.'

Black tie! He'd have to rent that. No, if he did go he'd buy it. He'd feel better in a suit he actually owned.

He considered the matter further, aware that Kerensa was studying him, waiting for his answer. He looked into her eyes, and suddenly knew it was important he did attend. If he dodged the issue now, he would somehow lose by it. If Rupert and Anthony did intend playing games then let them, for them to do so would only weaken their position and strengthen his.

'Buy yourself a new gown for the occasion and I'll pay for it,' he said.

Kerensa's face broke into a broad smile. 'You mean that?'

'Of course! And don't worry about the price either, get whatever takes your fancy.'

She went to him and kissed him lightly on the lips. 'You're an absolute poppet,' she breathed.

'And you're at work. Hop to it, woman, I'm waiting for my tea.'

'Coming right up, boss, sir,' she joked.

A dinner party at Rupert's, he thought when she'd gone. He carefully marked the date in his diary, not that he was likely to forget.

It took Graham ages, but finally he managed to knot his bow-tie. The man in the shop had made it look easy, but it was far from that. He picked up his brand new white silk scarf and coat and went downstairs. Jennie whistled when he entered the kitchen.

'How do I look?' he asked anxiously.

Madge put her hands on her hips and stared at him. 'Prince Charming to the life,' she declared.

'Very elegant,' Jennie said.

Madge crossed to Graham and slightly readjusted his cummerbund. 'There, that's better.'

John gazed at Graham, his expression stony. Slowly he shook his head.

'Dad?' Graham queried.

'You don't want my opinion.'

'Yes, I do.'

John cleared his throat. 'You look like a toffee-nosed, upper-class degenerate.'

'Steady on!' Graham exclaimed, and laughed.

'You shouldn't go aping your betters. Nothing good will come of it, you mark my words.'

'That's enough out of you!' Madge snapped, furiously.

'He asked so I told him,' John protested.

His father's words made Graham even more nervous. He could still call it off, Graham thought. Go to Corfe Mullen and tell Kerensa he wasn't feeling well. That he had a sore stomach, perhaps due to something he'd eaten. Or he could . . .

Steady! he warned himself. He was panicking, that would never do. If he tried to call it off Kerensa would guess he was lying. No, he'd accepted the invitation and would have to go through with the evening.

'I've got some whisky in, would you like a drop before

you go?' John asked, offering it as an excuse to have a drink himself.

Just the thing, Graham thought. He was about to accept, then changed his mind. It was best he arrive at the dinner party stone-cold sober and stay that way. He'd allow himself several glasses of wine during the evening and no more.

'Not for me thanks, Dad,' he replied.

John's reply was to grunt, as he was already on his way to the sideboard where the whisky was.

'I'll be off then,' Graham said, shrugging into his coat and draping the scarf round his neck.

'Enjoy yourself,' Madge smiled, pecking him on the cheek.

'Have a good time,' Jennie added, kissing him also.

'Still think he looks like a toffee-nosed, upper-class degenerate,' John muttered, pouring whisky into a glass, and wishing the bottle was full instead of half-empty.

Graham's stomach was churning as he went out to the car.

Graham pulled up outside the Poundsberry house which was ablaze with light. Other cars were already parked on the sweeping carriage drive. The moment he'd been dreading had arrived.

'All right?' Kerensa queried softly.

'I'm fine.'

'Then let's go in.'

Graham got out of the Lanchester, then helped Kerensa out. 'You look wonderful,' he said for the umpteenth time since arriving at Corfe Mullen to pick her up.

The gown she'd bought was bottle green, cut low in the front, plunged at the back, and had a flared skirt. She was wearing a black lace wrap round her shoulders to ward off the autumn chill.

Graham took Kerensa by the elbow as they scrunched their way over chippings to the stone steps that led to the front door. The brass knocker on the large imposing door was shaped like a dolphin. Graham banged once.

The door was opened by a young housemaid who took Kerensa's wrap and Graham's coat and scarf.

'Kerensa darling, delighted you could come!' declared Rupert, appearing beside them.

Rupert was even more handsome than he recalled, Graham thought, as his heart sank. How could Kerensa possibly prefer him over such an Adonis? But she did, he reminded himself and was wearing his engagement ring to prove it.

'Graham, this is Rupert Poundsberry our host, and long-standing friend of mine. Rupert, Graham Forsyth.'

'Pleased to meet you Graham,' Rupert said, extending his hand.

Graham looked into Rupert's face as they shook hands, and saw nothing there to give him cause for concern. 'And I to meet you.'

'Congratulations on your engagement. You're a very lucky man.'

'I know,' Graham smiled.

'Now, come on through and have some fizz.'

'Are we the last to arrive?' Kerensa asked as they entered the drawing-room.

'No, another couple are still to come.'

Rupert lifted two champagne flutes from a silver tray atop an antique desk and handed them to Kerensa and Graham. As he was doing that a pretty dark-haired young woman joined them.

'Hello, India,' Kerensa said.

'Haven't seen you for yonks,' India replied, and smiled at Graham.

Kerensa introduced Graham who gathered from the ensuing conversation that India was Rupert's partner for the evening.

'Still as keen on riding?' Kerensa asked India.

'Rather!'

'India hunts,' Kerensa explained to Graham.

'I've just bought myself a new gelding. Seventeen hands, a beautiful beast,' India said.

'Excuse me a moment,' Rupert murmured, and went off.

So far so good, Graham thought, sipping his champagne as Kerensa and India discussed horses, a subject he quickly gathered Kerensa knew a considerable amount about.

'Do you ride Graham?' India asked.

''Fraid not.'

'You should try it sometime. Marvellous sport.'

Shortly after that the last couple arrived and were brought over by Rupert who introduced them to Graham as Geoffrey Malet and Davina Clewes.

The company was of mixed ages, Graham noted, glancing around. The eldest couple there he judged were in their late fifties. That particular woman looked rather fierce.

The conversation flowed smoothly. Rupert and Kerensa, between them, soon introduced Graham to everyone present. The fierce looking woman was called Jane Fitzalan, her husband, David.

Graham refused a top-up on several occasions by which time he realized he was actually enjoying himself. He was beginning to relax, his fears disappearing. The company couldn't have been more friendly.

Dinner was announced and they all trooped through to the dining-room where Graham found himself sitting with Jane Fitzalan on one side, Davina Clewes on the other.

The first course was vichyssoise during which Davina spoke to Graham about a play she'd been to recently. In her opinion George Bernard Shaw was more of an essayist than playwright. Though she had to admit, the Irishman was terribly clever.

In the middle of the main course Graham was addressed by Jane Fitzalan who enquired if he was new to the area.

'No, I've been here for years,' he replied.

'Strange I've never seen you before. Where do you live exactly?'

To Graham's horror he found that the table had gone quiet, and that everyone, without exception, was staring at him. Kerensa's expression suggested concern.

'Atherton,' he replied slowly.

'Then you must know Sir Reginald Tempest?'

'Not personally,' Graham informed her, his voice fractionally hoarse.

'I am surprised,' frowned Jane Fitzalan.

Graham didn't know whether he'd been set up or not, but if he had he decided to brazen it out. 'My father works for Sir Reginald at Wheal Tempest.'

Jane Fitzalan's eyebrows shot up. 'Really?'

'He was a miner but got hurt, so is now on maintenance duties.'

'Well, well!' murmured Jane Fitzalan.

'Graham's a self-made man. He recently bought the Stanton Brick Works,' Rupert stated quietly.

'And he and I are to be married in the spring,' Kerensa added.

Jane Fitzalan patted Graham on the arm. 'Good for you! I admire self-made people. Shows grit and determination, not to mention ambition. Good for you, Graham!'

The admiration in her voice was genuine. There was no hint whatever of her being patronizing.

'Thank you,' he replied with a smile.

'Jolly interesting,' Jane Fitzalan declared as the hum of conversation was renewed round the table.

Graham was grateful to Rupert for his support which was something he wouldn't forget in a hurry. It was the last thing he had been expecting.

Kerensa caught his eye and gave him a slight nod of approval. He'd done the right thing by being honest.

To Graham's surprise Jane Fitzalan later asked him and Kerensa round to their house for drinks the following weekend, which he was only too delighted to accept.

'Good to see you,' Mark Yeo enthused, ushering Graham inside.

'I got your message asking me to call round.'

'That's right. Your mother said you were working late when I knocked.'

Graham was wondering what this was all about, and hoped it wasn't trouble. 'I've been meaning to stop by since Ethel had the baby,' he lied. 'But it's just been one thing after another.'

'We understand, you've become a busy man,' Mark nodded.

'The business, getting engaged, buying a house. I could use thirty hours in the day rather than twenty-four.'

'Now, where's she gone?' Mark said, as he entered the parlour. 'Ethel was here just now.'

Ethel reappeared a few moments later having been taking off the apron she'd been wearing. 'Hello Graham,' she smiled.

He kissed her on the cheek. 'Hello yourself. How are you?'

'Don't let anyone ever tell you that looking after a new baby isn't hard work. I'm exhausted most of the time.'

She was pale, Graham thought. And there were dark bags under her eyes. 'I was just apologizing to Mark for not dropping by before now, but . . .'

'That's all right,' Ethel cut in.

'Do you want to see the baby?' Mark asked, his face glowing with pride.

Graham knew it was impossible for him to refuse, but the last thing he wanted was to see the damn child, a child he'd been having nightmares about since Ethel had told him she was pregnant.

'Of course,' he replied, forcing a smile on to his face.

'By the way, thanks for the card,' Ethel said.

'You got it then.'

'Oh yes,' she answered tightly, having hoped against hope for flowers.

God! Graham thought, this was awful.

'Follow me,' Mark instructed, and led the way through to the baby's bedroom which was painted a pale shade of blue with a matching fitted carpet.

Graham had to steel himself to look into the crib where the child lay fast asleep on her back. He realized immediately, elation leaping within him, her face bore a striking resemblance to Mark's.

He sagged, his shoulders slumping, unable to tear his gaze from that face he'd feared so long.

'Ethel was convinced we were going to have a boy which is why the room is painted blue,' Mark explained.

'I'd heard you'd had a girl,' Graham croaked. 'But not what you'd named her?'

'Catherine,' Mark replied.

Graham nodded.

'If she wasn't asleep I'd let you hold her,' Mark went on.

'Another time perhaps.'

'Another time,' Mark repeated. He bent over and smiled at Catherine. 'Sleep well my precious,' he murmured.

While Mark was doing that Graham turned to Ethel standing behind him. She'd been wrong on both counts, the baby's gender and sire.

They returned to the parlour where Mark told Graham to sit down. 'The reason we asked you round is that we want you to be Catherine's godfather,' he stated.

Ethel lit a cigarette and stared at Graham. Turmoil raged inside her at seeing him again, and being so close to him. She'd wept when she'd realized the baby was Mark's and not his. Even that had been denied her. She glanced at Mark, thinking how she despised her husband. She would have given anything to have had a magic wand that would make him disappear, and a Graham who loved her take his place.

'Godfather,' a bemused Graham repeated.

'So what do you say?'

'I don't know,' Graham prevaricated.

'Come on, don't let us down,' Mark urged.

Ethel smiled thinly, and puffed on her cigarette. 'Yes, don't let us down, Graham.'

He knew that to be a barb. 'I'm not sure I'm cut out to be a godfather.'

'Of course you are,' Mark insisted. 'You're a believer and regular church-goer, aren't you? And if anything did happen to Ethel and I, which heaven forbid it won't, then there's no-one I'd trust more to see that Catherine was taken care of.'

Graham relented. After all, he owed Ethel something. 'All right then,' he agreed.

'That's the ticket,' declared Mark, coming over and slapping Graham on the shoulder. 'Now I'll go and put the kettle on. I want to hear what you've been up to, and how that firm of yours is doing.'

An uneasy silence fell between Graham and Ethel when Mark had left the room. 'I thought your fiancée very pretty,' Ethel said eventually.

Graham nodded.

'Everything going well between you?'

'Extremely.'

Ethel's eyes glittered for a second, then the glitter was gone. She puffed on her cigarette. 'Don't worry, I'll never make trouble for you with her. I knew that was on your mind the day of the Down wedding.' She had another puff, then continued, 'Despite what you think of me, and what I feel, I'm not like that.'

'I must say it has . . . worried me from time to time.'

'I presume you've decided you are in love with her?'

Graham nodded again.

'And she's declared herself in love with you?'

'That's right.'

'Then I genuinely wish you both every happiness.'

He stared at Ethel, thinking he'd misjudged her. There was a lot more to her than he'd ever given her credit for.

Ethel desperately wanted to plead with Graham for them to occasionally get together, but didn't, knowing full well what his answer would be.

'Whose idea was it that I be godfather?' he asked.

'Mark's.'

'Truthfully?'

'Truthfully,' she stated.

'She looks just like her dad.'

Ethel blew a perfect smoke ring that rapidly expanded as it floated towards Graham.

'I've never seen you do that before,' he commented.

'A new trick of mine. To amuse myself.'

He mentally winced on hearing the bitterness in her voice. He'd hurt her profoundly, but had never intended to do so. He could guess how she must feel, the same as he would should he ever lose Kerensa. His heart, which belonged quite firmly to someone else, went out to her.

'How are things between you and Mark?'

Ethel shrugged.

'He's certainly enjoying being a father. He's taken to it like a duck to water.'

'He's been very helpful round the house. And with the baby, of course. He dotes on her, which I suppose is understandable after waiting for a family all these years. I was certain that . . .' She broke off and shook her head. 'Nothing.'

Mark breezed back into the room carrying a plate of biscuits. 'Tea won't be long. Or would you prefer coffee?'

'Tea will be fine,' Graham said.

Ethel rose when Catherine began to cry. 'That's her wanting her feed,' she explained. 'I'll leave you two to it.'

Ethel stayed with Catherine, taking her tea through in to the baby's bedroom.

Graham escaped as soon as he decently could.

*   *   *

Madge found George dozing in front of the range. He was snoring gently, his chest rising and falling in time with his snores.

'George!' she said, shaking his arm.

He woke with a snort. 'Madge!' Then, seeing the look on her face, panicked. 'What be wrong?'

She took a deep breath, still rattled. 'I was just about to turn up here when I ran into that damn Les Pack with his dog,' she explained. 'You should have seen the funny look I got.'

'That man's a menace,' George growled. 'So what did you do?'

'Kept on walking. "Evening, Mr Pack," I said to him, as normal and nice as I could make it, and just kept going. I knew he was staring after me, I could feel his eyes burning into my back.'

George rose. 'You sit here, Madge. Is there anything I can get 'ee?'

Madge shook her head. 'That's kind George, but no thanks. Fair gave me a turn that did.'

'He's always prying and snooping, that Les Pack. Putting two and two together and often making five. Do you think he realized you be coming here?'

'I don't think so. But it was a near thing. If it had been a few seconds later, and I'd turned up towards the house, then it would have been all round the village in no time at all that I was one of George Rattenbury's women.'

George balled a fist. 'Old man or no, if that had happened he'd have accounted to me. He'd tell no more lies and tales, or get up to mischief after I'd finished with the beggar.'

Madge fumbled in her coat pocket, took out a handkerchief and blew her nose. 'How are you anyway?' she asked.

'Fine. And yourself, Madge?'

'Oh, I had another row with John. Don't ask me over what, it just seemed to blow up.'

377

'I often thinks of you there with him and wishes you were here with me instead.'

She smiled up at George. 'So do I,' she confessed.

'I know he's your husband, but I got no time for that man of yours. He's a bad lot.'

Madge thought about that. 'I wouldn't say he was a bad lot, but he's certainly weak. Weak and lazy.'

'And a boozer,' George added. 'He's well known for his drinking.'

George pulled up another chair and sat facing Madge who remained in her coat. 'There is one solution to all this of course. Then it wouldn't matter what Les Pack saw or what.'

'Which is?'

'Leave your John and come live with me.'

Live with George! 'Are you talking about a divorce?'

'In time. Leave John, live with me and I'll marry you the moment your divorce comes through.'

Oh, the temptation! She gazed round the kitchen and could easily imagine it being hers. What joy it would be cooking George's meals here and sitting in the evenings, just as they were now, talking over the day's events. And then the nights together lying in George's arms. Sleeping in those arms, waking up in them.

She thought of the years of misery with John, her regret at ever marrying him. All that he'd put her through. One thing was certain, if she did leave him she wouldn't miss him one little bit.

'And you'd marry me?' she said to George.

He took her hand in his, and gently squeezed it. 'Like a shot, Madge.'

She gazed into his eyes, and smiled at what she saw there. 'I'll think about it,' she said.

'You do that.'

She rose, and shrugged out of her coat which George hung up for her. Then together they went through to the bedroom.

*   *   *

'Did you have a good time?' Madge asked Jennie who'd just returned home from being out with a chap.

'So, so.'

'Well, don't sound so enthusiastic!'

Jennie laughed. 'It was all right.'

'Where did you go?'

'Pictures.'

'The back row?'

'Mind your own business!' Jennie admonished.

Which probably meant they had, Madge thought with satisfaction. 'What did you say his name was?'

'Rob.'

'I've always liked that name. Is he tall?'

'No, he's a midget.'

'I was only showing interest!' Madge protested.

'Interest! I'd call it more like giving me the third degree.'

There was a few moments' pause, then Madge said, 'Nice, is he?'

'Pleasant enough.'

'And he's got a good job I believe you said?'

'He's a clerk with a company of wool exporters.'

That seemed sound enough, Madge thought. 'Are you seeing him again?'

'Maybe.'

Madge's face fell.

'Oh all right, yes I am. Next Saturday night. We're going dancing at the Roxy Ballroom.'

Madge couldn't conceal her delight.

'Now, can we change the subject?'

'Anything you say,' Madge nodded. She couldn't have been more pleased that Jennie was getting out and about again and had met a nice lad into the bargain.

Then she thought of George and George's proposal. Slowly the smile faded from her face.

'I've thought it through George and I can't come and stay with you,' Madge said.

George was clearly disappointed. 'Why not?'

'The children are the main stumbling block. How would it affect them?'

'They could stay here too if they wants. Be a bit cramped mind, and we'd have to move things around somewhat. But it could be done.'

'It's the scandal I'm thinking about, George. And how it would reflect on them, and me. I'm afraid things aren't as simple as I first imagined. There's Graham's business for example. The workforce would be bound to find out and that could embarrass him, or even make it difficult in his dealings with them.'

George scratched his chin.

'And there's Jennie. She hopes to make something of herself by going to night school. I wouldn't want to jeopardize her chances in the future which it's just possible a scandal might do. And what would Graham and Jennie think of me leaving John for another man, especially one who has the reputation – undeservedly I admit – you've got. They could easily lose all respect for me, and I couldn't bear that.'

When George didn't comment on those points, Madge continued, 'And what about the village? I'd never be able to hold my head up again knowing what they'd be thinking of me, and saying behind my back. You know what village gossip is like, they'd still be talking about it years from now. "There goes that Madge Forsyth who left her husband for George Rattenbury, him who used to carry on so much. And might still do for all she and we know."'

George's expression became grim, for what Madge had just said was true enough.

'Let's not forget the farmer, your employer. What would he say if I moved in? He's a stalwart of the church after all, and sees himself as a pillar of the community. In my opinion he'd sack you which would mean us having to leave this cottage.'

'There be other jobs, Madge.'

'But not in this area there wouldn't. Not for you with me in tow.'

'We'll go elsewhere then!' George exclaimed.

Madge shook her head. 'I don't want to move away. This is where my children are, and certainly in Graham's case going to remain. And that's another consideration, how would Kerensa's father and friends react to the news that Graham's mother had left her husband to live in sin with someone else. It would be simply awful for him, and a situation, regardless of my feelings for you, I'm just not willing to subject him to.'

'I can understand that,' George said quietly, nodding.

'Anyway, there's the financial aspect of a divorce. I made enquiries and they cost an absolute fortune. Far more than I'm sure you can lay hands on.'

George hadn't thought about that side of it.

'So I'm afraid us getting together isn't on,' Madge stated.

'You've certainly presented a powerful argument against it,' George commented, smiling thinly.

'Maybe things will change in time, who knows? But for now it's out of the question.'

George's mood had become a reflective one. 'Can I say something? And I'm not trying to change your mind. I accept what you've said, and that's that.'

'On you go then.'

'I thank God I met you Madge. You're the best thing that's ever happened to me. I swear it.'

Tears came into Madge's eyes, his words had touched her deeply. 'Even better than the girl you once wanted to marry?'

'Even better,' he stated softly.

She reached up and touched a weather-beaten cheek. 'You don't have much luck with women, do you George?'

'That's not the way they tells it in the village,' he joked.

'You know what I mean!'

'As you say, maybe things will change in time. In the meanwhile, we can continue on as we are.'

Madge thought of their love nest in the water meadows. She couldn't wait for summer to come again.

Kerensa stared at the sofa belonging to the three-piece suite which had been delivered that day. She wasn't at all sure she'd positioned it properly.

Graham gazed round the sitting-room of the cottage he'd bought for them. It was almost unrecognizable from his first viewing of it. Kerensa had worked wonders, and in a relatively short time too.

She'd organized everything herself: hordes of workmen who had descended one after the other, and following them, painters and decorators who had transformed the interior.

Kerensa frowned, and put a hand to her forehead. She closed her eyes, opened them again and sighed.

'Are you all right?' Graham queried.

'A sudden blinding headache. And look . . .' She took her hand from her forehead and showed it to him. It was wet with sweat.

'Sit down,' he instructed, pushing her towards the sofa she'd just been contemplating.

'Can I get you anything?' he asked.

'A glass of water please. My throat has gone dry.'

He hurried from the sitting-room, finding her with her head in her hands when he returned.

'Here, drink this,' he said, handing her a tumbler.

Kerensa gulped down the water and requested more. She drank the second glass slowly when it arrived.

'I think I'd better get you home,' Graham said.

'I must have caught a cold,' Kerensa declared.

'In which case bed is the best place for you.'

'The symptoms have appeared so quickly. I was perfectly fine when we got here.'

'Well, you're not now, so it's home.'

Kerensa stood, and staggered. Graham leapt to her side and steadied her.

'Wow!' she breathed. 'My legs just buckled under me.'

Graham helped her into her coat, and out to the car. When she was settled he went back to the cottage, turned the lights off and locked up.

When they arrived at Corfe Mullen he opened the door using her key and helped her inside.

'Head's spinning. Everything going round and round,' she said.

Anthony emerged from the drawing-room to stare at Kerensa in concern.

'She needs to go straight to her bed. If you do that I'll go for the doctor,' Graham said to him.

'No need for the doctor,' Kerensa mumbled.

'There's every need. Don't you agree sir?'

Anthony nodded. 'Look at her, she's white as a sheet. You're quite right, Graham. You go for the doctor and I'll get her into bed.'

It was a pity they didn't have a telephone at Corfe Mullen Graham thought as he sped through the night. That was something he'd had installed at his parents' shortly after buying the Stanton Brick Works.

Dr Court himself answered Graham's knock. 'I'll come right away,' he replied after Graham had explained the reason for his calling.

'I'll give you a lift if you'd like?' Graham volunteered.

'Fine.'

'It came on so suddenly,' Graham said as they headed back to Corfe Mullen.

Court, sitting with his bag in his lap, nodded. He was pretty certain he knew what was wrong wtih Kerensa, but refrained from saying anything until he'd examined his patient.

Graham and Anthony waited in the drawing-room while Court was upstairs with Kerensa. They both rose to their feet when Court eventually joined them.

''Flu,' stated Court, which was what he'd suspected. 'I've given her something and have written out a prescription which you can get in the morning Mr Sturt.'

Anthony accepted the prescription from Court, glanced at it, folded it and put it on the mantelpiece. 'I'll go to the chemist first thing,' he said.

'Better if I did that. Then Kerensa wouldn't be left on her own,' Graham suggested.

'Good idea,' acknowledged Anthony, and gave Graham the prescription.

'I'll drop by around midday tomorrow and see how she is,' Court said. 'In the mean time, keep her wrapped up warm and give her lots to drink.'

Anthony nodded that he understood.

Graham wanted to say good-night to Kerensa, but didn't think he could do so in the circumstances. 'I'll see you in the morning,' he said to Anthony.

He and Court then left Corfe Mullen.

''Flu,' muttered Madge sympathetically, immediately thinking of George whom she'd nursed through it the previous February; it was now February 1936.

'We've got a couple of men off at the mine with it,' John said.

'I've heard there's a bit of it about,' Madge stated. 'Though not as much as there was last year.'

'There was a lot of it then,' John agreed.

Graham thought of Kerensa, and wondered how she was; he hoped she was sleeping.

In bed or not he'd insist he saw and spoke with her next morning. He was her fiancé, after all.

'You look dreadful,' he said to Kerensa.

'Oh, thank you very much!'

'But still beautiful to me.'

'Creep,' she teased.

Anthony had already been up with the medicine

384

Graham had brought, and made sure Kerensa was fit to receive. She was sitting up in bed wearing a bedjacket sporting satin bows.

Graham laid a bunch of flowers in front of her, and a large box of chocolates beside that.

'Goodies,' he said.

She eyed the flowers which were a mixed assortment. He must have gone to a lot of trouble to get them at this time of year, she thought.

'Do I get a kiss in appreciation?'

'Not on the lips. I don't want you catching this.'

He kissed her on the cheek, noting as he did that her skin was very warm. She had a raised temperature he rightly guessed.

'How do you feel?' he asked.

'Weak.'

He nodded his sympathy.

'And shivery from time to time,' she added.

'Is there anything I can get for you?'

'Not really. Daddy is doing a marvellous job as a nurse.'

He sat on the side of the bed and took her hand. Her eyes, he saw, had an unnatural brightness to them.

'How was the medicine?' he enquired.

She made a face. 'Horrible.'

'Just as long as it makes you better, that's the main thing.'

'You should be at work, not here,' she said.

'You're more important.'

'Am I?' she asked softly.

'To me you are. You're the most important thing there is.'

She knew he meant it. If she hadn't been ill she would have hugged and kissed him.

They talked for a while, until Anthony appeared saying Kerensa really should get some more rest. Graham saw the sense in that and started to leave, but said he would return that evening.

385

Graham put the flowers in water before leaving, and Anthony took the vase up to her room.

'Stop bolting your food. You'll give yourself terrible indigestion!' Madge admonished Graham.

'In a hurry to go and see Kerensa,' he mumbled in reply. 'The doctor was calling in at midday.'

'How is she?' Jennie asked.

'As you'd expect with someone who's got 'flu.'

'It's a nasty thing,' Madge sympathized, thinking again of George and how bad he'd been with it.

'Anyway, must dash,' said Graham, rising from the table.

'What about your sweet?' Madge protested.

'No time for it. Bye!' And with that Graham fled the kitchen, and banged the front door shut behind him.

Madge lifted her eyes heavenwards.

Graham paused in what he was doing to glance over at Kerensa's desk where a Miss Smith now sat – he'd had the office enlarged but not sectioned as had been his original plan. Miss Smith was a temporary replacement while Kerensa was ill.

God, he missed her! He'd become so used to having her around all day. Still, it wouldn't be that long till she was back according to the doctor.

He'd take her more fruit when he went to Corfe Mullen that night, as she'd enjoyed the fruit he'd already given her. He must remember to buy a few more magazines for her to leaf through.

He looked at his watch. It was hours yet before knocking-off time! The minutes were dragging. They couldn't have gone more slowly.

He returned to his work, and tried again to concentrate.

But every so often he kept thinking of Kerensa, and on each occasion he smiled.

God, how he missed her!

'You're looking a lot better,' he enthused later, entering her bedroom.

'I feel much better.'

He placed the fruit to one side, then kissed her cheek. He noted it had cooled down. It also pleased him to see that the unnatural brightness had vanished from her eyes.

'How's Miss Smith doing?' she enquired.

'All right. But she's not a patch on you.'

'Flattery will get you everywhere,' Kerensa smiled. 'You haven't told me yet what she's like?'

'A real stunner. Nineteen years old with a figure that could send a man mad with desire,' Graham lied. In fact Miss Smith was a spinster in her early fifties who wore her pepper-and-salt hair drawn back in a bun and suffered from varicose veins.

'Hmm!' Kerensa mused.

'She's only got one fault,' Graham went on.

'What's that?'

'She's a rotten kisser.'

Kerensa realized she was being teased. 'Fool!' she exclaimed.

Graham then proceeded to make Kerensa laugh a lot, which she told him at the end of his visit had done her the world of good, and cheered her immeasurably, which was precisely what he'd intended.

'What do you mean, a turn for the worse?' Graham asked Dr Court who was already at Corfe Mullen when he arrived.

'Precisely that I'm afraid,' Court replied. 'She's developed bronchial pneumonia – a complication of her 'flu. She's most unwell, I have to tell you.'

Graham looked at Anthony whose face was tight and drawn.

'She went to the bathroom and collapsed,' Anthony said to Graham. 'I put her back in bed, then rang Dr Court from the nearest public telephone box. He was unfortunately out, but came as soon as he could.'

'Bronchial pneumonia,' Graham repeated to himself.
'Is that bad?'

'It can be,' Court answered softly. 'I've given her some
sulphonamides, which will hopefully help. All I, or any
other doctor can do, is continue with that treatment and
wait to see what happens.'

Court made a sympathetic face. 'I'm sorry,' he said,
addressing both Graham and Anthony.

'I must go up to her,' Graham said. 'I must be with
her.' He didn't care about proprieties any more. All he
could think of was being by Kerensa's side.

'She's sleeping for the moment,' Court said. 'When
she wakes encourage her to take lots of liquids. Milky
drinks, Ovaltine, that sort of thing.'

'I understand,' Graham said. 'Is there anything
else?'

Court opened his bag and took out a glass bottle which
he handed Graham. 'These are the sulphonamides, the
instructions are on the label.'

'Right,' Graham acknowledged.

'And I'll return in the morning.'

'I'll show you out, doctor,' Anthony said.

As Anthony was doing that a distraught Graham went
up to Kerensa.

Anthony quietly entered Kerensa's bedroom to find
Graham sitting by her bedside, the only light coming
from a small lamp.

'She's asleep again,' Graham informed Anthony.

'I've brought you some tea.'

'Thank you,' Graham replied, gratefully accepting the
proffered cup.

'It's gone midnight. Time you went home.'

Graham shook his head. 'With your permission I'll
stay right here.'

Anthony's initial reaction was to refuse. But there
again, where was the harm? And if Kerensa woke during

388

the night it might comfort her to have him there.

'All right,' Anthony agreed.

As Anthony left the room Graham went back to gazing anxiously at Kerensa.

Dr Court's expression gave nothing away as he examined Kerensa. 'How do you feel?' he asked.

'Terribly light headed.'

He nodded. 'I would have expected that.'

She coughed, a racking sound that rasped in her throat.

'Perhaps you might try a little soup later,' Court suggested.

'No appetite.'

'But soup would do you good.'

'I'll try then,' she said.

'Can you arrange that?' Court said to Anthony, who hesitated. Kerensa normally did all the cooking which wasn't exactly his forte.

'I can,' Graham stated.

'Broth would be best,' Court said.

'Broth it will be.'

Court looked again at Kerensa, and smiled. 'I'll pop in later and see how you're doing.'

'Thank you, doctor,' she croaked.

Dr Court then left the bedroom, Anthony following directly behind.

'Won't be a tick,' Graham told Kerensa, and hurried after them.

He joined the doctor and Anthony who were standing a little way down the corridor. 'I'm afraid her condition has worsened,' Court said grim-faced. 'But that must have been obvious to you.'

'Surely there's something else we can do or try?' Graham queried.

Court shook his head. 'What she's taking is the best available. However, feel free to call in someone else if you wish to have a second opinion.'

Graham let out a long sigh. 'No, if you say that's so then I'm sure you're right.'

'She's only had two doses of medicine, so there's still plenty of time for it to work,' Court stated. Then added brusquely, 'As I said to Kerensa, I'll pop in later.'

'And I'll organize that soup,' Graham muttered.

Graham returned to Kerensa while Anthony showed the doctor out, explaining to her where he was going and why, and promised he'd be back just as soon as he could.

'Where have you been?' Madge demanded. When he hadn't appeared for his breakfast she'd gone to his room to wake him to discover his bed not slept in.

He spoke quickly, the words tumbling from his mouth. His worry and anxiety were obvious.

'Of course I'll come,' Madge said the moment he stopped speaking.

Graham ran a hand over his unshaven chin. 'I'll put a few things together while you get ready,' he said.

Upstairs in his bedroom he made a small pile of clothes, then added a few other necessary items. All these he packed into a suitcase that had come down from Glasgow.

Madge had assembled everything she required in a wooden box, luckily having all the ingredients for broth to hand. She then made a lightning visit to the Post Office Stores where she explained the situation to Jennie and bought some lovely pork sausages for Graham's and Anthony's lunch.

Graham was waiting impatiently when she returned. 'Let's go,' he said.

'What about your firm, shouldn't you notify them that you won't be in?' Madge queried as the Lanchester pulled away from the kerb.

'I already have. Rang them while you were at the shop. I've instructed Miss Smith to call in Phil Crane who can take over my desk meantime. She's assured me she can cope until he arrives.'

Lucky she'd been home, Madge thought, she'd almost gone round to one of her WI pals for coffee.

En route they passed George on his tractor in a field and Madge remembered the chicken broth she'd taken him when he was ill.

Graham gently wiped sweat from Kerensa's fevered brow. Her skin had gone waxen, while her eyes had sunk right in on themselves. This was the fourth day of her bronchial pneumonia during which he'd rarely left her side.

Kerensa was awake, staring at the ceiling, a strange smile playing round her lips.

'Would you like some water?' he asked.

She seemed to bring herself back from another place, and focused on him. 'Please.'

He held her up and put the glass to her lips. She had several sips, then drew in a deep breath which rattled in her chest.

Graham laid her back on the bed, and wiped more sweat from her brow.

'I remember the day we met, at the fête. Such a lovely day,' she whispered.

'And a memorable one,' he said.

'Yes.'

A few seconds later he wiped more sweat away.

'You're saying she could die!' exclaimed Graham, horrified. It was a possibility he'd kept steadfastly from his mind.

'Well, I'm extremely concerned that she's not responding to the medicine. If she doesn't turn the corner soon . . .' Dr Court trailed off, and shrugged.

Kerensa die. Lose her! He glanced at Anthony who looked pole-axed.

'She's continuing to deteriorate,' Court went on. 'At this rate a few more days could easily prove too much for her.'

Too much for her . . . Too much for her . . . Those words shrieked repeatedly inside Graham's head.

'I'm sorry. I've done everything I can. Everything that can be done.' Court shrugged again. 'If only she would respond to the sulphonamides.'

Graham crossed to a chair and sat, Court and Anthony temporarily forgotten. He was numb with shock.

Too much for her . . . The words continued to shriek inside his head.

Anthony halted outside Kerensa's partially open bedroom door to stare at Graham sitting by her bedside. There were tears streaming down his face, a face twisted with anguish.

Anthony gazed at Graham, transported to see himself when he'd been told about Rebecca. He remembered only too well his own anguish before her death, and the terrible grief after it.

In those few moments his attitude to Graham completely changed. There could be no doubting the love Graham had for his daughter, that Graham loved Kerensa with the same depth and intensity of feeling that he'd loved Rebecca.

Anthony walked silently away, going to his own bedroom and there he, too, wept.

Please God, Graham prayed, hands clasped in front of him, don't let her die! I'll do anything to save her, give anything. Only please don't let her die.

If a life is necessary then take mine in her place. I offer it willingly. Take me, but save Kerensa. I ask you, I beseech you, I *beg* you, let Kerensa live.

Graham prayed and prayed till he could think of nothing more to say.

Then he started at the beginning and went through it all again.

* * *

Graham slowly woke up, realizing that sometime during the night he must have dozed off. He yawned and turned his attention to Kerensa.

He saw and heard the difference immediately. There was colour in her cheeks, while her breathing was back to normal. She'd turned that corner Court had mentioned, he instinctively knew it.

A great wave of elation burst inside him making him want to jump to his feet and shout with joy.

As she continued to sleep he hurried from the room to tell Anthony.

'You are on the mend I'm happy to say,' Dr Court pronounced to Kerensa who was sitting up in bed wearing her bedjacket.

'I knew it the instant I saw her this morning,' Graham declared, absolutely delighted.

'I still feel weak, but all right within myself,' Kerensa stated.

'You'll have to take things easy for a while,' Court warned her. 'Which, among other things, means not returning to work until you're fully recovered.'

'As her boss I'll see she won't,' Graham said.

'I'm not so sure about that Miss Smith though,' Kerensa joked.

'I'll tell you about her later,' Graham smiled.

'You know I don't think it was the sulphonamides that brought about her recovery, but her own body defences,' Court mused. 'It happens that way sometimes.'

'Whatever, she's going to get better. That's all that matters,' Anthony beamed.

'I'll second that,' Graham said.

'Now stay in bed for another couple of days, then you can start getting up for short periods at a time,' Court informed Kerensa. Then to Anthony, 'And she must have lots of nourishing food to build her strength back up again.'

Graham recognized the look on Anthony's face.

Madge had been dropping by to cook for them, but Anthony was thinking he couldn't expect her to go on doing that.

'I'll hire someone to cook and clean till Kerensa's properly on her feet again,' Graham said with Anthony's financial situation in mind. 'And in the mean time, my mum will be only too happy helping out. Kerensa is going to be her daughter-in-law after all.'

'I appreciate that,' nodded Anthony.

'Anything else?' Graham asked Court.

'Fresh air would be good for her. But, and I stress the point, not draughts.'

'Understood,' replied Graham.

'I'll stop by tomorrow to check on how you're progressing,' Court said to Kerensa.

Anthony escorted the doctor to his car leaving Graham with Kerensa.

'You gave me an awful fright,' he told her.

'I'm sorry.'

He sat on the edge of the bed and took her in his arms. He felt at peace once more, content, brimming over with love.

They were married in the spring as planned, a small wedding at Kerensa's request. Anthony scraped the money together and insisted on paying for it.

Chapter Eleven

'By the way, I'm going to London next week and shall be staying overnight,' Jennie announced.

John's fork stopped half-way to his mouth, and he stared at her in astonishment. 'I beg your pardon?'

Jennie repeated what she'd said.

'Don't be soft!' John declared, and continued eating. It was May 1936 and the newspaper he was anxious to get back to after his tea was full of the news that Italian troops had occupied Addis Ababa.

'I'm serious,' Jennie stated.

'Why are you going there?' Madge queried softly.

'For a job interview. I shall be staying at the Candida Hotel where I've booked a single room. I telephoned the hotel a little earlier while you were busy in here and Dad was reading. I'll naturally pay for the call.' Their telephone was in the hall.

Madge gazed quizzically at her daughter, as this was a real bombshell. 'What sort of job?'

The moment had finally arrived for Jennie to divulge the ambition that had driven her for several years. 'I have an interview with the Dean of the London School of Medicine for Women attached to the Royal Free Hospital. I've applied for a place there.'

'You're joking!' John exclaimed.

'I'm doing nothing of the sort.'

'You mean you want to go to this medical school?' Madge said.

'That's right, Mum.'

'To become what?'

'A doctor.'

John laughed, and bits of food flew out of his mouth. Madge turned and scowled at him.

'That's good! That's excellent!' he roared, and wiped a sleeve over his eyes.

'What's so funny?' Jennie frowned.

'That is. You're having us on, aren't you?'

'No, I'm not. I'm in deadly earnest.'

'You, a doctor!' John pounded the table, and continued to roar with laughter.

'You've never mentioned anything about this,' Madge said. 'Is it a new idea?'

Jennie shook her head. 'I've known for ages that I want to be a doctor. I never said because . . . well, I'd have felt embarrassed if I'd failed to get the necessary qualifications.'

'But you haven't sat your final exams yet,' Madge pointed out.

'The interviews are held before finals, although the outcome is dependant on the results. I wouldn't have applied if I wasn't more or less certain that I would do well in my exams. All my tutors have assured me that I should, unless something goes horribly wrong while I'm sitting them.'

'I see,' Madge mused.

'I've never heard such nonsense in my life,' John said.

'Why is it nonsense?' Jennie queried quietly.

'Women doctors! Whoever heard of such a thing,' John scoffed.

'Oh, they exist all right,' Jennie replied. 'There aren't that many of them yet I admit, but their number is steadily growing.'

John looked sceptical. 'Well, if there are such beings I bet they come from rich backgrounds and not plain working-class stock such as you. Why, it's ridiculous the idea of you becoming a doctor. Quite ridiculous!'

'It's nothing of the sort,' Jennie replied defiantly. 'And class has nothing to do with it. It's brains and ability they're concerned about, not the size of the house you live in and how much money you have in the bank.'

'Ideas above your station,' John snorted.

'That's the sort of accusation you made to Graham, and look how well he's doing,' Madge told him.

'Graham's a man,' John retorted. 'And anyway, he married into a posh family. Climbed in the back door so to speak.'

'I don't think I like what you're inferring,' Madge snapped, eyes glinting. 'Graham married Kerensa because he loved her and for no other reason.'

'So you say,' John said.

'You're despicable at times,' Madge declared.

'Let me simply say his marriage was very convenient, that's all.'

Madge turned to Jennie. 'Ignore him. He's ignorant.'

'I am nothing of the sort!' John exclaimed angrily.

'If they do accept you,' Madge turned to Jennie, 'does that mean you'll have to live in London?'

Jennie nodded.

'But how would you get by?'

'I've been saving part of my wages all this time. That will last me quite a while, long enough anyway until I can arrange some source of income.'

'And how long would your training be?'

'Five years,' Jennie replied.

Madge put down her knife and fork, suddenly losing her appetite. She'd known Jennie would leave home one day, of course, but not for London! She'd visualized her getting married and settling in the area if not in the actual village itself. Now this, and completely out of the blue.

'Remember you once asked me about calling in on Dr Court?' Jenny said.

Madge thought back, and remembered the incident. 'That's right, Jane spotted you coming out of his surgery.'

'And you asked if I was ill and I replied that I'd been seeing Dr Court about a project I had to do for night

397

school. Well, I'm afraid that was a fib. Dr Court has been advising me and helping me in all manner of ways. It was through him, for example, that I learned the Royal Free was the first hospital to open its doors to female medical students and where I would stand most chance of being accepted.'

'They'll never accept you, take my word for it,' John sneered.

'I'll get angry with you in a moment,' Madge warned him.

With another snort, John rose from the table, crossed to his chair, picked up his paper and began to read.

'So Dr Court was in on this,' Madge mused.

'He was the only one, and I swore him to secrecy.'

'What days next week?' Madge asked.

Jennie told her. 'I've already spoken to Mr Yendell and he's agreed to give me the time off. I explained to him that I had to go to London on important business, but didn't say what that business was.'

'That was decent of him,' Madge nodded. But then Bob Yendell was a gem, possibly the most-liked man in the village. If Bob could do you a good turn he would.

'A doctor,' John muttered in his chair, and laughed again.

'I can understand why you wanted to keep this to yourself,' Madge said, glaring at John.

'Ridiculous,' John repeated.

'The only thing round here that's ridiculous is you,' Madge declared.

'There's no certainty that I will get in, of course,' Jennie went on. 'There are only a limited number of places and from what I understand the competition is stiff. Medicine is a very popular career.'

'Among the nobs,' John said quietly, not taking his eyes off his newspaper.

'You can only try, no harm in that,' Madge said encouragingly to Jennie.

'Exactly.'

'And it's really what you want to do?'

'Yes Mum. Very much so.'

'Well, well,' Madge murmured, as it gradually began to sink in. She only hoped Jennie wasn't going to be disappointed. 'What will you wear for this interview? That's always important.'

'Well, I thought . . .'

The ensuing conversation was all about clothes, clothes Jennie already owned and clothes she might buy for the big occasion.

Madge watched in fascination as George consumed the huge mound of food heaped in front of him which she had cooked for him. It never ceased to amaze her how much he could eat.

George looked at her and smiled. 'Right tasty, Madge. You're a dab hand with the pots and pans.'

'I'm glad you're enjoying it.'

'Don't I always when you makes me something?'

Madge rose from the table and poured herself a cup of tea. George was drinking beer.

'And John has gone to the Band of Hope?' George said.

'That's why I'm free all evening and could come over and cook for you. Not only has he started going to their meetings, but he has signed the pledge with them. A drop of alcohol has not passed his lips since he did.'

'That'll please you then?'

Madge sat again at the table. It was lovely spending time with George like this, it was almost as if they were a married couple.

'I was surprised at what you told me about Jennie,' George said.

'About her wanting to become a doctor? I was too.'

'Good for her!'

'That's what I think. John, of course, is dead against it, says she's got ideas above her station.'

'Nonsense,' replied George. 'Why shouldn't she aim

high? She'll never get nowhere unless she do. Better to try and fail than not to try at all.'

'My sentiments precisely,' Madge said, cradling her cup between her hands.

'Besides, a lot of things have changed in this country of late. Many old barriers knocked down. We have the Great War to thank for that. And if Doc Court thinks she's got a chance then she surely has. He wouldn't let her make a fool of herself, would he?'

'True,' Madge acknowledged. She hadn't thought of that.

'Band of Hope,' George said, and chuckled.

'He is extremely religious,' Madge smiled. 'Always has been. Reads his Bible every Sunday evening without fail. At one time we all had to listen, but nowadays he mostly reads it by himself.'

'Curious chap,' George commented, spearing a potato.

'The worst thing about Jennie going to London, if she does that, will be the loss of her pay packet coming into the house. Theoretically anyway it would mean I was reliant solely on John's wage which is low.'

'How do you mean theoretically?'

'Graham slips me something from time to time. I'm sure he wouldn't see us go short.'

'He's a son to be proud of, your Graham.'

'I am. And of Jennie.' She hesitated then asked, 'Would you have liked children?'

'Oh, indeed! It's a sadness in my life that I haven't any. I would certainly have liked some by you, my lover.'

Madge blushed. 'That would have been nice.'

He placed a meaty, calloused paw over her hand. 'You gives me great pleasure, Madge. I can't tell you that often enough. You've brought sunlight into what had been a dull and dreary life.'

'And you give me great pleasure, George.'

'The offer's still open any time you wants to take it up.'

She knew the offer he was referring to was her living with him. She shook her head. 'Most of the old objections still stand, George. But if I ever feel I can then I'll say. You can rely on that.'

'Good.' He leaned across the table and kissed her lightly on the lips.

'So, how are things on the farm?' she enquired when the kiss was over.

He proceeded to tell her about his day, and about the farm in general.

Madge enjoyed it far more than when later she had to listen to John going on about the Band of Hope.

How dirty it was, Jennie thought as her train puffed its way past terraces of mean, grimy houses. Dirty and depressing were her initial impressions of London.

She stared through the window in dismay at the urban sprawl that stretched as far as the eye could see. London was so big, so vast!

'First time in "the smoke", luv?' asked a woman sitting opposite her in a strong London accent.

Jennie nodded.

'I could tell from yer expression you was impressed. There's nuffink like "the smoke". Whenever I go away I can't wait to get back again.'

Impressed! That was a laugh. She felt just the opposite.

'Nuffink like it,' the woman repeated, and sighed.

She's going to break into 'Maybe It's Because I'm A Londoner', Jennie thought, but mercifully the woman didn't.

Jennie went back to staring out of the carriage window.

'Here you are luv, this is where you want,' the cabbie said to Jennie.

Jennie got out and paid him, giving him what she considered to be a reasonable tip.

'Ta darlin',' the cabbie smiled, and drove off.

Jennie gazed up and down the length of Hunter Street. The air was so different here, she thought. There was a deadness about it, and it tasted of soot. She decided the smell was caused by so many people living densely packed together.

She stared nervously at the door through which she had to pass, where the whole course of her future would be decided.

Taking a deep breath to steady herself, she went inside.

'Miss Forsyth, you're next,' said the Dean's secretary.

'Thank you.'

'If you'll just follow me.'

They left the ante-room and walked down a corridor till they came to a door which the secretary opened. 'In here,' she instructed.

There was a solitary female sitting behind a table who rose and smiled as Jennie entered. 'Good-day, Miss Forsyth,' she said affably. 'I'm the Dean of the Medical School.'

They shook hands, then the Dean said, 'If you'd like to sit down we'll start.'

'Where is she?' cried Graham, bursting into the kitchen clutching a bottle of champagne. Kerensa strolled in after him.

Graham plonked the bottle on the table, took Jennie in his arms and whirled her round.

'Careful!' John warned.

'I couldn't be more pleased for you. Congratulations!' Graham said, and kissed Jennie on the cheek.

'Yes, congratulations. Well done,' added Kerensa, patting Jennie on the arm.

'Mum said on the phone that you were accepted there and then,' Graham prompted.

Jennie nodded. 'And the secretary promised to try and

arrange a grant for me which is icing on the cake.'

'Go on, tell Graham what the Dean said about you,' Madge urged.

'She said she was most impressed by my having gone to night school after leaving ordinary school at fourteen. She said I was the first applicant she's ever had who'd done that.'

'She's every right to be impressed,' Graham declared enthusiastically. 'What you've achieved through your own efforts is laudable.'

'I couldn't agree more,' Kerensa smiled.

Graham tore the foil off the champagne. 'Get some glasses, Mum. This calls for a celebration.'

'When do you start?' Kerensa asked Jennie.

'Late September.'

'And where will you live?'

'The medical school will fit me up with digs.'

'I see,' Kerensa answered.

There was a loud pop! and the champagne cork flew through the air. 'Here we go!' said Graham, filling one of the glasses Madge had laid out.

John watched this enviously, as he was still on the wagon.

'That's for you, sis,' stated Graham, handing her the first glass that he had now topped up.

'What about you, Dad?' Graham asked when the others had been given glasses.

'Not for me,' John grumbled.

'He can have some lemonade,' said Madge, and poured John out some.

'Here's to Jennie and her career as a doctor!' Graham toasted.

'I still have my finals to take,' Jennie reminded him.

'With the marks you've been getting to date you'll walk them. I have no doubts whatsoever about that.'

'I only hope you're right,' Jennie muttered.

'Jennie and her career as a doctor!' Madge and Kerensa chorused.

The contents of the bottle soon vanished leaving Graham wanting some more. 'Tell you what, let's all go to the pub and continue there,' he suggested.

'Good idea!' enthused Kerensa.

Why not? Madge thought. After all, it wasn't every day her daughter got accepted into medical school. 'I'm game,' she said.

'Coming for more lemonade, Dad?' Graham enquired.

John shook his head. 'Count me out. Pubs aren't any fun when you can't have a proper drink.'

'Aw come on, Dad!' Jennie urged.

'I said no, and I mean it,' he replied crossly.

'What did you think of London?' Kerensa asked Jennie as they left the house.

Jennie pulled a face. 'I thought it rather horrid really.'

'You'll soon get used to it. I know I did.'

'It's so filthy.'

'You stop noticing that after a while. London has a charm all of its own that I'm sure you'll like. And working in a hospital you'll meet lots of eligible young men. That's something to think about.'

They went into the pub where the women sat down and Graham took their orders. He then went up to the bar where he explained to the landlord and several regulars standing near by the reason for the celebration.

'Congratulations, Jen!' the landlord called over, sticking a thumb up in recognition of her achievement.

Madge glanced round and suddenly found herself staring at George sitting alone in a corner. If only she could have asked him over to join them, but, of course, that was out of the question.

He gave her the faintest of smiles, which she daren't return.

'So, tell me exactly what was said at your interview,' Kerensa asked Jennie.

Madge focused her attention on those sitting round her table. For the rest of her time in the pub she was acutely aware of George's presence, and wished he was sitting by her side taking part in their celebration.

'Madge?' John whispered, placing a hand on her thigh.

She mentally groaned. The only bad thing about John's non-drinking was that it had increased his libido.

'Madge, I know you're awake,' he said, the same hand now snaking up underneath her nightdress.

She hated John making love to her. But what could she do? They were married and shared the same bed. She couldn't even use his drinking as an excuse to cry off any more.

She closed her eyes and thought of George. It was so wonderful with him. If only she could leave John to stay with George. But she knew it was impossible, for she had to think of Graham and Jennie.

John grunted as he heaved himself on top of her.

Be quick! she thought. Please be quick! Still with her eyes closed, and saying nothing to John, she pictured George in her mind and tried to pretend it was he.

George, her dear friend and lover. George who made her laugh, and who listened so intently whenever she spoke. George whom she'd much rather have been with.

When it was over Madge turned her back on John and continued to think of George as she waited for sleep to descend.

Kerensa took a deep breath, then another. Her head was spinning round and round and she felt nauseous.

'Are you all right?' Graham enquired anxiously, moving towards her desk.

Kerensa ran a hand over her forehead. 'Just give me a moment,' she mumbled. Alarm flared in Graham, his mind flashing back to when she'd been ill with 'flu. 'Can I get you anything?'

'Some water.'

He rushed off, returning directly with the requested water.

'That's better,' Kerensa said after she'd had several sips.

'What was wrong?'

She gave him a weak smile. 'I think I'm pregnant.'

'What?' exclaimed Graham, delighted.

'It's certainly beginning to look that way. Pleased?'

'Pleased? I couldn't be more so. I'm bloody ecstatic.'

She'd missed two consecutive periods, where she'd never missed one before, and now this sudden attack of nausea. That's what it had to add up to. Anyway, she felt different within herself, as if a physical and mental change had already taken place.

Kerensa pregnant, Graham thought. He was going to become a father. He rubbed his hands in glee. 'But should you be working? Maybe you should go home and rest. I can always get . . .'

'Graham!' she interjected. 'Be a good chap and don't fuss. There's no reason I shouldn't go on working for some time yet.'

He couldn't wait to tell Madge, and knew exactly what her reaction would be. He'd ring her right away he decided. Anthony, too, his father-in-law should be informed.

A boy or a girl? Graham didn't care. Just as long as the baby was healthy and all its bits and pieces were in the right place.

'It'll be the first,' Kerensa said with a twinkle in her eye.

'Of course it'll be the first.'

'Of that dozen you wanted. Six of each, remember?'

He laughed, and kissed her on the lips. 'I remember.'

'Now let's get back to work. We've spent enough time on me as it is.'

'Right,' he agreed. 'Just as soon as I've rung Mum.'

'Not about this,' Kerensa stated firmly. 'I don't want you saying anything to anyone until I'm one hundred per cent certain. Understand?'

His face fell in disappointment, but he could see her

point. The treat of telling Madge would have to wait until another day.

Several weeks later that day dawned.

'I'm Jennie Forsyth,' Jennie announed to the plumpish middle-aged woman who answered her knock.

'And I'm Mrs Atkins.'

'How do you do?' said Jennie, extending a hand, which Mrs Atkins shook.

'Come in, you must be tired after your journey.'

'I am,' confessed Jennie. 'It was a long drive.'

'You motored then!' said Mrs Atkins, gazing over Jennie's shoulder to where the Hornet was parked.

'Yes,' acknowledged Jennie, picking up her two suitcases.

'Here, let me help you.'

They stepped through the doorway into a wide spacious hall smelling of beeswax and furniture polish. What friendly, reassuring smells, Jennie thought. There were framed photographs and paintings on the hall walls, some of the photos yellow with age.

'Your roommate arrived earlier,' said Mrs Atkins as they passed a comfy looking sitting-room containing overstuffed chairs, sofas and a host of knick-knacks.

'The water's hot so you can have a bath,' Mrs Atkins informed Jennie. 'But first I'll show you up to your room and bring you a cup of tea. You can have a bite after your bath if you wish?'

'That would be kind,' Jennie answered.

They began mounting carpeted stairs. 'Mr Atkins is a commercial traveller and away a lot. Taking in students gives me an interest as well as helping out financially. We don't have children of our own,' Mrs Atkins explained.

They arrived on a landing with two doors leading off it. 'The house is smaller than it looks from the outside,' Mrs Atkins said. 'There are only two bedrooms. Ours, and the one you'll be sharing with Miss Marshall.' She opened the nearest door. 'This is the bathroom, the other is your bedroom.'

Mrs Atkins knocked on the bedroom door. 'Miss Marshall, Miss Forsyth is here.'

Jennie hoped she was going to get on with this Miss Marshall. It would be awful if she didn't.

The door swung open to reveal a smiling red-headed girl with masses of freckles. 'Hello,' the girl said.

'Miss Marshall, Miss Forsyth.'

The two girls gave each other the once over, and both decided they didn't take exception to what they saw.

'I'm Esther.'

'And I'm Jennie.'

'I'll go and get that tea now. Would you care for a cup, Miss Marshall?'

'Please.'

Esther lifted the suitcase Mrs Atkins had set down and carried it into the bedroom. Jennie followed.

'I've already chosen a bed. Hope you don't mind?' Esther said.

'Not at all.'

Jennie gazed about her. The room was large with a high ceiling. It contained two single beds, two wardrobes, two chests of drawers, two Lloyd-Loom chairs and a dressing table. Like the rest of the house it had a warm, friendly atmosphere to it. She'd fallen on her feet here, Jennie thought.

'Where are you from?' Esther asked.

'Devon. A village called Atherton.'

'I'm from Canterbury in Kent. First time away from home on your own?'

Jennie nodded.

'Me too. Little bit scary, isn't it?'

'It is,' Jennie agreed.

'I can't wait to start tomorrow.'

'Me neither,' Jennie stated.

'I've always wanted to be a doctor. My father's one.'

'The idea came to me several years ago. And my father works in a copper mine.'

Esther's eyebrows shot up. 'Really!'

'He used to be a miner but hurt himself, so is now on maintenance duties.'

Esther sat on the edge of her bed and stared quizzically at Jennie. 'I'm nineteen, you look older than that.'

'I'm twenty-two.' Jennie hesitated, then told Esther about her leaving school at fourteen and subsequently going to night school to complete her education. Esther found that enthralling.

The two girls continued to swop facts about themselves, and by the end of that evening had become firm friends.

The following morning both girls were up bright and early, excited at what lay ahead. Neither could eat much breakfast as they were far too nervous. They then drove to Hunter Street – following Mrs Atkins' directions – for their first day at medical school.

When the thirty new intakes had assembled, they were welcomed and addressed by the Dean who concluded by wishing them all good luck. They were then issued with a timetable plus various sheets of explanations and instructions.

'So far so good,' Esther said as they headed for a lecture hall, the entire intake trooping along chattering nineteen to the dozen. Jennie gazed from face to face, thinking she was bound to get to know them all well during the next five years.

In the lecture room Jennie and Esther sat together and stared with interest at their lecturer, a thin-faced woman wearing horn-rimmed glasses.

'Physiology,' the lecturer announced, and the hall fell silent.

After a short while Jennie and the others began making notes.

Madge stared out over the water meadows, thinking about Jennie who'd rung home the previous night to say her first day had gone well, and that she was happy with her digs. It was a tremendous relief as, of course, she'd been worried.

She wondered where George was, and what he was up to, which made her smile. She often smiled when she thought of George.

Several crows flapped by. As they disappeared off into the distance her mind went back to Glasgow and her years there. What would have happened to them if they hadn't come down to Devon? she wondered. And what would they be doing now?

Life had been hard in Glasgow, hard and relentless. But not all bad, there had been happy times, particularly when she'd been younger, before she'd met and married John.

She remembered the street games she'd so loved, peever, kick the can, playing 'shops'. And the Saturday penny she used to be given when her da could afford it, a penny she'd instantly spent on sweets, the highlight of her week.

And then there were the tenements, stone-staired and gas-lit, grey canyons along which icy cold winds whistled in winter. A world, and culture, away from Atherton and the verdant lushness of Devon. Glasgow was a city of steel and iron, of noise and sparks and fire. A bigger contrast to her present surroundings would be hard to find.

She continued gazing out over the fields, drinking in their beauty and tranquillity. They were so calming to look at, so soothing.

A tractor appeared in the distance, but it wasn't the one George drove. She watched it trundle over the grass, the spikes of its rear wheels digging into the earth.

It was like some prehistoric monster, she thought, and recalled drawings of such animals in books Graham had brought home when young. There had been a period when he'd been absolutely daft on the prehistoric, and had bought a lead Tyrannosaurus Rex which for some reason he'd christened Bicky.

Thinking of Graham made her think of Kerensa and the baby that was on its way. She smiled again, this time at the prospect of being a grandmother. She'd enjoy that, and would spoil the baby rotten. Well, wasn't that what grandmothers were for! She'd already started sewing and knitting in preparation for its arrival.

She sucked in a deep breath, and sighed. Then she resumed her walk, an unleashed Brownie bounding along by her side.

'They say it's just like being on the Continent,' Esther declared to Jennie who was gazing wide-eyed about her. It was their first Saturday in London and they'd decided to come to Soho to take in the sights.

They stopped to stare in a shop window that was filled with all manner of foodstuffs quite unknown to either of them. Exotic delicacies from all round the world.

'Hmm!' murmured Jennie as the smell of strong coffee wafted over and around them.

'I'm enjoying this,' Esther said.

'Me too.'

They moved on to another shop that sold pastries. 'Yum, yum,' said Esther, gazing enviously and hungrily at those on display.

There was a chocolate-and-cream concoction that caught Jennie's eye which looked as though it would just melt in the mouth. 'My sentiments exactly,' she murmured.

Two men walked past jabbering in a foreign tongue. Both had olive skins, were unshaven and one had a cigarette dangling from his mouth that jerked up and down as he spoke.

'We've certainly nothing like this in Exeter,' Jennie commented as they continued down the road.

'Nor in Canterbury.'

Jennie nudged Esther and gestured across the street with her head where a coloured man in traditional African dress had emerged from a French restaurant. Both girls stared at him, mouths slightly agape.

The man noticed them staring and smiled to reveal gleaming white teeth. He then strolled on.

A few minutes later they passed a Chinaman who represented another first.

Graham read the figures before him, nodding to himself every so often. Business was booming as the figures showed.

He looked up, and over at Kerensa. 'I'm going to have to take on more men,' he declared.

She ceased typing. 'That'll please Norman Butt. He's been muttering of late.'

Graham tapped the sheets he'd been reading. 'It's now got to the stage where it's costing me more in overtime than it would to take on more men. So that's what we'll do.'

'How many?'

'Two to start with. And we'll see how we go from there.'

'Do you want me to draft an appropriate advertisement for the newspaper?'

Graham considered that. 'Tell you what. We'll put a board out front and see what reaction we get to that. In this instance, local men would be preferable.'

'Shall I go down and ask Norman to organize it?'

'You stay right where you are. I'll have a word with him,' Graham said, hurriedly rising and coming round from behind his desk.

'I don't have to be wrapped in cotton wool!' Kerensa protested. 'I'm quite capable of walking a short distance without doing myself an injury.'

Graham went to her and kissed her lightly on the mouth. 'Humour me. Besides you have to do as you're told. I'm the boss.'

'And what about at home?'

'Aren't I the boss there too?' he queried with a mocking smile.

'Of course,' she replied in a tone which said that wasn't really so.

'Graham,' she called out when he was at the door.

He halted, and turned to her.

'I'm very lucky to have met you. God was smiling on me the day I did.'

That brought a lump to his throat, and he experienced an even stronger tenderness towards her. 'I won't be long,' he said, and continued on his way.

She had another attack of nausea when he was gone, her most severe yet, but didn't tell him on his return as she didn't want to worry him.

The stench in the anatomy room was unbelievable and indescribable. It came from the formalin in which the cadavers had been pickled. Jennie found the eight naked bodies stretched out on trollies an awesome, and most disturbing, sight.

Jennie gulped. They'd been warned what to expect, but it was a shock none the less.

'Come in ladies,' said Dr Langton, the anatomist. Standing beside her was a man of a rather ghoulish appearance who was the technician. One of his duties was to saw the top off the skulls so that the brain could be exposed.

The new intake of students moved further into the room, eyes darting from body to body in combined horror and fascination.

Most of the bodies had belonged to old people, though some simply looked old because they'd clearly had a very hard life. It was rumoured that the bodies came from France, while others said they were vagrants who'd died on the streets.

'Four of you to each cadaver please, two on either side,' Dr Langton instructed. Two girls were left with one body and Dr Langton joined them.

413

'I take it you all have your dissecting instruments?' she said.

A murmur of agreement ran round the girls. They had supplied these instruments themselves.

'Good.'

Jennie gazed down at the cadaver she and Esther had chosen. The man's skin was brownish and waxy. He was thin and wasted, his chest covered in hair. His neck was scrawny, his cheeks sunken. Jennie thought he looked hideous.

'We start with the upper limbs, then move to the lower limbs. Then it's the head and neck, followed by the abdomen and chest,' Dr Langton smiled. 'Not all today though. I'm talking about the entire course.'

Jennie wondered who the dead man was and what his name had been? What sort of life had he led? Not a very good one from the look of him. She brought her attention back to Dr Langton who was speaking, and berated herself for letting her thoughts wander.

'Now if you'll all gather round here, I'll demonstrate what I want you to do.'

Finally, it was over and they could escape into the fresh air.

'That smell,' said Esther, and shuddered.

'It's still in my hair,' complained Jennie.

'Gruesome. Totally gruesome,' Esther went on, and shuddered again.

'But necessary if we're to learn.'

'Of course. I understand that.'

Jennie thought back to her cadaver and the sensation of slicing into his bloodless wrist. It was a day she would never ever forget.

Graham helped Kerensa climb on to *Waterwitch*, the first time he'd been aboard in ages. 'I've missed her,' he declared sadly. 'But since buying Stanton's I've been so busy I just haven't had the time to get down.'

'She is a beauty,' Kerensa said.

The deck could use a good scrubbing, Graham thought. And an overall lick of paint wouldn't go amiss. He'd neglected her, which saddened him even further. *Waterwitch* didn't deserve that.

He wondered how L'Corbin and Majohn were. He imagined they were still in the smuggling game no doubt, and doing well.

'I think I'll sell her,' Graham said. 'To someone who'll look after and use her, which I'm unable to do nowadays.'

'That's a pity,' commiserated Kerensa, knowing how much he loved the boat.

'Yes, but it's the right thing to do. For her sake,' Graham replied, making up his mind. He would drop by Pepperell's Boatyard on the way home and arrange matters.

'Maybe you'll buy another boat sometime in the future,' Kerensa said.

'I'd like that. For I certainly enjoy sailing.'

'Losing this one is one of the penalties for being such a successful businessman,' Kerensa said.

'And think, I have little enough time now. What's it going to be like when the baby arrives?'

'That's true,' Kerensa nodded. She hadn't thought of that. 'How about a last run out then?'

Graham frowned, he hadn't intended taking *Waterwitch* to sea. 'Are you up to it?'

'Of course I am. It's a beautiful day, a run out would do me good.'

'Could be choppy?'

'The choppier the better.'

He laughed at her enthusiasm. They were both dressed warmly, and there was other warm gear aboard. 'You're on,' he declared.

He made a few checks and preparations, then when ready opened the river doors.

They went down the Parry for the last time, in *Waterwitch* anyway, he told himself. He'd been right, the sea when they reached it was choppy, but neither of them were affected by the conditions.

They spent three glorious hours at sea, laughing and joking much of the time. It was a fitting last excursion for a boat Graham cared so much about, and which had served him well.

There was a hint of tears in his eyes when the boat-house was relocked and they were driving away. He felt he'd just said goodbye to a dear old friend, but a goodbye he knew in his heart of hearts was in the friend's best interests.

'Hey-yup!' said George, stopping the tractor and engaging the brake. He was on the downward incline of a hill, returning from towing some felled trees. He was on his way to another job that called for the tractor.

He jumped down and hurried to a sheep lying on its back. Once a sheep fell on to its back it was helpless and would stay in that position until it died.

The ewe gazed mournfully up as George approached, and frantically waggled its feet. It had been there for some time, George judged. 'Though not too long,' he said aloud. 'Otherwise you wouldn't be waggling thae feet the way you be.'

The ewe was heavy, but the weight wasn't a problem for George. He heaved and heaved, and on the third attempt managed to turn the beast on to its side.

The ewe scrambled to its feet. It panted deeply, staggered a few paces, stopped, shook itself, then walked groggily away.

Still on his knees, George smiled as he watched it go, now hurrying to join others grazing further along the hill. The ewe was lucky he'd happened along when he had, they weren't doing all that much work on this part of the farm at the moment. She could very easily have gone west.

He was still smiling and thinking about the sheep when he heard the noise behind him. He turned, and what he saw caused the smile to freeze on his face.

Even as he moved he knew he didn't have a chance.

Madge went into the Post Office Stores and queued behind Mrs Coffin who was consulting a written list.

'A packet of tea,' said Bob Yendell laying that beside the other items already assembled in front of her.

Mrs Coffin peered at her list and shook her head. 'Me writing's so bad even I can't read it,' she declared.

'Good-day, Mrs Forsyth,' said Bob.

'Good-day to you.'

He leaned slightly over the counter. 'Have you heard the news? I've just been telling Mrs Coffin.'

'What news is that?' Madge enquired.

'About poor George Rattenbury. He was accidentally killed when his tractor ran over him. They say it was a terrible sight.'

Madge went ice cold. It was some sort of grisly joke, it had to be. George dead! Why, only two nights ago she and he . . .

'Awful!' Mrs Coffin said. 'Did he die instantly, Mr Yendell, or did he linger for a while?'

Madge could have slapped the silly bitch's face.

'No-one knows. His body wasn't found till this morning. From what I'm told the catch somehow slipped off the brake pedal. Happens frequently I believe, and George had left the machine out of gear. It was on a hill and . . . Well, you can imagine what the rear-wheel spikes did to him.'

Madge wanted to open her mouth and shriek. She put a hand to her forehead. This couldn't be true. It couldn't be! She stared at the counter but couldn't see it properly, as it was obscured by a kind of haze.

George dead! Noooo! she wailed inside her head.

'Are you all right, Mrs Forsyth?' Bob asked.

She tried to answer, but no words came out. Must get out of here, she told herself.

She swivelled and blundered from the shop, not knowing where she was headed, not caring.

George dead. Dear, sweet George dead. Her world had just exploded into a million pieces.

She wished she was dead herself.

'What's wrong with you?' John demanded, having just arrived in from Wheal Tempest.

Madge sat slumped in a chair. She was pale, her cheeks tearstained, her hair awry. She looked up, and focused on John. Her first thought was, why couldn't it have been him instead of George.

'I haven't got round to making the tea yet,' she mumbled.

He came over and squatted beside her. 'What is it, Madge? You're in a right old state.'

'Have you heard about the accident?'

He shook his head. 'No.'

'George Rattenbury's been killed. Run over by his tractor. You know that horrible big thing with the spiked rear wheels.'

'Killed?' John repeated.

'Sometime yesterday. They didn't find the . . .' She couldn't bring herself to say the word body. She could think it, but not say it. 'They didn't find him until this morning.'

'That's dreadful,' John said.

'Yes,' she whispered.

John thought of the big man who'd always seemed so full of life. 'There will be a lot of women upset today I'm thinking,' he chuckled.

Madge fought back the urge to lash out at John. 'That's a stupid thing to say,' she hissed. 'Stupid and insensitive.'

'All right, keep your hair on. I didn't mean any disrespect.'

'Well, it certainly sounded that way.'

John frowned. 'Anyway, why are you so upset? It

wasn't as though you knew him very well.'

'No, I didn't,' she lied. 'But I thought him a nice man. Very pleasant and polite, always said hello or gave me a nod in passing.' She drew in a deep breath. 'I suppose it was the manner of his death that got to me. Quite ghastly.' The latter was true, if only part of the truth.

John nodded, and rose to his feet again. 'I'll put the kettle on shall I?'

'Please.'

'There's no whisky in the house otherwise I'd offer you some.'

'No whisky, coffee will be fine. And while you're making it I'll go and wash my face.'

In the bathroom they'd had built a number of years previously Madge gazed at herself in the mirror as water gushed into the sink. The lines on her face stood out in stark relief, and there were lines where she'd never noticed any before.

She felt sick with grief, bereft. Bile was churning in her stomach.

She turned off the tap, and dropped her head to stare at the now still water. And in that water saw George astride his tractor. He was smiling, waving at her.

And as she continued staring at him, his image as real to her as though he was there in person, she began to weep again.

A few hot tears that quickly became a flood.

Madge pulled the large collar of her coat up to her ears as protection against the cold. Luckily for her John had been going out to a Band of Hope meeting which meant she didn't have to invent an excuse to leave the house.

She halted, gazed about her to make sure she wasn't being observed, then turned up towards George's cottage. She was banking on the fact that there wouldn't be anyone there, and there wasn't. She scouted round it, making absolutely sure the coast was clear, before going inside.

Her hands were shaking as she lit the lamp in the kitchen, its warm yellow light illuminating the room.

Across his chair was an old, well-worn cardigan that had been a favourite. She picked it up and pressed it to her face, drinking in the smell of him that impregnated the wool. She held it to her as she moved around the room, gently touching, caressing items that would be forever associated in her mind with George and this cottage.

Silently she flitted through to the bedroom where she closed the curtains. That was the hardest, and sweetest, place of all for her to go – they'd made love so many times in there.

She gazed at the bed, her mind filled with memories of what had taken place there.

'Oh George!' she whispered.

Still clutching the cardigan she sank down on to the bed, her arms extended.

And lying there, as though crucified, she began to cry yet again as grief once more overwhelmed her.

'Go to the funeral, why ever for?' John queried. 'It isn't as though he was a friend or anything like that.'

'He was friend enough to you the night he found you drunk and incapable,' Madge retorted.

John nodded, what Madge said was true enough. He'd forgotten that incident.

'Anyway, we'll go as a mark of respect,' Madge stated firmly. 'That would be right and proper.'

'If you insist,' John replied with a shrug.

She left it there. John had agreed. They'd go. She'd had her way.

George's funeral – wild horses wouldn't have kept her from it.

Jennie stopped reading and rubbed her eyes. Then she

yawned. She was in the medical school library studying with a number of other girls including Esther who was sitting beside her.

'Want to go back to the digs?' Esther queried.

Jennie thought about that, glanced at the wall clock, and shook her head. 'Not yet. Do you?'

'I suppose not. Though to be honest I'm so tired I can hardly think straight.'

Jennie was exactly the same. 'Another half-hour, eh?'

'Another half-hour,' Esther agreed.

Jennie returned to the book opened before her and read:

THE KIDNEYS

The two kidneys flank the aorta and the inferior vena cava to which they are joined by stout blood vessels. The most important function of the kidneys is to maintain constant composition and volume of the body fluids. This control comprises . . .

The coffin was carried in by six pallbearers led by George's brother from Newton Abbot way. The farmer whom George had worked for was another of the pallbearers, the other four being farmhands.

George's brother didn't look at all like him, Madge thought, in fact you'd never have guessed the two were related.

Feeling absolutely numb inside she watched the coffin progress slowly down the aisle. A coffin containing George, her George who'd come to mean everything to her. George who'd brought light back into her life. George who'd raised her to heights she'd only hitherto dreamed of, and then afterwards been so incredibly tender and gentle. George, whom she'd never see again.

Madge's eyes were rivetted to the brass-handled coffin as it swayed its way down the aisle. She put a hand to her mouth and bit into her thumb, at which point something inside her snapped.

'Madge, for God's sake, what is it?'

The voice came from a long way away, and was one she vaguely recognized. Where was she? Who was the man peering down at her? And what was that noise?

The noise, she realized, was the sound of someone keening, someone completely distraught. But who?

She gazed up at the man now shaking her by the shoulders. Why was he doing that?

'Snap out of it, Madge. This is ridiculous.'

Gradually things started coming back. She'd been in church. Yes, that's where she'd been, in church. It had been a funeral, and the coffin had been brought in. Whose coffin?

George's of course. It had been George's funeral. That was the last thing she recalled, thinking about George.

'Madge?'

The man had released her and was staring down, a fierce, puzzled, expression on his face.

'I loved him,' she said.

'You what?'

'I loved him. I loved George.'

There was a pause, then the man queried softly. 'George?'

'Whom we buried today. I loved him.'

The man's expression changed to one of disbelief. 'What are you havering about?' he demanded.

It was dark outside she saw. What had happened to the time since the funeral? The many hours? Where had they gone?

The man squatted and stared at her. 'What are you going on about, Madge?'

'George, I'm talking about George.'

'Rattenbury?'

'Yes, George Rattenbury. Such a sweet, lovely person. He was buried today.'

'I know. I was there. With you.'

'Me?'

'You, Madge.'

'Oh!'

The man took hold of her hands, and squeezed them. 'What's this guff about loving George?'

'I did. And he loved me.'

'That can't be so. You're confused. Acting strangely.'

She gave a sharp, brittle laugh. 'I know what I'm saying all right. Don't worry about that.'

The man's face darkened in anger. 'Are you telling me you were one of George Rattenbury's women?'

'He didn't deserve the reputation he had, it wasn't true. He once told me he didn't do anything about the gossip because it appealed to his sense of humour. Made him laugh.'

'You actually slept with him?' John queried, voice quivering.

'Yes, often,' Madge smiled, picturing the pair of them together in their love nest by the river.

Quick as a darting snake John's hand flashed to crack against Madge's cheek. She cried out, and was knocked sideways.

'You tart! You fucking tart!' he yelled, beside himself with fury.

The smack brought Madge back to her senses. She blinked, and blinked again. What had she done? What had she said?

John grabbed her and yanked her to her feet. 'You bitch! You fucking rotten bastarding bitch!' And with that he began to repeatedly slap her.

Graham heard the commotion as he came through the front door. He broke into a run when he heard his mother's voice pleading with his father to stop.

He burst into the kitchen to find John still slapping Madge round the face and shoulders. He flew across the intervening distance and caught hold of John.

'Get off!' John snarled, and tried to push Graham

away. He only half succeeded. Turning his attention back to Madge, he again raised his hand.

That was it for Graham. His fist went smashing into John's face with all the force behind it he could muster. It landed on the side of John's nose which immediately spurted blood. John spun away to bang into a chair and then go crashing to the floor.

Graham took Madge into his arms. 'Are you all right, Mum?'

Madge gulped in deep breaths. Her cheeks were stinging, as was her neck, but apart from that she was unhurt. 'Yes,' she whispered in reply.

John rose on to his knees, then using the table as a lever hauled himself upright. 'Bitch!' he choked, and stumbled from the room.

Graham stared after him, aghast at what he'd just witnessed. He'd seen fights between his mother and father before, but nothing like this.

'What happened?' he queried.

She couldn't tell Graham what that had been all about. How could she? And she doubted John would ever reveal the real reason for what had occurred, his pride would see to that. 'Thanks for your help, Graham. It was good you came when you did.'

He smoothed back her hair. 'Can I get you anything?'

She shook her head.

'A cup of tea perhaps?'

'Well, maybe that.'

'Here, sit down.'

He assisted her to the nearest chair, then filled the kettle and put it on. He was puzzled and perplexed.

'What brought you here?' Madge asked.

He stared at her. 'You knew I was coming. We arranged it this afternoon.'

'Did we?'

'Why, don't you remember? I stopped the car and spoke to you in the street. You were chatting to the Scotts at the time.'

Madge recalled none of that. It was part of the blank between her being in church and a few minutes ago. 'How did I seem to you then?' she asked.

'Fine. A little distracted perhaps, but fine otherwise.'

She gently massaged her temples and thought about John going berserk when she'd told him about her and George. But then what man of his background and temperament wouldn't?

Told him about her and George. God! And when she'd done so she hadn't even recognized John as her husband.

'Are you going to explain what it was all about?' Graham asked softly.

'I can't, son. It was very personal. Strictly between your father and I.'

'It must have been something pretty horrendous for him to react as he did.'

Horrendous all right, she thought. No wonder John had flown completely off the handle. Why if Graham hadn't turned up when he had there was no saying how it might have ended. John could even have killed her! It happened in circumstances like that. She shivered as she considered what she'd just been through and what might have been.

'I think you should come and stay with us tonight,' Graham suggested.

Not a bad idea, she thought. It would give John a chance to cool down. 'Yes,' she nodded.

Graham was relieved to hear her agree. 'You'd better pack whatever you'll need.'

She put her hands to her cheeks which were still tingling, and then noticed she'd developed a dull ache in her right shoulder. Later, when she undressed she found a large black-and-blue bruise there.

'I'll get those things,' she said, coming to her feet.

Like his father Graham too was filled with fury, but with him it was the ice cold variety.

*　　　*　　　*

425

John lurched into the pub and up to the bar. 'Give me a pint of scrumpy and a double whisky,' he said to the landlord.

The landlord stared at him in astonishment. 'Hello, John. Haven't seen you in ages. Heard you'd signed the pledge.'

'The Band of Hope,' someone sniggered.

John swung round and glared at the sniggerer who was a chap called Clifford Copinger. 'Watch your mouth. Any more cracks and I'll take that pint pot and shove it up your arse,' he said, his Glasgow accent thicker than normal.

The smile vanished from Clifford's face. 'Only a joke, pal.'

'I didn't find it funny.'

'Sorry.'

John turned again to the bar where the landlord was regarding him curiously.

'Well, are you serving or just standing there?' John demanded.

'Of course.'

The landlord poured a large whisky which he set before John. As he was moving to get a glass for the scrumpy John picked up the whisky and threw it down his throat.

'Another of the same,' John instructed.

'Before or after the cider?'

'Before.'

The second large whisky vanished as quickly as the first. Madge and George Rattenbury! He hadn't even suspected there was someone else. And yet all this while . . .

The most galling thing was what Madge might have said about him behind his back, for the two of them must have discussed him, in all manner of intimate detail!

'Another,' he snarled.

'Hold on a bit, John,' the landlord said, placing the scrumpy in front of him.

426

'I said another,' John repeated, and chucked a pound note on to the bar.

His mind was churning. Madge with another man, with George sodding Rattenbury.

He wanted . . . He didn't know what he wanted to do.

Madge lay in bed staring at the ceiling. She was in Gone To Ground's spare bedroom. On the bedside table a clock was ticking.

She'd racked her memory, but still couldn't remember anything between George's coffin being carried down the aisle and the incident with John.

From what Graham had said she'd carried on as normal after the ceremony, going through the motions. But she recalled none of it. Where she'd been, what she'd done, who she'd spoken to were totally erased from her memory.

How was she going to live without George? She simply didn't know. The prospect was appalling. Life without George, but with John. John for whom she had neither love nor respect. John who was a millstone round her neck, and always had been.

Fresh tears crept into her eyes. She seemed to have done nothing but weep since George's death. Weep, and writhe inside with anguish.

'George,' she whispered.

You gets some sleep Madge, you needs it my lover, his voice in her mind replied.

She smiled. 'George?'

You gets some sleep now. Do as George says. He knows best he does.

'Yes, George.'

She closed her eyes.

That's it, my darling, my pretty. Proper job.

She dreamt they were in their love nest by the river. And afterwards they walked hand in hand through the water meadows.

* * *

427

John had consumed a great deal of alcohol, yet for some reason remained stone-cold sober. He walked towards home, hands deep in his pockets, head bowed. He was confused, bewildered and angry.

Rattenbury was dead, that made all the difference. He doubted he could have coped with the situation if Rattenbury had remained alive.

He let himself into the house to find it in darkness. Madge must have gone to bed he reasoned, and went upstairs.

He clicked on the light, then stared in surprise at the empty bed. Where was she? He tried Graham's old room, but she wasn't there. Nor was she in Jennie's.

So where had she gone? What had happened? Had she left him, and if so was it for good?

He went back downstairs and made himself a cup of tea. He couldn't believe she'd left him. She'd be spending the night with one of the neighbours. Or Graham more likely. Yes, that would be it. She must be at Graham's.

He thought of the telephone, and ringing, but decided against that. It was late and he might wake them.

He sat in front of the dying, cherry-coloured fire, grateful for the heat it was still giving off. Madge and George Rattenbury, he could never forgive her. The most hurtful thing of all was that she'd said, insisted, that she loved Rattenbury, loved him!

What was to happen now? What was to be done? He just didn't know. And what if she had left him for good, how would he get by without her? Who would cook, wash, clean? He cringed at the thought of coming home to an empty house every night. That would be awful, and so lonely.

He had a sip of tea, and sighed deeply. How could she do this to him? How could she? The humiliation, the loss of face. Thank God no-one would ever find out. Her adultery would remain a secret between the two of them. Unless George had said something? But no, George had

428

been well known for his discretion where women were concerned.

He heaved another sigh, this one of relief. He shouldn't have hit her earlier, but her confession had completely and utterly thrown him. He hadn't had the slightest inkling she was playing him false.

He still found it hard to believe that Madge had gone to bed with another man, and George Rattenbury of all men! He would have thought that if someone like George had made an advance she'd have run a mile. It just showed how you could misjudge someone.

He ran a hand through his hair, and scratched what was rapidly becoming a bristly chin. He then closed his eyes.

His mind jumped back over the years, and suddenly he was looking at Anne Moore. The lovely Anne. He started to remember the times they'd had together, and smiled in memory. As he smiled a line from the Bible came to him: 'Let him who is without sin . . .'

'Mum!' said Graham, shaking her gently. 'I've brought you a cup of tea.'

Madge blinked her eyes open, and stared up at Graham. 'Why, thank you, son,' she said, pulling herself into a sitting position.

'How are you this morning?'

'All right.'

'Sleep well?'

'Like a top.'

'That's good,' he declared, and sat on the edge of the bed. 'Have you decided what you're going to do?'

'How do you mean?'

'You're welcome to stay here as long as you like. Even move in if you wish to.'

Madge considered that. 'It's kind of you and Kerensa. But no, not with a baby coming. I'd only be in the way.'

'No, you wouldn't!' he protested.

'Oh yes I would. In the way and under Kerensa's feet.

429

There's an old saying that two women should never share the same kitchen and I believe that it's true.'

'I could always make other arrangements for you, if you wanted that?'

'Thank you, Graham, but your father and I will sort things out between ourselves.'

'Are you sure?'

'I am.'

'Last night frightened me, Mum, he could easily have injured you.'

'He frightened me too,' Madge said softly. 'But what happened was entirely my fault.'

'Your fault!' Graham exclaimed. 'I find that hard to believe.'

'It's true none the less.'

'And you won't say what it was all about?'

She shook her head. 'And please don't ask again.'

'If that's what you want.'

'It is,' she stated emphatically.

'Right, well, I'm just off to work. There's no need to get up right away, and when you do go downstairs Kerensa will cook you a nice breakfast.' Kerensa had finally given up work the previous month, and had been replaced by a Miss Flindel.

He leaned over and kissed Madge on the cheek. 'Take care.'

'And you, son.'

Graham was a good lad, she thought when he was gone. She was very proud of him, and Jennie of course. Jennie who was doing so well at medical school.

After a while she slipped out of bed, had a long soak in the bath, then went downstairs where she insisted she make her own breakfast, not wanting to trouble the large, waddling Kerensa.

Kerensa had been warned by Graham, and the previous evening wasn't mentioned.

John came out of Wheal Tempest with Steve Campbell

and Drew McIntyre, talking avidly about the day's graft and various problems and aggravations they'd encountered.

John was walking on the outside of the threesome and was nearest the Lanchester when it slid to a stop alongside them. Graham reached across and opened the door.

'See you!' John said to his two mates, and got inside, closing the door behind him.

Without uttering a word, Graham re-engaged the gears and drew away from the kerb.

John was now nervous and it showed. There were a few moments of silence between them, then he said, 'How's your mum?'

'A decent night's sleep has done her the world of good.'

John nodded. 'I guessed she'd gone home with you.'

There was another silence, which John eventually broke by asking hesitantly, 'What are her plans?'

Graham glanced at John, then focused his attention back on the road. 'I offered to let her stay with us, but she refused. She says you and she will sort things out between yourselves.'

John's shoulders sagged. That was a relief. 'I see,' he muttered.

'She wouldn't tell me what happened last night, but insisted it was strictly between the pair of you.'

'It was,' John said. 'Strictly.'

'Then I just want you to know one thing. If you ever lift your hand to my mother again you'll regret it for the rest of your days. I promise you. Understand?'

John, bitterly ashamed, didn't reply.

'I mean it, Dad. One way or another I'll ensure it'll be the biggest mistake of your life.'

'I understand,' John replied, thoroughly chastened, and somewhat frightened. He knew his son well enough to know the threat was no idle one.

'I hope you do.'

John thought of George Rattenbury with a seething hatred.

He found Madge busy in the kitchen. 'Your tea's ready. I'll put it on the table when you've had a wash,' she announced.

'Can we talk first?'

She paused in what she was doing, and looked at him.

'I'm sorry about last night,' he stated quietly. 'I shouldn't have hit you.'

'You've done so before, though never like that.'

'Yes,' he acknowledged. Damn, he wanted a drink, but there wasn't any alcohol in the house.

'Do you want me to leave?' she asked.

'No!'

She stared him straight in the eye. 'I don't know what came over me yesterday. I think I had some sort of breakdown. That's the only explanation I can come up with. When I told you about George I didn't even realize you were my husband. At the time you were a complete stranger. It wasn't until you hit me that I mentally returned from wherever it was I'd been.'

'You hurt me Madge,' he said, piqued.

'And you hurt me. Not only last night but for nearly all our married life. What with your drinking and laziness and all the rest of it. You've never cared one fig for me.'

'But I have! I swear.'

'Then you've had a funny way of showing it.'

He took a deep breath. 'I suppose I have been greatly at fault. I can't deny it.'

That confession gave Madge some grim satisfaction.

'I think it's best we both forget what happened and let bygones be bygones,' John said. 'Rattenbury's dead after all, there's no altering that.'

'No,' Madge whispered, staring at the carpet, there wasn't. George was gone. She'd never see him again, not in this life anyway.

432

He thought again of Anne Moore. 'And I'll try to be a better husband to you. How's that?'

She nodded.

'Good. So it's settled then?'

They would go on as before. Husband and wife, living together. Despair welled up in her to mingle with her grief. Oh George! she wailed inside her head. Why did you have to go and get yourself killed. We had such a short time together. A short, but glorious time she reminded herself. A time, and happiness, no-one could ever take away from her. A time and happiness to treasure for the rest of her days.

'It's steak and kidney,' she said.

'Terrific! My favourite.'

'Get your hands washed then and I'll dish up.'

John paused at the door. 'I'll never mention this business with Rattenbury ever again if you won't? It'll be as if it never happened.'

'Hurry up,' she said.

When he'd left the room she gazed about the kitchen, seeing George there the night he'd brought John home. Seeing and hearing him. She smiled weakly. George might be dead, but as long as she was alive he would always occupy a place in her heart and mind.

She turned her attention to the boiled potatoes and began draining them.

'No boyfriend yet?' Madge asked Jennie who was home for the Easter break.

''Fraid not. To be honest, with the amount of work I have there's not really all that much chance to socialize. Most days my nose is hard to the grindstone, morning, noon and night.'

'But you are enjoying it?'

Jennie gave her mother a broad smile. 'I love it, Mum. I find medicine a great joy.'

That pleased Madge immensely. 'Now tell me more

about this Esther Marshall you've become so friendly with.'

Jennie was in the middle of describing her new friend when the telephone rang. Madge went to answer it.

She returned to the sitting-room, face flushed, eyes bright. 'That was Graham. He's had to rush home, the baby's on its way.'

Jennie clapped her hands in glee. This was wonderful.

'I told him I'd go right over there. Will you come?'

'Of course!' said Jennie, jumping to her feet.

'A week early,' said Madge a few moments later as she pulled on her coat.

'That shouldn't matter,' stated Jennie.

They drove to Gone To Ground in her Hornet, finding the doctor's car parked outside when they arrived. Graham answered their knock.

'Dr Court is with her now,' he said, ushering them inside.

'How is she?' Madge asked.

'All right, as far as I know.'

'She's certain the baby's started?' Jennie queried. 'I mean, it isn't a false alarm?'

'Her waters have broken so it's the real thing,' Graham answered. He thought of Anthony whom he'd rung in Wiltshire where he was visiting a friend. Anthony had said he'd catch the first available train home.

'Isn't this exciting!' Madge enthused.

'Do you have everything in that you'll need?' Jennie asked Graham.

'I believe so.'

They chatted until Court appeared from upstairs. 'Everything's fine and in order,' he announced. 'Nothing to be worried about. I'll leave you now and go and find Mrs Morpeth the midwife, the very best we have I might add. She'll be along directly.'

'Is there anything I can do?' Jennie queried.

Court beamed at her. 'How are your studies going, Jennie? Getting on all right?'

'The studies are going well, doctor. I'm progressing nicely thank you very much.'

He patted her on the arm. 'I have great hopes of you, my girl. Great hopes. And yes, there is something you can do, you can stay with Kerensa until Mrs Morpeth gets here.'

'Can I be with her too?' Madge volunteered.

Why not? Court thought, and nodded. 'But I suggest Graham remains here. It might upset him to see her in pain, then she might be distressed at his distress which wouldn't do her any good at all.'

'I'll stay put,' said Graham. The truth was he had no wish whatever to be present during any part of the forthcoming proceedings. The very thought made him squeamish.

Jennie and Madge went upstairs while Graham saw the doctor out. They found Kerensa lying in bed with her hands on her hump.

'How do you feel?' Jennie asked with a smile.

'Apprehensive.'

'Any discomfort?'

'Not at the moment.'

'Anything we can get you?'

'I would love a cup of hot chocolate. There's some in the kitchen.'

'Leave that to me,' declared Madge, and left the room again.

Jennie plumped up Kerensa's pillows and generally tried to make her more comfortable.

'I'll be glad when it's all over,' Kerensa confessed.

'I can imagine.'

'You won't leave me alone, will you Jennie? Having you here is such a comfort.'

'Of course not,' Jennie replied, flattered by the request.

They chatted until Madge arrived back with the hot

chocolate, and shortly after that Mrs Morpeth showed up. She was a no-nonsense type of woman somewhere in her fifties. She immediately issued a string of instructions which Madge and Jennie hastened to carry out.

Kerensa's face screwed up in pain. She moaned, then gasped in relief when the contraction subsided.

'Dr Court mentioned you're at medical school,' Mrs Morpeth said a little later to Jennie.

'That's right.'

'Do you want to help me deliver?'

'Oh, yes please!'

Mrs Morpeth nodded her approval. She liked Jennie's enthusiasm. 'Have you been present at a birth before?'

'No, this will be my first.'

'Right, then pay attention and you might learn something.'

Minutes turned into hours, during which Dr Court popped back twice to see how things were going. He pronounced himself satisfied on each occasion.

When the interval between contractions had narrowed considerably Mrs Morpeth sent Madge out of the room. Then, with Jennie acting as assistant, she made the final preparations for the baby's birth.

'That's right, let it all come out. Don't worry about us or anyone else,' Mrs Morpeth crooned as Kerensa shrieked in agony.

Downstairs an ashen-faced Graham was worrying his nails while being comforted and assured by Madge. He jerked like a gaffed fish every time there was a fresh scream.

Jennie wiped sweat from Kerensa's brow, face and neck. 'Won't be long now,' she smiled.

Kerensa opened her mouth to reply, but before she could do so another contraction occurred. She gave her loudest and longest shriek yet.

'You're doing fine,' said Mrs Morpeth. She beckoned Jennie to her side and in quiet tones explained exactly what was happening and what would happen next.

Soon after that the baby's head was born, followed quickly by the trunk and legs. It was a little boy.

Mrs Morpeth cleared the baby's air passage, then smacked him on the bottom which produced a healthy wail of protest.

'Is everything as it should be?' Kerensa queried anxiously.

It was a question Mrs Morpeth was regularly asked directly after the birth. 'He's a real beauty,' she declared as she completed an examination of the child.

Mrs Morpeth wrapped the baby in a cloth and handed him to Kerensa who was exhausted.

'He's gorgeous,' said Jennie, smiling at the child who suddenly opened his eyes to stare at her. His eyes were a pale, washed-out blue colour.

'How do you feel?' Mrs Morpeth asked Kerensa.

'Incredibly tired.'

'I'm not surprised. It's hard work having babies.'

'He's so tiny,' commented Kerensa. 'It didn't feel like that when he was coming out.'

Jennie laughed. 'I'll bet.' She'd just watched something she hoped she herself would experience one day.

'He's got lovely eyes,' she stated.

'All new-born babies have blue eyes. Did you know that?' Mrs Morpeth said.

Jennie shook her head. 'I didn't.'

'We'll just tidy mother and baby up a little then you can call the father.'

A few minutes later Graham, concern written all over his face, was ushered into the bedroom where he found Kerensa sitting up in bed holding the baby.

'How are you?' he asked Kerensa, and kissed her on the cheek. He then stared in wonder, pride oozing out of him, down at his son.

'Not too bad.'

'He's . . . lovely!'

Kerensa gave a small laugh. 'I think so too. Want to hold him?'

'Can I?'

'Of course,' said Mrs Morpeth.

'I hope I don't drop him,' muttered Graham, taking the baby from Kerensa.

'You'd better not,' warned Madge who'd come into the bedroom with Graham.

Graham cradled the baby in his arms and made clucking noises. The blue eyes slowly closed and the baby fell asleep.

'You obviously have the touch,' smiled Jennie.

'I just hope he can keep that up,' commented Mrs Morpeth drily, knowing what lay ahead for Kerensa and Graham.

'What are you going to call him?' Jennie enquired. 'Any ideas?'

'We've already chosen a name,' Kerensa answered. 'It was going to be Fiona if we'd had a girl. But as he's a boy it'll be George after my maternal grandfather.'

Madge was stunned. 'George?' she queried softly.

'Don't you like it?' Graham asked.

Of all the names, they couldn't have chosen one that would have pleased her more. One George had gone, now another had arrived. 'I like it very much. George Forsyth,' Madge said, and nodded her head. She wasn't aware of it but a tear had trickled from her left eye.

'Then George it is,' smiled Graham.

'George it is,' Madge repeated, voice husky with emotion.

Chapter Twelve

Jennie broke into a run, it would be unforgivable if she were late for Mr Sherry's ward-round. He was the consultant and leader of the firm, which is to say team, she was attached to. It was January 1939, her fourth month on the wards.

She glanced at a wall clock as she flew by. She was cutting it fine. Damn, she thought, she should never have allowed herself to get caught up as she had.

She knew full well what would happen to her if she was late, Mr Sherry would be caustic in the extreme, and embarrass her in front of the others. She wasn't at all fond of Mr Sherry whom she considered to be cruel, though it had to be said he was an excellent surgeon.

She came to a pair of swing doors and barged straight through them, hitting something on the other side.

With a cry the white-coated doctor went tumbling to the floor to bang his head against a wall. When he sat up his nose was bleeding.

Jennie stared at him in horror. 'I . . . I'm terribly sorry,' she said.

'Christ!' the doctor muttered angrily, wiping blood from his nose and face.

Jennie groped in her pocket for a clean handkerchief which she offered to him. 'I'm late you see. I . . .'

He took the hanky and pressed it to his nose, glaring at her as he struggled to his feet.

'Look, I can't stay. I really am sorry. Miss my ward-round,' Jennie cried, as she chased off.

The man watched her rush away. 'Bloody medical students!' he exclaimed. They were nothing but trouble.

439

He swore under his breath. He'd go and see Sister Lancaster, she'd help him. He could easily have broken his nose, he thought as he strode away. Easily!

He wondered who the stupid girl was. He'd never seen her before and hoped he never would again.

Later that day Jennie was in the canteen. She was eating with some friends, when she suddenly spied the doctor she'd hit with the door earlier. He was in conversation with a colleague, the pair of them in earnest discussion.

Should she or shouldn't she? It would only be good manners after all. And he did require a fuller explanation and apology after what had happened.

'I'll just be a minute,' she said, pushing her empty plate away and rising to her feet. Nervously she made her way towards him.

The man ceased talking when he saw her approach. His face darkened in anger.

She stopped beside him and attempted a smile which came out all lop-sided. 'Hello again,' she said.

He didn't reply.

'Hello, Miss whoever you are,' his companion said.

'Forsyth. Miss Forsyth. I'm a student.'

'And a very pretty one at that,' the companion replied charmingly.

Jennie turned her attention again to the other doctor. 'I really am sorry. I was late for my ward-round which is why I was running.'

'Out of control,' the man said.

She swallowed. He clearly wasn't going to make this easy for her. She wished now she hadn't come over.

'Is she the one who . . . ?' the companion queried, and laughed when the man nodded.

'How is your nose?' Jennie asked.

The man lifted his cup of tea and sipped it. He then slowly returned the cup to its saucer. 'Sore.'

Jennie could see his nose was puffed and bruised,

440

which made her feel even worse. 'I wish there was something I could do.'

'There is.'

'What?'

'Go away.'

How rude! Jennie thought. She was in the wrong, but there was no need for him to be like that.

'Steady on, old chap,' chided the companion.

The man gingerly touched his nose, and frowned To him it felt the size of a melon and blinking painful. 'I'll have you know that because of you I had to change my entire morning schedule,' he said to Jennie. 'It was ages before I stopped bleeding like a stuck pig.'

'Again, I'm sorry,' she mumbled.

'Sorry doesn't help my nose or compensate for the morning I've had.'

'Oh, come on, Eliot,' the companion admonished. 'Be a bit more gracious.'

'Why should I?'

'You might if you were a gentleman,' Jennie snapped. Then, 'Oh!' when she realized what she'd said.

The glare returned. 'So I'm not a gentleman, am I?'

'You're hardly acting like one,' she retorted, amazed at her own audacity. This was a doctor, after all.

'Good for you, Miss Forsyth,' the companion said.

'Is that a fact?'

'It is,' she stated, wishing again she'd never come over.

'Go away,' Eliot repeated.

'I will!'

She was angry now. Cross with him, cross with herself. She whirled round, and in the process accidentally knocked the table with her thigh.

Eliot's cup and saucer slid across the highly polished surface, over the side and on to his lap. He yelled in surprise and alarm as the hot tea soaked into his trousers.

Jennie couldn't believe what had happened. She gazed

at Eliot in shock as he leapt to his feet and literally danced on the spot. People all around stared at them, many of whom began laughing.

'You . . . ! You . . . !' Eliot spluttered, his face having gone puce, while his eyes stood out like ping-pong balls.

Jennie nearly reached over to wipe down the sodden material, then realized she could hardly do so because of its location.

'I'm so sorry,' she said yet again.

The companion leaned right back in his chair and hooted with laughter, thinking that Eliot dancing up and down was a truly comic sight.

'Are you burned?' Jennie asked tremulously.

'Go away!' Eliot roared.

To the sound of laughter Jennie beat a hasty retreat, fleeing from the canteen.

'You're joking!' Esther breathed. It was that evening and she and Jennie were in their room.

'I'm not. The tea went straight on to his lap. You should have seen him, he was cavorting about like a Red Indian.'

Esther put a hand to her mouth, and sniggered. 'I wish I'd been there. It must have been some sight.'

'Oh, it was,' Jennie nodded. 'It was most certainly that.'

'And was he burned?'

'I don't know. I asked him but he just yelled at me to go away. So I did.'

'Poor chap. First you bang his nose, then pour tea into his lap.' Esther shook her head. 'Talk about winning friends and influencing people!'

'I should say I influenced him all right. But not the way I would have wished,' Jennie commented wryly.

Esther sat on top of her bed and crossed her legs. 'So, what was he like?'

'How do you mean?'

'As a man!'

As a man? Jennie wondered. She thought back to the canteen. 'Mid to late twenties I'd judge.'

'And?' Esther prompted.

'You mean his looks?'

Esther sighed with exasperation. 'Of course I meant his looks, dummy!'

'Dark hair,' Jennie said slowly. 'Not short, but not all that tall either. A little taller than me I'd say.'

'Handsome?'

'Well, he wasn't ugly.'

'Eyes?'

'Two.'

'Jennie!'

Jennie laughed. 'I can't remember. Brown I think, though I wouldn't swear to it.'

'You're not exactly observant, are you?'

'Both occasions we've met, or should I say, encountered each other, have hardly been normal ones.'

'True,' Esther conceded.

'He had a reasonable build though, I did notice that,' Jennie said.

'Broad shoulders?'

'Fairly.'

'Complexion?'

'All right. He certainly wasn't covered in pimples or blemishes if that's what you mean.'

'And he was called Eliot? I like that name. It's different. Do you think he's a houseman or registrar?'

'I've no idea. Could be either.'

'Lucky for you it wasn't a consultant you'd taken to abusing,' Esther teased.

'Hardly abusing!' Jennie protested. 'Both incidents were pure accidents. And with the teacup he more than deserved what happened. That'll teach him to be so rude to someone who's doing her best to apologize.'

'Yes, that was uncalled for,' Esther agreed.

'Black!' Jennie suddenly exclaimed.

'I beg your pardon?'

'I've just remembered, he had black hair. Black as opposed to merely dark. Black as his temper.'

'Sounds quite nice really. Apart from the rudeness, that is.'

'Well, he certainly didn't impress me,' Jennie stated. 'Far from it.'

'What about his friend, the pleasant one. Tell me about him?'

Jennie went on to describe and pass comment on Eliot's companion.

Graham stared with satisfaction at the almost completed extension that was being added to the existing building. When the new machinery he'd ordered was installed and running he'd be able to increase his productivity by fifty per cent.

Fifty per cent! Maybe more. He mentally rubbed his hands in glee. Business couldn't be better.

He now had eighteen men working for him on the shop floor, and would shortly be hiring more. The company now also boasted two reps, as Phil Crane had been joined by Percy Clapp who hailed from St Thomas in Exeter. Percy was proving a big success, though he wasn't quite in the same league as Phil Crane. Miss Flindel had acquired a junior called Mavis.

Yes, Graham thought, things couldn't have been better. Profits were again up on the previous year, and, of course, would leap next year thanks to their increased capacity.

He thought of Kerensa and George, and smiled. The baby was in the rudest health and growing fast. Kerensa had transpired – as he'd been sure she would – to be a devoted and doting mother. For a while now she'd been talking about a brother or sister for George, and both of them felt that it would only be a matter of time before one appeared.

Happy? Graham couldn't have been happier. Hands

444

deep in his pockets, and smiling broadly, he returned inside and got on with his work.

A lump rose into Madge's throat, which it always did, as she stared down at George's grave. In her clasped hands she held a small posy of winter flowers.

She didn't come to the grave all that often in case she was seen, and she brought flowers even less frequently.

Madge bent and laid the flowers on the grave, stood up straight again and smoothed back her hair which was blowing in the wind. It was now over two years since his death, but it seemed like yesterday.

She looked up at the sky which was pale grey and filled with scudding clouds. Off in the distance a flight of swans was traversing the horizon. It was a cold and blowy day, but pleasant none the less.

Memories flooded into her mind of all the good times George and she had had together.

She shouldn't stay any longer, she told herself. People came and went all the time. If she was observed standing over George's grave it would cause tongues to wag. At least she didn't have to worry about Les Pack any more, the old goat had passed on the previous year and was buried somewhere in this same cemetery. At the time it had been the talk of the village that there had been such a small turn out for the funeral service. But that had been hardly surprising, Les had never been much liked.

As she walked away she imagined George smiling, watching her leave.

'I hear they don't come any nicer than Mr Ralston,' said Henrietta Hull as they made their way to the out-patients clinic where they were to join a new firm. There were four in the group, Henrietta, Jennie, Rachel Levi and Emily Browne.

'Who's the registrar?' asked Rachel.

'Someone called Greenstone. He's relatively new here, I believe.'

'And the houseman?'

'Amanda Fryer. I've met her, she's a great laugh.'

They arrived at out-patients, had a word with the receptionist and then went into the Ear, Nose and Throat clinic as instructed. There they found the firm was awaiting their arrival.

Mr Ralston was talking to the registrar who had his back to them. The consultant was a small, bald-headed man, thin as a stick. The houseman hovering close by was a 'jolly hockey-sticks' type with a somewhat unfortunate horsey face and large teeth.

'Ah, the students!' smiled Ralston, at which point the registrar turned to face them.

Jennie's heart sank, for the registrar was none other than Eliot. 'Christ!' she muttered under her breath.

When he saw her, Eliot's welcoming expression changed to a scowl. He shook hands with Jennie very unenthusiastically, only holding her hand for the briefest of moments before releasing it again.

This was awful, Jennie thought. How on earth was she going to work with someone who clearly disliked her, someone on whom she'd made such a bad impression?

Mr Ralston spoke to them for a short while, explaining a little about ENT in general, and telling them about some of the cases they would be observing.

During this Jennie became acutely aware of Eliot staring at her. She turned to him and attempted a smile, but before she could do so, he'd quickly glanced away.

She focused again on Mr Ralston.

Try as hard as she might Jennie's mind kept wandering as Mr Ralston droned on about a mastoid operation he would be carrying out the following day. The patient, a nine-year-old boy, was sitting up in bed looking apprehensive about what lay ahead.

Mr Ralston suddenly stopped talking and singled Jennie out. 'I do wish you'd pay attention, Miss Forsyth.

I'm teaching for your benefit as well you know,' he admonished in a quiet, disapproving, tone.

Jennie immediately coloured. 'I'm sorry,' she mumbled, horribly aware that all eyes round the bed were now focused on her.

'I should think so,' Mr Ralston murmured, and resumed where he'd left off.

God! Jennie thought. How embarrassing. And look at that Eliot Greenstone smirking at her discomfort.

She forced herself to concentrate.

'What's wrong with Miss Forsyth, she seems to be permanently distracted?' Mr Ralston said to Eliot when they were alone.

'Yes, I've noticed that too.'

'Yet I'm told she's done extremely well up until now. Charlie Muir was her last consultant and he couldn't speak too highly of her. Says she shows great promise.'

Mr Ralston paused, and looked contemplative. 'Maybe it's me. Perhaps I put her off in some way.'

Put her off? Suddenly the penny dropped as Eliot considered those words. Of course! He should have realized. 'I think I may be able to sort her out. Leave it to me,' he said.

'Good chap! Now what did you make of that . . . ?' Ralston launched into a discussion about a particularly interesting case of cochlear disorder they had examined earlier.

Esther looked at the tray of sticky buns and sighed. 'I daren't,' she said to Jennie. 'I'd love to but I daren't.' She patted her tummy. 'Can't be too careful. Not with my metabolism you can't anyway.'

Jennie and Esther were heading for some of their chums when Eliot Greenstone appeared beside them, carrying a cup of coffee.

'I wonder if I could speak with you please Miss Forsyth?' he requested politely.

Oh no! she thought. What was this all about? 'Certainly,' she replied.

He smiled at Esther. 'Hello, I'm Eliot Greenstone.'

Esther also smiled, but hers was a quite different smile to his. 'And I'm Esther Marshall. Pleased to meet you.'

'And I you.'

They shook hands.

'There's an empty table over here,' Eliot said to Jennie, indicating the one he meant.

'See you later,' Jennie said to Esther.

'Lovely to have met you, Mr Greenstone,' Esther told him. 'Goodbye.'

'Goodbye,' he replied, and started after Jennie who'd moved off.

When she'd sat she stared down into her cup, and hoped he wasn't going to be rude again.

'How are you enjoying ENT?' he asked when he too had sat down.

'It's interesting.'

'You can learn a lot from Mr Ralston, he's a top man in his field.'

'So I believe.'

'Yes, a top man,' Eliot repeated, studying Jennie over the rim of his cup. 'I understand you got on extremely well with Mr Muir?'

'I did,' she acknowledged.

'He speaks very highly of you apparently.'

'That's kind of him.' She hesitated, then said, looking directly at Eliot for the first time since sitting down, 'Is this about Mr Ralston telling me off during the ward-round?'

He decided honesty was the best policy. 'Yes.'

'I see,' she murmured.

'Your lack of attention and general distraction since joining us on Monday has been quite noticeable.'

Jennie bit her lip.

'It's me, isn't it? I'm the problem.'

She nodded. 'I get nervous when I'm near you. Stupid really, but there we are.'

'Because of what happened?'

'They were both accidents, and then you were so rude. I keep expecting you to be rude again. Or get back at me in some way.'

'Oh dear!' Eliot said softly. 'Yes, I was rude that day. Quite unforgivable really. Please accept my apology.'

She relaxed a little when she heard that. 'Only if you accept mine?'

'Accepted,' he smiled.

'Yours also.'

'Good, that's that then. It's pax between us, right?'

'Right,' she agreed, feeling as though a great weight had been lifted from her shoulders.

He solemnly offered her his hand which she shook.

'I nearly died when I saw you were the registrar on our new firm,' she confessed.

'And I wasn't exactly happy to see you. That walking disaster area was how I thought of you.'

She blushed. 'I'm not normally like that. I assure you. Were you burned?'

'No,' he replied. 'Though hot tea on my crotch isn't an experience I'm anxious to repeat. And certainly not in a situation with half the hospital staff laughing at me.'

'You looked very funny.'

'I'm sure.'

He was quite pleasant really, she decided. Not at all the ogre she'd imagined. She thought his dimpled chin most attractive.

'I was told you're relatively new at the Free,' she said. 'Where did you come from?'

'St Thomas's. I trained and did my house jobs there. I jumped at the chance of working with Mr Ralston, and consider myself very fortunate to be his registrar.'

'Good for future prospects?'

'Among other things,' he nodded. 'By the way, call me Eliot.'

'And I'm Jennie.'

'Forsyth's a Scottish name,' he mused.

449

She told him the story of how her family had moved to Devon from Glasgow.

'I come from Harrogate myself,' he said.

'You don't sound a northener?'

'Oh, it's there if you listen hard enough. But I'm not broad. I've my grandmother to thank for that. She was well spoken and insisted I was also.'

'Was she a big influence on your life?' Jennie asked.

Eliot looked away, then back at Jennie. 'She brought me up. My father died when I was very young, and my mother a few years later. It was rather sad.'

Jennie was shocked. 'How awful for you. What did they die of?'

'My father's appendix ruptured, my mother of TB. She was never a well woman and went right downhill after his death. I think maybe losing them was the motivation for my becoming a doctor.' He shrugged. 'But enough of me, tell me about you?'

He listened in fascination as she spoke about leaving school at fourteen, then attending night school later on. She was quite a remarkable young lady he realized, and a pretty one at that.

They chatted until it was time to report to the outpatients' clinic which they walked to together.

On duty again she reverted to calling him Mr Greenstone, but from there on they remained on first-name terms.

'Excellent port,' commented Anthony Sturt, wishing he could afford port of such quality.

'More stilton?' Kerensa queried.

'Please.'

He cut himself another portion of cheese, and then helped himself to a Bath Oliver. Food for the gods, he thought. He adored dining with Graham and Kerensa.

'I've a proposition to make,' he announced.

'Oh?' said Graham.

'As you know when I die Kerensa will inherit Corfe

Mullen. Which, I may add, I'm rattling around in like a pea in a pod since she left.'

'You have Mrs Peters,' Graham interjected. She was the housekeeper he'd hired for Anthony, and whose wages he paid.

'It's not the same at all! She's staff, not family. I can't talk to her or be with her the way I was with Kerensa. She doesn't sit down in the evening and discuss the day for example.'

'But you've no complaints about her?'

'None at all. She's excellent. But a housekeeper none the less.'

Graham nodded, he understood.

'The house seems so damn big and lonely nowadays,' Anthony went on. 'Which I suppose is a sign of my advancing years. Also, it has to be said the house needs money spent on it, and has done so for a long time. Take the roof for example, it really does need renewing.'

'So what are you driving at?' Graham prompted.

'Why don't we swop?'

'Swop!' Graham exclaimed. 'You mean Corfe Mullen and Gone To Ground?'

'Exactly.'

'I see,' murmured Graham, bemused.

'It makes sense if you think about it. You can afford to renovate and maintain the place, plus you're young with a family, which may be added to at any time I presume. And as I said, Corfe Mullen will be Kerensa's anyway, so why not move in now before it becomes too run down and dilapidated.'

'It's certainly a thought,' Kerensa said.

'And you wouldn't mind living here?' Graham asked Anthony.

'I'd feel far more comfortable. Kerensa's turned it into a beautiful home. With your financial backing I'm sure she'll do wonders at Corfe Mullen.'

'What do you think, darling?' Graham asked Kerensa.

'It's a wonderful idea. I'm all for it.'

451

'Then we'll swop,' nodded Graham, excited at the prospect.

Anthony toasted them in the port he was so enjoying, and hoped that when Graham and Kerensa moved they might leave something of their cellar behind – like a case or two of this port.

'Why on earth do you want to take up pottery?' demanded John, astonished.

'Now that the family has gone I have time on my hands. Pottery would be a good hobby for me,' countered Madge.

John shook his head. 'Well I never!'

'You don't object do you?'

He considered it. 'I suppose not.'

It wouldn't have mattered if he had tried to put his foot down, she'd just have gone ahead anyway, she thought.

'It's only two evenings a week,' she said. 'And you can hardly complain, between one thing and another you're out a great deal yourself.'

That was true, he told himself. Now he'd given up the Band of Hope he'd become very active again in the church.

'I'm sure I'll enjoy it,' Madge said. 'And if I don't, then I can always stop.'

His family never ceased to amaze John. First Graham with his business affairs, then Jennie becoming a doctor, now Madge wanting to take up pottery of all things! What on earth would they come up with next? he wondered.

She was really looking forward to the pottery classes, Madge thought, resuming her knitting. She was making John a pullover that he badly needed.

She was certain they were not only going to be enjoyable but fun, which they indeed proved to be on both counts.

'Stay on at Corfe Mullen with you?' Anthony repeated.

452

'That's right,' Kerensa nodded.

'Have you spoken to Graham about it?'

'Of course. In fact it was he who suggested it.'

'One big happy family, eh?'

'That's it.'

Anthony was very tempted. But caution warned him to think this through. The last thing he wanted to do was make a mistake.

'You'll see lots more of George then,' Kerensa said.

'And you.'

'Every single day,' she smiled, and kissed him on the cheek.

He reached up and touched the spot she'd kissed, thinking of Rebecca who was never far from his thoughts. 'Have another cup of tea,' he said, and poured her some.

'So, what do you say?'

He took his time refilling his own cup. 'No,' he stated eventually.

Her face fell in disappointment. 'Why not?'

'I get on extremely well with you and Graham as things stand. If we were all to live together in the same house that relationship might alter. You might find me a nuisance, or someone who gets under your feet, or forever interfering.' He held up a hand to silence her when she opened her mouth to interject. 'I appreciate the offer, and will tell Graham so, but I really do believe it's best that I don't live with you.'

'Think it over, Daddy. You may change your mind.'

Anthony shook his head. 'I won't. But thank you both for asking. Your doing so means a great deal to me.'

'Well, the offer's always there.'

'Bless the pair of you.'

Maybe he was right, Kerensa reflected. It would be terribly sad to damage the warm, congenial relationship the three of them now enjoyed. And her father did have his little ways, as she well knew. But then, so did she and Graham.

*   *   *

Jennie watched Eliot operate, thinking how skilful he was. He had an artist's hands.

He glanced up, and suddenly his eyes were boring into hers. He smiled, and she returned the smile, as goose-bumps prickled her back.

He began speaking again, informing the students present what he was doing and how he was going about it.

He was a very good teacher, Jennie thought. He had the ability to make everything clear and somehow simple. Nor did he ever get irritable when questioned as did so many of the other surgeons.

Pity it was her last week with this particular firm. She was going to miss Eliot a great deal. They'd become good chums during her time with the firm.

Still, she'd continue to see him round the hospital. They'd bump into one another all the time.

'Now here . . .' said Eliot.

She craned forward to get a better view.

Graham let himself into Corfe Mullen, threw his coat over a chair, and sighed. It had been a long, hard day and he was dead beat. All he wanted was to put his feet up and drink a very large whisky and soda.

He found Kerensa in the drawing-room, sitting on the bare boards surrounded by samples of carpet and fabrics.

'I'm glad you're home. You can help me choose,' she said.

'You'll have to do that by yourself. My brain is so tired it's switched itself off,' he replied.

'Oh darling!' She jumped to her feet, hurried to him and enfolded him in her arms. 'That bad?'

He nodded.

She kissed him on the lips. 'Come and sit down. Is there anything I can get you?'

'Coming right up,' she said, hastening towards the whisky decanter when he'd told her that was what he wanted.

Graham slumped into a chair and gazed at George

contentedly playing with some cardboard boxes in a corner. Staring at George, and thinking of recent events, made him frown.

'Thank you,' he said, accepting his drink from Kerensa. 'Aren't you joining me?'

'I'll maybe have one later. But not now.'

Kerensa kneeled beside him. 'Mr Maunder finished painting our bedroom today so I can put the curtains up tomorrow.'

'Good,' he nodded. It had been cold in the bedroom without curtains. 'What about the carpet?'

'I've telephoned instructions for that to be laid as soon as possible.' The carpet in question was a pretty green Wilton that she'd chosen.

'You really do enjoy all this, don't you?' he said, stroking underneath her chin.

'Hmm! It's fun.'

He thought of the roof and how much that had cost him. Taking over Corfe Mullen was an expensive business, but one he could afford. The brick works continued to do splendidly. Though he didn't know how long that would last.

'Have you read today's newspaper?' he asked.

'Yes.'

His lips thinned. 'It's looking more and more as if war is inevitable.'

'The Territorial Army is to be doubled in strength,' she said.

'It's very worrying.'

She thought so too. 'What happens if there is a war?' she queried.

'How do you mean?'

'At Stanton's.'

He drank some of his whisky, and instantly felt better. He had another sip. 'That's the big question, isn't it?' he replied thoughtfully.

Kerensa shivered. 'Someone just walked over my grave,' she said.

He looked at her, thinking how much he loved her. She and George were everything to him.

'Cheer up, it might not happen,' she said.

'Maybe not.'

'And if it does, we'll just have to cope somehow. But I have to admit, war is a scary thought.'

'I was seven when the Great War ended,' he said slowly. 'I can remember soldiers returning home from the Front. A long line of them, four abreast, marched past our house. I was waving and cheering, as were lots of others. Many of the women were crying, there were handkerchiefs everywhere.'

'And now there's the possibility of it occurring all over again,' Kerensa murmured, shaking her head in disbelief.

'So it would seem.'

'Stupid,' Kerensa said. 'Totally stupid.'

Graham thought of his men at Stanton's, the majority of whom, including himself, were of fighting age, and wondered how many of them would come back should such a conflict take place.

'I think it's a terrific effort. Good for you Mum!' Jennie enthused.

'Not too bad considering I haven't been doing it long,' Madge said with pride. They were both studying a pot she'd made.

'I like the colours,' Jennie declared. Madge had interwoven various shades of pale blues and greens.

'So did my instructor. He says I have a good eye for colour.'

Jennie handed the pot back to Madge who placed it on top of the sideboard. 'I'm going to use it as a fruit bowl,' she stated.

'It'll be ideal for that.'

'She's certainly coming on with her pottery,' John commented from his chair.

'It's a very interesting and relaxing hobby,' Madge declared.

'You're clearly enjoying it.'

'I love the classes. They're the highlight of my week.'

Jennie crossed to stand in front of the fire where she held out her hands to the flames. She was home on holiday, having arrived back shortly before tea.

It suddenly struck her how relaxed her parents were in each other's company, this was something new. They seemed more at ease with one another.

John excused himself, and went to the toilet, taking his evening newspaper with him.

'How's his drinking?' Jennie asked when he was gone.

'Not so bad. He still likes a tipple, but doesn't go at it the way he used to. He's quite changed in that respect, I'm happy to say.'

'I'll bet you are!'

'He's changed in other ways too. All for the better.'

'There's certainly a different feeling between the pair of you,' Jennie commented.

'Not so much of the underlying aggravation you mean?'

'Exactly,' Jennie nodded.

Jennie was right, Madge thought. She and John rubbed along far better nowadays than they ever had in the past. John had mellowed considerably, was far less dogmatic than he'd been. As for herself, emotional heartbreak and inner turmoil at losing George had gradually given way to a state of mind that might have been termed serene.

Her mother had aged, Jennie thought. There were far more lines on her face than she recalled, and certainly a lot more grey in her hair. But her eyes remained clear and sparkling, with a great deal of humour in them. Determination too, there was no mistaking that.

'So, what do you intend doing tonight?' Madge enquired.

'I want to go over to Corfe Mullen and see the baby.'

'Good idea!' said Madge, clapping her hands. 'I'll come with you.'

'We'll both go after we've washed the dishes.'

Madge glanced at the dishes stacked by the sink. 'Tell you what, your father can do them. How's that?'

Jennie raised an eyebrow. 'Will he?'

'If he's told he will.'

My, my, Jennie thought.

They put on their coats and waited for John to reappear. 'Aye fine,' he replied when Madge had explained what she wanted him to do.

'Are you going to the pub later?'

'I might pop in for a short while.'

She nodded. 'See you when we get back then.'

'Take care, and give my love to all at Corfe Mullen. Particularly that baby.'

Jennie stared in amazement as her father donned an apron. She had to flee the house not to burst out laughing in front of him.

'Jennie!'

She stopped and turned as Eliot came hurrying up to her. 'Hello,' she smiled.

'Hello. How are you?'

'Tired. You know how it is.'

'Oh, I do!' he said, remembering his own houseman days and the long hours that one was expected to work. 'Are you on duty tonight?'

'No, I'm off.'

'Excellent!' he beamed. 'It's my birthday today so a small crowd of us are going to have a few drinks in the Pakenham to celebrate. Will you join us?' The Pakenham Arms was a nearby pub favoured by hospital staff.

'I don't know,' she hesitated. 'I had planned to wash my hair.'

'Oh, come on, don't be a stick in the mud! And from what I can see your hair doesn't need washing.'

'Well . . .' She trailed off.

'That's settled then. I'll expect you there at eight. And don't worry about money, that'll be taken care of.'

'Eight then,' she agreed.

'Now I've got to dash. We'll talk later.'

He squeezed her arm, then walked swiftly away.

Drinks with Eliot, and others of course. She'd have to get him a present, she thought.

There were eight of them, Jennie and Thelma Hart the only females present. Thelma was a registrar on an orthopaedic ward.

Jennie was sitting flanked by Eliot on one side, with a chap called Hector on the other. She was thoroughly enjoying herself, relishing the company, Eliot's in particular. He swung from being outrageously funny one moment, to darkly intense the next. She was finding him quite mesmeric.

'Your turn to go up to the bar, Giles,' Eliot said, indicating a pile of money in the centre of the table.

Giles groaned. 'Is it really?'

'It is,' was chorused in reply. Giles was notoriously lazy, a terrible shirker whenever possible.

'Same again all round?' Giles queried, rising and finishing off his pint.

Jennie wondered if she should risk another gin and tonic. She'd already had three. Oh, what the heck! she thought. It was a birthday celebration after all.

Eliot had been delighted with the two all-white cotton handkerchiefs she'd given him. She'd apologized saying they weren't very original or exciting, but the best she could do in the time she'd had. He'd replied they'd be jolly useful and that he couldn't be more pleased. He'd also scolded her for spending money on him which he'd said she shouldn't have done.

Jennie was deep in conversation with Eliot, talking shop, when a dark-haired woman suddenly appeared at their table. 'I made it after all,' she said to Eliot who jumped to his feet.

'Helen!' he exclaimed. 'I'd given you up.'

'I managed to get someone to look after the children

459

in the end, but it wasn't easy. That's living in London for you,' she replied.

Who was Helen? Jennie wondered. Whoever, she was pretty in a sultry sort of way, though not all that marvellous a figure – more of a boyish shape than anything.

'Now let me see, who don't you know?' mused Eliot. 'Thelma for a start. Thelma Hart, my wife Helen.'

Jennie was stunned. *Wife!* She hadn't known Eliot was married. He'd never mentioned her. No-one had.

Helen and Thelma shook hands.

Jennie felt sick and strangely, betrayed. Why had no-one said anything?

'Jennie Forsyth, my wife Helen.'

Jennie rose and shook hands with Helen, acutely aware that her smile had a fixed quality about it. 'I'm very pleased to meet you,' she lied.

'And I you.'

'Jennie's a houseman,' Eliot explained. 'All the way up from sunny Devon.'

'How interesting,' smiled Helen. 'I went to Devon once, there were cows everywhere.'

'We do have quite a lot in the county,' Jennie replied, wondering if that was some sort of veiled barb. She decided it wasn't. Helen had meant exactly what she'd said.

When the introductions were complete Eliot asked Helen what she'd like to drink, then went up to the bar to get it for her.

'How many children have you got?' Jennie enquired when Helen had sat.

'Two. A boy and a girl.'

'What are they called?'

'The boy is Peter, the girl Cassandra. Cass for short.'

'And their ages?'

'Peter is the elder, he's five. While Cass has just turned three.'

'How nice,' Jennie said.

'Were you a nurse?' Thelma asked. 'So many doctors seem to marry nurses.'

'No, I wasn't,' Helen answered. 'I knew Eliot from Harrogate where we both come from.'

'Yorkshire is a lovely part of the country. I adore it there,' Thelma commented.

They continued chatting till Eliot rejoined them with Helen's drink. He now sat with his wife rather than with Jennie.

Eliot was nothing to her anyway, Jennie thought, at least not that way. They were simply good friends, and would continue to be so.

But she did wish she'd known!

'May I join you?'

Eliot snapped himself out of his reverie, having been lost in thought. 'Of course,' he said, half-rising.

Jennie sat facing him. They were in the hospital canteen, half-way through the afternoon. It was the week after his birthday, and the first time since then she'd managed to catch him alone.

'You looked very pensive?' she prompted.

'Just thinking about a case.'

'A difficult one?'

'It was. But I believe I've solved the problem. So, how are you?'

'Tired, as usual. Thank you for the other evening. It was most enjoyable.'

'We certainly enjoyed ourselves.'

The word *we* grated on her. 'I hadn't realized you were married.'

'No? It's common knowledge. I thought you knew.'

She shook her head. 'And two children to boot!'

His face lit up. 'I shouldn't say so but they're smashing children. We've been extremely lucky.'

That damn word *we* again! 'Who do they take after, you or their mother?'

'Both of us. A bit of each.'

461

He was a good dad, she guessed correctly. 'Has Peter started school yet?'

'He's going in the autumn. He's looking forward to it.'

'That will make life easier for Helen. Children are quite a handful.'

He nodded his agreement. 'She's looking forward to his going too.'

They both laughed at the dryness of that statement.

'You're clearly very fond of your children,' she said.

'Is it that obvious?'

'To me it is.'

'Yes,' he smiled. 'I am. Extremely so.'

A pang of jealousy stabbed through Jennie. 'So tell me about you and Helen. How long have you known one another and how did you meet?'

'We were childhood sweethearts, I suppose,' he replied. 'She lived not far from where we did.'

'That's your grandmother and you?'

He nodded. 'I met Helen when I was about twelve. It was during the summer holidays and she and some other girls were putting on a little garden play which I and a few of my pals went to see. The whole thing sort of grew from there.'

'Childhood sweethearts, how lovely,' Jennie repeated, the merest trace of acid in her voice. 'And how long have you been married?'

'Seven years now.'

'Does Helen like London?'

'She isn't all that keen,' Eliot answered. 'She'd much rather be home in Yorkshire. Perhaps we'll return one day, who knows?'

'You might get a consultancy there?'

'Exactly. I can but try.'

'And what about you, do you like London?'

'Let's say I don't dislike it, with certain areas appealing more than others. I can't deny that it's interesting and filled with surprises. What about yourself?'

Jennie considered that. 'Like you, I don't dislike it.

But I can't envisage myself staying here for ever. I may not be country born but I'm country bred, which tells.'

'I know what you mean.'

Jennie wanted to ask him if he and Helen were happy together, what state their marriage was in, but didn't feel she could do so. From what she'd observed in the Pakenham they certainly seemed happy enough, which filled her with despondency. She hadn't realized how . . . fond she'd become of Eliot. Initially she'd thought of him as a sort of brother figure, but he'd somehow become more than that. Trust her to take a shine to someone who was unavailable!

'We're going up to Hampstead Heath this Sunday,' he said. 'The children adore it there. Have you been?'

She shook her head.

'They think it a wonderful place. There's a pub called the Spaniard's Inn which we often sit outside, weather permitting, and have a drink and a bite to eat.'

She could just picture them in her mind. Eliot, Helen and their two children whom she hadn't yet met. She could hear childish laughter, and visualize Eliot's expression of contentment as he watched them. And then there was Helen, speaking to him, reaching out and taking his hand . . .

Jennie sucked in a deep breath and banished that picture from her mind. It had upset her, brought back the jealousy. For she wanted it to be her sitting there, her reaching out.

Ridiculous! she thought. She was letting her mind run away with itself. She should get a grip. He was a married man after all! Unavailable, someone else's husband. The father of two young children by that someone else – the boyishly shaped Helen.

At least she had a better figure than Helen, fuller and more feminine. There could be no disputing that. She only wished he'd notice. There again, maybe he preferred skinny women.

She mentally wagged a finger at herself. Stop being

unkind! Helen was probably a very nice person, worth-while in the extreme.

Jennie focused on Eliot's dimpled chin, and thought how sexy it was. She would have adored to touch it, play with it.

'Jennie?'

She blinked. 'Sorry, what was that?'

'I was talking about the case I mentioned earlier.'

Had he? She hadn't heard a word. 'Yes, go on,' she urged.

Fascinating dimple, she thought, as he continued speaking.

'A tennis party?' Jennie repeated.

'Yes, there will be four of us. Helen, myself, Jack Spencer from gynae and you. What do you say?'

'I would have loved to come Eliot, but unfortunately I'm on duty this Sunday.'

His disappointment was obvious. 'Oh! What a pity.'

'I could have used the exercise, not to mention the fresh air. But I'm on and there's no way round it.'

'Well, perhaps another time.'

'Perhaps,' she smiled.

'See you then!'

'See you.'

She watched him stride away. Damn her being on duty, but as she'd said there was nothing she could do about it.

She turned and walked slowly down the corridor, her thoughts focused on Eliot and the tennis match that might have been.

'Blast!' she muttered aloud.

Jennie gazed round the Greenstone's tastefully decorated sitting-room. There were several elegant pieces of furniture and a magnificent Victorian mirror facing the fireplace. On a round mahogany table, which she'd looked at when she'd first arrived, were an assortment of knick-knacks and various framed photographs, including one of a young Eliot.

It was odd being in his house, she thought, being where he lived. Odd and exciting.

She didn't like the dark green velvet curtains, she decided, nor the large peculiar potted plant standing in a corner. There was a brass Buddha on the centre of the mantelpiece which she thought looked rather splendid and imposing, and quite unusual.

'How are you for wine?' Eliot enquired, coming up to her and a chap called Edward Thurston whom Eliot had introduced to her as his best friend from Harrogate. There were twelve of them at the dinner party all told, which included their hosts.

'I'll have a top up,' Edward said quickly, proffering his glass.

Jennie wasn't at all impressed with Edward, thinking him a crashing bore. While he'd been wittering on, mainly about Yorkshire, her mind had been elsewhere.

'Not for me thanks,' she smiled to Eliot when he raised an eyebrow to her.

'We'll sit down shortly,' he said.

'Good, I'm famished,' declared Edward, who was somewhat on the tubby side.

'Is he keeping you well entertained?' Eliot asked Jennie.

'Very much so,' she lied politely.

'Knows nowt about cricket though. Pity,' Edward said.

'Helen's the girl for that. She's a fanatic.'

'I know. Grand lass is Helen. One of the best.'

'Lovely wine,' commented Archibald Bates-Owen, joining them and holding out an empty glass. He was a registrar on a renal firm.

Jennie had been surprised and delighted to be invited to the Greenstone's dinner party, something they arranged about four times a year she'd since found out.

She hoped she wasn't going to be sat next to Edward, anyone but him!

'Is there anything else I can get you?' Eliot asked her. 'There are soft drinks.'

'No, I won't bother. But I would like to go to the bathroom.'

'Certainly. It's upstairs on the right. You can't miss it.'

That would get her away from Edward she thought with satisfaction, going out into the hallway. When she came back down again she'd join one of the other groups.

She went upstairs, stopping to look with interest at several pictures *en route*. On reaching the landing she turned right as instructed.

There were two open doors, one the bathroom, the other a bedroom where various lights were on. Out of curiosity she stepped inside and glanced about. It was unmistakably Eliot's and Helen's.

Her gaze came to rest on a double bed covered with a pretty pink quilt. Their bed she thought, the one Eliot and Helen slept in together, where they made love.

It had been a mistake to enter the bedroom, she shouldn't have done. It had been extremely foolish of her.

Whirling round she hurried from the room to the bathroom where she remained until she'd regained her composure.

Esther Marshall buffed a nail, wishing she didn't have to keep them so short, but anything longer would have been impractical and certainly frowned upon. It was one of the small penalties a woman paid in medicine.

She glanced over at Jennie lying on her bed staring up at the ceiling. She'd been lying there for ages without speaking.

'What are you thinking about?' Esther asked.

'Eh?'

'I said what are you thinking about?'

'Eliot,' Jennie replied dreamily, then started when she realized what she'd confessed.

Esther's expression became one of disapproval. 'You two are getting very friendly I've noticed.'

Jennie rolled on to her side, cross with herself for being caught out like that.

'He's a married man, don't forget. A heavily married man.'

'I know!' Jennie answered, her crossness betraying her.

'You are attracted to him, aren't you?'

Jennie didn't reply to that.

'I just don't want you getting hurt,' Esther said softly. 'And you will do if you take up with him, sure as eggs are eggs.'

'There's no question of that,' Jennie snapped.

'No?'

'No!'

'I hope not. For your sake.'

'We just get on well together, that's all. Enjoy one another's company.'

'That can easily lead to other things.'

'Anyway, he's besotted with his family. He's told me so.'

'Is he aware of how you feel?'

'And *how* do I feel?'

Esther pulled a face.

'I like him. He's fun.'

'And dangerous, as far as you're concerned. Be warned, I'm telling you.'

'It wouldn't be jealousy speaking, would it, Esther Marshall?'

'No, it wouldn't. I assure you. I've got too much sense to get mixed up with a married man.'

'I'm not mixed up with him.'

'Yet.'

Jennie glared at her roommate. 'Not yet, or at any time in the future.'

Esther shrugged, and continued buffing. 'I hope you stick to that.'

'Besides, what business is it of yours?'

'Temper!'

Jennie could have slapped Esther. Instead she bounced from the bed. 'I'm going out for a walk,' she announced.

'Like me to come with you?'

'No!'

'I'm only thinking of your own good, Jen.'

Jennie's shoulders slumped, and the anger drained out of her. 'I know that, Ez.'

'Just don't get involved, I beg you.'

'I have no intention of doing so, even if approached, which is highly unlikely. And I've changed my mind, why don't you come with me.'

'All right,' smiled Esther, tossing her emery-board aside.

It was a beautiful night with a full moon shining palely out of a bluey-black sky. They had a long walk to the Angel and back, during which Eliot wasn't mentioned once.

Madge entered little George's bedroom and crossed to his bed where he lay fast asleep. She was caring for him while Graham and Kerensa attended a function in Exeter.

He was a gorgeous child, she thought, and very like Graham at that age. Looking down on her grandson brought back so many memories of Graham and Jennie when they were young.

She sighed, then bent and stroked his brow. 'Sleep tight,' she whispered, and padded from the room.

Downstairs again she considered turning on the wireless, but decided against it. She settled into a comfy chair and closed her eyes.

As she often did she thought of her own George, George Rattenbury, and the good times they'd had together. They were memorable times.

A frown creased her face when her thoughts turned to the possibility of war, a war many now said was inevitable.

Fear clutched at her thinking of Graham becoming caught up in the war, as he was bound to. She bit her lip. She'd lost George, and couldn't bear the idea of losing Graham as well. To lose Graham, her darling boy, would be too much, too cruel.

How many brave lads had died in the Great War, hundreds of thousands of them. Surely another war, against the same enemy, would be a repeat. Hundreds of thousands of lads now alive would march off to such a war and like their fathers not come back.

It was an awful prospect, an appalling one. Why couldn't the politicians do something to avert such a conflict? Herr Hitler was to blame, that terrible man with the funny Charlie Chaplin moustache. She'd seen him in the Movietone newsreels and thought he looked pathetic. A little weed given to rantings, ravings and hysterics. To think she could conceivably lose her Graham because of him. It made her want to spit.

But maybe it wouldn't come to war, maybe it would all blow over.

'What happened to your cheek?' Jennie asked in concern.

'I nicked it shaving. You should have seen the blood! I thought I was in the operating theatre,' Eliot joked in reply.

Jennie laughed.

'Anyway, what I wanted to ask you was, are you on duty this Sunday?'

'Why?' she queried.

'I wondered if you would like to make up a foursome at tennis?'

She considered that. She was very tempted but Esther's warning rang in her ears, she knew it was good advice.

469

'No, I don't think so,' she replied tightly.

He frowned. 'Why not?'

'I have other plans. Sorry,' she lied.

'Oh!'

She kept her expression blank as he scrutinized her face. 'How are Helen and the children?' she asked.

'Fine.'

'What's Helen doing today?' she enquired pointedly.

'I'm not quite sure. I think she's having coffee with a friend this afternoon.'

'A friend with children also?'

'Yes,' Eliot nodded.

'That'll be nice for her. Now I must be off. See you around.' And with that she walked away.

She hoped he'd got the message.

When Sunday came round she found herself at a loss for what to do. She and Esther could have done something together, but Ez was on duty. She was considering calling on some of the other students when the idea struck her.

She drove through Islington to the Archway Road, approaching the heath via Highgate. When she found a suitable spot she parked.

Hampstead Heath was larger than she'd imagined. She gazed out over London thinking what a vast city it was. There were lots of people around, courting couples, some individuals walking their dogs, an old man with a stick which he kept waving about as he talked to a young boy who might well have been his grandson.

It was lovely to breathe fresh air again, she thought, drawing in a deep lungful. That was something she missed more than anything.

She strolled until she eventually reached the Vale of Health. There she turned and retraced her steps.

As she walked she thought of Eliot and his family who often came here. It was right that she hadn't made up the foursome she told herself for the umpteenth time.

Getting more involved could only lead to unhappiness and grief. If their friendship had been strictly on a platonic level that would have been all right, but she knew how her feelings were developing, and they went beyond mere friendship.

She wondered yet again what Eliot felt for her. Did he view her simply as a friend, an interesting companion, or was there more to it than that? He'd never said, though several times she'd caught him looking at her in a way that made her catch her breath and blush.

She wondered whom he'd got to make up his foursome? Someone ugly she hoped, and laughed.

When she got back to her car she drove to the Spaniard's Inn where she ordered herself a snack and a half-pint of mild.

She took her lunch outside and sat at a table, wondering which table the Greenstones had used last time they were there. Perhaps they'd occupied the very table she was now at, perhaps Eliot had even sat on her chair!

She was being silly, she told herself, and very childish. The best thing she could do was put Eliot completely out of her mind, and forget him. Even though she would continue to see him at the hospital, she would just have to think of him in a different light and never forget he was a married man with children.

'I think he's going to ask you up,' Esther whispered to Jennie.

'Who?'

'The tall chap coming this way. Do you know him?'

Jennie located the chap in question. 'No.'

'He's been eyeing you for minutes now.'

They were at the Empire Rooms in Tottenham Court Road where the hospital staff was holding a summer dance. Jennie had already danced with various partners.

'Here he comes!' said Esther, turning away.

'Hello,' the young man smiled at Jennie. 'I'm Harold.'

471

'I'm Jennie.'

'Would you care to dance?'

'Please.'

She walked out on the floor with him where he took her into his arms. 'I'm not the world's best dancer I'm afraid,' he apologized.

'That makes two of us,' she lied. In fact she was a very good dancer but had said that to put him at his ease.

'Are you a nurse?'

'Yes.'

'Thought you must be.'

'Are you a doctor? I haven't seen you round the Free.'

'I'm an architect actually,' he replied. 'I'm here with a chum who is a doctor though – Tom Braine.'

'I've worked with Tom,' Jennie acknowledged. He was part of a general surgery firm.

They were still chatting when she suddenly spied Eliot and Helen dancing a little way off. Eliot, who'd been staring at her, nodded when she spotted him. She nodded back.

'And where do you live?' she asked Harold.

'Camden Town. And you?'

She told him, explaining she shared a room with Esther, the girl she'd been standing with. She risked a glance at Eliot, and found he was still gazing at her. Unless she was mistaken his expression implied jealousy.

The dance ended and they applauded. She prayed Harold would ask her to stay up, which he obligingly did. So, too, did Eliot and Helen she noted.

When she and Harold resumed dancing she snuggled up closer to him, taking up a more intimate pose. Harold, needless to say, was delighted.

They stayed up for five dances in all, then Harold suggested they might have a drink at the bar. Afterwards they returned to the floor and continued dancing.

While they were applauding the last dance Harold asked if he could see her home.

'I have a car,' she informed him.

'Oh!' he exclaimed, disappointed.

'Do you?'

He shook his head.

'Then I'll take you home.'

'Terrific!'

'Just let me have a word with Esther first to explain the situation.'

'Don't worry about me, I'll get the bus,' Esther said.

'You can come with us if you wish. I can drop him and . . .'

'Don't talk nonsense,' Esther interjected. 'I don't want to play gooseberry and spoil your fun. You go ahead and enjoy yourself. You can tell me all about it when you get home. Give me the gory details.'

'Not too gory I hope,' Jennie replied lightly.

'See you then.'

As she was queuing for her coat she spotted Eliot again. She turned her head away when it looked as though he might come across and talk to her.

'Ready?' Harold queried when she'd retrieved her coat and put it on.

'Ready,' she confirmed, taking his arm.

As they left Jennie was aware that Eliot was watching them.

Graham switched off the wireless and stared grimly at Kerensa. It had finally happened.

'God help us all,' he said.

Kerensa wiped a tear from her eye. Right up until the very last she had hoped, prayed . . .

'War,' she said, and shivered.

'War,' Graham repeated. 'I'll pour us both a large drink.'

She certainly needed one, Kerensa thought. 'War,' she said yet again, and shook her head in disbelief.

It was Sunday, 3 September 1939. Graham was twenty-eight years old.

473

Chapter Thirteen

'What's wrong?' Graham demanded, having just arrived home from work. Kerensa's expression was one of abject misery and despair. Her answer was to point to a letter on the hall table.

He knew what it was the moment he saw it. His call-up papers had arrived.

'I see,' he murmured.

He lifted the envelope, and opened it. He read the contents, then threw the pieces back on to the table.

'How long?' she asked.

'I have an interview on Monday.'

She dusted an imaginary speck off the table. They had known it was only a matter of time, that his call-up was inevitable, but that didn't make it any easier.

'I'd love a cup of tea,' he said.

'There's a meal in the oven.'

He shook his head. 'If you don't mind I've lost my appetite.'

She fully understood. She felt the same way.

'How's George?'

'Around somewhere. Playing no doubt.' George was very good at getting on and playing by himself. He had a tremendous imagination.

Graham followed Kerensa through to the kitchen where she filled the kettle. 'I'd better ring Mum,' he said. Madge was an integral part of the arrangements he'd made to keep the business going. She was to look after George during the day while Kerensa ran the firm. Seven men had already gone, to be replaced by women. His instructions to Kerensa had been simple, just keep things ticking over until he arrived back.

Graham had long since decided that he'd go into the Navy. The sea appealed to him, he'd be happiest there. In a funny way he was looking forward to it.

'Have your tea before you ring,' Kerensa said, her voice choked with emotion.

'There's no way round this,' he said.

'I know.'

'I have to do my bit like all the others.'

'I know that too. But I'm not married to the others.'

'But many of them, too, have wives who're having to show a stiff upper lip.'

She glared at him. 'Shut up, Graham, and stop talking like an idiot.'

'All right,' he murmured softly.

She put a hand over her face, and her head drooped. 'Sorry,' she mumbled after a moment.

'I understand. This isn't easy.'

'I know but . . .' She drew in a deep breath, and smiled at him. 'I'll try and do better from here on in. Now, how was your day?'

After a while he phoned Madge, then played with George who was thrilled and excited when told his daddy was going off to fight the nasty Germans and Italians.

Jennie stared at the night sky which was cherry red in parts. In the distance she watched the flashes and clatter of anti-aircraft guns, while her ears were filled with the shrill bells of fire engines and ambulances.

'Hello, I thought I recognized you,' said a voice behind her.

She turned to find a haggard Eliot smiling at her. She'd seen him in passing from time to time, but it was ages since they'd last spoken.

'I'm just going off-duty,' she replied.

He nodded. 'Me too. How long were you on for?'

'Two days. I'm dropping.'

'Same here.'

He came to stand beside her and they both gazed up at the sky, now dominated by planes. 'Lightning war. That's what *blitzkrieg* means, lightning war,' he said.

She didn't reply.

'I've just finished operating on a little girl of nine,' he stated. 'We had to amputate both legs above the knee.'

Jennie stared at him, seeing the pain in his face. She could have told him a dozen horror stories, all of which he could have matched.

'The world's gone mad,' she murmured.

'Yes. Stark-raving bonkers.'

'I must get home and get some sleep,' she said.

'Me too. Though I'm going to have a stiff drink first. I've got a bottle of armagnac in.'

'Lucky old you,' she smiled.

'How have you been anyway?'

'Fine. And you?'

'The same. Helen's taken the children up to Yorkshire away from this lot.'

'Best thing to do,' Jennie replied.

'That's what we thought. They're staying with her parents, which, of course, delights the parents. And Helen always enjoys getting back to Yorkshire.'

Eliot stopped speaking and cocked his head. 'Listen,' he muttered.

It was a far-away whine that very quickly got louder and louder. He knew exactly what it was.

He grabbed hold of Jennie and bundled her against the wall, shielding her with his body. When it went off the explosion was deafening.

'Near thing,' he breathed, releasing her.

'Too near,' she said, shaken by the experience.

'Look!' he exclaimed, pointing.

One of the German bombers had been hit by ack-ack and, with cockpit ablaze, was plummeting from the skies.

'Good riddance,' Eliot said with satisfaction.

Jennie thought of the poor souls trapped in that

cockpit, and shuddered. It didn't bear imagining what they were going through.

'Why don't you come home and have a drink with me?' Eliot suggested.

She stared at him, quite taken aback.

'We don't live all that far from one another after all. Do you have your car with you?'

She shook her head. 'I'm low on petrol. Besides, it's so damned dangerous driving in the blackout. I hate doing it.'

He could well understand that.

Her thoughts were whirling. Go back and have a drink with him? She shouldn't really. Common sense told her not to. And she was dead beat into the bargain. She opened her mouth intending to say no. 'That would be nice,' she heard herself saying instead.

'Let's go then.'

They walked side by side through the darkness. She took his arm after she'd stumbled, finding that easier and feeling more secure.

'When are you on again?' he enquired.

'First thing tomorrow.'

'Me too. Then it'll be another long stint as there's no sign of this abating.'

'I wonder how much of London will be left after this is all over?' she mused.

There was always the possibility that the whole bloody lot would be flattened, he thought grimly, then told himself not to be so stupid. He was allowing his imagination to run away with itself. London would survive – if not in its entirety.

Another German plane spiralled earthwards, this one blazing from front to rear. They heard the explosion when it hit the ground.

They had to bypass a street where a bomb had demolished a building which had subsequently fallen across the street and effectively blocked it. Lone figures moved among the rubble.

They finally reached Eliot's house and went inside. He grasped her by the hand and led her into the sitting-room. 'Wait here till I deal with the curtains,' he instructed.

When he'd closed the blackout curtains in that room he quickly went through the rest of the house closing others. When everything was to his satisfaction he returned and switched on a light.

'Drink?' he said.

Jennie slumped into a chair where she shivered, for it was cold in the house.

'Do you want me to put on a fire?' he asked, handing her a balloon glass containing a generous measure.

'Don't bother. It's not worth it. I won't be here that long.'

He sat in a chair facing her. 'It's lovely being with you again.'

She sipped her brandy.

'You've been avoiding me this long while. Why?'

'You know why, Eliot.'

He smiled thinly. 'I wanted to hear you say it.'

'You're a married man with two children. That says it all.'

'But you were attracted – are attracted.'

She didn't reply to that.

'Me too.'

She still didn't speak.

He looked into his glass, and swirled round its contents. 'It's a funny thing war, isn't it? One moment you can be alive, the next dead. Or worse, like that little girl I mentioned earlier.'

Jennie shuddered.

'And it changes everything. Stands everything on its head. Somehow normal rules don't seem to apply in wartime. At least, that's how it strikes me.'

She could see now he was even more tired and haggard than he'd first appeared. But then many of the staff were like that. It had been, and would continue to be, an exhausting time for them all. She herself felt totally drained, wrung out like an old dishcloth. She put her hand to her hair which hung limp and lifeless, and realized that it desperately needed washing. But it wouldn't be done that night or the next if she had to work through again.

'How's the boyfriend?' Eliot asked casually.

'Boyfriend?'

'The chap you left that summer dance with?'

'Oh, Harold! I stopped seeing him some time ago. He was pleasant enough but not for me.'

'Doctor?'

'No, architect.'

'And there's been no-one since?'

She smiled. 'What is this, the third degree?'

'Sorry,' he apologized. 'Just being nosey I suppose.'

'I did go out with someone else after him. Fellow called Simon. But that eventually fell through as well.'

'Gave him the elbow, eh?'

It had actually been the other way round, but she wasn't telling him that. 'How are you and Helen getting on?' she asked instead.

He shrugged. 'Same as always.'

'What does that mean?'

'Exactly that. We have our ups and downs, just like any other married couple.' He paused, then said, 'I've thought about you a lot, Jennie. I used to enjoy our getting together.'

'And I've missed you, Eliot. I enjoyed it too.'

'But I'm a married man with two children.'

'Unfortunately,' she smiled.

'Yes,' he agreed.

His agreement made her chest tighten, and emotion clog her throat. She should never have come, she told herself. What had she been thinking of? It had been so long since she'd seen him that she'd have thought emotions would have changed between them, but they hadn't. The same attraction still existed.

She leaned back in her chair and closed her eyes. It would have been so easy for her to fall asleep. If she let go mentally for an instant she'd drop over the edge.

There was something very pleasant and satisfactory about being so tired, she thought – almost exhilarating.

Her eyes snapped open in surprise as his lips touched hers. She hadn't heard him leave his chair.

She started to struggle, but he put a hand on her shoulder, restraining her.

Nor did she want to struggle, she realized. She desperately wanted him to kiss her.

Their tongues touched, and intertwined. His hand that had been on her shoulder fell to her waist. He dropped on to his knees so that his face was level with hers.

Finally the kiss was over, and he was staring at her, smiling. 'I've wanted to do that for so long,' he confessed.

She brushed away a stray lock of hair, confused now, and angry with herself for allowing the kiss to happen. But she had loved it, she would have been lying to say otherwise.

'I must go,' she said simply.

'Not yet.'

'I must, Eliot.'

'Let me kiss you again?'

'No.'

'Please?'

'No.'

He reached up and stroked her cheek. 'You've got beautiful skin.'

She nearly touched his dimple, but fought back the impulse. She wanted to enfold him in her arms, hold him, smother him with kisses.

'Are you sleeping in a shelter?' she asked. 'Or have you a cellar?'

'A shelter out back. But I shan't be using it, not tonight. Tonight I'm so damn tired I'm crawling into my own bed to get a proper sleep, that's if I can with all this noise going on. And if the *Luftwaffe* blows me to smithereens then that's just tough luck for me.'

She laughed. 'I have to share our shelter with Ez, my roommate, and Mr and Mrs Atkins. He snores dreadfully.'

'How awful for you. I snore too.'

'Do you?' she smiled.

'But only occasionally. And then all you have to do is turn me on to my side and I stop.'

'Is that what Helen does?'

'Who else?'

Helen, her heart sank to think of Eliot's absent wife.

'Have some more armagnac?'

'Not for me. One was enough. It was delicious.'

'Jennie?'

She stared back at him. 'What?'

'Let me kiss you again. Please?'

'I said no.'

'Don't make me beg.'

'Persistent, aren't you?'

'In some cases that can be an admirable trait.'

He leaned closer till their faces were only inches apart. 'One last kiss and then I'll walk you home.'

She relented, desiring the kiss every bit as much as he. 'One kiss and I'll walk myself home.'

She wriggled with pleasure as his lips brushed hers. Kissing Harold or Simon had been nothing like this. This was sheer, unadulterated bliss!

Jennie gazed at the Atkins' house. She was still exhausted, yet at the same time her spirits were soaring. Incongruously in the circumstances – with German bombers still droning overhead, searchlights piercing the night sky, the clatter of ack-ack and the stridency of ringing bells – she could have shouted for joy.

She thought of Esther and the Atkins in the rear garden shelter, Mr Atkins having been home for several months now due to the war situation. Well, if Eliot could stay in his own bed that night so too could she. Sod the Nazis! She would sleep in her own comfy bed and dream lovely dreams. Dreams of Eliot, she had no doubt.

And what was it he had said again? If the *Luftwaffe* blew him to smithereens then it would be just tough luck. Well, same for her. If the *Luftwaffe* got her then just too bad. But her comfy bed it was going to be, bombs or no bombs.

Laughing quietly, and feeling wonderful, if horrendously tired, she went inside.

Jennie paid for her coffee, then took it over and joined Henrietta Hull and Rachel Levi. 'How are things?' she queried.

'Don't ask!' said Rachel Levi, pulling a face.

'I know how you feel,' Jennie sympathized.

Jennie tasted her coffee. 'Awful,' she pronounced.

'At least it's hot and wet,' Henrietta muttered.

'Which is about all that can be said for it,' Jennie qualified.

They were chatting generally, basically bemoaning their lot, when Jennie spotted Eliot sitting with a bunch of colleagues. Her heart immediately leapt, and she tingled all over.

A few seconds later he glanced across and saw her staring at him. He smiled, and she smiled in return.

She thought of a few nights previously when they'd kissed, and a tremor ran through her.

'Jennie?'

She broke off the eye contact, and turned to her companions.

'Are you all right? You're shaking. Maybe you've got a cold coming on?' said Henrietta.

'No, it's not that. Simply tiredness.'

Henrietta and Rachel nodded their understanding.

'Anyway, as I was saying . . .' Rachel went on.

Jennie tried to listen, but her mind was focused on Eliot.

Kerensa laid down her pen and then ran a hand across her brow, which she then gently massaged.

She sighed, and gazed at the framed photograph of Graham standing on her desk. Miss Flindel and Mavis were both absent at that point, running errands in other parts of the works. She was entirely alone.

She touched the envelope that lay at the bottom of the photograph, the most recent letter she'd had from Graham.

He was well, training hard, and would shortly be going to sea. He hoped to be home on leave before he left.

She offered up a silent prayer that he would get leave. For once he went to sea who knew how long he might be away! It could be a year or more. It all depended on the ship and where it was posted.

She kissed the tip of a finger and placed it against his lips. 'For you my darling,' she whispered.

How lonely life was without him at home, she thought. She had George, of course, the source of great comfort, and her father was forever popping in. But life wasn't the same.

It was the nights that were the worst, they seemed to stretch interminably. Some nights she gave in and brought George into bed with her so she could cuddle him, but she considered that a bad habit which she didn't indulge in too often.

Work, she thought, I must get on! Graham most definitely wouldn't approve of me day-dreaming like this – even if it is of him.

She pulled a folder in front of her and opened it. Soon she was lost in its contents.

'Go on Brownie, fetch!' urged Madge, throwing the stick as far as she could. It was a Sunday morning and she was walking the dog in the water meadows.

She was worried silly about Jennie, from all accounts London was taking an awful hammering. She'd have given anything to have Jennie back safe and sound in Atherton, but of course that was impossible.

Brownie came racing up to her with the stick clamped firmly between his teeth. 'Good dog,' she said, taking the stick and patting him on the head. Brownie furiously wagged his tail. He adored going for walks with Madge.

'Again?' she queried, knowing full well that was precisely what Brownie wanted. He'd be happy if she threw the stick all day long.

'On you go then!' she said, and chucked the stick in a different direction.

Jennie had rung the previous week and had sounded cheerful enough, shrugging off the continuing Blitz as no more than a temporary inconvenience. But Madge was horribly aware it was far more than that.

Nor was London the only city being devastated. Coventry was taking a pounding as well and had lost its beautiful cathedral.

She crossed two fingers. 'Keep lucky, Jennie,' she whispered. 'We're all praying for you.'

That night the Germans tried to torch the City of London by dropping at least 10,000 fire bombs on it. The resulting inferno could be seen for miles.

Jennie came up short as Eliot emerged from a door directly in front of her. 'How are you?' she queried.

'The usual. A candidate for the knacker's yard. How about yourself?'

'The same.'

'I've got to hurry. I have a list waiting.'

'Oh! Right.' That meant he was due in the operating theatre.

He hesitated. 'I, eh . . . Are you on later? I mean this evening.'

'I'm due off. But you know what it's like.'

He gave a hollow laugh. He knew only too well. 'I'm definitely off, and shall be at home. Why don't you come round for another drink and a chat?'

'Helen still away?'

He nodded.

'I thought so. And you're lonely?'

He realized he was being teased. 'Dreadfully.'

'I see.'

'So, will you come?'

She considered the invitation, common sense telling her she should turn him down flat. What was to be gained after all? 'I'll think about it,' she replied at last.

'Good,' he nodded.

'But don't be upset if I don't turn up.'

'I'll be there waiting if you do.'

'Bye,' she said, and hurried on past him.

As she went down the corridor she caught herself smiling.

John entered the kitchen with a drawn, haggard face. 'Nine o'clock before we got away. Nine o'bloody clock – I ask you!'

'There is a war on and they're desperate for copper,' Madge reminded him.

'Maybe so, but these long hours are killing me,' he grumbled, throwing himself into his favourite chair.

'I'll get your tea.'

He yawned. 'Someone should go and see Tempest personally, complain about these inhuman hours. They're working us like beasts of the field, I tell you.'

Madge smiled wryly. The idea of John working like a beast of the field was completely at odds with her comprehension. She knew him only too well. He might be putting in the hours but the work accomplished by him during those hours would be the minimum he could get away with. She was in no doubt on that score.

'Cauliflower cheese, how's that?' she queried.

'Sounds fine. Light on the cheese, I suppose?'

'What do you think with supplies as short as they are? And it'll get worse. Rationing can't be all that far away.'

'Rationing,' John repeated, and groaned. What next to plague him?

'I'd like to see Tempest working the hours we do,' John went on after a few seconds' sullen pause. 'It would be a different story then.'

'Oh, stop moaning!'

'Or you, come to that. You're not in that dark and damp hole for the entire day.'

There were occasions when John could be extremely tiresome and irritating, and this was one of them. She switched the gas on under the pot containing the cauliflower.

'The sooner this war's over and done with the better,' John muttered.

She eyed him darkly. 'If I was you I'd be thanking my lucky stars I'm in a reserved occupation and not at the sharp end.'

'It wouldn't bother me if I was,' he lied.

'No?' she laughed.

'No, it damn well wouldn't. I'm not scared of the Germans. In fact the Army might be preferable to being stuck in that awful mine. And can you hurry up, I'm starving!'

'I'm being as quick as I can.'

'The new figures were posted today. Production is up on last week. That's the fifth week running.'

'Good for the lads at Wheal Tempest.'

'More money for Sir Reginald you mean. He's not giving it away free, you know. Not by a long chalk!'

'Stop going on,' Madge admonished.

'I'm entitled to. You haven't had the long day I've had!' John retorted angrily.

This could easily become a row, she realized. He was in that sort of filthy mood. But she couldn't resist. 'You should be thankful you're on light maintenance duties. Think of those doing the actual grafting and what it's like for them.'

'My duties aren't that light,' he protested.

486

'They're light by comparison, as you're well aware. So don't try and flannel me.'

John made a 'humping' sound at the back of his throat. 'That Staddon's a slave driver,' he went on sourly. 'If he was allowed to use a whip I'm sure the bugger would.'

'Don't be ridiculous,' Madge mocked.

'I'm not being ridiculous at all! What the hell do you know? You don't work there.'

'I know what I hear from other wives. Staddon's a decent man by all accounts.'

'Decent my arse!'

'Don't use language like that to me,' Madge snapped.

'He's a bastard through and through.'

'Maybe with you, but not with others. Perhaps he has a down on you because he saw through you years ago. Remember when he caught you sleeping on the job.'

'That's right, cast that up again!'

'Well, he did, didn't he?'

John came to his feet and thrust his hands deep into his pockets. 'I wish we could unionize the mine. I'd show Staddon and Sir High and Mighty Reginald a thing or two then. By God, I would!'

'They'd eat you alive. You're nothing compared to either of them. And if you think you are you're kidding yourself. All you boil down to is a big mouth.'

He glared at her. Why did he always feel she got the better of him? When he had conversations with her in his head he never lost. But in reality it was always the opposite.

Madge glanced over at the pot containing the cauliflower, and frowned to see the gas had gone out. She crossed to the cooker and twiddled the knob to no avail. Nor was gas coming through any of the other burners.

She went to the cupboard under the stairs and examined the meter, but the problem wasn't there.

'Bad news,' she declared, returning to the kitchen. 'There's been a gas cut.'

'A what?' he exploded.

'A gas cut. You'll have to wait for your tea.'

His face went red, and his lower lip started to quiver.
'That's it then, I'm off to the pub!'

He stormed out of the house, slamming the front door
behind him.

'Wouldn't bother him to be at the sharp end, not
scared of the Germans,' Madge repeated, and laughed
derisively.

As John was storming down the street Jennie was
arriving in front of Eliot's house. She still really hadn't
made up her mind whether she was going in or not.

There had been a raid earlier, but now the skies were
quiet. It was a lull, the planes undoubtedly would be
back.

She chewed a thumbnail as she considered her
dilemma. She'd come this far, she told herself, so deep
down she must want to knock.

But there again, he was a married man with two
children. Any relationship could only end up being
hurtful to both parties concerned. And she knew if she
went in there would be a relationship. She wasn't that
naïve. Not after the way they'd kissed, and the feelings
she'd experienced, when she'd been here before.

She remembered those kisses and how blissful they'd
been and knew she craved more.

Well, she thought, you can't stand here all night.
Either knock at the door or go away.

She'd go away. And with that she turned on her heel
and strode back the way she'd come.

Within a dozen paces she began to falter. Was this
what she really wanted? It was certainly the intelligent
thing to do, the sensible thing. There could be no
disputing that. But was it what she really wanted?

'Blast!' she said, and turned round again.

He opened the door to stand framed in darkness. 'You
came,' he smiled.

'No, it's a trick of your imagination,' she replied caustically.

When the door was closed behind her he switched on the light. 'A very real looking trick,' he commented.

Suddenly she was nervous. 'Thank you,' she said as he helped her out of her coat.

He hung the coat up then led the way to the sitting-room. 'Would you like a glass of wine?' he asked.

'Please, that would be nice.'

'Back in a tick,' he said, and vanished.

She crossed to the magnificent Victorian mirror facing the fireplace and gazed at herself, patting several stray strands of hair back into place. There were dark smudges under her eyes, but that was common to most of the hospital staff, many of whom looked far worse than she.

'Mirror, mirror, on the wall, who is the fairest of them all?' Eliot quoted, having come back into the room.

'Not me, that's for certain,' she laughed, accepting the glass of red wine he handed her.

'Well, I think you're gorgeous.'

She sipped the wine. 'Hmm!' she murmured.

'It's Pauillac. A good bottle opened in your honour,' he informed her.

'You were so certain I'd come?'

'Not at all. But I wanted to give you something special if you did.'

That touched her. 'And if I hadn't turned up?'

'Then I'd have drunk the lot myself.'

She smiled at that. 'Do you keep much wine at home?'

'A bit. We have a larder that doubles up as a cellar.'

She sipped her wine again, closing her eyes appreciatively as its mellow warmness slipped down her throat.

'I'm glad you like it,' he said.

'I certainly do.'

'Shall I put a record on?'

'That would be nice.'

He went to a gramophone that she would have sworn

hadn't been there during her previous visit, opened the lid and then wound up the mechanism. The record he played was 'Whispering Grass'.

'How about a dance?' he suggested.

Why not? she thought. She put her glass on the mantelpiece beside the brass Buddha and moved towards him. Once in his arms they began to dance.

When that record was finished he replaced it with 'A Nightingale Sang In Berkeley Square'.

While they were dancing to that he kissed her lightly on the neck. When she didn't object he did so again, this time allowing his lips to linger a little longer.

'Let's sit down,' he whispered when the record came to an end.

He took her by the hand and led her to a sofa, pulling her down beside him. She gave a tiny moan as his tongue slid into her mouth to find hers, his hands fluttering up and down her back, touching, caressing.

She broke apart from him and gulped in air. 'You don't waste any time, do you?'

He stared at her, studying her. 'Jennie?'

'What?'

'I'm not quite sure what I feel for you. But whatever, it goes deep. If I wasn't married, I . . .'

'But you are,' she interjected. There was a moment's pause, then she said, 'Do you love Helen?'

'I thought I did. Now I'm not so sure.'

She kissed his dimple and then licked it.

'Oh Jennie,' he murmured, placing a hand over her breast.

She closed her eyes as he massaged the breast, and caught her breath as he removed the hand and started unbuttoning her blouse.

He pulled the blouse apart and lifted up her bra, freeing her breasts. He then began kissing them.

'Oh!' she gasped. 'That's so good.'

She started when his hand went up under her skirt and total panic suddenly engulfed her.

'No!' she cried, tugging his hand away. 'Stop it! Please stop it!'

'Jennie, I . . .' he said thickly.

She pushed him from her. 'No, Eliot, no! This is wrong. I don't know what possessed me to come here. I knew something like this would happen. But it's wrong. Completely wrong.'

He stared at her, perplexed and hurt. 'I'm sorry.'

She jumped to her feet and hastily rearranged her clothes. Her heart was hammering and she was still filled with panic.

'I have to go.'

'I didn't mean to upset you.'

'I know that.'

'Stay, finish your wine.'

'No, I have to go.'

'Look, I've made a mess of things. But don't hold that against me. It's simply that I feel so strongly about you.'

She felt exactly the same about him, which was why she must go and never return. She'd been insane to come in the first place, completely out of her head. What had she been thinking about? He was a married man with a family, there was no way round that.

She looked at her hands. They were shaking, almost uncontrollably. She felt sick, and somehow cheap. It was small comfort that he didn't think of her like that, that he wasn't out for an easy conquest.

'I'll get my coat,' she said.

'No, I will.'

She gazed after him as he hurried from the room. She blamed herself for what had occurred. She should never have taken up the invitation, but stayed well away. Fool! she berated herself. Fool!

He returned with her coat. 'Can't you stay and talk? I swear I won't lay another finger on you.'

'No, Eliot. It's best I leave.'

'Damn!' he muttered.

491

'It's just not to be,' she said, attempting a smile which didn't quite come off. 'We must be philosophical.'

'Don't think badly of me.'

'I don't. I assure you. But anything between us would be wrong. No matter how attracted we are to one another, it would still be wrong.'

'I suppose you're right,' he said, rubbing his forehead.

'I am. Believe me. Now see me to the door and I'll say goodbye.'

He switched off the hall light before opening the door. 'Will you kiss me good-night?' he asked.

She didn't even have to think about that. 'No,' she replied, and stepped outside.

As she hurried home through the blackout, the air-raid sirens began to wail, a wailing that was echoed in her heart.

'Mavis, it's time for you and I to take a walk,' said Miss Flindel.

Kerensa glanced up in surprise, a look of delight flooding her face when she saw Graham grinning at her.

She almost knocked over her chair in her eagerness to get to him. 'Oh, it's so good to see you!' she exclaimed, falling into his arms.

'And to see you.'

When Miss Flindel and Mavis were gone he kissed her.

'How I've missed you,' Kerensa said.

'And I've missed you, terribly.'

'How long?'

He gave her a wry, lop-sided smile. 'Monday.'

'That all!'

''Fraid so,'

'It's only four days,' she protested.

'There's nothing I can do about it.'

'I know that.'

She found she was trembling. This was so unexpected.

492

'I thought you still had several weeks' training left and wouldn't get leave before then?'

'The powers that be changed their mind. I'm to report to Portsmouth on Monday evening.'

'What sort of ship?'

'A large one. I can't tell you more than that.'

'Walls have ears and all that sort of thing?' she teased.

'It's true what they say about careless talk.'

'Any idea where you're off to?'

'None whatsoever. And that's the truth.'

She hugged him tight. 'Oh God, it's good to have you back.'

'And it's good to be back. I've dreamed about it almost from the moment I went away. Coming back to you.'

She placed the tip of a finger on his cheek and traced a line. 'Don't accuse me of not being conscientious, but I'm taking time off till Monday. Miss Flindel will cope, I'm sure.'

He frowned. 'I, eh . . .'

The finger went from his cheek to cover his mouth. 'No arguing, husband mine. We're going to spend every single minute of your leave together. And that's that.'

He smiled, and kissed her. 'Yes, boss.'

'Starting now. Let's go.'

'Where to. Home?'

She thought about that. 'No, a pub first where we can have a drink and a chat. Then home.'

'Done,' he smiled.

They found Miss Flindel, told her what they planned, then drove off in the Lanchester to a little pub that was a favourite of theirs.

Graham pulled up in front of Corfe Mullen, and switched off the engine. Then he and Kerensa got out. It was early afternoon after their visit to the pub where they'd had lunch.

What a magnificent house it was, Graham thought,

493

stopping and staring at it. To think that he and his family owned it and lived there. He laughed.

'What's so funny?' Kerensa asked.

'I was just thinking. It's a long way from the house we lived in in Glasgow, and where I was born, to this.'

'And to owning your own successful firm,' she smiled.

'That too.'

'Well, you deserve it all, Graham. You've worked hard enough for it.'

And taken chances, he thought, remembering his smuggling days. 'Let's go in and surprise Mum,' he said.

Kerensa hooked an arm round his. 'Let's do that.'

When Madge caught sight of Graham she let out an almighty shriek that woke up little George who'd been sleeping.

Jennie was *en route* to her current ward when she caught sight of Eliot in the company of Mr Ralston, the ENT consultant, the pair of them heading for the ENT ward just ahead. Ralston started to gesticulate, making some point or other, to which Eliot nodded several times in agreement.

Outside a raid was in progress. The drone of planes could be heard, and the clatter of anti-aircraft fire. There were several batteries only a short distance from the hospital.

'Make way!' someone shouted.

Jennie pressed herself against the wall as an emergency on a trolley went hurtling by. The patient was a young man with blood-soaked bandages round his head.

Jennie dismissed Eliot from her mind as she continued on her way. She had masses to do and might well be working through the night. The prospect filled her with dread, knowing what those long hours would be like. Only that morning a houseman had keeled over from exhaustion and had had to be put to bed.

She'd have a shower later, she thought, which brought

a smile to her face. That would be lovely and make the night go more easily – a relaxing shower in piping hot water.

She was turning a corner when it happened. A huge explosion lifted her off her feet and threw her flat. A chunk of plaster hit her on the back of the head to spatter away in bits. When she looked up the air was thick with swirling dust and other small debris.

A child was screaming hysterically, others yelling and calling. She stared in horror at a woman lying just a few feet away, her back against the wall. The woman's expression was one of incredulity. Her neck had been clearly severed by flying glass.

A porter went running past, then returned to Jennie. 'Are you all right, love?' he demanded.

She nodded. 'I think so. Go and help where you're needed.'

He didn't reply to that, merely rushed off.

She sat up and examined her limbs one by one. None were broken, though there was a graze on the back of her left hand. She felt her trunk, that too undamaged.

She came to her feet and hurried after the porter, intending to render what assistance she could.

She halted to stare at a pool of blood in the middle of which was a human arm. The body to which the arm belonged was nowhere to be seen.

An old man staggered up to her. 'You seen my Edna?' he asked.

'No, I'm afraid not.'

'She's got an appointment, see. We were on the way to the clinic, and suddenly she was gone.'

'I'm sorry,' Jennie replied.

'Don't want her to be late, do we? She might miss her appointment.'

He continued past Jennie. 'Edna? Where are you, Edna? You playing silly beggars, gel?'

Chaos and confusion reigned. Further down the

corridor she bumped into Mary Hopton, a student like herself. Mary was wandering round aimlessly, clearly in a state of shock.

Jennie took Mary into a nearby sterilizing room and sat her down. She tried the tap and, luckily, it was still working. She poured Mary a glass of water which she forced her to drink.

What to do next? Jennie hadn't a clue. What was certain was that there would be others needing her help more than Mary.

She had a few words with Mary, who nodded that she understood, then left her, intending to find someone to report to.

'A bomb. A bloody great big one. Seems to have hit the eye ward,' someone called out.

Jennie stopped short. The eye ward was adjacent to the ENT ward where Eliot had been. She broke into a run, racing in that direction.

'Oh Christ!' she exclaimed when she came in sight of the piles of rubble that were all that remained of the ENT ward. On top of one pile lay the body of the ENT Sister, Sister McCafferty.

'Eliot!' she sobbed.

A fireman appeared, then another and another. They began tearing at the rubble, heaving great chunks of it aside. She joined them, bloodying her hands as she frantically clawed at the bricks, plaster and battening.

Dead patient after dead patient was found amidst the wreck of beds and tables. She was surrounded by firemen and policemen now, all working flat out.

'It'll be a miracle if anyone survives this lot,' a fireman commented to his mate.

Jennie glanced at him and realized she was crying. She couldn't believe that Eliot might be dead, that she'd never see him alive again, or talk to him. The man she loved had been killed.

Further down one of the corridors an internal wall collapsed. Jennie gave no thought to any personal danger she might be in as she continued removing the rubble in a frenzy.

She stopped to stare when they found Mr Ralston. Eliot would be next, she thought, the two of them were together. But he wasn't. They found the houseman instead.

'Jennie?'

She looked round to find Eliot gazing at her in concern. He was extremely pale and there was a dry trickle of blood below his nose.

'You're alive!' she croaked, unable to believe her eyes.

He nodded.

She came to her feet. 'But I saw you and Mr Ralston heading for the ward. And we've found him.'

'He sent me on an errand. I was some distance from the ward when the bomb hit.'

Profound relief washed through her. Tears reappeared to roll down her cheeks.

'Oh Eliot!' she whispered. 'I thought . . . I thought . . .'

He took her into his arms and held her tight. Then he was crying too.

She knocked at his door, and waited. He was off duty, but that didn't necessarily mean he'd be at home. She knocked a second time.

Eliot opened the door. 'Jennie! What a pleasant surprise.'

'Can I come in?'

'Of course.'

When the door was closed again he switched on the hall light, then ushered her into the sitting-room where he'd been reading a medical journal. It was the evening of the day after the bomb had hit the hospital.

'Drink?'

'Please,' she smiled.

'Wine? Scotch?'

'Scotch would be perfect. A small one, with water.'

497

'Coming right up.'

He left the room, returning shortly with two crystal glasses containing their drinks.

'Cheers!' she toasted.

'Bottoms up!'

They both had a sip from their respective glasses.

'Now, to what do I owe this honour?' he asked.

'Do you mind if I sit down?'

'Please do.'

She perched on the sofa, he on a chair.

'I've been thinking about yesterday and how I felt when I thought I'd lost you,' she began. 'Quite simply it made me realize, or admit to myself perhaps, that I've fallen in love with you.'

This time he had a large swallow from his glass. Nor did he take his eyes off Jennie as he drank. They remained riveted on her face.

'I've also been thinking about several comments you once made to me,' she went on. 'One was that war is a funny old thing. One moment you can be alive, the next dead. Or worse. Yesterday we had an excellent example of that. Also that war changes everything, stands everything on its head. And that in wartime, normal rules don't seem to apply.' She paused, then said softly, 'I've come to the conclusion that I agree with these sentiments. Wholeheartedly.'

'I see,' he murmured.

'I was beside myself with grief when I thought I'd lost you, completely bereft. And then, as though by magic, there you were. Restored to me.'

'I could so easily have been in that ward,' Eliot mused. 'Should have been. If Ralston hadn't decided he wanted . . .' Eliot broke off, and shivered.

'I love you, and I'm going to enjoy you while I can. That's my decision,' Jennie stated.

'Does that mean what I think?'

She nodded.

'I think I love you too. In fact, sitting here looking at

498

you, I'm certain of it. Perhaps yesterday focused my emotions as well.'

'Mrs Atkins won't think anything of it if I stay out all night. She's quite used to that by now.'

He smiled. 'The bedroom or the shelter?'

'You choose.'

'Let's live dangerously and use the bedroom.'

'Then the bedroom it is.'

He laid his glass aside, rose and crossed to her.

'I'm a virgin,' she stated.

'I thought as much.'

He brought his mouth to hers and kissed her tenderly. After a while they went upstairs.

'Write as often as you can, I treasure your letters,' Kerensa said to Graham leaning out of the carriage window. They were at the railway station, as she was seeing him off to Portsmouth.

'The leave has simply flown by, but then I knew it would,' Graham said sadly.

'But we had a lovely time, didn't we, my lover?'

He laughed at her using that term. It was rare for her to speak 'Devon'.

'Wonderful,' he agreed.

The guard blew his whistle, and waved his green flag.

She wouldn't cry, Kerensa told herself. She hadn't cried when he'd gone away the first time, nor would she now.

The train juddered and, with a clank, slowly began to move. Graham waved, and Kerensa waved furiously in return.

'Good luck!' she called out, then, quietly to herself whispered, 'Good luck my darling.'

She continued waving till he was finally lost to view.

'Helen's arriving home today,' Eliot said to Jennie. 'One of the letters I picked up just before we left the house was from her.' The mail had been delivered only moments before they left for the hospital.

This would be Helen's first trip back since decamping to Yorkshire with the children. 'For how long?'

'It could be some time, she didn't say. The letter was more of a note really.'

'Well, that puts paid to that,' said Jennie, disappointed.

'Just the nights together. We can still meet.'

'It won't be the same though, will it?' she declared.

The worst of the Blitz was over. There were still occasional raids by day and night, but nothing compared to the bombardment at its height.

'Let's wait and see what happens,' he said.

Jennie thought of Eliot with the boyish Helen in that bed she'd come to know so well, and red-hot jealousy stabbed through her. It was Helen's marital bed after all, she reminded herself, she was the interloper.

'If you give me the key I'll nip back there at some point and change the sheets,' Jennie said. 'Any idea what time Helen is due in?'

'She mentioned late afternoon. But you know what the trains are like, it could be midnight before she shows up.'

'None the less I'll get over there as soon as I can and tidy up. I don't want her finding anything suspicious or incriminating.'

'Listen, I must get on. I'm frightfully busy,' Eliot said.

'Right. Give me the key and I'll return it to you later.'

'You're a poppet, Jen.'

During the past weeks it had almost been as if she was married to him, that she was Mrs Eliot Greenstone. Now the genuine article was about to reappear, and she felt sick.

Still, she'd known what she was getting into. She hadn't deluded herself in any way. But it was excruciating to think of Helen in bed with Eliot, and not her.

She put a hand to her brow to discover it was covered

in cold, clammy sweat. She had to put these thoughts out of her mind, she told herself.

'Only home for a few days!' Eliot exclaimed in surprise. 'I'd have thought you'd stay longer than that.'

'I want to get back to the children,' Helen replied. She was very tired, as it had been an extremely long and tedious journey. The train had kept stopping, apparently for no reason, and then standing for ages before continuing.

'How are they?' Eliot asked eagerly. He adored his children.

'Fine. Couldn't be better. Peter is well settled into his new school and Cass is growing like a weed.'

He made a face. 'It's a pity you couldn't have brought them with you?'

'The way things are! Don't be ridiculous, Eliot. London isn't safe and well you know it.'

'It's nothing like it was though.'

'Bringing them home before the end of the war is out of the question, and that's final,' she stated firmly.

'You're looking well,' he said.

'And I feel it. As I wrote to you, I'm doing some warwork, which is hard but worthwhile. And there's always plenty to do – a paper drive, jumble sale, oh lots.'

'The main thing is that the children are safe,' he said.

'Exactly!'

'But I would have thought you'd have stayed for more than a few days – for some while actually.'

'Impossible,' she snapped irritably, realizing she was developing a headache.

'I'll come up and visit just as soon as I can get time off,' he promised. 'But it's been bedlam at the hospital as you can well imagine.'

'Poor Mr Ralston,' she sympathized. 'Such a clever, kind man.'

'I nearly bought it that day I can tell you.'

'So you said in your letter,' she nodded.

'Gave me quite a turn.'

'No doubt. But listen, let's talk further tomorrow. I'm whacked.'

'Bed then,' he said.

There was something in his tone which made her frown. 'Now, don't you be getting any ideas. At least not with regard to tonight. All I want is sleep.'

'I understand,' he replied, in a way rather pleased.

'I don't suppose you've had time to be lonely with so much work to do?' she said.

He thought of Jennie. 'That's right.'

'The children ask after you, of course. It's always Daddy this and Daddy that.'

He smiled, picturing Peter and Cass. 'I miss them a great deal.'

'It's a pity you can't also spend the war in Yorkshire. But, of course, you're tied up here.'

'Until I get my consultancy. And then we can only hope.'

She yawned. 'I'm going up. What about you?'

'I'll follow in a few minutes.'

She came across and kissed him on the lips. 'I'd say you've lost weight.'

'I may well have done. As I've told you, things have been hectic.'

'Don't wake me in the morning. I'll have a long lie in.'

'Right.'

He watched her walk from the room. He'd loved her once, and perhaps in a way still did. He was certainly very fond of her. She was the mother of his children after all. But it was Jennie he really loved. He knew how she would react when he told her Helen was only home for a few days – she'd be delighted.

When he went up to the bedroom several minutes later he found Helen already in bed fast asleep.

Chapter Fourteen

'I hate it when she's down,' Jennie complained as Eliot joined her. They were in a café close to the hospital where they'd arranged to meet. It was February 1941 and the newspapers were full of the continued British advance across Libya where the previous week they had taken the town of Benghazi after a dash from Tobruk. Also there was plenty of news about the Afrika Corps which had landed in Tripoli under the command of the German General Erwin Rommel.

'I know,' he sympathized.

'Do you?'

'That's a silly question, Jen.'

She shrugged. 'I suppose it is. She is your wife when all's said and done.'

'I do believe you're jealous,' he teased.

She glared at him. 'Now who's being silly. Of course I am! You know how I feel about you.'

'Ten days isn't for ever,' he said.

Jennie groaned. 'It is in the circumstances. She's not usually here as long as that.'

'It's ten days on this occasion because Edward Thurston gave her a lift in his car, and he won't be returning until then when he'll give her a lift back up again. You remember Edward, you met him at our house.'

'Your best friend?'

'That's him.'

'I thought he was boring.'

Eliot laughed. 'I suppose he can be at times. But I like him. He's always been a great pal to me.'

503

'Is he home on leave or something?'

Eliot shook his head. 'Edward isn't in the forces. He works for the War Department. Don't ask me what he does there, something hush, hush.'

'A civil servant in other words,' she sneered.

'That's it.'

'Based in Harrogate?'

'Leeds actually.'

'Easy war for him,' she said, thinking of Graham at sea with the Royal Navy.

'Someone has to do the job, I suppose. And from all accounts he's terribly good at it.'

'So why's he in London?'

'In connection with the WD. He bumped into Helen apparently, mentioned he was motoring down and she cadged a lift off him. Which brings me to the question, how would you like to come to another dinner party in our house?'

'You mean with Helen?' Jennie exclaimed in surprise.

'No reason why not. She knows nothing about us. And besides, she liked you. Said so only this morning.'

'But we've only met twice.'

'Nevertheless, she remembered you favourably. She said we needed another female to make up the numbers, and when I suggested you she agreed at once saying you'd be perfect. You'd made quite an impression on her apparently.'

Jennie stared at Eliot. 'Are you sure this is a good idea?'

'Whether or not you come is entirely up to you.'

'When is this dinner party?'

'Friday night. And before you say anything, I know you're off duty.'

That was true enough. 'Who else is going to be there?'

Eliot mentioned a few names from the hospital, then the name of a couple who were friends of Edward's and lived in Knightsbridge.

'The thing is,' Eliot smiled, 'Helen has brought down a

rather excellet baron of beef which she intends serving.'

'A baron of beef!' Jennie repeated, her mouth watering. With the current food rationing such a luxury was unheard of, at least in London.

'You've just talked me into it,' she said.

Eliot laughed. 'Thought I might.'

'And she doesn't suspect a thing?'

Eliot shook his head.

'You're sure?'

'Course I'm sure. She doesn't have an inkling that I have someone else.' When he saw the look on Jennie's face he qualified that remark. 'That I love someone else.'

'Better,' she nodded.

A dinner party at Eliot's! With Helen there. Now what should she wear?

Mr Houlihan was a most eccentric Irishman, and a consultant general surgeon, who had been known in the past to kick inattentive or stupid students and housemen on the bottom during ward-rounds. His eccentricity was only matched by his brilliance with a scalpel and his reputation with a bottle. It was said he could operate dead drunk – and often did – and be as good as when he was stone-cold sober. The only means of telling the difference between one state and the other were the fumes that emanated from him.

Jennie and Esther were working together for once, the rest of the firm consisting of a student called Antonia Brackett, Jilly Soames, the houseman, and Alexandra Johnson, the registrar, all of whom now gathered round Houlihan who gazed at them rather devilishly from behind thick curling eyebrows.

'Shall we proceed?' he said and, without waiting for a reply, strode off into the ward where his round was due.

Sister and Staff were waiting for him and, after a curt nod from 'the great man', joined the little group.

On arriving at his first patient Houlihan lifted the

notes from where they were hanging at the bottom of the iron bed and flicked through them. While he was doing this Sister gave him a few reminders and observations about the patient in question.

'And how are you today, Mr Tinker?' Houlihan enquired.

'Not too bad, sir.'

'Sister says you're fit enough now to have your op. So I'll put you on tomorrow's list. How's that?'

Mr Tinker swallowed hard. 'That'll be fine, sir.'

'Good.' He turned to Sister. 'Make the necessary arrangements will you?'

'Yes, Mr Houlihan.'

At the next bed Houlihan spoke at length with the patient, pointing out various aspects of the man's wound to his junior colleagues, and asking the students pertinent questions. He asked Jennie two, both of which she was able to answer fully and correctly, which obviously pleased him.

They progressed up one side of Nightingale Ward, then started down the other.

'Mr Alford, is it?' Houlihan said pleasantly.

Mr Alford didn't reply, he was gaping at Jennie who hadn't actually looked at him yet. When she did her face dropped in surprise.

'Jennie!' Mr Alford exclaimed.

'Andy!'

Houlihan looked amused. 'What's this, reunion time?' he said, but not unkindly.

Jennie blushed. 'Sorry, Mr Houlihan. Andy and I come from the same village in Devon. We went to school together.'

'Did you now!' Houlihan said. He glanced again at Andy's notes. 'You're a soldier, Mr Alford?'

'That's right, sir.'

'And just arrived in last night. It says here you've been shot in the thigh.'

Andy nodded.

506

'Hmm!' Houlihan mused, reading further.

Jennie glanced again at Andy who was smiling broadly at her, and smiled in return. Here was a real turn-up for the book – Andy Alford at the Free!

'Let's have a look, shall we?' Houlihan said, replacing the notes. 'Sister!'

Sister and Staff began undoing the bandages that swathed the upper part of Andy's leg.

'Much pain, Mr Alford?' Houlihan enquired.

'A bit, sir.'

'Have you been sleeping?'

'With some pills, sir.'

Houlihan nodded that he understood.

When the bandages and dressing had been removed Houlihan peered at the wound. 'Not healing as it should,' he murmured.

'That's right, sir.'

'Which is why they've sent you to us.' He beamed at Andy. 'They need the beds, you see.'

'So I understand, sir.'

Houlihan moved slightly to get a better vantage point. 'You'll certainly be laid up for a while, Mr Alford. I think I can safely guarantee that. Now . . .'

He swung on Sister and issued a stream of instructions which Sister carefully noted down. When he was finished Sister correctly repeated them.

'We'll see you tomorrow then, Mr Alford,' Houlihan said.

'Thank you, sir.'

'Speak to you later,' Jennie whispered as the firm moved on.

'I'll look forward to it.'

The next case was a post-operative patient who was making good progress. They lingered there for less than a minute before moving on again.

Before going off-duty Jennie returned to the ward to pay a visit to Andy. She had the screens put round him so they could talk in private. 'Hello again,' she smiled when the screens were in place.

'Hello, Jennie. Or is it doctor?'

'I'm not a doctor yet, only a trainee. So Jennie will do.'

She sat on the edge of his bed. 'What a coincidence, eh?'

'You could have knocked me over with a feather.'

'How's Poppy?'

'Never better. Same with the maid, proper job!'

Jennie smiled to hear those familiar expressions. 'And the little boy?'

'Freddy's terrific from what Poppy writes. He's three now, you know.'

'And Ruth?'

'She'll be seven later on this year.'

He reached out and touched her hand. 'You can do me a favour, Jennie. I'd certainly appreciate it if you did.'

'Name it?' she smiled.

'I could write, but that would take time. And I'm no great shakes at writing anyway. Your mum's on the telephone. If I pay for the call could you ring your mum and ask her to tell Poppy where I am so she can maybe come visit?'

'Of course!' said Jennie. 'I'd be only too happy to do that for you.'

'Thanks, Jennie. I sure appreciate it.'

'I'll ring this evening. How's that?'

'Grand.'

He stared at her. 'Oh, but it's good to see you again. It's a real whiff of home.'

'And it's the same for me seeing you.'

His face clouded over. 'I always felt . . . guilty about you, Jennie. I gave you a raw deal.'

Jennie looked down at the top sheet.

'I had to do what I did. There was no way round it.'

'Poppy was pregnant by you, wasn't she?'

508

His lips thinned, and he nodded. ''Twas that old year's night dance, remember? You and I had a fight and you left me. Well, I got chatting to Poppy and . . . she was more amenable than you. The sad thing is, it was only the once.'

The old year's night dance! That confirmed the guess she'd made when Ruth was born.

'I was right bitter at the time, I can tell you,' Andy continued. 'It was so unfair. One little bit of fun and that as the result.'

When she still didn't comment he went on, 'What happened broke my heart, Jennie. Particularly at the wedding. When I saw you there I realized just how horrendous a mistake I'd made. A mistake I could never rectify, and would have to live with for the rest of my life. And for what? A couple of minutes' fun in the garden shed.'

'The garden shed?' she exclaimed, appalled.

'Yes,' he whispered.

She thought that awful, and degrading, but didn't say anything.

There was a few seconds' hiatus, during which they were both introspective, then he spoke again. 'Though I have to say it has more or less worked out all right. Poppy and I do get on. It took a while, but eventually we settled down together. She's not you, of course, and never will be. But in a funny way she's right for me, and me for her.'

'So there aren't any regrets?'

'I wouldn't say that. But we've both made the best of how things have fallen out.'

'I'm pleased,' Jennie said sincerely.

He looked her up and down, taking in her white coat and professional air. 'When I knew you, you worked in the Post Office Stores and was a village girl. Now look at you! Almost a doctor. No, perhaps things worked out best in the long run. You were too good for me. I didn't see it at the time, but you clearly were. I would only have made you miserable.'

He was right, she thought. She would never have been fulfilled married to Andy. She would never have been able to spread her wings as she subsequently had. 'I owe you a lot,' she said.

'Me!'

'If it hadn't been for you I'd probably never have gone to night school, and if I hadn't gone there medicine would have been nothing more than a dream. So if you view it that way some good did come of our relationship.'

'You're a born lady, Jennie, while I'm just a country bumpkin. Remember the old rhyme?

'Devon born, Devon bred, strong in the arm . . .'

'Thick in the head,' she finished for him.

They both laughed.

'You're a tonic, Jennie. A real tonic. And I'm sure that between you and your Mr Houlihan you'll have me up and about in no time.'

'Was it bad where you were?' she asked.

His smile faded. 'Fairly. I can't talk about it. But yes, it was. I lost a great many mates. All fine men.'

'I'm sorry,' she said.

'Their wives and sweethearts will be even more so.'

'I'm sure,' she said softly.

Jennie rose from the bed. 'I'll place that phone call later. You can rely on it.'

'And make sure your mum tells Poppy I'm all right and that there's nothing to worry about. She's a terrible worrier is Poppy.'

'I will. See you at tomorrow's ward round. By the way, how's the thigh?'

He screwed up his face. 'Could be better. But mustn't complain.'

On impulse she bent and kissed him on the cheek. 'Try and get a good night's sleep.'

'Jen?'

She stopped, and turned to him again.

'Are you happy?'

She thought of her career, and Eliot. 'At the moment, very much so,' she replied.

'I'm glad. I truly am. Good friends you and I?'

'Good friends,' she agreed.

He raised a hand in farewell as she disappeared through the screens.

For someone well brought up Edward Thurston ate dreadfully badly Jennie thought, having been watching him for the past few minutes. He held his knife and fork in an extraordinary way, and spoke with his mouth full. It didn't seem to faze Helen, who was sitting beside him, one little bit.

Edward and Helen were talking cricket, with the emphasis on Yorkshire cricket. Names, scores and events on and off the field were being bandied non-stop between them.

Eliot shot Helen a dark, disapproving glance, thinking she was neglecting their other guests in favour of Edward whom she was allowing to monopolize her.

'Do you like jazz, Jennie?' enquired Julian Barnes, sitting on her right-hand side. He and his wife Madeleine were Edward's friends from Knightsbridge where they lived in Hans Crescent.

'Very much so,' she replied.

'I adore Jelly Roll Morton myself, whom I believe hasn't been all that well recently.'

'Really!'

'Mind you, they live a frightfully decadent lifestyle these black musicians. Up to all sorts, some of which I wouldn't dare mention at a dinner table. But interesting none the less.'

'Quite,' Jennie smiled.

Eliot was getting angry with Helen, she noted. And Helen was aware of that anger and ignoring it.

'Beautiful beef,' stated Humphrey Hall, a gynaecologist there with his wife, Zoë.

'Rather!' Zoë agreed.

511

Eliot glanced at Jennie, and a warmth crept into his eyes. He thought he'd never seen her look lovelier.

Jennie looked from him to Helen, and couldn't help but think of the two of them going to bed later. That irritated her, and made her jealous.

She started when she found Helen returning her gaze. It seemed to her Helen could read what was in her mind. Don't be stupid, she berated herself, how could Helen possibly know!

'Enjoying yourself, Jennie?' Helen enquired.

Was her tone condescending? Jennie wondered, then dismissed that as her imagination at work. 'Very much. It's a delightful meal.'

Helen nodded her acceptance of the compliment. She was an excellent cook who enjoyed being praised.

'Lucky old you being able to get hold of meat like this,' commented Thelma Hart to Helen.

'One of the advantages of rural and small-town life,' Helen retorted. 'This cow, for example, was running round a field only a few days ago. The farmer and I are great chums.'

'Is that Roger?' Eliot asked.

'Yes.'

Eliot laughed. 'Oh him!'

'And what's wrong with Roger?' Helen demanded.

'Nothing. If you don't mind them in-bred.' Eliot said that purposely knowing it would annoy Helen.

'He's nothing of the sort!' she protested.

'You know full well he is. Why, his mother and father were related in all . . .'

'Nonsense!' interjected Helen.

'Roger's her second cousin,' Eliot stated, the inference clear.

'How interesting,' murmured Hector, Thelma's partner for the evening.

'There's nothing like a little touch of incest to add sparkle to a conversation,' Eliot said.

'There's no incest in my family,' Helen snapped.

'Of course not,' Edward agreed in a rather pompous tone.

'If you say so, dear,' Eliot murmured, slicing a piece of beef.

Eliot was in for it after they'd gone, Jennie thought, loving his several barbs and jibes at Helen. She knew what he was really saying – that he preferred her company and wished they were alone.

God, how she loved him! To death and distraction. If they'd been sitting together she'd have played footsie with him, or tried to entice him upstairs. As her imagination ran riot, she almost burst out laughing, so it was lucky when Hector launched into an anecdote about something that had happened to him at the hospital the previous week, which was rather funny and well told.

'Could you pass the horse-radish, please?' Thelma asked Chris Knobsworth when Hector was finished. Chris was another registrar at the Free.

While the horse-radish was being passed round, Helen glared briefly at Eliot, not having been in the least bit amused about the in-bred – incest conversation.

Oh dear! Jennie thought, catching the glare. She glanced at Eliot who was smiling wickedly back at his spouse, which was infuriating Helen even further.

There would be words later on, Jennie thought with a combination of glee and grim satisfaction.

Eliot laid down his knife and fork, and rose. He picked up a silver-lidded claret jug and started round the company.

'And how's your beef?' he asked Jennie when he reached her.

'Delicious.'

'Good. We try to please.'

She blushed slightly, knowing full well it wasn't the beef he was referring to.

'More wine?' he asked.

'Please.'

As he bent over to pour the wine he contrived to brush

against her which sent a spasm of excitement and sexual thrill through her insides.

'Thank you,' she said when he'd finished pouring, her voice tight.

He had such a sexy bottom she mused as he bent over again. She could hardly resist . . .

'Getting back to jazz . . .' said Julian Barnes.

Jennie wrenched her thoughts away from Eliot, and Eliot's bottom, forcing herself to concentrate on what Julian was saying.

Jennie stopped just inside the ward to stare at Andy's bed. A plumpish woman was sitting on the chair beside him, whom she recognized as Poppy Alford. Putting a smile on her face she walked towards them.

'Jennie!' Andy exclaimed with pleasure as she approached the bed.

Poppy looked round, saw her and immediately stood, adopting a deferential posture.

'Hello Poppy, how are you?' Jennie smiled.

'Fine thank you, doctor,' Poppy replied hesitantly.

The years hadn't been all that kind to Poppy, Jennie noted. If anything she looked plainer than she had when she was younger. And she was certainly carrying far too much weight.

'As I've told Andy, I'm not a doctor yet. So it's still Jennie,' she replied lightly.

Poppy shifted, clearly uncomfortable to be in Jennie's presence. Because of Andy? Jennie didn't think so. Probably because she was now someone in authority. Doctors, even trainees, were held in very high esteem and were very much part of the 'them' not 'us' syndrome.

'Thank you for ringing your mother, Jennie. I'm much obliged,' Poppy said.

'It wasn't any trouble.'

'And saved time in letting you know what was what,' Andy chipped in.

'Yes,' agreed Jennie. 'The mail can be all over the place nowadays. But then what can you expect with a war on?' When there was no reply to that she said, 'And how are the little ones?'

'They be fine, jim dandy,' Poppy replied enthusiastically. 'I wish I could have brought them to see their dad, but that just really wasn't on.'

'I understand.'

'But I got presents, things they made and drew for me,' Andy beamed.

'That's nice.'

'Andy's going to be all right, isn't he, Jennie?' Poppy asked anxiously.

'Of course he is,' Jennie reassured her. 'He'll get nothing but the best of care here, I promise you.'

Poppy gazed at Andy, adoration shining from her eyes. 'He's been ever so brave. A real hero,' she gushed.

Andy's face clouded. 'Here, none of that. Our mob were all heroes. I was certainly nothing special.'

'Well, to me you were, and are,' Poppy said.

'Ah, that's different,' Andy told her with a smile.

'I'll leave you two, I have to get on,' Jennie said. To Andy she added, 'I'll see you later.'

Poppy went to Jennie and grasped her by the hand. 'Thank you ever so much, Jennie. I know you'll look after him as best you're able, and send him home to me soon.'

'How long are you staying in London for?'

'Just one day and night. I have to get back to the children. Besides, I don't fancy the idea of hanging about London. Too big and frightening for my taste.'

Andy laughed. 'She's scared the white slavers will get her.'

'It does go on,' Poppy said, wide-eyed, to Jennie.

'Though hardly in wartime,' Jennie teased.

'That's true,' Poppy muttered. 'Hadn't thought of that.'

'She reads too many novels, she does,' chipped in Andy, grinning.

'Nothing like a good read,' protested Poppy.

'You'd get on well with my brother Graham. He's another for books,' Jennie said.

'How is he?' Poppy asked. 'In the Navy I was told.'

'He's fine, when last I heard. Kerensa, his wife, thinks he's in the Mediterranean, though she's not absolutely certain about that.'

'I understand,' said Poppy. 'Let's just hope everything stays all right with him. Nice man, your brother Graham.'

Jennie said her goodbyes and left them. When she glanced back before leaving the ward Poppy and Andy were deep in conversation.

Funny how things worked out, she thought. At the time she'd been so upset at his dropping her to marry Poppy. Nice chap that he was, she could see now what a lucky escape she'd had.

Andy was right. In the long run he'd only have made her miserable. And if she'd married him she'd never have met Eliot.

Eliot yawned. 'Are you going to be much longer?' he asked Helen who was sitting at her vanity table. It had been a long day that had included several cases which had been exceptionally demanding.

Helen peered at herself in the mirror, sniffed, and rose from her chair. She put out the overhead light, then padded to the bed and climbed in.

Eliot switched off his bedside light, and the room was plunged into darkness.

'So what have you planned for tomorrow?' he asked.

'Actually, Edward has asked me to lunch at his club. Do you mind?'

'Not in the least.'

'Good!'

'It'll give you something to do while I'm at the hospital.'

'Precisely what I thought. And I do enjoy eating out, it can be such fun. And Edward is excellent company '

'How's his business down here going?'

'He's never said. And I would never dream of enquiring.'

'Of course not,' Eliot murmured.

She leaned over and pecked him on the lips. 'Good night, darling.'

He put an arm round her as she started to move away again, and pulled her close. 'What's the hurry?'

'No hurry . . .'

The rest of the sentence was lost as his lips covered hers.

'Nice,' he said when the kiss was over.

'Very. But not tonight Eliot.'

'Why not?'

'I have a sore tummy. Besides which, I just don't feel like it. I'm sorry. Perhaps tomorrow night.'

He allowed her to escape to her own side of the bed where she snuggled down.

'I do miss the children,' he sighed.

'So do I.'

'Except you'll soon be back with them.'

She turned and looked at him in the darkness. 'You can be a marvellous father, you know. It's something I've always admired about you.'

'Thank you,' he smiled.

'You're very loving and caring towards them. It's most commendable.'

'So are you.'

'But I'm their mother. Mothers and fathers are quite different.'

'I can't wait to see Peter and Cass again. And the changes in them.'

'Edward thinks they're marvellous. He told me on the way down here that he hopes he's blessed with children as lovely and sweet as ours when he eventually marries. He said we were very lucky.'

'And so we are. Very.'

There was a silence, then Helen murmured, 'I wish you didn't have to work so hard. This war is being quite beastly to you.'

'It's being quite beastly to a lot of people,' he commented drily.

'You know what I mean!'

Somewhere in the distance an ack-ack battery opened up, and then another. A small raid was taking place.

'Bloody Germans,' Helen muttered, and shivered.

'Scared?'

'What do you think? The thought of being blown up in my bed gives me the jitters.'

'Want to go to the shelter?'

She considered that. 'There's no real danger, is there? I mean, it's hardly what it was like six months ago?'

'Hardly,' he agreed.

She imagined getting out of her lovely warm bed and trailing out into the cold garden, and even colder shelter and decided she'd stay put.

'Good night Eliot,' she said.

'Good night Helen.'

She soon fell asleep, and began to snore. And as she did so Eliot, still wide awake, thought of Jennie who would never have refused him, no matter how sore a tummy she had.

But then Jennie and Helen were two very different animals.

Graham reeled as yet another wave of acrid smoke enveloped him. All around him men were coughing and spluttering.

A young seaman cried out for his mother, then keeled over and died. A large section of his back completely stove in.

Forster, who had the bunk above Graham, put his hands to his face, and screamed hysterically when what had been his face seemed to dissolve beneath his fingers.

518

He sank to his knees and screamed again, a scream that was quite inhuman.

A tongue of flame licked out, followed by several larger ones, then a surging sheet of fire scorched and sizzled everything it touched.

He had to get out of there, Graham thought. They all did. He moved, and immediately stumbled over someone lying prostrate. He knelt and turned the person over. It was Lieutenant Warrington, dead as mutton.

The ship rocked violently, and heeled over slightly. She'd been hit yet again.

'Assist the wounded,' Graham instructed authoritatively. 'And we'll make for a sea deck.'

'Fuck the wounded!' said John 'Taffy' Jones. 'I'm looking after number one, see.'

Graham strode quickly over and hit Jones across the face. Jones recoiled with an oath.

'We're all mates here, we look after one another,' Graham said.

'Screw you!'

'Run now and I'll personally see you're for ever branded a coward,' Graham stated.

Jones tried to stare Graham in the eye, but couldn't. He swallowed hard. 'There's no need to be that way about it, Gray.'

'Then do as you're told.'

Graham crossed to Forster who was now keening and helped him to his feet. 'It's all right, Billy lad. We'll take care of you.'

'My face!' Forster wailed.

'We'll soon get it attended to. Now come on, one foot in front of the other. There's a good chap.'

Graham's lungs felt as though they were on fire from the billowing and swirling acrid smoke that would kill if they remained much longer where they were.

He got Forster through the hatchway, which was a start. They had three decks to manoeuvre before they reached the lowest sea deck. And who knew what lay between where they now were and there?

Graham glanced backwards at the shadowy figures moving about. 'Doing your bit, Taffy?' he called out.

'I am indeed, you black-hearted Scotch bastard,' came the reply.

Despite the conditions Graham smiled.

'I can't see. I can't see a fucking thing!' Forster wailed.

'Hush,' Graham said, as if he was talking to a child, which in a way he was, for Billy Forster was only seventeen years old.

When all living men had left where they'd been, Graham, supporting Billy Forster, led the way towards the nearest companionway.

'I've been meaning to ask, is Helen's family really incestuous?' Jennie queried, lying curled up beside Eliot in his bed where they'd just made love.

'Oh frightfully!'

'I'm serious.'

Eliot smiled down at her. 'Like many old families of that sort there are certain . . . irregularities, shall we say, in its past, not to mention present. Nothing infuriates Helen more than to be reminded of them.'

'I enjoyed the dinner party. There were all sorts of lovely undercurrents going on.'

'She got me annoyed that night. She shouldn't have allowed Edward to monopolize her as he did. Bad form when she was the hostess.'

'Or were you really annoyed because of me?'

He glanced at her in surprise. 'Why should I have been that?'

'I don't know. Because I was there, and so was your wife.'

'Could be,' he mused.

She stroked his buttock. 'Anyway, she's gone now. As far as I'm concerned that's all that matters. You're mine again. All mine!'

'We get on so well together, you and I,' he murmured.

'Better than you and Helen?'

There was a pause, then he said, 'Yes.'

That admission thrilled her. 'We're a natural combination, you and I. Like bacon and eggs.'

'You're a funny old thing at times,' he smiled.

'What does that mean?'

'It means I like you very much, as you well know.'

Her expression became grave. 'I don't just like you Eliot, I love you.'

'And I, Lord forgive me, love you.'

She opened her mouth to utter further, but he covered it with his hand. 'Don't say anything more for the moment.'

She laid her head against his breast and closed her eyes. She smiled as the hand that had been over her mouth started to caress her, quickly re-arousing her.

They were in the middle of making love a second time when the sirens sounded and battery after battery of ack-ack opened up.

They would later discover that the Blitz had returned with a vengeance as the Germans launched a new spring initiative.

Esther Marshall pushed the textbook she'd been studying away, she'd had enough for one night. Her mind felt as if it had been dipped in cement, and allowed to set. She sighed, then stared over at Jennie towelling her hair, which she had just washed.

'I hate being back in that shelter,' Esther complained.

'Then don't use it.'

Esther shrugged. 'Better safe than sorry.'

'You're a born conservative through and through,' Jennie mocked.

'I won't argue there. For example, you wouldn't get me taking up with a married man.'

Jennie stopped towelling. 'Now don't start that again!'

'I only mention it for your own good.'

'Well don't!' Jennie snapped.

'Suit yourself.'

Esther picked up an American film magazine she'd come across at the hospital, gazed at its front cover, then tossed it aside. She'd already read it through several times.

'The finals aren't all that far away,' she said.

'I know that!'

'Then what?'

'How do you mean?'

'You and lover boy. What happens then?'

'I've no idea,' Jennie replied irritably.

'That sort of relationship wouldn't do me at all. You're on a hiding to nothing, mark my words. They never leave their wives, or very rarely anyway.'

Jennie didn't reply to that.

'You must have broached the subject with him, surely?'

Again Jennie didn't reply.

'Jen?'

'No, I haven't actually.'

'Then how do you know he isn't just using you for a good time while his wife is elsewhere?'

That suggestion infuriated Jennie, and it showed. 'I just know, all right! We love one another.'

'You certainly love him, that's obvious.'

'And he loves me.'

'Maybe so,' Esther said quietly.

Esther lit a cigarette, having recently taken up smoking. 'For my money you're on a one-way road to nowhere. What prospects have you got with him, I mean?'

'Will you shut it Ez, please?'

'Only trying to help, after all. What else are friends for?'

'Minding their own business,' Jennie replied tartly, for what Esther was saying and driving at had hit a particularly raw nerve. It was a subject she didn't like to

522

think about, far less dwell on. If only Eliot would say something! But he never did. He seemed happy to maintain the status quo.

Esther attempted to blow a smoke ring at the ceiling, and failed miserably. It was a skill she was determined to acquire.

Jennie tossed the towel aside and began combing her hair. There was a lull in the raids which would begin again shortly. Then she and Esther would go down to the shelter. Eliot was at the hospital working.

'How do you think you'll do in the finals?' Jennie asked.

Esther shrugged. 'Who knows!'

'You must have some idea?'

'Let me put it this way, I'm working hard and keeping my fingers crossed. *You* won't have any trouble though, everyone knows that.'

'Do they now!' Jennie exclaimed.

'That's the word. You're expected to come out somewhere near the top of the heap. Jobs will be yours for the choosing.'

'I wish I was so confident,' Jennie declared, though she had to admit, the extra tuition she'd had from Eliot had been an enormous help. He'd spent countless hours going over things with her.

'I met someone nice today,' Esther said dreamily.

'Did you!'

'Yes. His name's Nathan.'

'So?' Jennie prompted when Esther failed to elaborate.

'Well, it was like this . . .'

Jennie listened intently, and afterwards was full of questions, some of which Esther could answer, others she couldn't.

Kerensa shot out of her chair when she heard the taxi draw up outside Corfe Mullen. She flew to the front door and threw it open.

'Graham!' she squealed. She'd been awaiting his arrival, as he'd telephoned her from Euston Station to tell her he was coming.

'Keep the change,' Graham told the delighted cab driver, and turned to Kerensa running helter-skelter towards him.

He swept her into his arms, and whirled her round. Then he was kissing her, eagerly, passionately.

'You said three weeks' leave on the telephone,' she stated as the taxi drove off.

'That's right. Three glorious weeks all to ourselves.'

'And George, of course.'

'Of course,' Graham smiled. He couldn't wait to see his son who was now four.

'He'll be home later. He's at his nursery which he thoroughly enjoys.'

'Good,' nodded Graham.

He stared at Kerensa, drinking her in. He pulled her back into his arms and hugged her again. 'How I've missed you,' he murmured.

'And I you.'

'I've got news,' he declared, pushing her to arm's length. 'News I've kept till I could tell you in person.'

'And what's that?'

'I've been selected to become an officer. When I finish leave I travel to Brighton where I begin training.'

'Oh Graham, that's wonderful!'

'Yes, I'm pleased.'

'And how did they come to select you?'

His expression changed to become sombre. 'They seemed to think I showed leadership qualities during the . . . during the final engagement.'

'You mean when your ship was sunk?'

He nodded. 'So many good men were lost. Lots of them friends.'

'But you survived, that's all I care about.'

'I survived, yes,' he said, sighing.

'Was it awful?'

'Fairly. The worst part was a young chap called Forster. It's a long story, but I did my damndest to save him, which I succeeded in doing. Then he went and died under the surgeon's knife.'

'I am sorry,' she sympathized.

'I took that very personally. Silly of me really, but I did.'

Something in his eyes made her cringe inside. It was clear he'd been through a great deal.

'You're home now, that's the main thing,' she said soothingly.

'Yes.'

'Would you like a drink? I've got some Scotch in.'

'Let's knock back a few together,' he smiled. 'And I'll teach you about sippers.

'Oh, Kerensa!' he exclaimed suddenly, and hugged her yet again, this time as though for grim death. When he finally released her there were tears in his eyes.

'Let's get that drink,' she said. 'And you can tell me all about it.'

He picked up his case, and then arm in arm they went inside.

Jennie decided to have a word with Sister before visiting Andy. She knocked, then went into Sister's office when bid.

They exchanged the usual pleasantries, after which Jennie asked, 'How is Mr Alford this afternoon?'

'Not so hot, I'm afraid,' Sister replied. 'As you're aware his wound has become infected, the wound itself is starting to break down. Both conditions, despite frequent change of dressings and the wound being regularly cleaned, continue unabated, I'm afraid.'

Jennie's lips thinned. This wasn't good, not good at all.

'We're doing everything we can,' Sister went on.

'I appreciate that. You don't mind if I speak to him?'

'Not at all. Perhaps you can cheer him up. He's terribly down in the dumps.'

Jennie left Sister and made her way to Andy's bed where she found him staring disconsolately at the ceiling. He was even more drawn than the last time she'd seen him, and dark patches had appeared under his eyes.

'So, how's my favourite patient?' she asked jocularly.

'Terrible.'

'It's not that bad, surely?'

'I've got a splitting headache and my leg is throbbing like you wouldn't believe.'

She picked up his notes, read the new additions, then replaced them at the bottom of the bed. 'Can I take your temperature?'

'Help yourself.'

That was up on the previous reading, which worried her.

'What's wrong, Jen? No-one will tell me.'

She hesitated, then said, 'Your wound has become infected. Which was always on the cards when it wasn't healing properly. However, it's nothing we can't sort out.'

'It's sore.'

'Bound to be,' she smiled. 'Now is there anything I can get you?'

'I'd adore a glass of lemonade.'

She nodded. 'I'll see what I can do.' That wouldn't be easy the way things were, but she'd do her best. There must be some somewhere.

'I've been craving it all day,' he explained.

'I understand. That sort of thing happens when you're ill.'

'I'm all hot and sweaty.'

'I'll speak to Sister about another bed bath, or at least a rub down.'

'Thanks, Jennie,' he said.

'Have you written to Poppy?'

'I started, but couldn't go on. I was having trouble focusing on account of my headache.'

'If you dictate I'll finish it for you?'

His face lit up. 'Would you Jen? You're a brick.'

When she'd finished the letter she addressed the envelope and said she'd post it for him. He was extremely grateful and thanked her profusely.

'You mustn't let it prey on you. You must try and be objective even though he's a friend,' Eliot advised. He and Jennie were in his shelter while an intense and fierce raid raged outside. The Germans were attacking in greater numbers than ever before.

'That's so difficult. We went to school together, don't forget. I keep seeing him as a little boy.' She paused, then said, 'A little bugger actually who used to pull my hair and nip my arm.'

Eliot laughed.

'It's no laughing matter,' she chided.

'Of course not. It was simply the way you said that. You're fond of him, aren't you?' He knew about Jennie and Andy, as she had previously explained the situation.

'Yes. I mean, he was part of my life. I don't want to see anything happen to him.'

'You can rely on Houlihan doing everything he can.'

'Oh Eliot!' she exclaimed softly, and wriggled even closer to him. Pressing her flesh against his.

He held her, and rocked her gently, while outside bombs rained down all over London.

'Sit down, Jennie,' Houlihan instructed. When she'd done so he opened a drawer and took out a bottle of sherry and two glasses. 'Can I tempt you, me darlin'?'

She shook her head. 'No thanks.'

'I think you should. If for no other reason than to keep an old Irish dipso company.'

She smiled at that. 'All right then. But only a small one.'

His small one transpired to be an extremely large one by normal standards, while what he poured himself

527

might have been a beer measure. 'Bottoms up!' he toasted.

'Now then,' he said when they'd both drunk. 'I want to speak to you about Mr Alford. To put it bluntly, I'm going to have to amputate.'

Jennie went pale. This was what she'd feared. 'There's no other way?'

He was kind to her, seeing how distressed she was. Any other colleague would have received a sharp retort. 'If there was I'd take it.'

She realized her bloomer. 'I'm sorry, I . . .'

'That's all right. I fully understand. It's always different when it's personal.'

She swallowed more of her sherry. Amputation! Poor, poor Andy. 'When?' she asked.

'The sooner the better. Tomorrow's list.'

She nodded.

'Now the thing is, do I tell him, or you? Which do you think would be better?'

She considered it and concluded that such awful news had to be better coming from her than any other member of staff. 'Me I suppose,' she answered.

'I thought that would be your reply. I've had the screens put round his bed. No time like the present, eh?'

No time, she thought.

'Unfortunately these things happen,' Houlihan went on quietly. 'It might have gone either way. Sadly for him it's turned out as it has.'

Of all the nasty things she'd had to do, and take part in, since coming to the Free this was undoubtedly the worst. He wasn't just any patient, but Andy whom she'd gone out with, and come very close to marrying. If matters had transpired otherwise it would have been her husband who was about to lose a leg.

She laid what remained of her sherry aside. 'Right!' she declared, standing. 'Best get on with it.'

Houlihan watched her leave the room, taking care to close the door behind her. When she was gone he swore viciously, then poured her drink into his own and, in one swallow, saw off the lot.

Andy stared at Jennie in horror. 'You don't mean that,' he managed to say at last.

'I'm afraid I do.'

'But . . . but . . .' He trailed off, and gagged.

'Do you want a basin?'

He tried to speak, but couldn't. He nodded instead.

Jennie rushed out from behind the screens, collared a passing nurse, told her what was needed, then returned to Andy who was trying to contain his urge to vomit.

He managed to control himself until the basin arrived, then he let go.

When he was finally finished Jennie used the towel the thoughtful nurse had also brought to wipe his mouth, and after that his forehead, beaded in sweat.

'Jesus, Jennie, you can't let them do that to me,' he pleaded, hands knotting and unknotting.

She asked the nurse to leave them alone as she laid the foul-smelling basin on the floor. 'There's no alternative, I'm afraid.'

'I had no idea. You said . . . You promised everything would be all right. That there was nothing wrong with me you couldn't sort out.'

She would have given anything to be elsewhere, other than in the situation she now faced. 'I'm sorry,' she mumbled.

'You lied. You're just like all the rest of these poxy doctors, you fucking lied!'

Now she was sweating. She could feel it under her arms and coursing down her back. 'I'm sorry,' she repeated.

'Sorry! What sodding good is that to me? I'm going to lose a leg and all you can say is you're sorry. Well, fuck you, Jennie Forsyth. I hope you rot in hell. I hope you . . .'

He broke off when a stern-faced Sister appeared

inside the screen. 'Please stop shouting, Mr Alford. You're disturbing the other patients,' she said in a stern yet sympathetic voice.

'Screw the other patients! I don't give a shit about them. All I care about is me. They're going to cut my bloody leg off tomorrow. Do you understand that? My bloody leg!'

Sister glanced at Jennie, and partially raised an eyebrow. Jennie knew what she was being asked, and nodded her assent. Sister swiftly vanished.

Andy reached out and grabbed Jennie's arm. His tone became pleading again. 'Please, Jennie, please? Don't let them do this. Please?'

She stared into his bulging eyes, seeing pain, shock and terror. She felt like Judas Iscariot, as if she were personally responsible for what had to happen. As if she'd personally failed him in some way. She knew that was nonsense of course, but none the less it was how she felt. And it hurt.

She grimaced as he squeezed her arm even more forcefully, a squeeze that was going to leave a bruise. 'You could die if we don't amputate,' she answered.

'No, I don't believe you!'

'It's true.'

'You're a butcher like all the rest of them. I thought you were different, Jennie, but you're not. You've become like them, a bloody butcher!'

Sister returned carrying a loaded hypodermic syringe. Staff was with her to lend assistance.

Andy panicked totally when he saw them. 'I'm getting out of here. You're not cutting my leg off!'

He sat up and threw back the bedcovers. He then attempted to swing his feet off the bed, but Sister and Staff were on him before he could do so.

Jennie helped, holding him down while he ranted and raved, calling her and Houlihan all the foul names he could think of.

Sister was quick and efficient. The needle slid home

and she depressed the plunger shooting the swift-acting sedative into a muscle.

'What are you doing? What the hell are you doing?' he cried.

'It'll calm you down,' Jennie muttered through clenched teeth.

'I don't need calming down. I need to get out of here.'

'We'll talk about that,' she said.

'I want my clothes. I want . . . I want . . .' He faltered as the sedative started to take effect.

'There, there, Andy,' Jennie murmured soothingly.

'There's a good man, back into bed,' Sister said.

His gaze fastened on to Jennie. A gaze that reminded her of a trapped and helpless animal. A gaze that almost broke her heart.

'Jen? Please?'

The frenzy had gone out of him now, his eyelids had begun to droop. 'Best you sleep,' she replied.

'Don't let them take my leg off. I couldn't bear that. Better I was dead. Honest!'

'Nonsense. Think of Poppy, and Ruth and Freddy, you've got them to live for.'

'Poppy won't want me with only one leg.'

'Yes, she will. She loves you.'

'She . . .'

'She loves you,' Jennie repeated.

'Yes,' Andy said dreamily. 'She does. Just as I once loved you.'

Jennie shot Sister a glance, then Staff. Both tactfully averted their gaze.

'Just as I once . . .' His shoulders sagged, and he began to snore.

'Leave him to us now. We'll take care of him,' Sister stated.

'I, eh . . . He's an old boyfriend,' Jennie said simply.

Sister smiled. 'That's none of our business, is it Staff?'

Staff shook her head.

Jennie, thoroughly shaken, left them to it.

Eliot lay with his arm round Jennie while she whimpered in her sleep. He knew her thoughts obviously focused on Andy who was to be operated on the following day.

She muttered something unintelligible, then whimpered again. If only there was something more he could do! He'd done everything possible before she'd fallen asleep. All that remained was to be there as a comfort, while she slept and when she woke.

Life could be a bastard at times, he thought, a real bastard.

'Eliot?' she said after a while.

'I'm here, Jennie.'

She crowded in closer to him, and promptly fell asleep again.

Funny how it could get to the stage where you were able to sleep through almost anything, he mused. Pain, bombs, bells, air-raid sirens.

He listened to the strident clamour of an ambulance that went past the house to recede into the distance towards the hospital. Casualty would be bedlam again, he thought, as indeed it was most nights.

Her hand emerged from underneath the bedclothes, searching. He took hold of it, and she sighed.

Life could be a bastard, he thought again, a real bastard.

'The next patient is Mr Alford,' Theatre Sister announced to Mr Houlihan.

He looked at Jennie and smiled. 'There's no need for you to be present at this one, Miss Forsyth. Unless you wish to?'

She shook her head.

'Then go and have a cup of tea. In fact, take the rest of the list off.'

'Thank you, sir.'

The swing doors opened and a trolley was wheeled in on which lay the anaesthetized Andy.

Houlihan made them wait until Jennie had left the theatre before allowing them to transfer Andy to the operating table.

Jennie waited anxiously, watching the minutes tick by on a nearby wall clock. Every so often she sipped at the cup of tea she was holding.

The ward Staff nurse appeared, her job to return Andy to the ward. She glanced at the clock, then at Jennie. It was the same Staff nurse who'd helped inject Andy the previous day.

'That tea looks good,' she said.

'There's plenty left in the pot.'

Staff considered it and decided she still had time for a quick cup.

Jennie finished her cup and laid it aside. 'He should have been out by now,' she fretted.

Staff glanced again at the clock. 'I wouldn't worry if I was you. I'm sure Mr Houlihan has everything in hand.'

Five minutes later Theatre Sister appeared pushing Andy. 'All went well,' she announced breezily.

Jennie went to Andy's side and gazed at him. It would be a while yet before he woke from his general anaesthetic.

'I'll accompany you if I may?' she said to Staff.

'I'll be glad of the company.'

Jennie swung on Theatre Sister. 'And there were no complications?'

'None. It all went smoothly. As it should.'

That was a relief, Jennie thought. You never knew with even the simplest of operations. All sorts of unforeseen things could go wrong and often did.

Jennie helped Staff wheel the trolley back to the ward.

Andy's eyes fluttered open. For a few moments he looked puzzled, then his memory returned. 'Water!' he croaked.

Water was forbidden for the present. So Jennie used a

previously prepared damp flannel to wet his lips and tongue.

'Again!' he begged when the flannel was removed.

'Later,' she promised.

'How . . . how . . . ?'

'It all went exceptionally well, Andy. There were no problems or complications.'

He stared at her, his gaze piercing and unblinking. 'Went well?' he repeated.

'Yes.'

He took a deep breath, then slowly exhaled. He reached down and felt where his leg had been.

'Oh my God!' he cried, tears appearing in his eyes.

'It's best you rest now,' Jennie advised.

He turned his head away from her and stared in the opposite direction. Nor did he reply when she spoke to him again.

She left shortly after that, appreciating that he wanted to be alone with his thoughts and grief.

Before going she told him she'd be back later. He didn't reply to that either.

'I'm so looking forward to seeing the children!' Eliot enthused, and smacked one fist into the other.

Jennie grinned at him. 'You're like a child yourself.'

'I can't wait to get on that train to Yorkshire tomorrow. I hope they're at the station to meet me. Though with delays and things it's hardly likely.'

'Still, you never know your luck.'

'True enough!'

'A whole week,' Jennie said. 'It's going to seem a lifetime.'

'Nonsense. It'll fly by.'

'For you perhaps, but not for me.'

He smiled at her, and placed the fingers of one hand against her cheek, a cheek he found cool and soft, a cheek he also found strangely erotic. 'I'll miss you, Jennie. And think of you every single day.'

534

'And I'll miss you and think of you every single hour,' she countered.

He laughed at that. 'Even when asleep?'

'*Especially* when asleep.'

He knew exactly what she meant, and was flattered. 'We get on so well, you and I,' he said, repeating something he'd often told her.

'I wish you weren't deserting me.'

'I am not deserting you,' he protested. 'Merely going to visit my children.'

'Not to mention *wife*.'

'So that's it. You're jealous.'

'Of course I'm jealous, you fool. What else do you think I'd be?' she riposted waspishly.

'Pleased?' he teased.

'Pleased!'

'With regard to the children.'

'And what about with regard to Helen?'

'Understanding?'

She punched him in the stomach. 'And I hope that hurt.'

'You're lethal,' he complained, rubbing the sore spot.

'Not half as lethal as I could be. So you watch it.'

'Oh, I shall,' he promised.

She threw her arms around his neck. 'Have I ever told you that I love you?'

'Not for at least half an hour. And I love you.'

'Say it again,' she prompted.

'I love you, Jennie Forsyth.'

'Now kiss me.'

He did. And then she kissed him.

'I wish you didn't have to go.'

'Don't be selfish. Think of the children.'

'There's also their mother.'

'There's no need to be jealous of her,' Eliot said softly.

'No?'

'No.'

'You're not just saying that as a sop?'

'Would I do such a thing?'

'You might,' she answered. 'Men do.'

'Well, I'm not. I swear.'

She took a deep breath. 'Oh Eliot, I'll be so lonely without you.'

'It'll give you a good chance to do work for your finals. They're looming up, you know.'

'Don't remind me.'

'You'll sail them,' he said. 'I'd put money on that.'

'I hope you're right.'

'I know I am.'

'Then it's head down with the books while you're away,' she promised.

'I'll make it up to you when I get back.'

Her eyes twinkled. 'Promise?'

'Double promise.'

'I'll hold you to that.'

'I have no doubt you will,' he commented drily.

'You don't know what I have in mind,' she teased.

He was certain he did.

Cass Greenstone squealed with delight as the box-kite Eliot was controlling looped the loop. 'Do that again, Daddy. Do it again!' she cried, her cheeks red from the keen wind that was blowing. She, her brother Peter and Eliot were on Marston Moor, the scene of a famous battle in July 1644 between Prince Rupert and Cromwell. Cromwell's victory had been the turning-point in the Civil War.

Eliot wasn't at all sure he could repeat the manoeuvre, but much to his delight, and theirs, he managed to do so.

Cass laughed, and clapped her hands in glee, while Peter shouted, 'Good for you, Dad!'

Eliot glanced at his son, relishing the boy's praise. How he enjoyed his children's company, and especially entertaining them. It gave him enormous pleasure.

Eliot paid out more line, allowing the kite to gain altitude. It was a marvellous day for kiteflying, and he was surprised they were the only ones on the moor. There again, he reminded himself, many of the fathers who might have been thus engaged were away at, or tied up with, the war.

'Can I hold it, Daddy? Can I?' Cass requested.

'Not fair!' Peter immediately complained. 'I'm the boy and I'm older. I should have first shot.'

'But *I* asked first,' Cass countered hotly.

Peter glared at her. 'Flying kites is for boys, not girls.'

'Not so!'

'Is too.'

Cass crossed her eyes and stuck out her tongue, which infuriated Peter, as she knew it would.

Eliot was amused by this interchange, thinking how much they'd grown since he'd last seen them. Both were enjoying the prep schools Helen had managed to get them into.

Eliot brought his attention back to the kite which was suddenly diving groundwards. A few tugs and pulls levelled it out, then it started regaining height.

'There's an art to this,' he declared, aware of how pompous that sounded, but he wanted to impress the children.

'Is there really, Daddy?' Cass exclaimed, wide-eyed.

He stared at her, unsure whether one so young was capable of teasing him. He decided that was precisely what she was doing.

'Maybe not an art exactly,' he prevaricated. 'Let's change that to skill.'

'You're very skilful, Daddy,' Cass commented, still wide-eyed and laying it on with a trowel.

You'll go far in life young lady, Eliot thought, visualizing her winding countless beaux and suitors round her little finger.

'Let's have a go then Dad?' Peter urged.

'Cass asked first.'

'But she's a girl.' He said that as though it was something inferior.

'Better a girl than a smelly old boy,' Cass jibed, tongue in cheek.

Peter rose to the bait. 'I am not smelly!'

'Oh yes, you are. Smelly pooh.'

This time his glare was venomous. 'You're loathsome,' he stated.

'And you're smelly. Rotten socks and rotten feet.'

'I have not got rotten socks and rotten feet!'

Cass grinned, she had her brother right where she wanted him in the palm of her hand. 'Sez you!' she retorted.

'All right, enough,' Eliot commanded.

Cass dismissed Peter, and turned to beam at her father. 'Me first, that right, Daddy?'

'Tell you what, let's toss?' he suggested.

The beam changed to a scowl, while Peter's expression brightened. 'Yes, let's toss,' Peter agreed.

'Don't know,' mumbled Cass.

Eliot produced a half-crown. He wound the line round his wrist as he spun the coin.

The coin flashed through the air to be deftly caught by Eliot who banged it on to the back of his hand. 'You call, Cass,' he said.

'Heads.'

He removed the covering hand and heads was revealed. 'I win! I win!' Cass shrieked in delight.

You would! Eliot thought wryly. Never mind, he'd make it up to Peter somehow.

When they later returned home he told Helen it was one of the best days he'd ever had and meant it.

Jennie woke to find her stomach heaving. She was going to be sick! she thought in alarm.

She threw aside the bedclothes, slipped her feet into mules, grabbed her dressing-gown and ran for the bathroom. She made it just in time. Falling to her knees she vomited into the toilet.

When she'd finished throwing up she sat back on her haunches. What had brought that on? she wondered. When she ran a tremulous hand over her forehead she found it covered in cold sweat.

She must have caught something, she decided. 'Flu? Could be. She returned to her bedroom and sat on the edge of the bed, glancing over at Esther still fast asleep.

She was nauseous, light-headed and shivery. She should forget the hospital and stay at home, she told herself. But with the finals so close . . .

She glanced at the clock and saw there was still a good half-hour before the alarm was due to go off. Gratefully she climbed under the covers and sank back on to her pillow.

Trust her to fall ill just before finals. Of all the luck! Still, it might be one of those twenty-four- or forty-eight-hour bugs. Please God it was! She simply couldn't afford an extended period off at this stage, not with the finals almost upon her.

She drank some of the water she kept by her bedside, which helped. She then closed her eyes, and waited for the inside of her head and body to calm down.

She said nothing to Esther when it was time to get up, or *en route* to the hospital. By mid-morning the symptoms had passed and she was as right as rain again.

'It's a lovely restaurant,' commented Jennie, gazing about her. This was Eliot's treat for her having finished her finals.

'It was recommended. I've never been here before myself,' he replied with a smile.

She studied the menu, fairly limited because of the war. The last thing she wanted was a fancy dish, something simple would suit her.

A waiter approached with the bottle of Chablis Eliot

had ordered. He opened it, poured a small amount for Eliot to taste, then filled their glasses when Eliot pronounced the wine satisfactory.

'Here's to good results!' Eliot toasted.

She sipped, and thought the wine delicious. She hoped it wasn't going to give her heartburn which she'd been a martyr to of late.

'So how do you really think you did?' he asked.

'All right.'

'Just all right? What about the . . . ?'

'I want to speak to you,' she interrupted.

He halted in mid-sentence, and stared at her. 'Of course. About what?'

'Me.'

'I'm all ears.'

'*I'm* pregnant.'

She watched his face fall in surprise and consternation. She'd intended being more delicate when she told him, but somehow it had just spilled out.

He swallowed hard. 'Pregnant?'

She nodded.

'You're certain?'

'Oh yes. There's no doubt about it.'

'How . . . er . . . ?'

'Two months. Approaching three.'

He was shaken, and it showed. 'But we were so careful,' he said slowly.

'Clearly not careful enough.'

She stared at him, but he refused to meet her eye. 'So what do I do?'

'Do? Well, let's think about it. I suppose you could keep it, but at this stage it would ruin your career.'

Sadness crept over her. That wasn't what she'd wanted to hear at all.

He drank some more wine. Then he began nervously twisting his fingers together. 'This is a real bombshell. The last thing I expected. Oh Jennie, I am sorry!'

She sipped her Chablis, and said nothing.

He was mentally writhing, she observed objectively. Her sadness deepened.

'So, what do I do?' she repeated. 'I've been worried sick.'

'My poor love, what an awful thing to happen. But I don't think we have got any choice. I can't leave Helen because of the children which I'm sure you understand. Why don't you leave it all to me. The medical profession takes care of its own. You won't be the first amongst our ranks to be caught out, or the last. There are ways and means.'

'It's an abortion then,' she said.

He nodded. 'Anything else would be madness on your part.'

Your part, she repeated those words to herself, and smiled cynically. She wondered if he even began to realize the pressure she'd been under leading up to and during the exams. The pressure of, amongst other things, keeping this to herself. Why, she hadn't even confided in Ez. In a way she wished she now had.

'I'll pay for everything, of course,' he said.

She fought back the impulse to hit him. That and the urge to jump to her feet and stalk out of there. *Your* part indeed!

'At least the finals are over and you've got time to yourself. Time in which to have this done,' he said.

'Yes,' she nodded hollowly.

'What about jobs. Any offers yet?'

'A number. Providing my results merit them.'

'They will. Sure as eggs are eggs.'

The last thing on her mind was her results. At the moment they didn't seem to matter at all. The baby she was carrying did. His baby. Eliot's and hers. How she'd managed to concentrate on the finals she didn't know, but somehow, miraculously, she had.

'You're sure there's no mistake?' he queried again.

'There's no mistake,' she assured him. 'I'm pregnant.'

Suddenly she wanted to leap to her feet and scream

like some demented banshee. She felt bloody hysterical!

She didn't quite know what she'd expected from him, but more than this almost obscene hurry for her to have an abortion.

'Will you excuse me? I have to go to the bathroom,' she apologized.

'Of course.'

He half-rose as she stood.

She kept her dignity and composure until she reached the bathroom. Once in the cubicle, and with the door locked behind her, she broke down and silently wept.

At that moment she hated Eliot. Hated and despised him.

Mrs Atkins poked her head round Jennie's door. 'There's a gentleman here to see you, luv. Says his name is Greenstone.'

Jennie sat up in bed. It was the first time Eliot had been to the Atkins'. 'He's a doctor colleague,' she explained. 'Show him in.'

Eliot entered somewhat shame-faced. 'Thank you, Mrs Atkins,' he said politely.

'Shall I close the door or leave it open?' Mrs Atkins asked Jennie.

'You can shut it,' she replied.

When the door had clicked shut Eliot crossed to Jennie's bed and perched on it. 'How are you?' he queried anxiously.

'How do you think?'

'I just couldn't get there to pick you up. The list went on and on, and there was simply nothing I could do.'

'I understand.'

'I felt awful. Truly I did.'

'I managed all right,' she said. 'They arranged a taxi which brought me here. And I came straight up to bed.'

'Mrs Atkins doesn't . . . ?'

Jennie shook her head. 'Not even Esther. Only you, me and the hospital know about what I had done.'

'So, what have you told Mrs Atkins?'

'That I was taken unwell at the hospital and had to come back. There was no question of her not believing me.'

Jennie paused, then said reproachfully, 'You might at least kiss me.'

'Sorry. I was so concerned I forgot.'

He kissed her on cold, bloodless lips. 'Was it terrible?'

How could she explain her emptiness? An emptiness that made her feel like a hollow, scooped out, shell. All she wanted to do was to burst out crying. Weeping for her lost child, and herself. She kept thinking how unfair it was that she'd had to have an abortion. It had turned her into a murderess. There was no other way of putting it. She'd murdered what would otherwise have been a viable and healthy child.

'Pretty,' she replied enigmatically.

'I am sorry, Jen.'

Are you? she wondered, peering into his face. She didn't think so. He wasn't worried at all, but relieved.

'I've been thinking,' she said. 'The best thing for me to do would be go home and recuperate there.'

'Good idea!' he enthused.

She suddenly experienced the urge to hit him.

He saw her expression, and quickly qualified himself. 'From the medical point of view, that is.'

'Of course,' she said, giving him a razored smile.

'When will you leave?'

How anxious he was to get rid of her, she thought. 'Just as soon as I feel up to the journey.'

'Will you motor down?'

She nodded. 'I'll need my car when there.'

'Perhaps I can prescribe you a tonic?'

'Atherton will be tonic enough,' she answered.

'I meant . . .'

'I know what you meant,' she snapped.

'Sorry.'

She reached out and took hold of his hand. 'Ignore me, I'm all jangly and irritable.'

'To be expected in the circumstances.'

'I suppose so. Now you trot off and let me sleep. I'm so tired I feel I could do a Rip Van Winkle.'

He laughed, but the laugh she noticed was forced. 'All right then.'

They kissed again, then exchanged a few words together, after which he took his leave.

She settled back, and stared at the ceiling, wishing he'd never bothered to pay her a visit.

Her thoughts turned to Andy as she began drifting off. He was making a fine recovery now that he'd accepted his situation. She couldn't have been more pleased. It shouldn't be too long before he'd have a false limb fitted and be up and about.

She frowned, thinking again of Eliot, and thought how disappointed she was in him.

Jennie drew up outside the family house in Atherton and gazed at it in fond affection. How many good memories she had of that house, and the village in general. It was marvellous to be home.

She got out of the Hornet, and locked it, deciding she'd deal with her luggage later. She went to the front door, opened it and slipped inside. She'd purposely arrived late in the evening hoping that both Madge and John would be home.

She halted outside the kitchen, smiling to hear the familiar voices coming from within. John was talking about an incident which had occurred earlier that day at Wheal Tempest, while Madge was commenting on what he said.

'Hello everyone, how are you?' she said, breezing in. She hadn't informed her parents she would be coming back, wanting to surprise them.

Madge gawped, then her face broke into a huge smile. 'Jennie!' she exclaimed.

'Well, I'll be . . .' John declared, trailing off.

Madge came to her feet and hurried to Jennie, sweeping her into her arms. 'We didn't expect you,' she said reprovingly. 'How long are you here for?'

'A while.'

'Let's have a dekko at you.'

Madge thrust her daughter to arm's length and stared at her. 'You look dreadful,' she pronounced.

'Thanks!'

'Very pale,' John nodded, obviously delighted to see his daughter.

'Haggard,' Madge said, worry appearing on her face.

'I haven't been well. A bad bout of 'flu,' Jennie explained, lying. 'And of course I had my finals. So all in all I'm about done in.'

'Poor lass,' John sympathized, rising. 'Come and sit yourself in my chair. As you know it's the comfiest in the house.'

'I am honoured,' Jennie replied.

'And I'll put the kettle on,' Madge said. 'Tea or coffee?'

'Coffee if you have it.'

'We do. Are you hungry?'

'Not for the moment, but maybe I will be later,' Jennie answered, enjoying the waves of heat washing over her from the fire. She closed her eyes; the drive from London had tired her considerably, far more than she'd thought it would. She wasn't nearly as strong as she'd imagined. The abortion had taken a tremendous amount out of her, mentally and physically.

Madge stared at her daughter. Best thing for her was a bowl of good soup, she thought. She had some mutton in which she'd use to make broth tomorrow morning. Mutton, vegetables from the garden, and pearl barley. That would put a bloom back on Jennie's cheeks.

'A while you say,' Madge repeated. 'How long is that?'

'Oh, till I've had my results and, hopefully, secured myself a job. A month at the minimum.'

A month! Madge was delighted. She dived into a cupboard where she had a piece of sultana cake that she'd been keeping for a special treat.

The treat would now be Jennie's.

Jennie sipped the schooner of sherry Kerensa had poured her and continued to watch George playing. He was absorbed with some lead soldiers and a wooden fort.

Kerensa was talking about Stanton's, but Jennie was only half listening. It was George who had captured her attention.

How like Graham he'd become. She could see Kerensa too, but he had far more of Graham in his face than of his mother.

She couldn't help but think of her own child, the one she'd lost, and wonder what he or she would have looked like? Would it have taken after her or Eliot? She tried to picture such a child, and conjured up an image that made her heart sink.

'Bam! bam! bam!' George cried, shooting the 'enemy'. He then toppled the shot enemy soldiers over so that they fell dead. He beamed at the 'bodies'. And, to make quite sure they were dead, used a 'friendly' carrying a rifle with a bayonet attached to stab them each several times.

'Bloodthirsty brute,' commented Kerensa, referring to George.

'Yes,' Jennie answered vaguely.

A boy or girl? What was it she'd been carrying? That was something she'd thought about a lot. A little Eliot or little Jennie? And what would they have called it? Her own preference would have been for James if a boy, Lucinda a girl.

She could imagine herself breast feeding, and changing nappies – several dabs of vinegar on the inside of the nappy would prevent nappy rash, Madge had once told her.

Emotion suddenly rose up to clog her throat. Staring

at George she felt bereft, lost. She found herself trembling all over.

'Jennie?'

She roused herself from her reverie to gaze at her sister-in-law through eyes now sparkling with tears.

'Are you all right, Jennie? You've got the strangest expression on your face.'

Jennie knew she had to get out of there.

'It's the 'flu I had, I don't think I'm completely over it yet,' she lied.

'Is there anything I can get you?'

Jennie laid her schooner aside. 'No, thank you, Kerensa. But I think I'll leave and go home to bed.'

'Of course. Are you fine to drive?'

'Perfectly, thank you very much.'

There was further conversation as they walked to the door. But later, thinking back, Jennie couldn't remember any of it.

On the return journey she had to pull off the road and stop. 'Oh my baby!' she whispered, not merely trembling now but shaking badly.

'Oh my baby!' she repeated, and collapsed over the steering wheel in a heap.

'Half a pound of nice and tasty please,' Jennie asked Bob Yendell. She was doing some shopping for Madge at the Post Office Stores.

He pulled a face. 'Can't do half a pound, my lover, but can give you four ounces. Sorry about that. But with provisions in such short supply I have to try and see that everyone gets a fair crack of the whip.'

'Quite right, Bob. I'll have four ounces then.'

Bob used a wire to cut the cheese, giving her closer to five ounces as she was an ex-employee, and wrapped it in greaseproof paper. 'Anything else?'

'Yes, I'd like a . . .'

She was interrupted by the shop door banging open. 'There's been a terrible accident at the mine,' Mrs

Turton announced breathlessly, her large chest heaving from the exertion of running.

A silence fell on the shop which was full of customers. Then Jennie galvanized herself into action. Her basket and shopping were forgotten as she manoeuvred her way to Mrs Turton's side.

'Terrible you say?'

Mrs Turton nodded. 'Cave in. I just heard. They've sent for Dr Court.'

Then they'd need her as well, Jennie thought. She hurried past Mrs Turton, out into the street, and wondered whether it would be quicker to go home for her car or go straight there. She decided to go straight there.

When she arrived at the mine she found men milling about in confusion. An enquiry informed her that Dr Court hadn't yet arrived.

She spotted Steve Campbell and Drew McIntyre, and went over to them. From their glazed eyes and the disjointed way they were talking she guessed they were both in shock. Steve finished one cigarette, used the stub to light a fresh one, and threw the stub away.

'It happened so suddenly,' Drew McIntyre said to Jennie. 'There was a rumble, and noise, and then all hell broke loose. We were lucky not to be near the actual cave in.'

'Lucky,' Steve Campbell repeated.

She spotted Staddon, waving his arms about and issuing orders. She raced over to him.

'No civilians allowed in here. Get out!' he snarled at her.

'I'm a qualified doctor, Mr Staddon. You might need my help,' she informed him.

He blinked, then nodded. 'Sorry, I forgot. Of course we might need your help. You hang on till we see what's what.'

'Are many hurt?'

'Some. They're bringing out the casualties now.'

'What happened?'

548

He shrugged. 'God knows. But something went wrong, that's for sure.'

The tram appeared at the mine entranceway, rattling noisily into view. The driver yelled that he had injured aboard.

The driver was Dick Horrell. His face was streaked with dirt and there was a nasty gash on his left cheek. The tram clanked to a halt, and he leapt to the ground.

'Your dad's here!' he shouted to Jennie.

The shock of that stopped her in her tracks for a moment, then she continued towards the tram. The living were in the foremost carriage, the dead in the second.

John was lying on the carriage floor, his eyes closed, his face a ghastly shade of green. The breath was rasping loudly in his throat.

Tam Scott lay beside John, one of his arms twisted at such an angle Jennie immediately knew it was broken. There were two others in the carriage with John and Tam.

'Look to your dad first,' Tam said. 'He's the worst of us here.'

Jennie climbed into the carriage and knelt beside John. A cursory examination informed her that his chest had been badly crushed.

His eyes fluttered open. 'Hello lass,' he said, giving her a strained smile.

'Hello Dad. Got yourself in a mess again I see.'

He tried to laugh, but instead his face screwed up in pain. 'That's right.'

'Dr Court will be here shortly. I'll give you something from his bag.'

He coughed, and dark blood splashed, then ran from a corner of his mouth. 'I've had it, girl,' he said.

'Don't be stupid!'

'I'm not being stupid. I'm being realistic. I know I'm an ignorant old man, but I still know what's what. I'm done for, and that's a fact.'

'Oh Dad!' she whispered.

'Who would have thought . . . this morning . . . I was in such a rush I never even said goodbye to your mum. Now there's a thing.'

She used her hand to wipe the blood away from his mouth and cheek. As she did she prayed Dr Court would get there soon.

He frowned up at the sky. 'Is the sun shining?'

'Yes.'

'Funny, I can feel the heat, yet it seems overcast to me. A strange sort of . . .' He broke off to cough again.

'You're going to be all right, Dad, I promise,' she said, her voice crackling with emotion.

'Don't make promises you can't keep, lass.' He paused, then went on, 'I can't complain really. I've had a good innings. One that, despite everything, might have been a lot worse.'

'How are you, John?' Norman Lead enquired, he was one of the other injured in the car, and lying furthest away from John. He'd just come round, having been unconscious for the past few minutes.

'Fucked,' replied John, then, apologetically, 'Sorry Jennie, forgot you were there for a moment.'

'That's all right, Dad,' she smiled. 'I've heard a lot worse.'

'Aye, you would. Being all grown up and a doctor now. I'm proud of you, girl. Real proud. You and your brother both. Tell him that from me, will you?'

'Tell him yourself.'

'No, I'll need you to do that.'

He stopped to struggle for breath. 'The pain,' he mumbled, 'like a furnace in my chest.'

Jennie bit her lip, and looked again for Court of whom there wasn't yet any sign.

'Jen? Lass.'

'Yes Dad.'

'Take my hand, hold it.'

She did so.

'I want you to give your mother a message from me. Will you do that?'

She nodded, tears dripping from her eyes.

'Tell her . . . despite everything . . . no matter how things might have seemed . . . I did love her. And always have.'

'I'll pass your message on, Dad.'

'God bless you, girl. God . . .'

The words trailed off and, to the accompaniment of a great sigh, his eyes closed.

Jennie, sobbing, felt for his pulse, but there wasn't one. John was dead.

She gathered him into her arms, and held him there while rocking him back and forth.

She allowed herself that indulgence for the space of a minute, then began tending the others as best she could.

Shortly after that Dr Court, who'd been with a patient on the outskirts of the village, put in an appearance.

'It's Sir Reginald Tempest,' Kerensa announced, having answered the knock on Madge's door.

Madge gave a startled cry and rose from where she'd been sitting. This was totally unexpected.

A grim-faced Sir Reginald entered the sitting-room where the family were foregathered. 'I'm sorry to intrude at this time of grief,' he apologized to Madge.

'Not at all, Sir Reginald. Will you sit down?'

'Thank you.'

'Can I get you a drink, Sir Reginald?' Anthony Sturt asked. He was there with Kerensa; George was at his nursery.

Sir Reginald shook his head. 'No thank you, Anthony.' The two men knew one another, having frequently met socially. Sir Reginald turned his attention to Madge. 'I'm extremely appalled and distraught at what occurred. Please accept my sympathy and condolences.'

Madge nodded.

He smiled thinly at Jennie. 'And thank you for your help, Miss Forsyth. I'm delighted to hear you're now qualified.'

'Thank you, Sir Reginald. Can you tell us what the final tally was?'

His expression darkened even further. 'Four dead, I'm afraid. Twelve injured, five badly. There's never been anything like it in the history of Wheal Tempest.'

'An evil day,' Anthony muttered.

'Have you been told how your husband was injured?' Sir Reginald asked.

'As a result of the cave-in,' Madge replied.

'Not quite. He wasn't affected by the original fall. But with another threatening he, all on his own, raced to the scene of the tragedy, and was desperately trying to free those trapped when the second fall took place. The three men who came out on the tram with him all owe their lives to your John.'

Madge was astounded. 'You mean he could have escaped unscathed?'

'Most certainly. He was at least fifty yards away from the original cave-in when it happened. And what's more, he knew danger still threatened when he attempted his rescue. Your husband, Mrs Forsyth, was an extremely brave man, and an example to us all. I take my hat off to him.'

Madge was dumbfounded – John a hero! That's what Sir Reginald was saying. She could hardly credit it. Her John!

'I'm glad I was the one to inform you,' Sir Reginald went on.

'Thank you, Sir Reginald. I had no idea. The other families of the injured, including the Scotts who are close friends of ours, are still at the hospital.'

Sir Reginald rose. 'I'll be on my way then.'

'What caused the cave-ins?' Jennie queried.

'That still has to be established, Miss Forsyth. But I think the findings will probably be that, because of the desperate need for copper in this war, they're crying out for it, corners have been cut that otherwise shouldn't have been. I say that realizing the full import of my words, but I don't wish to be thought of as dodging or shirking any responsibility in this matter. Demands have been made of me and the mine by the authorities, and I have simply been trying to comply with these demands. Your father and the others are as much victims of the war as those killed and wounded at the front line.'

Jennie nodded. 'I understand.'

'Could you see me out, Mrs Forsyth? I'd like a private word,' he requested.

At the front door he halted and turned to Madge. 'I don't want you to worry about the funeral expenses, I'll take care of those. And there will be adequate compensation, rely on that. Furthermore, you needn't be concerned about this house, we'll come to some amicable arrangement.'

Madge was profuse in her thanks – that was a huge load off her shoulders.

'Good day to you then, Mrs Forsyth.'

'Good day to you, Sir Reginald.'

He left her, walked to his car and got inside. She watched him drive away.

Her John a hero! To have done what he did! It just showed you how, even after a lifetime of marriage, you never really knew someone.

And he had truly loved her! She hadn't known that either.

'Jennie, do you have a moment?' Dr Court asked.

'Of course.'

John's funeral had taken place earlier, and the mourners were now back at the house for a buffet and refreshments. It was a sombre occasion.

Dr Court took Jennie into a corner where he smiled at her. 'You coped well at the mine the other day,' he said.

She shook her head. 'It was little enough.'

'None the less.'

'I only wish . . .' she trailed off.

'John was a dead man before he came out of the mine. There's nothing you or anyone else could have done that would have changed that.'

'I know,' she replied, then, with a shrug of the shoulders, she sighed, 'Still . . .'

'So tell me, have you made up your mind yet? Are you going to be a hospital or family doctor?'

'I'm contemplating both. Each has its attractions.'

'I see,' he mused.

'At the moment I could go either way.'

Court sipped his sherry, eyeing Jennie over the rim of the glass. 'Ever since you first came to ask my advice I've thought of you as something of a protégée,' he confessed.

'Why, thank you.'

'I've followed your career to date with great interest.'

She was aware of that. 'I'm pleased I haven't let you down.'

'On the contrary, your results have all been excellent, including your finals. And now you're qualified you have a year to put in before registration. Will you do that in its entirety at the Free?'

'I hadn't planned otherwise.'

'Medicine is your first job, correct?'

She nodded.

'And then after that there's a further six months of gynaecology and obstetrics.' He paused, then said softly, 'How would you feel about coming to work for me?'

That threw her. 'I beg your pardon?'

'I'm getting on, and the population of Atherton is steadily increasing. I could use some help. So what about it?'

'Work for you?'

'Why not? You know everyone and they know you. You're a natural for the position.'

This was the last thing she'd expected.

'You don't have to give me an answer straight off.

554

Take advice. But I tell you this, it would give me great pleasure if you were to say yes. And of course you must remember, as I've just said, I'm not getting any younger. One day in the not-too-distant future the practice would be yours.'

Her mind was whirling. All she could think about was Eliot and their relationship.

'This is very kind of you, doctor, very kind indeed.'

'You'll consider it then?'

'I can assure you I'll give it very serious consideration. Chances like this don't exactly present themselves every day.'

'You and I would be a fine team, Jennie. I have no doubt about that. There's a lot I could teach you – and would.'

'How long before I have to give you an answer?' she queried.

'Take your time. There's no rush. Give me an answer when you're sure it's the right one.'

A family doctor in Atherton! The prospect appealed very much indeed.

He drained his glass and held it out to her. 'In the mean time, how about some more of this excellent sherry? It's quite the best I've had in ages.'

The sherry, along with all the alcohol, had been provided by Sir Reginald Tempest – who was present with Lady Tempest – from his private cellar.

'Will you excuse me for a minute,' Jennie said, refilling his glass, and left Dr Court.

She couldn't wait till later to tell Madge about Dr Court's proposition.

The Camden Head at Islington Green was a pub Eliot and Jennie often used. It was rough and ready with a charm all its own. During peacetime it was much favoured by traders from the adjacent Camden Passage antique stalls and the nearby Chapel Market.

From where she was sitting Jennie watched Eliot

ordering their drinks at the bar. Hazel, the head barmaid, blond and busty, burst out laughing at something he said as she was serving him.

'You made an impression there,' Jennie teased when Eliot set a half-pint of mild in front of her.

'Just a little joke,' he smiled.

She studied him, his dark hair, the dimple she knew so well and a great warmth welled within her.

She dropped her head and stared into her glass. The atmosphere between them immediately changed.

'Jennie?'

'I've given this a lot of thought, Eliot,' she said quietly. 'And I've come to the conclusion that things just can't go on as they've been.'

His expression had become sober during this speech. 'How do you mean, Jen?'

'I never want to experience what I've been through recently again.'

'You mean the pregnancy and abortion?'

She nodded. 'It was . . . ghastly.'

'I can understand that,' he said sympathetically.

She looked up and stared him straight in the eye. 'Our local doctor at Atherton has asked me to join his practice after my six months of gynae and obstetrics.'

A hiatus ensued during which Eliot sipped his beer.

'Exactly what are you saying?'

'Simply that the time has come for you to make a choice. Helen, or me.'

'Oh!' he exclaimed.

'I'm sorry, but that's how it is. I have my own self-preservation and future to think about.'

'Naturally. Would you like to work in Atherton?'

'Very much so. I would also like to be with you, but not in the way our present relationship stands.'

'You want marriage?'

'It wouldn't be easy for anyone concerned. But yes, that's what I want. The mistress role just doesn't suit me.'

He blanched to hear that. 'I never thought of you exactly as my mistress.'

'How else would you describe me?'

He spread his hands. 'All right! I suppose you have been. But I never thought of it that way because I love you.'

'And I love you. However, I still can't go on as we have been.'

'So it's either yours truly or Atherton?'

'It would appear that way,' she answered.

He fingered his dimple, rubbing the edge of his thumb up and down its cleft while he thought.

'I hated you when you proposed the abortion, and particularly the manner in which you proposed it,' she said suddenly. 'Hated and despised you.'

'And now?'

'And now I believe we should get matters sorted out between us – one way or the other.'

'If I did leave Helen it would be quite some time before a divorce came through. In the mean time, we'd have our careers to think about.'

'Make a decision first, then we'll worry about things like that and any complications which might arise,' she replied.

He nodded. She was right. His decision was of primary importance. 'Life's a peculiar old business, isn't it?' he mused. 'More ups and down than a game of snakes and ladders.'

For some reason that made her think of her father – a drunk and malingerer who'd amazed everyone by dying a hero.

'Yes,' she agreed, 'it is.'

Hampstead Heath wasn't at all like Marston Moor, Eliot thought as he wandered down through it. He remembered the day spent on the moor with Peter and Cass flying their kite.

He smiled, recalling how much he'd enjoyed it. It had

been one of the best days he'd ever had, he'd later told Helen.

Peter and Cass, he pictured them as they'd been on the moor – his son and daughter whom he idolized. How he wished they weren't in Yorkshire, but still in London.

How he wished . . . He considered that, and it was as if a dagger had been stuck in him and twisted. For weren't they the nub of the matter? Not Helen, or even Jennie, but Peter and Cass.

How he loved them. Of course they were apart now, but he was able to visit occasionally, and eventually the war must end and they'd all be back together again.

But that wouldn't be the case if he divorced Helen, then he would only see them occasionally, with them all growing steadily apart. And what if Helen should one day remarry? That would mean them having a step-father, a usurper in his place.

He swore, picked up a stone and threw it as far as he could. It spun through the air to land with a satisfying thump.

If only matters were simple and straightforward – divorce Helen and marry Jennie. But matters weren't simple, far from it. If nothing else his background saw to that.

He thought about how he had felt when his father had died, and then his mother a few years later, how awful that had been. He'd felt betrayed, forsaken, abandoned, a different species of animal to his friends who still had their parents. There had been the long, lonely nights when he'd cried himself to sleep, the question he'd asked himself again and again – why him?

Certainly his grandmother had done her best, and it would have been considerably worse for him if she hadn't been there, but that hadn't gone anywhere near compensating for his parents.

There had been no mother to turn to when he needed her, no father to take him places, or talk to him.

Tears appeared in Eliot's eyes at these memories. Of

course his divorcing Helen wouldn't be the same for Peter and Cass as it had been for him losing his parents, but the two situations certainly had something in common.

Could he bring himself to knowingly inflict even a portion of the grief he'd suffered on to his own children? Even a portion would hurt them dreadfully. Could he live happily knowing he'd done that?

And then there was the possibility of the step-father he'd already envisaged. For he had to face it, Helen was still relatively young, and attractive in many men's eyes. What if such a step-father turned out to be a dud as far as the children were concerned? A step-father who resented them, and wanted his own family, in which case Peter and Cass would be relegated to second-class citizens.

Would Helen allow such an eventuality? She might, if she was in love with the chap. He shuddered to think of his babies as Cinderellas. It would be unforgivable on his part.

There again, Peter and Cass could live with him and Jennie. He knew that wasn't a possibility even as he thought of it. He knew Helen only too well, she'd never give them up – not in a month of Sundays.

This was so complex and convoluted. It was easy for Jennie to make demands! And they were so difficult for him to fulfil.

The children, in the end that was what it all boiled down to, the children, and how much he cared.

He swore again, and kicked a clump of grass. He glanced up at the sky, and envisaged a kite flying there.

And below the kite two children laughing, Peter and Cass.

Eliot sat facing Jennie in the Camden Head, his entire demeanour one of total wretchedness. 'I can't,' he stated simply. 'I just can't.'

Jennie had known he was going to say this from the

moment they'd met up. She sipped her drink and didn't reply. For the time being, her outward manner would remain strong. Reaction, as she was well aware, would set in later.

'I can't inflict on my children some of what happened to me as a child. If I hadn't lost my own parents, been an orphan . . .' He stopped almost overwhelmed with emotion.

'I love you desperately,' he finally went on in a cracked voice. 'But I also love them. A different sort of love, but love none the less.'

'I understand,' Jennie said softly.

'Do you?'

She nodded.

'I can't bring myself to deprive them of a father, even if that arose through divorce and not death as happened in my case.'

'This really has put you in the most awful quandary, hasn't it?'

'Yes,' he breathed.

'And you've made your choice.'

'I am what I am, Jennie, moulded by the cards life has dealt me. It would be a terrible mistake for me to divorce Helen feeling as I do. My guilt towards the children would become a canker that would eat away at our relationship, eventually destroying it. That I genuinely believe.'

He was probably right, she thought. If only his past had been other than it was.

'I'm sorry,' he husked.

'So am I. It would have been good between us.'

'If it hadn't been for the children,' he qualified.

She took a deep breath. What she wanted more than anything suddenly was a long walk in which to sort out her thoughts.

'That's it,' she said.

'I suppose so.'

'We must break it cleanly, Eliot. Less pain that way. Don't you agree?'

He nodded.

She paused, then said, 'I want you to know your decision does you credit, and I admire you for it.'

'Jen—'

'No!' she interjected. 'You've said all you need to say. I understand and, in many ways, applaud you. But that doesn't make it any easier. In future I'd prefer if we just smiled when we bumped into one another at the hospital. We needn't talk, unless it's necessary. We might get thrown together professionally, after all.'

She took a sip of her drink, wishing she possessed a magic wand which she could wave and cause herself to disappear. 'I'm not going to say goodbye, just get up and go. All right?'

'Jennie, come home with me for one last night. Please?'

She smiled thinly, and rose.

'Don't go, Jen!' he pleaded. 'Not yet.'

Break it cleanly, she repeated to herself. The decision had been taken, now she must walk away, for both their sakes.

She couldn't resist one last kiss. She bent over and kissed him lightly on the lips. Then she moved out from behind the table and headed for the nearest door.

Outside she paused for a second, then headed towards the nearby canal for that much-needed walk.

Their last drink together had been a short one, but long enough for her future to be decided – a future without Eliot.

Esther held Jennie close while Jennie cried her eyes out. This was what she'd feared all along.

'There, there,' Esther crooned. 'You'll get over it.'

'You warned me not to get involved, that I'd get hurt if I did. And you were so right. God, how right you were!'

'Just put it down to experience. That's all you can do,' Esther replied, stroking Jennie's hair.

561

Jennie pressed an already sodden handkerchief to her face. 'I wish I was dead,' she moaned.

'No, you don't. Not really. In the meanwhile, you must keep in mind that time will heal. Time always does,' Esther counselled wisely.

Jennie clutched her stomach, a stomach that had so recently carried his baby. Now the baby was gone, and so was he.

Her agony was such that her entire body began to convulse.

Eliot stared at the letter announcing his appointment as the junior ENT consultant at St James's Hospital, Leeds. It was three months since that fateful evening in the Camden Head when he and Jennie had broken up, and just over five weeks since he'd heard about the vacancy at St James's.

St James's was perfect for him, of course, exactly what he'd wanted. He would be based in Yorkshire on a permanent basis, reunited with Helen and the children. He couldn't have been more thrilled or delighted.

His smile faded when he thought of Jennie whom he badly missed. Badly? No, it went far deeper than that. A day never went by when he didn't think of her, imagine what it would have been like if . . .

He broke off that line of thought, dismissing it from his mind. That episode in his life was over, finished, through his choice.

He knew Jennie would be pleased for him that he'd landed this particular post, and wondered if he should seek her out and tell her? They hadn't spoken since the parting.

No, he decided, best not to initiate matters. She'd hear the news on the grapevine and perhaps speak to him about it.

In the event she did, and didn't.

A gaunt and battle-weary Graham watched the coastline

of Sark emerge out of the early morning mist. The coastline made him smile. He wondered if L'Corbin and Majohn had survived the war and hoped they had. Bless them both for the couple of villains they were.

The war was over, the Axis powers and Japan defeated. He still found it hard to believe that the end had finally come about after so long, and at last the Allies were victorious.

But victorious they were, and now HMS *Bloodaxe*, a Hunt class destroyer of which he was captain, was on its way home to Pompey and an uncertain future. For himself and the majority of his crew, it would be the end of their last voyage, and a return to Civvy Street.

He thought of Kerensa, it was eleven long months since he'd last seen her and little George. According to her letters, she'd kept Stanton ticking over, maintaining its head above water despite all the problems imposed by wartime conditions.

Shortly he, Lieutenant-Commander Forsyth, would be back at the helm, and he could hardly wait. In postwar Britain, bricks were going to be in enormous demand, particularly for the first few years when badly bombed cities like Exeter and Plymouth would have to be rebuilt. Stanton's would be among the foremost suppliers of the great reconstruction, of that he was determined.

He intended building an empire which one day George would inherit – an empire based round Stanton's, with its heart in Corfe Mullen.

Graham rubbed his hands in anticipation.

Chapter Fifteen

Madge held the bowl at arm's length, studied it critically, and then nodded her satisfaction. It would do. In fact it was one of her better efforts. She hummed as she wrapped it in tissue paper and carefully placed it in a cardboard box.

It was the summer of 1948, and since the war Madge had acquired something of a name for herself as a potter. Her technique had improved vastly since Graham, as a birthday present, had turned what had been the outside toilet into a kiln. Between there and her kitchen, which doubled as a workshop, she spent many blissful hours working to her heart's content, and making a small living into the bargain.

Not that she needed the money; Sir Reginald had been most generous and Graham was always there if she needed extra. That was rare these days, as her basic requirements were few.

She thought of Graham and smiled. Stanton's was booming, expanding yet again, taking on even more staff. Nor could he and Kerensa have been happier; they continued to be as much in love as they'd always been, while Saskia, who'd been born eighteen months previously, kept Kerensa run off her feet.

George, now eleven, was doing well, making quite an impression at prep school where he'd gained a well-deserved reputation with both bat and ball.

And then there was Jennie. Madge sighed inwardly. Whatever was to become of her? How she despaired of her daughter. A great success as a doctor, but in her private life . . .

Madge's thoughts were interrupted by the front door bell ringing. Probably Jane dropping by, she conjectured, *en route* to answer it. But it wasn't Jane, but rather a strange man smiling nervously.

'Mrs Forsyth?' he queried.

'That's me.'

'Then I've come to the right house.'

Jennie was walking Brownie in the water meadows – not the Brownie George Rattenbury had given Madge, but a successor bearing the same name – when she spotted a snakelike figure carving its way up river.

Otter! She hadn't seen one in goodness knows how long and then recalled it wasn't far from where she was now standing that she and Christine Cook had been shown another by Andy Alford all those years ago, the first otter either she or Christine had ever seen.

She watched the otter disappear into the undergrowth, probably hiding from Brownie who was cavorting about some distance away. She was about to summon the dog to her side so they could start the journey home when she noticed the blurred outline of a man walking in her direction.

She screwed up her eyes, trying to identify the man, but with the blazing sun directly behind him it was impossible.

She whistled, then called, 'Brownie! Here boy!'

Brownie bounded up, furiously wagging his tail. He was a cross between a lurcher and spaniel which she had jokingly named a splurch – a strange looking dog, but extremely affectionate.

She rubbed Brownie's head and ears. 'Come on, let's go,' she said.

The man was close now. He stopped and stared at her. 'Hello Jennie.'

He shifted his body slightly, and suddenly she could see his face quite clearly. It wasn't a face from the village or thereabouts, but one she knew none the less. And then the penny dropped.

'Eliot!' she exclaimed, stunned.

Smiling, he came nearer. 'Your mother told me where to find you. I called at the house.'

'Eliot,' she repeated, lost for words.

'You look terrific,' he stated.

Jennie swallowed hard, and found her voice. 'What are you doing here?'

'I've come to see you. All the way from Leeds.'

'To see me?'

He nodded. 'You've been in my thoughts a lot recently. And when I found myself with some time off I decided to drive down to Devon and try to find out what had become of you. And now here you are.'

He continued to stare at her, drinking her in. 'It's been so long,' he said.

'You, too, are looking well, and prosperous.'

He glanced around. 'So, these are the famous water meadows. I remember you mentioning them.'

'Did I?'

'Your mother says you've never married. I asked.'

'Did she now?' That angered Jennie. Madge shouldn't have discussed her private business.

'I often wondered whether you'd married,' Eliot went on.

'Well, now you know,' Jennie replied somewhat waspishly. 'How's Helen?'

'Fine. Couldn't be better.' He paused, then added, 'She left me.'

'Left you?' Jennie queried in surprise.

'For Edward Thurston. Remember him?'

'Of course. He ate atrociously.'

Eliot laughed. 'He still does. It transpired that he and Helen had been having a long-term affair. Something that started during the war when she moved back to Yorkshire. At least so she says, I have my suspicions that it was going on even before then.'

Jennie murmured sympathetically.

'I only found out when she informed me she was leaving me for him.'

'You had no idea?'

'None at all, not an inkling. Knew they were great chums, of course. But didn't realize it went further than that.'

'Has she taken the children with her?'

'I'm afraid she has,' Eliot replied, voice tinged with sadness.

'How old are they now?' Jennie queried.

'Peter is fourteen, Cass twelve.'

'Ironic really,' Jennie mused.

'Yes,' he agreed. 'But the children are older now. Quite grown up in many ways. Not like when you and I . . .'

'Can I ask you something?'

'Go ahead.'

'Do you regret that decision?' It was a cheeky thing to ask, but she wanted to know. It was important.

He thought for a minute. 'It depends what you mean by regret. But no, I don't believe I do. I did what I considered right for them, and us. As I told you at the time if I'd left with you, our relationship wouldn't have survived because of my guilt. I'm sure of that.'

Jennie bent and picked up a stick which she threw for Brownie. Then she ran a hand through her hair. 'I can't get over you suddenly reappearing like this. It's so unexpected.'

'I thought it might surprise you.'

'You, Helen absconding with Edward Thurston, it's one surprise after the other,' she retorted.

He laughed, and relaxed a little. 'Did I say terrific? Let me amend that to fabulous.'

Now she laughed. 'Stop trying to flatter me.'

He had aged, she thought, though not unkindly. There were lines on his face where none had been before. His face had assumed a sort of crumpled, lived-in, quality. And she'd noticed a small bald spot on his crown.

'I believe you've been very successful at Leeds,' she stated.

'How do you know that?'

'I have contacts in far-flung places. Word of your progress has filtered back to me upon occasion.'

He gazed up at a dreamily blue sky. 'I didn't hear a sausage about you.'

'Did you try to find out?'

He shook his head. 'No. I thought it best that way. Let sleeping dogs lie, so to speak.'

'I understand,' she replied.

She took the stick that Brownie had retrieved and threw it again. 'Shall we walk?' she proposed.

'It's beautiful countryside,' he declared, falling into step beside her.

'I think so.'

'So, tell me about yourself?' Eliot prompted.

'How do you mean?'

'Your job, your life here, whatever.'

'My life here is very satisfying. I couldn't ask for more.'

'You enjoy being a family doctor then?'

'Very much so. It's hard work, but rewarding.'

'How about boyfriends?' Eliot asked casually.

'Scores,' she teased.

'Really! I'm not sure whether to be impressed or scandalized,' he replied. 'Seriously?'

'Seriously? There was one serious relationship. His name is Jonathan and he's a solicitor for one of Exeter's foremost legal firms.'

'Was?' Eliot probed.

'We went out for quite a while, then broke up.'

'Can I ask why, or would that be rude?'

Jennie shrugged. 'He asked me to marry him, and we subsequently got engaged. He comes from an old, well-connected Exeter family, and the ceremony was to be a large one in the cathedral. Only I called it off before it got that far.'

She glanced sideways at Eliot, wondering whether or not to explain further. Finally she decided, she would. 'I called it off because he simply wasn't the man for me. He was good-looking, charming, well-off, but . . .' She hesitated, then said, 'Boring, I'm afraid.'

'I see.'

'He eventually married someone else, a woman called Sally. They're happy together I understand.'

'And that was the closest you came?'

'There's no need to put it like that!' she snapped.

'Sorry,' he apologized. 'I wasn't trying to be funny or have a dig at you.'

'I should hope not.'

He swished a bit more with his stick. 'Do *you* have any regrets?'

About Jonathan?'

'For one.'

'Not in the least. I would have hated being married to him, nice chap that he is. When you've . . .' She stopped abruptly, and bit her lip.

'Were you about to say that when you've experienced the real thing second best is hard, if not impossible, to settle for?' he queried softly.

She didn't answer that.

'Because if that's so I'd wholeheartedly agree with you.'

Brownie flushed a rabbit and set off in hot pursuit.

'I've thought about you a great deal as well,' Jennie suddenly stated.

'You have?'

'Of course, idiot, you were a huge thing in my life after all.' She added quietly, 'Perhaps the biggest.'

'Your mother has asked me to stay for tea,' he said.

'Has she?'

'Was quite insistent about it too.'

Good old Madge, Jennie thought. That went someway

to making up for discussing her private business.

'I could live here,' Eliot stated, waving his stick at the countryside. 'It appeals.'

Jennie's heart began to beat faster. Was there more to this visit than she imagined?

'When did Helen leave you?' she asked.

'Just after Christmas. She suggested we go out to a restaurant, just the two of us, and she told me there.'

'A restaurant! I would have thought she'd have done that at home.'

Eliot's lips twisted into a cynical smile. 'I never asked her, but perhaps she thought being in a restaurant would stop me creating a scene.'

'And would you have?'

'Create a scene? No, I don't think so.'

They walked a little way in silence. 'What happens now?' Jennie asked.

'Eventual divorce.'

'And how do you feel about that?'

Eliot whacked the top off a thistle with his stick, the purple head arcing away in a graceful curve.

'Relieved in a way. Extremely sad in others. The children are taking it well, thank heavens. I was flabbergasted when Helen told me she'd been having an affair with Edward,' Eliot went on. 'She never seemed the type somehow.'

'I'm sure lots of wronged husbands think that,' Jennie commented drily. 'Did she ever find out about us?'

'No.'

That was a relief.

Brownie flushed a mouse and went chasing after that. He was thoroughly enjoying himself. Some geese, their long necks straining out in front of them, flew overhead.

'There are so many questions I want to ask you I hardly know where to begin,' Eliot said.

He reached out and ran the tip of a finger down her cheek. 'It's marvellous to see you again, Jennie, I can't tell you.'

She felt exactly the same about him.

'You know in a way I envy you being a family doctor,' he said.

'How so?'

'You must deal with such an infinite variety of problems.'

'That's true,' she acknowledged. 'One patient can have an earful of impacted wax, the next a carcinoma of the lung.'

'The trouble with specializing,' Eliot went on, 'is that it all becomes a bit repetitive after a while. Oh sure, you can do research and write papers, none the less it is repetitive.'

'Do I detect some discontent?' she teased.

'A little I suppose,' he admitted. 'And what there is has been worse since the Helen affair.'

'But surely you wouldn't give up your godlike status as a consultant?' she further teased.

'Stop riling me,' he retorted.

She laughed at that.

Brownie was barking again. 'He's found something, though goodness knows what,' Jennie said.

Eliot drew in a deep breath. 'What a gorgeous day. Quite perfect.'

How true, Jennie thought.

'Let's sit somewhere?' Eliot suggested.

They stopped at some levelled tree stumps and sat on two of them.

'Have you been seeing anyone since Helen?' Jennie enquired.

'Good heavens, no!'

Seven months wasn't all that long after all, she thought. Give the poor man a chance. 'I'm sure you'll meet someone nice eventually,' she declared.

He heaved his stick into the river where it was borne away in a swirl of water.

'Jennie, can I be honest?'

She nodded.

'I feel very vulnerable at this point. I'm worried that I could look extremely foolish.'

She didn't answer that.

'Well?'

'Go on, I'm listening.'

He paused, then said, his voice quavering slightly, 'I came down here hoping that there may be a chance of salvaging something between us. I say hoping because I didn't know your situation or what your present feelings were about me. It is a long time after all.'

That took her breath away. 'Salvaging something between us?' she repeated.

'Probably ridiculous! Probably—'

'Shut up, Eliot!' she interjected.

He did so immediately.

Her mind raced in turmoil. And now she'd gone very cold despite the summer heat. She gently rubbed her hands together.

'How do you feel about me?' she asked eventually.

'I've never stopped loving you.'

She glanced at his face and saw he was speaking the truth. That was obvious.

'Leaving you broke my heart,' she said.

'It didn't do me a lot of good either.'

She giggled to hear that, breaking the emotional tension.

'If you want me to go I'll go?' he offered.

'You were right,' she said. 'I never married Jonathan because he was second best. I realized that I'd never stopped loving you and part of me refused to compromise.'

'And you still—'

'Yes,' she cut in.

He paused, then said, 'So, I still love you and you still love me. Where does that leave us?'

'You tell me. You're the one who's popped up like a genie out of a bottle. You tell me.'

He suddenly swore. 'I'm asleep and dreaming this.'

'No dream, but reality,' she smiled.

'Can I kiss you?'

She didn't reply, but her expression told him the answer.

He took her face between his hands, and brought his mouth tenderly on to hers.

The kiss, the closeness of him, his scent, brought so many memories flooding back. As the kiss continued, Jennie found herself trembling all over.

He sighed when it was finished. 'You were always special,' he said.

'You weren't so bad yourself.'

He ran a hand over her face, and through her hair. 'I've dreamt so often . . . you've no idea.'

But she had, for she'd had her own dreams, dreams that had caused her to wake smiling, and at other times filled with a cold fury.

'Would you consider marrying me?' he asked.

Those words sent a thrill through her, for they were words she'd so desperately wanted to hear.

'You and I are made for one another, we both know that,' he went on.

She couldn't disagree. 'What about the children?'

'They're so much more grown up now. And anyway, Helen has altered the status quo.'

'Done what you couldn't?'

He smiled wryly. 'She didn't have the background I did. She doesn't have those terms of reference.'

He was suddenly like a child himself, she thought, wanting to envelop him in her embrace. What a sad childhood his must have been. And how profoundly it had affected him.

'You've done your best, your duty by them,' Jennie said. 'Now you must live what's left of your life to your own advantage.'

'So, will you marry me?'

'I'll tell you what I won't do, and that is go to Leeds. Not with Helen in the vicinity.'

'Oh!' Eliot exclaimed, disappointed.

'Just how discontented are you with being a consultant? Discontented enough to contemplate an alternative?'

He frowned. 'What sort of alternative?'

'I'm in practice with Dr Court who is shortly due to retire. You could take his place.'

'In Atherton you mean!'

'Why not? Then the two of us would be working together in what could be a partnership in more ways than one.'

'A family doctor,' Eliot smiled.

'Small beer I know compared to the exalted position you now hold. But it would have its compensations,' Jennie said, tongue in cheek.

'There you go again!'

Jennie laughed at his pretended outrage.

He gazed out over the water meadows, thinking how serene and tranquil they looked. If Peter and Cass were to spend holidays with him here, he was certain they'd both enjoy themselves.

'And how would your Dr Court feel about me taking his place?'

'He'd be delighted,' Jennie replied enthusiastically. 'Particularly after I'd explained the circumstances.'

'You and I working together,' Eliot mused. It sounded wonderful.

'You'd have a lot to learn, of course, but we'd soon teach you.'

Excitement gripped Eliot. This was simply too good to be true. 'You still haven't answered my question,' he reminded her.

'I'll marry you just as soon as you're free,' she replied.

'Oh Jennie!' he exclaimed, eyes shining.

'In a way it's as though I've known all along this was going to happen and have been waiting for you,' she stated quietly.

He drew her up into his arms. 'God, how I love you.'

'And I you.'

He kissed her again, this time deeply.

'I've had a thought,' she murmured when their lips parted. 'My brother's father-in-law died a couple of years ago, which means his cottage is standing empty. I'm sure Graham, who owns it, would be pleased to let it to you. It's called Gone To Ground.'

'Gone to Ground!' Eliot laughed. He liked that. It tickled his fancy.

'You could live there till we got married, then we both could,' she said.

'Perfect.'

'Totally,' she qualified.

He threw his head back. 'I'm so happy!' he exclaimed.

'Me too.'

He pulled her even closer. 'How do you feel about us having a family?'

'At my age!' She was thirty-four years old.

'It's not impossible. One anyway, if we hurry the divorce along.'

'Then you'd better do so,' she said.

He took her by the hand. 'Let's go and have that tea, I'm absolutely famished.'

Off they went, laughing and talking animatedly as they strode across the water meadows, with Brownie padding alongside. The past behind them, a bright future beckoning, a future together.

THE END

A SELECTION OF FINE NOVELS
AVAILABLE FROM BANTAM BOOKS

THE PRICES SHOWN BELOW WERE CORRECT AT THE TIME OF GOING TO PRESS.
HOWEVER TRANSWORLD PUBLISHERS RESERVE THE RIGHT TO SHOW NEW
RETAIL PRICES ON COVERS WHICH MAY DIFFER FROM THOSE PREVIOUSLY
ADVERTISED IN THE TEXT OR ELSEWHERE.

☐	17632 3	**DARK ANGEL**	*Sally Beauman*	£4.99
☐	17352 9	**DESTINY**	*Sally Beauman*	£5.99
☐	40427 X	**BELGRAVIA**	*Charlotte Bingham*	£3.99
☐	40163 7	**THE BUSINESS**	*Charlotte Bingham*	£4.99
☐	40428 8	**COUNTRY LIFE**	*Charlotte Bingham*	£3.99
☐	40296 X	**IN SUNSHINE OR IN SHADOW**	*Charlotte Bingham*	£4.99
☐	17635 8	**TO HEAR A NIGHTINGALE**	*Charlotte Bingham*	£4.99
☐	40429 6	**AT HOME**	*Charlotte Bingham*	£3.99
☐	40072 X	**MAGGIE JORDAN**	*Emma Blair*	£4.99
☐	40298 6	**SCARLET RIBBONS**	*Emma Blair*	£4.99
☐	40321 4	**AN INCONVENIENT WOMAN**	*Dominic Dunne*	£4.99
☐	17676 5	**PEOPLE LIKE US**	*Dominic Dunne*	£3.99
☐	17189 5	**THE TWO MRS GRENVILLES**	*Dominic Dunne*	£3.50
☐	40364 8	**A SPARROW DOESN'T FALL**	*June Francis*	£3.99
☐	40407 5	**THE GREEN OF THE SPRING**	*Jane Gurney*	£4.99
☐	17207 7	**FACES**	*Johanna Kingsley*	£4.99
☐	17539 4	**TREASURES**	*Johanna Kingsley*	£4.99
☐	17151 8	**SCENTS**	*Johanna Kingsley*	£4.99
☐	17504 1	**DAZZLE**	*Judith Krantz*	£4.99
☐	17242 5	**I'LL TAKE MANHATTAN**	*Judith Krantz*	£4.99
☐	17174 7	**MISTRAL'S DAUGHTER**	*Judith Krantz*	£2.95
☐	17389 8	**PRINCESS DAISY**	*Judith Krantz*	£4.99
☐	17503 3	**TILL WE MEET AGAIN**	*Judith Krantz*	£4.99
☐	40206 4	**FAST FRIENDS**	*Jill Mansell*	£3.99
☐	40360 5	**SOLO**	*Jill Mansell*	£3.99
☐	40361 3	**KISS**	*Jill Mansell*	£4.99
☐	17209 3	**THE CLASS**	*Erich Segal*	£2.95
☐	17630 7	**DOCTORS**	*Erich Segal*	£5.99
☐	40262 5	**FAMILY FORTUNES**	*Sarah Shears*	£3.99
☐	40261 7	**THE VILLAGE**	*Sarah Shears*	£3.99
☐	40263 3	**THE YOUNG GENERATION**	*Sarah Shears*	£3.99
☐	40264 1	**RETURN TO RUSSETS**	*Sarah Shears*	£3.99

All Corgi/Bantam Books are available at your bookshop or newsagent, or can be ordered from the following address:

Corgi/Bantam Books,
Cash Sales Department
P.O. Box 11, Falmouth, Cornwall TR10 9EN

UK and B.F.P.O. customers please send a cheque or postal order (no currency) and allow £1.00 for postage and packing for the first book plus 50p for the second book and 30p for each additional book to a maximum charge of £3.00 (7 books plus).

Overseas customers, including Eire, please allow £2.00 for postage and packing for the first book plus £1.00 for the second book and 50p for each subsequent title ordered.

NAME (Block Letters) ....

ADDRESS ....

....